Praise for *The Day I Died*

"Part police procedural, part psychological thriller, Rader-Day's literate, understated novel shines a spotlight on domestic violence, loneliness, and the deadly secrets that lurk just below the surface of small-town America."

—Sara Paretsky, *New York Times* bestselling author of *Brush Back*

"Secrets lie behind every loop, slant, and swirl of *The Day I Died*, Lori Rader-Day's compelling story of a handwriting analyst searching for a lost boy. Richly written, complex, and imaginative . . . this is a perfect read for fans of Mary Higgins Clark."

—Susanna Calkins, Macavity Award–winning author of the Lucy Campion Mysteries

"A stunning exploration of fear and choices—and their consequences. Lori Rader-Day is a major new talent."

—Leslie Budewitz, two-time Agatha Award–winning author and past president of Sisters in Crime

"A vividly imagined and beautifully written mystery, *The Day I Died* is also a fully realized novel about domestic abuse and the past as tether. The book's protagonist, a woman who can see other people's secrets but desperately hides her own, is tied by that tether to the decisive moment of her life. The pull of the past draws her back to that fatal, fateful day as surely as Rader-Day draws in her readers."

—Terence Faherty, Edgar Award–nominated author of *The Quiet Woman*

"In her masterful novel *The Day I Died*, Lori Rader-Day offers readers one of the most compelling and original voices in literature today. This is a psychological thriller, yes, but so much more. At heart, it's a wise and compassionate exploration of loss—loss of self, of home, of direction, and for a while, even of hope. I found it beautifully written, satisfying on every level, and I couldn't help but love it. I guarantee that you will too."

elling author

"*The Day I Died* firmly establishes Lori Rader-Day as one of the most important voices currently writing mystery fiction. Her taut prose grips the reader and never lets go as she focuses on Anna Winger, a handwriting expert and small-town single mother, who is pulled into a murder investigation that forces her to see the writing on her own wall. Anna not only has to solve the murder, but she has to save the person she loves the most. Rader-Day's sharp understanding of the human condition has been on display since her brilliant debut, but here, it glows and is even more jaw-dropping and insightful. You won't want to miss a sentence. Especially the last one."

—Larry D. Sweazy, award-winning author of *Where I Can See You*

Praise for *Little Pretty Things*

"Rader-Day again proves herself (after *The Black Hour*, 2014) a deft manipulator of dark atmosphere, witty dialogue, and complex, charismatic characters. Highly recommended for psychological thriller groupies, especially those who walk on the literary side of the genre and favor books like Tana French's *Faithful Place* (2010) and Cornelia Read's Madeline Dare series."

—*Booklist* Starred Review

"Once again, Chicago author Rader-Day delivers a breathless psychological thriller with a killer first line, an irresistible mystery, and lean chapters soaked with suspense. Comparisons to Tana French (*A Secret Place*) and Paula Hawkins (*The Girl on the Train*) have become all-too-common in the mystery genre, but with two consistently great novels now under her belt, Rader-Day has proved their equal in crafting taut, literary mysteries with fascinating heroines."

—BookPage

"[One of the] most arresting crime novels of 2015." —*Kirkus Reviews*

Praise for *The Black Hour*

"A perfect thriller for summer . . . Rader-Day's addictive prose is atmospheric and laced with dread."
—BookPage

"Captivates from page one. . . . This reviewer was bowled over by the novel's alternating points of view, superb storytelling, and pitch-perfect take on academia."
—*Library Journal* Starred Review

"An exceptional debut. . . . An irresistible combination of menace, betrayal, and self-discovery."
—*Publishers Weekly* Starred Review

"An unputdownable read."
—*Booklist* Starred Review

"A terrific whydunnit! This dark page-turner of a puzzle—well written, with bite and style and edge and simmering conflict—will keep you riveted from page one."
—Hank Phillippi Ryan, author of *Say No More*

"*The Black Hour* is the rarest of mysteries: one that wants to keep you turning pages in a cold sweat, suspecting every character you meet of both the best and the worst motives; and also one that has something complicated and important to say about the forces that impel us toward death . . . and life. It's an extraordinary debut, marking the arrival of a major new voice in literary suspense."
—Christopher Coake, author of *You Came Back*

THE
DAY
I
DIED

Also by Lori Rader-Day

THE DAY I DIED

A Novel

WILLIAM MORROW
An Imprint of HarperCollins*Publishers*

To Amanda Lumpkin and Trisha Tyree Cathey.

And to my parents, Melvin Rader and Paula Dodson, who gave me a happy childhood and yet I still turned out to be a writer.

On the day I died, I took the new oars down to the lake. They were heavy, but I was saving myself the second trip. The blades rode flat along the ground, flattening two tracks through the wet grass.

It was morning. The air was cool, but down on the dock, the slats were already hot. I noted a lone fishing boat out on the water. Inside, two men hunched silently over their tackle, their faces turned out across the lake. Beyond them, mist rose off the water, nearly hiding the far shore.

This moment. This is what I return to.

Later, I will note the long crack in the new oar, just before my head goes under, just before the flume of blood rises off my skin under the water like smoke. I will come back to this moment and think, if I had just gone back up the steps to the house immediately. If I had just stayed up at the house in the first place.

If I had just.

Part I

Chapter One

By the time the search volunteers arrived at my door with a handful of flyers, their zeal and concern had worn to a polish. I'd been watching the news and was a little tired of the kid myself. But I couldn't look away. A baby, really, gone all day. He had bottomless brown eyes and tousled hair like the fuzz of a baby bird. He was two. He hadn't toddled down the street to pet the neighbor's dog, wasn't found halfway to the convenience store with a handful of pennies for candy. The real thing, this kid. Missing.

"Have you seen this little boy?" asked one of the women. The other yawned into the back of her hand. They wore yoga pants and Parks Junior-Senior High School Booster Club sweatshirts. One had pigtail braids, like a child, and the other one, the tired one, had her hair pulled back in a band, probably growing out bad bangs. Behind them, the street was overlit with neighborly porch lights.

"I saw him on the news," I said, taking the offered flyer and reading the details I'd already heard: Aidan Ransey, height, weight. So small. "How long's he been gone?"

"Since this morning," said the one with pigtails, but the other woman didn't like me being curious, I could tell. Either she'd tired of the questions or she thought mine wasn't the right kind. "From his own bed," pigtails said, her voice catching. I was reminding this woman to be worried for other children now sleeping in their beds or waiting up for their mommies to come home from their good deeds. "I can't believe it," she said, shaking her head.

The other woman shot her friend a look. She could believe it. "Look," this one said, getting down to business. "Can you put a flyer in your . . ." She glanced behind me, toward the staircase with its worn carpet, then toward the back hallway with the overhead light dangling, waiting for a new bulb. I lived upstairs, but none of the other neighbors would bother to answer a knock on the front door. Truthfully, I usually didn't, either, but I knew from the news that there would be canvassers. Better to open the door. Better to take the flyer. ". . . in your laundry room or something?" the woman said finally. "Call the number if you hear or see anything, OK? We need to keep moving."

"Wait a minute," the one with the braids said. "I know you from football pickup. Are you Josh's mother? I'm Caleb's mom, from Boosters?"

"Joshua," I said, my tongue thick in my mouth.

"We haven't heard from you about helping with concessions," she said. "And the pancake breakfast is coming up—here, let me give you my number." She folded a flyer in half, Aidan's face cut in two, and pulled out a pen. "We really count on all the parents to help."

Her friend smirked as I took the flyer. "Thanks," I said. It was the second time in one evening I'd been asked to volunteer for something. My activism was normally confined to dropping the occasional quarter into fund-raising buckets. But not for anyone who rang a bell or stood in street intersections. They were assholes. "Pancakes," I said.

"It's the most popular fund-raiser for the team we do all year," Caleb's mom said. "And so much fun."

Headband and I exchanged a look. "Great, well," I said. "I hope they find that little boy soon."

A shadow passed over Caleb's mom's face. "They will," she said. "As soon as they find his—"

"Come on, Steph," her friend said. "We need to get this street done."

They were down the sidewalk, the reflective stripes on their athletic shoes flashing, when the door at my shoulder opened to the chain's length. The neighbor, Margaret, put one myopic eye against the opening. "What did she say? As soon as they find his what?"

"His mother," I said.

Margaret pressed her ear up to the door opening. She wasn't hard of hearing. She caught every noise we made upstairs and let us know about it, thumping a broom handle at her ceiling. She wrestled with the chain to open the door wider. Her twiggy legs stuck out of her housecoat. "How d'you know that?"

I looked again at the flyer, at the infant cheeks of Aidan Ransey, and handed it to her, then at the other copy, with a phone number and the woman's name—*Stephanie Bux*—written in round, cheerful shapes. The *i* was dotted with a fat circle; the fours in her phone number were pointy, defensive. No—protective. The other woman would fill her in on their way down the street and then Caleb's mom would be sorry she'd written anything down for me, even if we all knew I had no intention of calling.

I turned to Margaret. "Haven't you heard?" I held the folded flyer to my forehead. "Apparently I'm some kind of voodoo priestess. I can see into the future. I seeeeee . . . a small boy, brown eyes. Yellow, almost white hair . . . I see pudgy hands and a full diaper—"

Margaret huffed and closed the door.

I lowered the flyer. After a moment of watching the street, I reached for the switch for our porch light and flicked it on. I didn't believe in wishful thinking, even though it was all I seemed to do.

THE NEXT MORNING at the café on the courthouse square, the *Parks County Spectator* was sold down to a few copies. A handwritten sign above the cash register read *NO CHANGE SORRY*. I paid for a paper and a weak tea, glancing between the careful, narrow warning on the sign and the careful, narrow man behind the counter.

Outside, the courthouse rose over the square like a castle on high. People scurried over the lawn, between a set of imposing limestone pillars, and through the doors. The mechanical chimes from the clock at the top of the rotunda counted out the hour. I crossed the street and sat on the low wall encasing the courthouse lawn, my back to all the activity.

The same baby photo from the flyer graced the front page. I flipped through the article, then searched the rest of the paper's photos and captions, paging past high school football scores and gardening club news, chili suppers, a notice for that pancake breakfast. On the back page of the newspaper, a furniture store's proprietor had signed his name to an advertisement as a guarantee on his low prices. His short, everyman name was embellished with a sweeping flourish. Someone had a Napoleon complex. I paused over the prices. Joshua could use a chest of drawers, but it was too early for furniture that wouldn't fit in the back of our SUV.

None of the photos showed me the county sheriff, the man I was not rushing to meet.

At last I stood, discarded the tea, and followed the bustle of activity into the courthouse. In the lobby, under a lofty stained-glass dome, people in uniforms and with ID cards dangling from their necks outnumbered the civilians. Their faces grave and important, they rushed in and out of an area cordoned behind makeshift walls. I joined a long line snaking toward a set of metal detectors.

"Is all this fuss for that one kid?" said a man ahead of me in line.

"You know whose kid it is?" said one of the guards, taking all the cords and adapters out of my laptop bag and inspecting each piece as though we had all the time in the world. "Seen enough of them Ranseys come through here to last me the rest of my life."

"Good to know the law will hup to for anyone at all when the time comes," the first man said. He noticed me listening and hurried away.

The line for the elevator was short, but I took the stairs anyway. They were mottled marble, white with gray threads, worn by generations of shuffling feet. Best of all, they were empty of people, empty of pleasantries given and expected in return.

At the top of the third-floor landing, rather too quickly, the Parks County Sheriff's Administrative Office announced itself self-importantly, gold paint on opaque glass.

I straightened my shoulders, took a deep breath. Then another. A minute ticked by. No one went in or came out.

I could tell Kent I didn't want to do it.

But I couldn't. Not really.

The door opened onto a wide gray room crowded with closely aligned desks, each covered with spilling files and old paper cups. At my right, a reception desk sat unmanned. Behind the door, a low black sofa suggested guests, but none were in evidence. No guests, no hosts, no one at all.

A single sticky note was pasted to the front desk. I glanced around, stepped in, and plucked it up.

Square note, yellow. In thick black felt-tip—no. I peered more closely. In thick purple felt-tip, the note said *Back in a jiff!* The letters were round and rolling.

At the back of the room, a light showed through an open door. I put the sticky note back and made my way there. I had raised my knuckles to the door when something inside slammed. I startled backward.

"What do you want?" a man's voice said.

I nudged open the door. "I—"

A man in a brown uniform and black ball cap sat behind a cluttered desk, his elbows on his knees and his hands steepled in front of his face. He opened his eyes and lifted an arm, crossing-guard style, to hold me at the doorway, and jutted his chin toward his desk.

"We want the same thing you do, Russ," a woman's voice said, scratchy through the speakerphone.

"Do we?" he said, waving me away. I backed out of the doorway a bit but studied him. He was younger than I would have predicted—my age, give or take. I had painted all small-town police officers with the same brush as the ones I'd known growing up: pudgy, doughy, bellies hanging over their belts. This one was trim with muscular, tanned arms. Such a shame. I didn't have time for handsome.

"The truth," she said. "What the hell is going on over there?"

"I don't know yet and I don't see how jumping the gun on this will help us get to the truth of it all," he said. "I just wish you'd give us a little more time"—his hard look turned uneasy—"to confirm some things. I haven't talked to Erickson yet this morning, for one thing. Have you?"

"We have a deadline," the woman said.

"You can't tell me that it's within the next two hours," the sheriff said. "People are still waking up to yesterday's paper, Kay, for crying out loud. Our deadline's more important than yours, anyway, or you'll be printing two—" His eyes caught mine. He lifted the receiver on the phone and swiveled in the chair, his back to me. "I can't tell you what to do. But it's not time for guessing. Sure as hell not time for blame. We don't know what happened to him yet."

A shiver went up the back of my neck. I'd watched the news again after the volunteers had gone the night before, held hostage by the kid's brown eyes. This morning after Joshua went to school, I watched a top reporter from one of the Indianapolis stations standing with her microphone in front of a row of dirty, peeling houses with sagging porches. "Citizens of Parks, Indiana, are asking themselves today," she'd said, giving her blond bob a punctuating dip, "how could this happen—*here*?"

Here—she'd said it with all the wonder and disbelief I still felt after three months.

At the newscaster's elbow, a thick, hardy woman with gray hair falling out of a bun grimaced into the camera. "He's a good boy," she said, peering into the lens. Her voice sounded like concrete rolling in a mixer. Her deeply wrinkled face folded into itself in pain. The bottom of the screen announced that this was Aidan's grandmother.

"Mrs. Ransey, have you heard anything about Aidan's whereabouts?" the reporter asked.

In Parks, there were no forests to search, no standing bodies of water to drag. How much danger could the kid get into, here, where there was nowhere to hide except cornfields and shallow ditches and everyone so eager to help? He should have been asleep in a pile of dirty clothes or behind a closet door. They should have found him within an hour.

I'd only just pointed the remote at the set when the grandmother sobbed and grabbed at the reporter, then the camera. The world shook loose. "He needs to be home with his gramma," she wailed, the sound terrible and mesmerizing. The camera stabilized, refocused. I turned off the TV before the smug reporter could tut-tut the story to a false conclusion.

"Thank you, Kay," the sheriff was saying. "I appreciate that. I promise: the second I can give you anything, I will, OK?"

He leaned forward to hang up the phone, the mechanics of his chair squealing in protest. When he turned back to his desk, he seemed surprised to see I was still there. "Help you?"

"I'm Anna Winger," I said.

He pulled his cap low over his eyes. "You got a lead, headquarters is moved out into the lobby. You couldn't've missed it."

"No, I'm—" I struggled to say the right thing. The introduction would set the tone. "Kent Schaffer asked me to come by."

I let the sheriff take his time placing Kent's name, remembering the offer Kent must have made and the specialty service I could provide. When he looked away in impatience, I knew he'd put the pieces together.

"You're a fed?" he said.

"A . . . subcontractor."

He snorted, shook his head. But before he said anything else, before he stood and introduced himself or shook my hand, before he did anything at all, he did what they all did. He surveyed his desktop, closed a folder. He selected a single page from the mess of papers and files on his desk and turned it over.

I crossed his office to the window and blinked into the sun. Below, my neighbors made their way to the bank, the café. I could see the trophies in the window of the karate studio. I could see for a mile, actually. I'd read central Indiana had once been a dense forest, but I didn't buy it. A lone tree on the courthouse green had begun to change its colors.

"Well, OK, Mrs. Winger," the sheriff said finally. He came around his desk with his hand outstretched.

"*Ms.* Winger, please. Sheriff Keller, let's be clear." I let my hand glance off his. "I'm not here to analyze *your* handwriting."

He stayed straight-backed, level-eyed. The brassy details of his uniform seemed to make him taller than he was, though he was tall. The features I had discerned as handsome faded against the razor's edge of his demeanor. He was as hard and stern as a billy club, and probably considered it part of his job not to look away.

"I had no idea Schaffer was into this mumbo jumbo," he said.

"He's a leading international expert," I said.

"In *bunk*," he said. "And how did you become—whatever level of expert you are?"

"Training and apprenticeship, certifications—the way you become anything else."

"But you didn't become anything else," the sheriff said.

We considered each other. "I can go," I said.

"Kent Schaffer wanted you to help." The sheriff squinted at me so I would know that he didn't. He brushed past, swept a pile of newspapers and folders off the guest chair, and nodded toward it. "I'm in no position to turn away volunteers. The entire Indiana law enforcement community is camped out downstairs, and they've taken every resource we've got. I'm down to just me and my secretary."

I remembered the sticky note in the lobby. *Back in a jiff!* I could have told him his secretary was someone who couldn't quite control her emotions, someone who might be inappropriately confidential with a stranger, who might say too much or the wrong thing entirely. Probably the worst sort of person to have working with confidential information, but then no one had asked for that assessment. I didn't give it away for free.

"Anyway," Keller said.

I sat in the chair, waiting.

He returned to his side of the desk and sat, cleared his throat. "Anyway. This is what you do?"

"This is what I do," I said.

I listened to his knee bouncing under the desk. His handwriting probably had a kinetic wriggle.

"You can really make a living out of this—what's the word? Service? In Parks?"

"Most of my work is federal or for large corporations. None of them are headquartered *here*." I heard the tweak in my voice, not so different from the TV reporter's that morning. "I don't do a lot of—local jurisdiction."

He'd heard the tweak, too. His chin was pointed in my direction now. "I see. And what do you do a lot of? Exactly?"

I sat back and crossed my legs. I'd promised Kent I didn't mind going in person, but I did. I dealt with authority every day— by phone. By virtual, protected networks and hypersecure file transfer. Occasionally by sterile, anonymous package delivery. The justice and corporate work was faceless, often humanless. Under the stern control of technology and distance, the work had dignity. In the sheriff's office, the search for justice was close and, by the looks of things, in chaos. Papers, books, and binders stacked and falling and, underneath, the smell of the lockup. There was no telling who had been dragged in to sit in this very chair and face the music. I felt the slick of their sweat and blood on the armrests and pulled my elbows in. The office was stuffy and close, reminding me of—

The air, thick, over a Northwoods lake, blood rising like smoke in the water—

Keller narrowed his eyes at me.

I took a deep breath. "I've spent time with ransom notes, forgery, all manner of documents, prenuptial agreements, contracts," I said. "I work a little in corporate recruitment and with the FBI—"

"I heard you were a spy," he said.

"Better than fortune-teller," I said, remembering teasing my neighbor the night before. I needed to stop making jokes about my job. They'd get made by everyone else, given enough time. "I think my son might have started the one about me being a spy."

"Got his handwriting all over it, huh?" The sheriff grinned. "What's his name?"

I shouldn't have come. Kent should have never asked this of me. Other people got involved. Other mothers hosted pancake breakfasts. I was the kind of mother who checked the license plates of passing cars.

"His name is Joshua," I said.

"Joshua," he repeated. "How old?"

The sheriff was perfectly within his duties to ask questions, but I was perfectly within my rights to hate the sound of my son's name coming from a stranger's mouth.

"He's thirteen. Just. I'm glad you haven't had to meet him. Now," I said, retrieving a notebook from my purse. "How can I help?"

The sheriff wasn't satisfied, I could see that. But he flipped open the cover of a binder on his desk, taking care to tip his notes away from me.

Chapter Two

"Aidan Michael Ransey," the sheriff began. "Age two years. His father reported him missing yesterday morning, early. And wouldn't you know it? His mother also seems to be out rambling. She resided in Parks with the husband and son until just a few months ago and now can't be reached."

I heard the squeak of Keller's chair and looked up from my notes. He'd leaned far back in his chair to look over the wall behind him. A diploma, a few certificates with shiny seals, a sea of frames full of photos: Keller and campaign signs. Keller in a crowd of uniformed officers. Keller shaking hands, handing out accolades. In each photo, he held himself tight, his eyes focused somewhere beyond the camera. The people near him shook his hand, clasped his shoulder, leaned into him, and propped themselves up against him. Given half a chance, they might have crawled onto his back and let him carry them.

He spun back around. "So of course the mother is of special interest here. Stealing your own kid is an excellent way to avoid a custody battle."

I looked down at my notes. *Mother*, with the *t* crossed distract-edly. Wasn't it not yet time for blame?

"There's a snag, though," he continued. "Couple of them, ac-tually, but one is an anonymous note threatening to take the kid."

Finally I saw the door through which I'd entered. Kent hadn't given me the details. That was his style, to let me make all my own discoveries. All my own mistakes.

"They're trying to pull prints off the note now," he said. "So all I can get you is a copy of—"

"A copy isn't good enough."

A flat stare from Keller. "Sorry?"

"A copy isn't good enough," I said. "I'll need to see the real thing."

"Well, I'm not likely to get *my* fingerprints on the real McCoy until tomorrow sometime," he said, slapping the desk. Annoyed with either the question or the answer he'd had to give. "Don't even have a copy yet, to tell you the truth."

"I'm surprised Kent didn't tell you I would need the original."

"No, he did," he said. "I just—"

I sensed some piece of his pride was at stake here. Perhaps he hadn't wanted to admit that the only real crime likely to pass over his desk this year—maybe in his entire tenure—had been taken away from him, that he couldn't lay his hands on his own evidence. "You just?"

"I just wanted to get a look at you first."

I froze, but inside I was taking flight, my heart pattering. I glanced at the door. "Excuse me?"

The sheriff closed his notes with a snap. "Wanted to make sure I didn't let any . . . woo-woo in the door."

"And how do I stack up?" I said, willing myself to calm down. "Right amount of woo for you?"

"Now, don't take it personal—"

"To take it personally," I said, "I would have to care significantly more than I do about your opinion. As it is, I only care professionally—but if you don't trust that my profession exists outside the realm of voodoo, I'm not sure what I can do for you."

"You can prove me wrong," he said.

"Seems like you're pretty sure about most things," I said. I glanced up at the wall of accolades and adoration. "What don't you already know?"

He didn't like me shopping his wall. "Where that boy is, first off."

"What do you think the note might tell us about Aidan's whereabouts?"

"This is your area. They say. But the whole thing tells me to get nervous." He nudged his cap crooked on his head to draw his hand over his face. He needed a shave. "Not a lot of kids go missing and almost every one of them turns up somewhere on a playdate everyone forgot about or, if they're actually gone, with the noncustodial parent, simply being withheld. It doesn't make a lot of sense—to me."

I looked back at my notebook.

He said, "I do worry that the note seems to be . . . vague on details. And demands, actually. There was no ransom mentioned."

I nodded. Without comparing it to a sample of someone's handwriting, the note was a big unknown in the center of a lot of unknowns. Anyone could have written that note. If the father wrote it, he could be covering his own tracks. The kid could be in danger or hurt. Or dead. And the mother. Was she just not answering the phone or was she in a quick grave somewhere?

I turned my head. From where I sat, Keller's office window was filled with a span of perfect blue sky. Just the other day I'd been thinking: maybe. Maybe it didn't have to be so hard. I remembered hot dock slats under my legs, a warm arm thrown around me as the sun dipped into the lake.

"So I'm nervous, all right," the sheriff said. "I'm nervous that kid is really gone. Pedophile gone, or—but forgive me if I hope it's the mother who's got him. You know why, *Ms*. Winger? Not because it's easier to solve, but because it's so much more likely we'll bring Aidan back home, soon and safe."

I kept my face passive. Sometimes when I needed to keep my mouth shut, I ran my tongue over the backs of my teeth and counted off the states. Tennessee, Kentucky, Pennsylvania, Ohio. One of my teeth had cracked at some point, inviting rot, and I'd finally had it rooted and capped in Cincinnati. I always tried to land on that tooth when Ohio's turn came along. Then Illinois, now Indiana. I looked up. "What was the other snag?" I said.

"What's that?" he said.

"You said there were a couple of snags."

I didn't think he was going to tell me. No sample, not enough info. And now a stonewalling look instead of letting me in on what I was up against. There was no reason for him to treat me as a peer, but I didn't have to put up with being treated like a circus freak. I stood and reached into my purse.

"The other snag is the babysitter," he said. "She was missing, too." I waited, a business card in my hand. It was a quality card, simple, with only my name and number pressed into smooth, white paper.

Was. *Was* missing. I sat back down.

"Until this morning," he said, "when her body was discovered in an out-of-service latrine at Sugar Creek Park."

ON THE WAY home, I took a detour. There was absolutely no reason for my going there, but when I saw the sign for the park, I turned in. Under the canopy of trees, I took a deep breath. I drove slowly but no children darted into the lane.

The road abruptly ended in a parking lot with empty playground equipment on the far side. Beyond that, a concrete block structure sat surrounded by more trees and, this morning, several cruisers, local and state, with their lights turned off. A couple of unmarked vehicles—a dark SUV and a panel van, black, maybe a crime scene unit—sat nearby. I parked just in view of the taillights and got out, wandering over to a park bench in the grass and sitting at an angle to the activity.

Why this place? Of all the parks to bring a kid for a day out, this one seemed least likely. Fall was thinning out the leaves overhead as well as the nice-weather days left in the season. This particular park also seemed out of the way and abandoned, given the better-kept Memorial Park right downtown, mere blocks from where the Ranseys lived.

A hundred feet away or so, an older man in a rumpled sweater stood in the grass with a small white dog on a leash. "Come on, Trix," he was saying. "Come *on*."

He startled at seeing me and then recovered with a gesture toward the goings-on at the facilities. "Bad business in that latrine," he said. "Safe as houses, this place is supposed to be."

"The park?"

"The whole town. And the park."

"You spend time here, I guess," I said, looking at the dog.

"Until this week, I never bothered taking her anywhere else," he said. "We used to have druggie types around but the sheriff's deputies are always coming through, waving. After a couple of town meetings, you understand. But now they haunt it well enough, keep things tidy. They patrolled it this morning, for heaven's sake, before the body was found. Now my wife won't let our daughter bring the kids up to visit, not until this is sorted."

After a few minutes, the little dog did its business and the man picked up the mess with an inside-out plastic bag over his shaking hand.

On the way out of the park, I met another dark SUV coming in and turned my head. Safe as houses, except I'd only known houses to be as safe as anyplace else. Which is to say, not a guarantee.

"JOSHUA," I CALLED from the front door. "I'm home."

The bare white walls seemed to bounce my voice back to me. All that talk of the missing and the dead gave me the shivers. I felt equal parts relieved and silly when I spotted his backpack on the dining room table. Not where it should be, as usual, but here. *Here.*

"Joshua? Are you home?" I listened for the telltale sounds of his video games, but then he'd be using the new headphones he'd gotten for his birthday. His games were quieter and more private now, which kept Margaret from whacking her broom at us or, worse, from shuffling upstairs in her slippers to snoop and have her say.

Right now all I cared about was he was here. I'd just spent a good deal of the day talking about a little boy gone missing and a woman found dead. Keller had given me a look behind that cordoned area in the courthouse lobby, where it seemed most of his staff and several other battalions of law enforcement now holed up. No one offered credentials to make my next visit any easier. Outside again, I'd taken a slow walk around the square, stopping to look at listings in a real estate office's window. Cheap real estate was of no more interest to me than outlandishly expensive real estate, but I dutifully read the details on farmhouses and split-level ranches until an agent came out to chat me up. After the park I'd driven to the school to catch the end of junior high football practice, only to discover the field empty.

All the way home, I had felt the low sizzle of my nerves. Aidan Ransey was missing, and now any boy could go missing. Maybe I was being a little overdramatic, but that was fine. I had decided years ago to be anything I wanted to be.

But you didn't become anything else. That's what the sheriff thought. He was wrong, but it was better if he didn't know it.

I dropped my bag on the table. At Joshua's room, I pressed my ear to the door. The clacking of his thumbs on the game controller gave him away.

In my bedroom, I traded the skirt and blouse for a pair of sweats and a T-shirt. I pulled my hair into a bun, pausing to gather myself in front of the full-length mirror some unkind soul had attached to the inside of the closet door. The sweats did nothing for the waist I'd ended up with after thirteen years sitting behind a computer, and the T-shirt was plain and dumpy. The uniform of a stay-at-home spy.

In the hall, I hesitated at Joshua's door, then knocked. No response. I knocked again. Either he couldn't hear me or he didn't want to.

When I finally opened the door, he was sprawled on the floor on his back, his head propped against his red beanbag chair. His thick brown hair, always too long, hung into his long eyelashes, flicking when he blinked. I loved his eyelashes, and of course the eyes, a deep brown with flecks of colors that had yet to be named. I loved everything about him. I even loved the profile, the straight nose and high cheekbones inherited from another face.

At that moment, he grimaced at something happening on the screen. His nose sneered, his lip curled in disgust, and everything about him turned into his father. He tossed the game controller to the floor, disappointment changing his face back into his own. Then he saw me at the door, and his scowl twisted back into place.

"Mom, *God*, what?" he said, his voice too loud for the room.

I gestured for him to take off the headphones. He sat up and pried them off. "I wasn't even *being* loud," he said.

"No, I know."

He swiped the hair out of his eyes with the back of his wrist, irritated. At the game or at me, I couldn't tell.

"I just wondered how your day was," I said.

He rolled his eyes. "How my day was?"

Sometimes he reminded me to get mad in return. Sometimes he pushed me to a raw anger that made me almost understand things I'd never understood, and then the heat would rush away, replaced by emptiness. That hollow feeling explained a few things, too. Wouldn't I do almost anything to keep from experiencing it? I would. I had.

"Yeah," I said, swallowing everything else I might have said. I leaned against the doorframe, crossing my arms. I wished I'd kept my business clothes on. Maybe the scent of the jail would have still been on them. "Your *day*. We humans mark time in twenty-four-hour allotments. How was *yours*?"

He gave a sharp-shouldered shrug. "'s OK."

I glanced at the alarm clock next to his bed. "No football practice tonight, I guess."

He looked up at me, considered, then decided on a shake of the head. I didn't press the issue of having driven out to fetch him. He wanted a cell phone, and I was pushing off any evidence that he needed one.

"Well, I guess I'll go make dinner, and you'll do your homework," I said.

Joshua sighed. "Fine."

"I'll call you in just a few minutes, and I don't want to see that gentleman again tonight," I said, nodding toward the TV, where a muscled military man was frozen in midfrenzy, mouth wide in the rage of attack. The headphones hadn't been for Margaret's sake alone.

"I *said* fine."

I closed the door. Another twenty-four-hour allotment, another chance to see how much I could screw this up.

In the kitchen, I opened the fridge and stared in, going over its contents and the conversation again. It had gone off the rails, but where? At last I had to admit that it was the moment he'd seen me.

Normal teenage stuff. We'd always been close, but his wingspan was wider now. He wanted more rights—more than permission to get himself to school, to join sports teams, to have a TV and games in his own room, to let his hair grow. He wanted his own life.

Of course I would worry how far this would go, how fast. I worried. When he was little, I had feared dropping him, not feeding him well enough, mysterious fevers. In elementary school, he came home scuffed up and knees torn. From playing, he said, but I wasn't fooled and worried that he didn't fit in.

I had worried most that he would never feel safe and, now, that I'd made him feel too safe. I had protected him so well he had no idea what it was to be afraid. I was the only one on notice, so I got to be the warden. I got to be the bad guy.

Which was life's little joke on me.

But lately—the recoil when I tried to touch him, the appraising look he gave me when he thought I couldn't see, as though we were strangers. That's how it felt: the boy in this apartment wasn't the boy I'd raised, the playful one, the artist, the one who could be tickled into hiccups, the boy he had been not that long ago.

This boy—the closed doors, the slammed doors, the constant video games, the wary looks—this boy was a ghost boy, a haunted boy, and my son had vanished. Joshua was missing, just as gone as the little boy Sheriff Keller was looking for. Why was no one looking for Joshua? Who was getting my boy back to me?

I closed the refrigerator and wandered out of the kitchen, gathering some magazines, a sweatshirt, a few other loose items of clutter, then, no plan for them, stacked them on the nearest flat surface. I sat heavily on the couch and gazed around. *Here*. A two-bedroom rental with too-thin white walls and no yard or balcony. The same not-much we'd grown accustomed to. But I'd lived in worse, in places other people would abandon, in places that stank of decay and neglect. *Decay. Neglect.* These were crisp, precise words on the page that stood in for a reality most people didn't truly understand.

Tennessee, Kentucky, Pennsylvania, Ohio. Small towns, big towns one after the other, false starts, lost deposits. Mice in the walls and backed-up sinks. Old wallpaper with black freckles of mold.

Then Chicago, where I'd let us get too comfortable. A handful of miles to the Wisconsin border, and I'd started to entertain ideas of settling down, maybe buying a condo. And then—

Small towns were better. Towns with forgettable names,

apartments with two locks on the door. Indiana. You could clean the dirty ovens. You could put out traps. There were more important things than having your slice of the pie, of putting down some roots, but it didn't stop me from wondering. Maybe this was the place. Except it wasn't because there was only one place, and we couldn't go back there.

I went to the kitchen and put some water on to boil, then grabbed the mail from the counter and went to the window in the living room to sort it in the fading light. Across the street, the houses lined up like a hand of solitaire. Down below, people walking their dogs stopped to chat.

I glanced up and down the block. From the second floor, you could see pretty far, a precaution. But I would never get used to the scrubbed look of this place. The whole town, harvested. How long had it been since I had been among the stillness of trees, encircled by a stand of pines like a bunch of protective brothers? The only trees nearby were scrawny, scrub or planted, with no better reason to be here than I had.

I added noodles to the boiling water and then took myself to the table and dropped into a chair. I was tired. Not just exhausted from a day of playing upright citizen for the sheriff, but forever tired, in my bones, in my skin. Tired of days, tired of nights. From the table I watched the window darken, the outside world folding away.

In a minute I would go to the window and close the blinds. Another precaution. But did it matter? Here, in Plain Sight, Indiana, who was I hiding from anymore? I was afraid of thinking it through too fully.

I got up and grabbed the straps of Joshua's backpack to move it off the table but instead pulled it to me.

The guidance counselor had called yesterday, twice. So actually yesterday I'd been asked to do three things I didn't want to do—but I supposed it wasn't volunteering when it was your own kid in trouble.

Down the hall, Joshua's door was still closed.

A tangle of papers caught in the backpack's zipper. I fought it open, pulled out the papers, and checked the spines on the books at the bottom. Language arts, *Our World and Its People*, a ragged copy of *The Adventures of Huckleberry Finn*, which he'd finished a book report for weeks ago. Maybe it was a test, to see if I'd take it out. The math text, of course. I'd offered to help. I'd even learned the new alien way they did math in order to help, but he preferred to do it himself, badly.

From the wad of papers, I picked out a math worksheet. Proof. He'd received a well-deserved *D* in red pen.

I tried not to spend much time on the pinched belly of that red letter. So what if the teacher had a tendency toward small-mindedness? That didn't change the facts.

I flipped through a few more sheets, then dug deeper, flattening a few pages to take stock. More math, a report. They were just figures, or typed.

At last I found a short-answer workbook page at the bottom of the pack. It was incomplete—empty, actually, except for the large round zero in red at the top and a few meager pencil markings in a corner. His name, *JOSH*, all capital letters.

I stared at the name for a long moment, then stowed all the backpack's contents as best I could and closed it up, leaving it on the table.

In the kitchen, I stirred the noodles and wished I'd never looked. But I had, and now I knew. His handwriting—once so playfully dismissive of the horizon, so youthful and alive—was gone. His name, even written by his own hand, was false. It was built of sticks, each letter strategically rendered and apart, lonely and stripped. I'd never seen anything so desolate, so perfectly engineered to give away nothing at all.

Joshua was hiding in plain sight, too. And I was pretty sure he was hiding from me.

Chapter Three

The call, when it came, was from Kent.

"What did you get me into?" I said before he'd had a chance to say hello.

"You're up to the challenge," he said. I could hear the smile. Sometimes I thought I might be in love with Kent, even though I hadn't seen him in person in twelve years. What that said about me—well, it said everything about me that anyone could ever want to know. I'd been in love just the one time, a disaster. I'd had a few dates, if that was even the word. An awkward setup, once, and then the guy, the client, I'd met for a few weeks in a series of beige chain-name hotel rooms—but that was just sex. What I missed was the other person's hip against mine on the couch. The thoughtless moments of life spent together. When I started thinking like this, I wished Kent weren't twenty years older and completely in love with his wife.

"Kent, the kid was taken by his mother," I said. My cheek was growing hot against my cell phone. "Right? We've got the nanny, babysitter, whatever—spotted by the neighbors taking the kid

out in her car, early. We've got the nanny and kid witnessed at
the park. And then, poof. The woman's dead in the broken-down
ladies' john, the kid's gone, and the mother can't be found."

"The mother—yeah, I didn't think that through, did I? Maybe
she didn't do it." We both listened to that false tenor of his voice.
"OK, I can send someone else. But you're literally down the block.
You'd be saving your nation some serious travel expenses."

"I was thinking about charging my nation double this time,"
I said. "Anything that reminds me too much of home, I charge at
least time and a half."

He laughed, but we'd both heard it. *Home*. I couldn't think
what to say next.

He cleared his throat. "Was there anything you wanted to
know?"

I didn't think he meant about the dead babysitter. Some
things, it was better not to know. "How did she die?" I said instead.

"Badly," he said. I could hear the grim set of his mouth. He was
worried about me, or maybe it had nothing to do with me at all.
"Something heavy to the back of the head—"

"Got it. Sorry I asked. Did you know Keller lied about having
the note so he could try me out first? Friend of yours?"

"A little puffed up, but he's all right—good guy, really. Just
heard from him," Kent said. "He's got the note in hand and a few
other things for you to look at. I could look into sending someone
else . . ."

"I'm fine," I said. "I have an appointment at Joshua's school
later but I can go do this early, get it over with." I heard the words
I had used and cringed. "Not that I don't appreciate all the work."

"There's another package coming from me," he said. "Human
resources."

"My favorite." In fact, I liked the hiring cases that came through Kent less than I liked the little letters and notes people sent me from all over the country in response to a few well-placed ads of my own. My lonelyhearts. Given my preferences, I would never have to take Kent's subcontracts or talk, really, to anyone else ever again. But a few love letters sent from prison to analyze was no way to keep a roof over our heads.

"I knew you'd be excited. Did you see that article in the *Wall Street Journal* about so-called smart pens saving the art of penmanship?" he said. "Published online, with no irony whatsoever."

"I hardly go online at all," I said. "But I'm glad someone is saving handwriting, or we'll be out of business." I calculated our age difference again. He'd retire in a few years, and then what would I do? Joshua still needed to go to college. All those forms asking for information, social security numbers, phone numbers. Addresses where you could expect to be for a little while. In a few years, our life would need a solidity it didn't have just now.

I had met Kent in a university classroom. I was supposed to be cleaning it, and he had just spoken to the students there. I had listened from outside the door, rocking my sleeping newborn against my chest. Up until then, I'd been taking community center handwriting classes for fun. After the class, I let the students and then the visitor and the professor, deep in conversation, walk by and then carried Joshua in his car seat into the room. There were always so many coffee shop cups left behind. At the lectern, I found a lovely leather notebook filled with a geometric script. I was paging through it when the professor cleared his throat at the door. Kent introduced himself, eyeing the sleeping baby. "What did you see?" he said as I handed him the notebook. "Am I a serial killer?"

The professor had laughed, but then his face drew still as I told the visitor what I thought of his script: self-conscious, high-minded, literal, a little too process driven.

"High-minded?" Kent had said, grinning. "Am I really? I think you might be right." And he had handed me one of his cards.

Now Kent said, "You OK? Seriously, Anna, I didn't even think—"

I had taken a deep breath to calm myself, but he probably thought I was still thinking about the back of the babysitter's head. I was glad I hadn't heard about it while still in the sheriff's office. "It's fine," I said. "Really. And send me as much human resources or whatever else as you want. I'm grateful for everything you—"

"Going to stop you there," he said. "Get down to see Keller again today, and that will be all the thanks I need."

All the thanks, but I never got to say them. In this way I was reminded that we weren't friends. One of us had been a drowning person, and the other, a life raft. I was on land for the moment, and he probably only hoped he wouldn't have to rescue me again. "I'll go today," I said. Not love, not friendship, in some ways not even gratitude on my part. It was relief, pure and deep relief that I might never need anyone's help as much as I already had.

KELLER'S RECEPTIONIST SAT at her desk, listening to the local talk-radio station at a low volume. When I opened the door, she snapped the dial down and smiled with a recognition I didn't think warranted. Keller had been mouthing off about me, I figured. "Hey," she said, drawing out the word. "I'm Sherry."

I waited for the punchline. Sherry and the sheriff? It was a bad '70s sitcom, set in a diner with a laugh track and the same cop/doughnut joke in every script.

The woman was just as bright as the sticky note she'd left the day before, just as blond and ponytailed and open-faced as the dot over that *i* had promised. More than that, I could sense that she was sticky, too—curious, wheedling.

I didn't have the patience, not after my repeat trip through the cattle chute of security downstairs. I hadn't brought my laptop on purpose this time, hoping it would speed things up. But a gum-chomping uniformed woman with a nametag that read *Deputy Tara Lombardi*, a woman hardly older than Joshua with a pixie face and spiky black hair, had taken a long look through everything in my purse, including my Illinois driver's license. *Who would leave Chicago for this place?* she had said with sneer.

I had the same feeling now, in front of this receptionist's too-familiar smile, as I had with my purse opened to its guts on the table. "The sheriff left a packet for me," I said, all business.

"Oh, sure, let me get it." She pushed herself from her desk and hurried to the back.

Aidan's missing-child poster had been tacked to the wall over the woman's workspace. The same fluffy-headed photo from all over town. Below it, nearly hidden from public view, was a coloring-book page scratched with red and blue, with a few distended letters in green in the corner. *Mommy*, it read in unpracticed lines and a simple squat pumpkin of a circle. The child's handwriting telegraphed nothing except that he drew his *o*'s clockwise.

Sherry returned carrying a large flat manila envelope. "I had to dig up his desk to find it," she said. "That man, I swear."

I recognized the moment. I was supposed to respond in agreement, a roll of the eyes or a nod that said I also didn't understand the mysteries of men. No problem. I didn't.

"Is there somewhere I can take a look at this?" I said. "I shouldn't be long."

Sherry slid the envelope across the counter and watched my hand claim it. "Back there," she said. "Any of the desks that aren't . . . gross. They're all slobs."

I chose a desk near the sheriff's dark door. *That man*, Sherry had said, as though this one was worth distinguishing from another. I don't think I'd ever offered a wry smile over a man's endearing faults. I hadn't had much of a chance for fondness.

Just before I'd started formal training in handwriting, I'd moved into another new—old, actually—apartment, a house with three floors and tall ceilings. Kentucky. I was hugely pregnant and slow on the stairs, which attracted the attentions of the man on the top floor. He always managed to be getting his mail at the same time I was coming home. When he finally asked me to dinner, I couldn't imagine what he saw in me. I wasn't finding men at all attractive, then. But I'd considered his offer.

In my lonely life, even with another life growing inside me, those months were the most alone I'd ever been. I waited tables, and sometimes the other girls would cover me for an extra break out of pity, but we weren't friends. I took reduced-price classes at the community center, taught by retired accountants and résumé-building new college graduates, any topic anyone wanted to teach me. I hardly talked to anyone. I didn't know what I was doing during that time. I spun in place with energy, with freedom and possibility, but also with nerves jangling. Each evening was a struggle not to dial Ray's number and tell him where to pick me up. I missed him. I missed—everything.

My memories would flatten until I couldn't remember why I was somewhere he wasn't.

Then, in one of the community center classes, I learned a bit about handwriting analysis from a librarian who had taken it up as a hobby.

The world peeled away. My manager at the restaurant had a scribble as fast as a rabbit's heartbeat, panicked. The college student taking polls at the bus stop transcribed with a script so tight and hesitant that she seemed to grow smaller as she wrote. People began to reveal themselves on the page. In life, they might be working, playing with their kids, remodeling their houses. But on the page, most of them skirted the edges of complete chaos.

Once I'd scraped the bottom of the librarian's knowledge of handwriting analysis, I'd put together enough tips from the restaurant to order a used textbook. The package came while I was at work, and the nice upstairs neighbor signed for it, leaving it at my door with a note. He hadn't known he was giving me everything I needed.

His handwriting had been calming, elegant in a way I hadn't expected and hadn't ever seen. I put myself to sleep that night remembering the way his script rolled forward, confident and steady and hopeful.

But then every time I saw him afterward, he brought up the package and how happy he'd been to offer his John Henry for the delivery. He meant John Hancock. John Henry, the steel-driving man, had probably signed his name, if he ever had, with a shaky X. Was John Henry a real person? John *Hancock* was the one with the significant signature. Maybe it was a joke? I couldn't tell.

The neighbor only smiled, now with affection. What I saw

was possession. He didn't know me, didn't know what I'd come through to hold this precious freedom in my own two hands. But he was already breaking off a hunk of it for himself.

I started to use the back stairwell. After Joshua was born, his late-night cries drove off most of the other neighbors, including the man with the elegant hand.

That man might have been something to regret, if I was in the mood. But these days I only had time for the man I was trying to raise.

I was still holding the sheriff's assignment in my hand. I ran a finger under the envelope's sealed flap and slid out a single sheet of copy paper and a plastic sleeve. I shook the package upside down. Another, smaller piece of paper drifted to the desk.

I took up this one first. Pink, lined. It had been ripped without care from a notepad, probably beside the phone. Two edges of the paper were ragged. Felt-tip pen, black.

Content first:

MILK, CAT FOOD
AIDAN'S CRACKERS
PEANUT BUTTER
BANANAS
HAMBERGER

I went through the list again, then turned the paper over, looking at the points at which the pen had leaked through. I turned to the front again and studied each line. The lettering was all uppercase, rigid, each letter a hostage on the page. Each word had taken a lot of time. The author might have used a chisel and had similar results—except that *Aidan's crackers* had a little slant to it.

I looked for a long time at those two words, so heavy with attention and care. So laden with the unbearable love for the name a mother called her child.

Then I turned to the other sheet of paper. It was a copy. A color copy, but still a copy. Apparently Keller considered my time his to waste.

Like the grocery list, the note had been ripped from a larger piece of paper, ragged on two edges, too, from the looks of the thing. Pink again. Hearts in a slight darker pink lined the edges. It was unsigned, and the block letters of the grocery list were gone. The script here was slim and girlish, but uneven and hurried. Ballpoint pen, blue.

> *that I want Aidan with me. You figure out how to get money to us after. We'll go away*

I smoothed the paper under my hand, though it was perfectly flat. I kept reading the content over and over—though I hadn't been hired for content, had I? I was stuck here, hoping that the sentence would finish, that something would link up and make sense.

After a few seconds, I sat back.

"Tough case?" Sherry called from across the room. She sat forward in her chair, making me think of her open, overly giving handwriting, her *Back in a jiff!* Those round letters, the ending flourishes of those *ff*s, like an arm curled, beckoning.

I glanced back at the grocery list. "Pretty tough," I said.

She lit up and hurried to my side, looking down at the two samples for a moment. "I don't know how you can tell anything from that," she said. "Especially that one. Block letters all look the same, don't they?"

We stared at the pages. "Do you know the little boy's family?" I said.

"Yeah," she said. "I mean, doesn't everyone know everyone else around here?"

"No," I said.

"Yeah, but you're—well." She could have said *new to town*, but she hadn't.

"Tell me about the father," I said.

Sherry's eyes drifted back toward the note and list. "I thought it was the mother who wrote these."

"I was just wondering." I paused, uncertain. Probably it was wrong to prey on what I could tell from the big open bowls of Sherry's *a*'s and *o*'s. "Just wondering who had her so scared."

Sherry's mouth dropped open. She pulled a sample closer to her with a manicured finger. "You can tell that from just—from just a *grocery* list?"

"You can tell a lot from a grocery list," I said, enjoying the demonstration a little, despite myself. "She was young. She was poor. She loved her son. She had a cat."

"You can tell she had a *cat*—"

I pulled the list back toward me. "I'm not a psychic. Cat food's on the list."

"Oh," Sherry said with a shaky laugh. "Just like you can tell she likes peanut butter."

"Or Aidan does."

"I bet he does," Sherry agreed, her voice gone soft.

I had a vision of Joshua, age three or so, crying from being left at the bad day care while I worked a double shift. My little boy had loved peanut butter. He used to love everything, including me. I missed that age, his sturdy little legs figuring out the world, but always running back to throw himself at me. I hadn't wanted to leave him at day care, then or ever. In the time I was gone, I could imagine a hundred ways for him to be taken from me. A hundred impossible ways to lose him.

This was all wrong. I should be telling CEOs which executives not to hire, or mining the halting love letters my lonelyhearts sent me. I should be turning Sherry's attention back to the question she hadn't answered, about Aidan's dad. But it was surprisingly pleasant to be talking this way to another woman, another mother. I hesitated, thinking of the women at my door from the Boosters, and then said, "For about two years, mine wouldn't eat anything but creamy peanut butter sandwiches with the crusts cut off. Morning, noon, and night."

Sherry looked behind her, found an extra chair, and pulled it up next to me. Her bright ponytail swung over her shoulder. "Mine's five," she said. "I can't talk about him enough. How old is yours?"

My head felt a little light. "He's a teenager. I wish he were still five."

"Yeah, because at five you can still put them in your pocket, you know? Or at least pick them up and carry them out to the car if they're being jerks. In some ways I can't wait for Jamey to grow up and turn into what he'll be," she said. "But in other ways, I want time to stop. I want him to stay perfect, just the way he is."

Perfect ears, perfect hands. I was often startled by Joshua's beauty. How had something so perfect come from such a mess? "Except—" I stopped. Was my life so empty that I was turning into a person who confided in strangers? Sherry had her fist hooked at her chin, waiting. "Except that he was perfect before, and he's perfect now, and he'll be perfect tomorrow," I said. "Suddenly he's a different boy than the one you knew, but still—perfect."

"That's it," Sherry said, triumphantly. "That's exactly—"

Across the room, the door swung open, banging against the wall. Sherry jumped to her feet. I expected the sheriff or another officer but instead a tall, thick man in a grease-smeared zip-up jacket stood in the doorway.

This was Aidan's father. I knew it from the shifty look Sherry gave me as she returned to her desk. I slid the handwriting samples out of sight.

"He's not in at the moment, Bo," Sherry said.

"Is he on vacation? I need to know what's going on." The man's voice violated the silent room.

"He would call you if there was anything at all," Sherry said. "I can have him check in when he gets back."

Bo ran his meaty fingers through his hair, then jammed his fists into his jacket pockets. "I mean it, Sherry, I need to be kept up to speed here. Are they even trying to find my kid?" His eyes swept the room and located me. He froze. "You got some help in to find him or something? Those detectives—"

"She's just doing a favor for the sheriff," Sherry said. "Now, why don't you give us your number again and I'll let him know you were here." She scooted a notepad across the counter to him and held out a pen. He grabbed it and scratched at the paper while Sherry watched. "Put your name down, too," she murmured.

"Shit, Sherry, you don't think he knows my number by now?" But he didn't look up. His hand dragged across the notepad and thumped the pen down. "The second he gets in, all right? I want answers." He wrenched the door open, paused, gave me another look, and was gone.

We listened to his fading footsteps down the stairs. It felt as though he'd taken half the oxygen in the room with him.

With a flourish, Sherry ripped the message from Bo off the notepad and marched it back to me, held high over her head, a flag. "Looky what I got," she sang. "Would I not make the best detective? Sheriff won't let me do anything but take calls and stuff, but I say I've got what it takes." She slid the paper in front of me.

"I don't even need to see it," I said.

"I know," Sherry said, shrugging. "He's wearing it like an aftershave, isn't he? He didn't used to be so—well, maybe he always was. We all went to high school together, me and Bo and—but so what? What do you see?"

For a moment, I didn't answer or look at Bo's message. This wasn't what Sheriff Keller had asked me to do. He wouldn't like it, and I didn't, either. This sample would taint the process—though of course encountering Aidan's dad in person had probably already done that. I thought about the pressed block letters of Aidan's mom's grocery list, about the fear etched into such a perfect word as *bananas*.

I picked up the message. White paper, blue ink. It had come from a memo pad with designated blanks for the time and date and the caller's name and number. Bo had scribbled on the diagonal across the entire sheet. The numbers were uneven, his signature sloppy. He had what my training had taught me to call resentment lines, vertical strokes in letters that clawed across the page like shovels digging a grave. Hidden in each millimeter of ink—*Bo Ransey*—was insult sustained, offense calculated. Not to mention the coiled twirls in his *B* and *R*, lying in wait like snakes.

I looked up.

Sherry put her palms on the desk and sighed. "I know," she said. "I hope she gets away, too."

Chapter Four

After a long shared silence, Sherry went back to her desk. I laid the samples side by side and studied them again.

The plastic sleeve turned out to be the most interesting and confusing of the pieces provided. Inside was an original sample, several two-inch or smaller shreds of blue stationery ripped and charred. Only a few inches of writing was visible between them. I tried to puzzle the pieces together without taking them out of the sleeve—they would disintegrate if I tried. All I could do was study the few discernible words visible:

> to, and, *never your, need to, her, love*

I had the feeling the author was taking care to be clear—legible as well as firm in the message itself. I spent a long time on each curve, on the spaces between words.

Tearing myself away was like rising out of water. I looked around me, stretched. The sheriff hadn't returned. No one had come through the door. I pulled a notebook and pen from my purse.

About the first two samples, I knew what I had to say. I smoothed the paper and bent to the task, but the words wouldn't come. At last I had to admit that I didn't want them to. I pictured the sheriff coming back to a handwritten analysis, poring over my self-conscious script to find something to mock.

The librarian who'd taught me my first little bit of analysis had warned me. "It will mess up your own handwriting for a while," he'd explained to that small group of curiosity seekers at the community center. Kentucky. Everyone there had a slow drawl that twisted words into new formations. "You'll have to stop thinking about handwriting," he had said, "just to get the check for the light bill written out."

Aidan's mom's handwriting swam in front of my eyes. I hadn't brought my laptop because of the lobby security, and now I couldn't bring myself to leave behind anything handwritten. I would go home to type my report. It would take longer to be done with the project, but I still needed these precautions, these rituals. The sheriff would understand, or at least think he did.

I LEFT THE samples behind with Sherry, but thought about them as I left the courthouse and retrieved my truck from the square. Outside, the sky was still bright and inviting, one of those perfect fall days, maybe one of the last of its kind. When the turn came to return to the apartment, I drove on.

I meandered through the town, letting my hand dangle out the open window. At the end of town, real estate signs attached to fences enclosed fallow fields. They'd be a development of starter homes before too long. Parks was a nice place to start. Back in town, I found an enclave of older, nicer houses and turned in to shop them. Parks, it seemed, was a nice place to end up, too.

I drove back through town and out the other side, still restless. Passing over the highway, I slowed to watch the cars rushing along the ribbon of gray toward the horizon. On the other side of the interstate, I pulled into the parking lot for the Dairy Bar and sat with the key still in the ignition. This was the place in town I felt most at home. That was the embarrassing truth of the matter—more at home at the local ice cream shop than even the place I lay my head at night. I'd worked at a place just like this, same name, back when I was a kid. It was the only explanation for why I'd let this little ice cream shed dictate where Joshua and I would land this time around.

We had left Chicago that morning early with no plan. Maybe Ohio again. Ohio was quiet, and far. But not Cincinnati. Smaller towns were better. I took a different direction there, too, dipping south into Indiana with the notion of swinging around Indianapolis and then east until we found something suitable.

Only a few hours into the drive, though, we were miserable, baked to the seats and battered by the highway wind coming through the windows. When a patch of roadside facilities presented itself, we stopped to fill the tank and stretch. Then I spotted the Dairy Bar sign. The same lettering for the neon sign and everything.

"They have the best burgers," I said to Joshua through the window. "I used to work at the one back in Wisconsin." I allowed an image to climb through the opening in my memory: my best friend, Theresa, leaning into the sliding window to order a malted milkshake big enough to ruin dinner and maybe breakfast the next day, too. Making faces at me as I worked. Theresa, once a real person, was now only a regret. When she came to mind, I stuffed her back down into the locked bin of my mind. A lot of people lived there, but wondering about Theresa only led to black thoughts and bad dreams. Theresa and my mother. "I had no idea these were a chain," I said.

Joshua glared at the sign and back at me. He didn't want a cheese-burger or a hot dog. He didn't want anything, not even the chocolate malt I bought him. He wanted to be furious. He didn't remember being mad about moving to Chicago, didn't know that he would attach himself to the next place, too. And of course he didn't understand why we'd had to leave in the first place, why we always had to leave. After I finished my burger, I drove us not back to the highway but into the town. At the courthouse square, I admired the white pillars and bought a paper at the little newsstand café.

Joshua hadn't said more than a few words all morning, but he broke his silence when I returned to the truck and opened the paper to the ads. "You're going to pick a town based on a crappy malt?" he said.

"I'm picking a town based on cheap rent," I said. "And I think my friend Kent lives not too far away."

He narrowed his eyes. "You don't have any friends."

"My colleague, then. The crappy malt is just a bonus."

Not a bonus but a salvageable piece of my childhood, some-thing I could keep, something I could return to, for crying out loud. What was the harm in that? One good memory—was it too much to ask?

Now I leaned into the sliding service window to order. The woman inside wore the familiar Dairy Bar—pink golf shirt, the logo over the breast. I could see through the store out the back door to another woman, much older and stooped, smoking a cig-arette and wearing the same logo pink shirt. I had once owned that shirt, had once had the seventeen flavors of malted milk-shakes memorized. On the hand-painted menu at my shoulder now, the flavor count appeared to be a little higher. Next to the menu, Aidan Ransey's face peered out from one of his posters. I turned my back on him and watched the traffic.

I was sipping my milkshake at a picnic table when a county cop car pulled in next to my truck. The driver hopped out and headed for the window. I watched after him. I was starting to recognize a few of the faces from the courthouse lobby. Then the passenger door opened and the sheriff emerged.

"You on a stakeout?" he called. He wore sunglasses, his black ball cap pulled low over them. "Or shake out, I should say."

I raised my cup in a toast, hoping he wouldn't feel that he needed to be friendlier than that. He came over anyway.

"Did you get a chance to look at the ransom note?"

"The *copy* of the note," I said. "I'll do my best with the partial information I've received to get you a report this afternoon."

"Why don't you report right now?"

"Don't want to keep you from your malted," I said.

His eyebrows rose. He took off the glasses and hung them in the pocket of his shirt. "We're here on county business."

Free malteds, then. I made a noncommittal noise around my straw.

"I guess you know the Ransey family runs this place—"

The straw dropped out of my mouth. "They do?" The other officer stood at the service window, leaning low to talk to someone inside. Out of all the things I might have learned, the fact that the Ranseys dealt in ice cream startled me. I'd picked up a certain global disdain for the Ranseys that no one had yet explained—that surprise that anyone might "hup to" for them—but maybe I was only protective of the Dairy Bar for my own reasons. I had been elbow-deep in the ice cream cooler for a full summer, breaking in my teenage back rolling big bins of chocolate sauce and hauling heavy bags of powdered malt and ice milk crystals in and out of the storage room. My first job, my first chance at freedom.

"You didn't know? You come here often?"

Could he even hear himself? He could. He was blushing up to his hat.

"Once in a while," I said. "We had one of these places where I grew up."

"Oh?" He looked up at the Dairy Bar sign. "Where's that?"

I slurped at my shake for a time. "Did you want that report?"

The sheriff hitched a boot over the seat on the other side of the table and sat sideways to me.

"OK, first off, the two photocopied samples," I said. "I identified some markers—are you going to write this down?"

He grinned at me. "Are you?"

"I identified some markers in the two pink samples that lead me to believe the author is a single individual," I said. "Some of the letter shapes are highly idiosyncratic, even though the author wrote them in what seems like two different situations. Different pens, different styles, maybe with different levels of urgency. If you'd asked someone to produce two handwriting samples that looked completely different from one another, they couldn't have done a better job. But—definitely the same hand."

"The same hand," he said.

"The same person," I said. "I'm assuming that's what you wanted to know."

"So the mother took him?"

At the Dairy Bar service window, the other officer was leaning in, flirting with the girl behind the counter.

"I can't tell you that," I said. "I never said I could."

"The ransom note—"

"Did you read that note?" I said. "I'm less interested in the script than I am in where the rest of that note is. The *actual* note, not a reasonable facsimile."

He glared at me. "You can't tell me because the thing's ripped or what?"

"Because it doesn't make any sense," I said. "The third sample, the little pieces of nothing, make more sense than that note."

"OK, the pieces," he said. "What about them?"

"Different hand," I said. "But you probably didn't need me for that. Written by a man, I think, but that's a bit of a guess. Someone hesitant to say what he was trying to say, sort of—halting and stunted. Labored. He probably spent a lot of time on it, maybe started over a couple of times? He does this thing before his words where he taps the paper a few times with his pen, and then goes on. He might have been lying or saying something difficult—or both. That one was from the Ransey house, too?"

He didn't want to answer. "The nanny's room. From the garbage."

When did a young woman burn a letter with the word *love* in it? Either the love was over, going bad, or forbidden.

"Would you recognize the handwriting in the pieces again if you saw it?" the sheriff said.

"Out of context? It's hard to say." I remembered back to the feeling of sinking below the surface of the shredded sample into another life, a story not mine. "I had the feeling that he was being careful to be clear. His handwriting might be smaller and tighter in this note than in something he was just dashing off. But maybe."

"That doesn't leave us with much, does it?"

"Well, we didn't start with much, did we?" I said. "Here's what I can tell you. The same person wrote the first two samples, the list and the partial. If you say one is from Aidan's mother, then both are. If it's the nanny—" I recalled the slight slant to Aidan's name in the grocery list. No one else could have written that list.

"Fine. The mother wrote them both. But that doesn't mean she took him. Or if she took him—"

"What?"

"Nothing."

Keller pulled his other leg over the bench and faced me. "Is there more?"

Was it professional courtesy to tell him I could rule out Aidan's dad as the source of the third sample, having seen his heavy, thudding hand already? Or was it just stepping in a pile of trouble? Either way—I'd done the work I'd been hired to do. I had a lot of questions about the household the child was missing from, but not questions I had a right to ask.

"That's all," I said.

I could tell he didn't believe me. We both turned to see his partner coming across the parking lot with a malt in each hand. His knuckles had that particular splotchy pink sunburn across them I recognized from a long day spent with hands on the steering wheel. The burn ran down to both wrists. The officer nodded to me and held out one of the cups to Keller.

"I got you strawberry," he said.

The sheriff took the cup sternly. His ears were strawberry colored, too. He didn't glance my way until he'd dismounted the picnic table and reached the passenger door of the cruiser. "You'll send that all in a formal report," he said. It wasn't a question.

It wasn't a question for me, either. I wanted nothing more than to be done with the Ranseys and this man. I stood and fed my cup into the trash bin. "Yes, sir," I said to the retreating car.

Chapter Five

The junior-senior high school sat among harvested cornfields just outside of town, a sprawling single-story outlet mall of a place inconvenient to almost everyone. Joshua took the bus to school, but I could tell by the station wagons with mismatched doors and repurposed farm trucks in the lot that the older students drove themselves.

I checked in at the front office, got a pass, and was led to a waiting area for the guidance counselor. I didn't want to wait. The student receptionist glanced at my tapping foot. When the counselor's door finally opened, a lanky man emerged with his arm around the back of a young woman with puffy eyes. The man, dressed in a sleek gray suit more stylish and probably more expensive than anything I'd seen in town so far, shot me a conspiratorial smile and escorted the girl out of sight. In a few minutes, he was back with his hand extended.

The grip was loose, as though I might be in the same delicate state as the crying girl.

I'd seen this guy before and it took a moment to realize where.

He'd only recently moved back to Parks, a hometown boy from the right side of Main Street. The local paper had covered his return as though he were a Kennedy. A local sports hero, a graduate of an upper-tier school out east, and now—my son's guidance counselor? Probably a hushed story there.

"Ms. Winger? Joe Jeffries. So happy to finally meet you." He had the sharpness of a paper crane in the shoulders, but around his eyes, I sensed something more animal. He was attractive, and I held that against him and also against the people who'd hired him. I tried not to think about the arm he'd had around the student.

I followed him into the office, already leery of that word: *finally*. Fine on paper, but in execution it certainly put out a notice of deficiency.

"I've been so eager to talk to you," Jeffries said, gesturing to a chair. "For a couple of reasons, really. The first, as you might have guessed, concerns Joshua."

I appreciated Jeffries's efforts. I knew Joshua secretly went by "Josh" at school, but I wanted no part of that.

"I would imagine both reasons concern him," I said.

"Actually, no." He tapped a pencil on his desktop, and we both took the opportunity to look at the pencil instead of each other. "I heard through the grapevine what you do for a living. I find it incredibly fascinating."

My heart fluttered. It was as if the alarm had sounded. Someone knocking on the door. A phone call in the night. Sometimes it struck me how unfair it all was. I was not the one who had ruined our lives—but I was the one who had to deal with the fallout, flitting from perch to perch. I was the one who had to decide, each time. Is it time to go?

In Kentucky, it was a phone call in the night, a familiar voice asking for a name I was starting to forget. In Chicago, years later, a woman on Michigan Avenue stared at me and said, *It's you, isn't it? You're that girl got herself drowned in Sweetheart Lake.*

I drew a deep breath and tried out my voice. "It can also be quite tedious," I said.

"Well, I'm fascinated," he said. "And I think our students would be, too. Maybe you could come in for an afternoon to talk to the Honors Society or something?"

I shifted in my seat. How quickly news traveled in this town. "It's not a sideshow act or anything," I said. "I don't do party tricks."

I didn't sound as certain of that as I normally did.

"Of course not," he said. "No, I didn't mean to suggest—I just thought the students would enjoy it." He leaned over his desk, and the scent of him—soap, shaving cream, minty breath— wafted across the desk, an assault. The weight of his gaze made me wonder if I'd ever been really looked at. The sheriff—he'd had a good look at me at our first meeting. He'd really seen me, too, more than I wanted him to. "I just think—what a window into the soul," Jeffries continued, poetic. Then he smiled. "And you must run up against some real damage. What's the most disturbing thing you've ever learned from someone's writing?"

The chiding in his smile was familiar and, though it had been a while since I'd seen it, a little sexual.

I shook my head. "It's not really like that."

But it was. Until this week, I might have pulled some anec- dote from my work with the lonelyhearts, the lovelorn people who send me scraps of letters and canceled checks believing that I can tell them something promising about the person they want to trust. Like the woman who'd sent me a love letter from a federal prisoner, in the hopes he was reformed. He wasn't. Or

I might have hidden enough details to tell a story from the confidential case files from working with Kent. But now of course it was Joshua's incomplete classwork that came to mind. My son didn't trust me, and he would lose himself to hide from me.

Across his desk, Jeffries waited. What he wanted was a sensational story that would turn my modesty false, something to retell in the faculty lounge later. I straightened in my chair and said, "I'll think about your offer to join the lecture circuit. What was the other reason you wanted to see me? About Joshua?"

"Right, of course." Jeffries reached for a file folder from his desk and riffled through a few loose pages. "Well, you probably aren't surprised to hear he's struggling. Math, especially. You might go over his homework with him each night, if you're confident in your seventh-grade math, which—don't be afraid to say that you aren't." He glanced up. Joshua didn't want my help and he certainly didn't want me looking at anything he'd written by hand. You could tell a lot from zeroes and twos. I shook my head. "Well," he said, "you can try just checking to see that he's done it. That's a first step."

"I can ask," I said.

"What's really bothering me about Joshua is less concrete. A couple of his teachers have mentioned he seems distracted or withdrawn. He's missed a few assignments. In some of his classes, he doesn't seem to be doing his homework at all, particularly some worksheets from his social studies class. Last week he refused to come to the board when one of his teachers asked him to . . ." He ran his finger over some notes. "Mrs. Tyler, English. She asked him to write a sentence across the board from their reading for some activity she had planned and he absolutely refused. She chose someone else but found it odd. Does this sound like your son?"

It didn't sound like my son, but it sounded exactly like the stranger who'd moved into his bedroom.

"I'm not an expert in seventh-grade math or seventh-grade boys, Mr. Jeffries," I said. Over Jeffries's shoulder, a title in the bookcase caught my eye: *Your Child in Conflict*. Then another: *The Age of Innocence Is Over*. The spines of a hundred books and journals begged for my attention. No one was an expert.

I had to get it right, but the cracks were starting to show. For a moment, I let myself imagine Mr. Jeffries's comforting arm around my shoulder as I confided in him. But: *grapevine*.

"I'll talk to him," I said. "About his attitude. And the math."

"Well, if it helps, you can tell him that if his grades drop any further, he'll be cut from football," he said. "That would be out of my hands, though I'd hate to lose him."

I stared at him. "Oh, you're the—"

"The assistant coach, yeah."

"Sorry I didn't . . . I've been meaning to stop by practice."

"No worries," he said, flashing the smile again. "We have our first game coming up soon. Hope to see you there."

Afterward, I walked the hallway, thinking about what Jeffries had said. The football team might be the bargaining chip I needed. Being on the team represented the most freedom Joshua had been able to negotiate. He'd worked so hard to make his case. But I'd never seen a schedule of the games. I was sure one existed, that it was being kept from me on purpose. But I couldn't have it both ways. I couldn't be mad the schedule wasn't pinned up on the fridge when I didn't want to go sit on hard bleachers and chitchat with the other parents.

A few minutes later, I realized I was lost inside the school. I turned back toward the guidance office, but couldn't find it again.

Three boys were sitting in a row outside a closed door. They had the same limp hair in their eyes, the same skinny legs. As I hurried past, one whistled. They laughed, and one of them, grown bold, called after me in a sultry voice, "Hey, baby."

They were Joshua's age. Over my shoulder, I gave the boys what I hoped was a warning glare. But then I thumped into something, hard, and started to fall. I felt arms trying to catch me and grabbed at them. "Whoa, now," a man said.

I looked up. Bo Ransey held me in his arms. "Sorry," I whispered, pulling out of his reach.

"No problem, my fault." He released me without a glance. "Steve-O," he yelled down the hall. "What the hell am I getting called in for now? Get your stuff and get out to the truck."

One of the boys separated from the others, high-tops dragging.

"Is that your son?" I asked. "I mean—your other son?"

Bo turned back to me. He was gray around the eyes. "Oh," he said. "No, this here is my sister's kid." The boy stood at our elbows, his eyes on the floor. Down the hall, the other two were having fits on his behalf. "Good as mine, though, right, Steve-O?"

The kid's eyes darted between us. "Yeah," he said. I recognized the little creep's voice. *Hey, baby.*

Ransey knocked his nephew on the shoulder. "Go on. Be there in a second."

The boy seized his opportunity as Ransey turned to me. "Look, really," he said, his voice going soft. "Do you know anything? Are they not telling me something?"

"About Aidan?"

"Yeah, Aidan. What else could I—?" He looked tired. "Do you know where she took him?"

"I don't—I don't know anything," I said, which was the truth.

Nothing was certain except that a baby was missing and a woman was dead. Nothing. For all I knew, this man in front of me had killed his family, that nanny. And he was tainting my process, big-time. "It's better that you talk to the sheriff. All I was doing there was—"

"The note, right?" He shook his head. "I heard about what you do. I don't believe in that crap, I can tell you that." He drew his palm over his face. "I don't believe in it at all, but if it helps find my boy and gets him back OK, I'll believe Santa Claus is married to the damn Easter Bunny, all right?"

His voice rang down the hall. The boys had gone still.

Finally Ransey folded his arms and took a step back from me. "Look," he said, gentle again. "Who knows what you see when you look at me—I'm not perfect. But I just want my kid back. She had no reason to take him. No reason to take him away from me."

I stood under his pleading eyes, believing him. But then I'd often taken things at face value. People were liars. In the end, and maybe after a long time, they would show you who they really were, how far they would go.

I only trusted what was written down. I might also give some credence to things I'd witnessed myself. What I'd seen was that love was no guarantee, that you could grieve the damage you'd done yourself, that being sorry wouldn't keep you from doing it again. The same hand that could caress you could swing at you with velocity. The same hand.

I nodded to Bo Ransey and let myself pass him, ready if he reached out to stop me. I followed the path the nephew had taken, anxious to be away from this place. Outside, I took a deep breath, skirted the Ransey truck with the boy inside the cab, and kept going. If Aidan's mother had taken him away, there was a reason. If I couldn't believe that, I couldn't begin to sleep at night.

Chapter Six

On the way home from the school I stopped at the café on the square for a copy of the *Spectator*. As I dropped the change into the man's hand, I noticed a few checks taped to the back counter, almost out of sight. The account numbers were marked out, and the narrow man's narrow hand had scrawled *DO NOT ACCEPT* across each one. I recognized the snakes-coiled twirls in *Ransey* in the signature line of one of them.

"On second thought," I said, "I'll take a hot tea, too." While the man turned to make my drink, I dug out more cash and leaned low over the counter to get a better look. The second check was also a Ransey, I thought, maybe even the hand of Aidan's mother. But the writing was so small I couldn't quite read the name. The third check taped to the wall was older and curled in on itself. As I squinted at it, the proprietor placed the steaming cup under my chin and narrowed his eyes at me.

Outside, I cast the hot water into the trash without even adding the teabag and sat at one of the sidewalk tables with my paper. A beautiful young woman smiled out from the front page, a small child in her arms. I checked the caption. The nanny, Charity Jordan, with an infant Aidan.

I skimmed the article. She was twenty-four. The child of Mr. and Mrs. So-and-So Jordan. Unmarried. She had cared for Aidan Ransey since he was six months old, living in most days but retaining residence at her parents' house. Sheriff Keller had given a similar recitation of the facts the morning I'd met him. His delivery had seemed coldhearted, considering the subject. But now I recognized his approach. Bullet-pointed thoughts were how I dealt with important details, too. The higher the stakes, the more important it was to be clear, concise, free of sentimentality.

Though it seemed a little sentimentality might be spared. Only twenty-four, still living with Mom and Dad, and found on the floor of a public toilet with her head bashed in.

Lower on the same page, another photo. This one was full color, too, but it didn't need to be. The woman in it was thin, small, stark against a white wall. Shifty. How could a single photo convey so little confidence in a human being? It had the feel of a mugshot. Wasn't this woman, Aidan's mother presumably, also technically missing? The caption gave her name as Leila (Coyle) Ransey.

I paused over the name, the first I'd seen it. *The mother. His mom.* She had been called many things in my presence but not her own name.

I looked between the two images for a long moment, bothered, but by what?

Deeper in the story, a "source" was claiming that a note left behind at the Ransey household was the work of Mrs. Leila Ransey. A handwriting expert had been called in.

I swallowed hard. Well, at least they hadn't mentioned my

name or my FBI connection. That was the sort of statement that packed our suitcases.

This "source," though—was this Sherry, unnamed, giving away secrets or was it the sheriff, giving the reporter what she'd demanded, anything he could offer, in lieu of the kid's whereabouts and a suspect in handcuffs? In any case, it was a big fat guess, since I hadn't given any information in time to be featured in this issue.

I looked up, watching a few cars passing by the courthouse. Across the square, that pixie-faced deputy from the security line was leading Bo Ransey out of the courthouse doors by the elbow. I raised the paper higher and watched over the top of it as Bo ducked out from under the girl officer's hold and stormed off. What did you have to do to get escorted off county property during the investigation of your missing kid? Deputy Lombardi waited, her hands on her hips, until the guy had cleared the grounds. She was turning to go inside when Bo pulled out of his parking space, squealing the tires.

I put the paper down. I couldn't wait to turn in that report and be done with these people.

A woman carrying a small child in her arms pushed an empty stroller past me.

And then I knew what was bothering me about the photos in the newspaper. The babysitter had been given the golden opportunity, in death, to cradle the missing boy, but his mother was treated as a suspect in a lineup. There would be no baby in her arms, not in the newspaper or, one might assume the editor had decided, ever again.

It was practically decided here on the front page of the *Spectator*. The sitter: beautiful, loving, and good. The mother: a villain. There were no pictures of Bo, no mention of details about the family, other than an address. No hints of any discord or bad checks, of offenses past or present.

"Hey there," a woman's voice said.

I startled back to attention. The two Booster Club moms from the night Aidan disappeared stood in front of me. Only this time, the bored one who couldn't be bothered with me was leaning in with a grin on her face. The other one held back. "Hi," I said. "Stephanie and—"

Stephanie's head snapped in my direction.

"Grace," the other one said, smiling. I thought she was more pleased that I'd remembered Stephanie's name, that I might have studied what Stephanie had written on the flyer for me, than she was thrilled to see me again. "We thought we saw you out at the school yesterday."

"Oh," I said. "Yeah, some paperwork we missed. In the transfer."

"There was some trouble out there yesterday," she said. "Thought maybe yours was in on it. Mine *definitely* was. Any trouble there is, he's in the thick of it." She seemed almost proud of it, the trouble her kid could cause. Then she looked at me more closely. "What transfer?"

"From his last school," I said.

"I can't believe anyone would choose this place over anywhere else. Especially Chicago."

Grapevine indeed. Everything Grace said was a leading question without the indignity of having to ask.

"It's so unsafe there," I said finally. "You've heard the stories."

"And then to land here in the middle of all this," Grace said, poking at the paper in my hands. I closed it and folded it under my arm.

"Well, the joke's on me, I guess."

"Are you the source?" Stephanie spoke up. She was watching me warily. "In the paper? The one who said it was the mother's handwriting."

"No," I said.

"But you're the one they've called in, aren't you? That's what you do, isn't it?" Grace asked.

"It's not all I do," I said. I couldn't see a way out of this conversation, and then suddenly, I could. "You seem interested. Did you want me to look at your handwriting?"

"No," Stephanie barked.

"Bet your ass," Grace hissed, grabbing for a pen from her purse. Through a few negotiations, it transpired that the only paper available was the one tucked under my arm. I handed it over, and she wrote a few words down. "And then my signature? Do I sign it?"

"Whatever you want," I said. I'd thought they both would have raced away in horror, but that just goes to show how little I knew about people, off the page. Now, even though I'd promised the school counselor I didn't do parlor tricks, I'd tricked myself into doing them.

Grace handed back the paper. "Do your worst," she said.

She'd written *You are so full of shit. Love, Grace Mullen.*

"You have . . . a healthy skepticism," I said.

"Oh, my God," Grace said. "Steph, it's like going to the creepy fortune-teller at the county fair. You have to do it, too."

My eyes were drawn to the bowls of the rounded letterforms, her *o*'s, *e*'s, *c*'s. They should have been cupped and open but were actually quite narrow and stingy. Maybe not quite healthy, really, all this lack of generosity. I'd seen the same tendencies in incarcerated women, in men trapped in jobs they felt they had to keep. In my mother's handwriting, in fact. A trapped woman who had never wanted anyone else to make it out alive. I wondered what the county fair fortune-teller might tell Grace, and what might be left out. There may have been a lot left out already, a great deal withheld. I looked up into Grace's greedy eyes. Nothing to be gained by telling the whole truth and, anyway, this wasn't a job.

"You have a natural openheartedness," I said, studying the letters for other lies I could tell. "You only wish you could do more. And, oh, that's interesting—"

"What?" Grace leaned in.

"Well, I see some markers that lead me to believe that you might be"—for the first time her expression edged into apprehension—"really fun to work with at the Boosters concession stand," I said.

Her face registered a twinge of confusion, then relief. "I *am*. You might not be so bad yourself."

Steph shot me a curious look. It *was* just like going to the county fair. I was the midway barker offering to guess weights, and I'd undercut by a good fifty pounds so that everyone could keep having a good time.

"Joshua lost the team schedule already," I said, using the tone I knew they'd expect. Boys will be boys. "How can I get a copy? And I guess I should sign up for some shifts?"

Stephanie handed me a card this time, preprinted and not likely to give anything else away. I took it, noting the twee little house design on it. *Sommer House*, it said under her name, though it didn't say where the house was located. I took the card, smiled, sent them off with pleasantries. It pained me. The entire episode was pantomime—and yet. At the end of all things, there was my kid. What was a little dignity thrown in, after everything else I'd lost?

BACK AT THE apartment, a flat white envelope addressed to me had been propped against the wall below the mailboxes. The rest of the mail was junk and catalogs, stuff directed to past tenants and to "the customer" at this address. I paused over a flyer, one of those things that advertised appliances or rug-cleaning services on one side and used the blank spaces to put out missing kid alerts. This one was a teenager from Nevada. I had no reason at all to study the face as carefully as I did. Sometimes, when the missing kid was old enough, a runaway, I found myself admiring her ambition.

I pawed through the rest of it: a catalog of women's clothing, all linen and large cuff bracelets as though the modern woman lived her life dressed for patio dining. I couldn't help flipping through a few pages. Who lived this linen kind of life?

I was halfway up the stairs when I turned to the next catalog in the stack and nearly dropped the lot.

Sweetheart Lake Adventures.

My knees shook. I sat heavily on the nearest step, the rest of the mail falling and sliding to the landing.

It couldn't be.

The photo collage on the cover contained every tourist option available to those visiting my hometown: children with chocolate faces in front of the fudge shop, a Paul Bunyan lookalike marching in a parade, fishermen lined up with their catches still on their lines, a gorgeous sunset cut through with purple and gold, and a long, scenic view of a dock with the calm, green-dark lake behind.

On the back of the magazine: my name, my address.

I pawed back through the thing, my throat hurting with tears held back. All of my childhood laid out before me so easily and—it was beautiful. The grocery store we used, the old movie theater. The long street through town toward the river, a celebration banner overhead. I had trouble believing it, really. It was a put-on. It couldn't be real. It couldn't still look like this.

It couldn't be *here*.

How could this thing be here in my hands?

I picked up all the mail again and hurried up to the apartment. I tossed all the junk into the trash and spent a few minutes tearing the Sweetheart Lake magazine to shreds, tinier and tinier, before I put them all into a plastic bag, tied the handles, and buried it at the bottom of the bin.

After a few minutes, I dug it out and hustled down the stairs to the back door and out into the parking lot to the Dumpster and threw it in.

How? When you didn't give out a phone number or an email or an address anywhere, turned down coupons and incentives every chance you got, never signed up for any list, ever—how could you still be located and have your heart sold back to you?

Back upstairs, I paced until I thought Margaret might pick up her broom and then finally returned to the table.

I'd saved the newspaper with the story about the sitter, Charity Jordan, and now I distracted myself by flipping through the pages. Her photo was oddly cheerful in the blank apartment. Probably chosen specifically to show how bright a young life had been snuffed out. I compared Charity's robust good looks to Aidan's mother again, who seemed small, almost fragile, in comparison. The police presumably had a theory about how young and buxom Charity had been felled by her delicate employer, but damned if I could come up with a different one. Maybe she was one of those women whose adrenaline allowed them to pick up the ends of Volkswagens off their imperiled children. I hoped never to have to put my own lymphatic system to the test. I had chosen flight over fight every chance I got.

I turned to the back page and caught up on the day's announcements: arrests at the local bar, a DUI out on the interstate, some spray-paint vandalism on a bridge outside of town. I turned back to the front, hungry for more information about Leila. Nothing new had been revealed, except that the address they'd had for her in Indianapolis turned out to belong to an organization, and she'd lived not at those coordinates but in a home run by that group. The former address was not repeated; the new address was not given. The group went unnamed. The lack of details seemed to be a point of view, a throwing up of hands. Halfway house, drugs, incompetency, suspicion. Whatever it was, it was odd, wasn't it? That a mother had left her young child in the care of other people to move into some *situation*—it wasn't right. It was all there, unspoken.

When I folded the paper up again, there was Grace Mullen's message and signature. And below it, a photo I hadn't looked at very closely. Some civic event, an award handed out, handshakes given. And standing to the side of the activity and commendations stood Sheriff Keller.

Which reminded me that I hadn't finished up the report that would release me from any further conversations with the man. I shook off the panic. It was all a fluke, a marketing list gone bad. This report to Keller was the real urgent project here. I opened my laptop and got to work.

BY THE TIME I realized I'd forgotten to pick up Joshua from football practice, it was too late. I heard his stamping feet on the stairs, the key in the lock. He walked through the door and dropped the dreaded backpack on the table.

"I am so sorry," I said.

"I caught a ride with a friend," he said. I thought perhaps he was torn between making me feel guilty I'd forgotten him and making sure I knew he had solved the problem himself. "His dad said I could ride with them every night, if I wanted. They go right by, he said."

"Well, I would need to meet this dad, you know. That's not how it's done."

Joshua wiped a shank of sweaty hair from his eyes and looked at me blankly. It's possible that he knew—and I didn't—that this was precisely how it was done. No need for background checks or jotting down license plate numbers. Just blind trust that the village would reach in and help raise the child? That was not how it was done around *here*.

"Well, he said they went right by. He said it was no trouble."

"We can talk about it," I said finally. What we needed to talk about was math, but that could wait until the issue was upon us and the books came out. I had a sort of after-adrenaline hang-over from the magazine in the mail. "Go get cleaned up."

He headed to the shower, pleased with himself. I hadn't even brought up the issue of the backpack dropped where it shouldn't be. We were speaking, at least. Why ruin it?

Also, I was shaking a little. I'd forgotten him. I'd never forgotten him before.

After a long moment, I went back to fussing over the wording of the file I would send into Keller's office about the Ransey handwriting samples. I wanted to get it right, demonstrate the right level of professionalism—and, yes, maybe I wanted to show Keller how it was done. Before long I was engrossed again. When I next looked up, the apartment was dark and quiet around me. The backpack and the homework inside lay untouched. He'd gone to his room and his video games.

Outside Joshua's room, I took a deep breath. We were going to talk about math?

I pounded on the door, waited for the mumble I could inter-pret as an invitation, and opened it. He lay on his stomach on the floor with a game controller in his hands, his headphones dangling around his neck.

"Just five more minutes, OK?" he said.

"Actually," I said. "I have to go somewhere for a few minutes. Just a quick errand. I need to—come with me."

"I have homework."

"Which you never do anyway. If you did, I wouldn't have been called in to your school today."

He dropped his face to the floor. "Oh," he said into the carpet.

"Yeah, it was a good time for everyone," I said. "I got to hear all about your stellar work ethic and some incident with a chalk-board."

He looked up, wincing. In a strange way, I liked him like this. I said something, he reacted. Better than silence. At least I knew he could hear me.

"Or maybe I should say *not* involving a chalkboard. And now Mr. Jeffries wants me to come to your school and show everyone the magic of handwriting analysis—"

Joshua rose from the floor so quickly, I jumped back.

"You're not going to, are you?" He threw the game controller to the floor and stared at it. So much like Ray just now, busting up his toys. "*That's* what I need."

He yanked the headphones off and sat heavily on the edge of his bed. I waited for him to swipe at his bangs. He did.

My mind raced to catch up with him. What was I learning?

"I won't go if you don't want me to," I said slowly. "But—come with me now. We'll grab burgers and malts at the Dairy Bar, and I'll help you with your homework after."

He turned a creased forehead toward me. He'd gotten so much from me, even if he did have Ray's profile, his eyes. Look at the disbelieving expression on his face. Look at his suspicion. Look at his doubt. I'd given him that. Every bit of that was from me.

Chapter Seven

In the car, Joshua tucked himself into the passenger door. I fidgeted with the radio, finally deciding on silence. It was a cool evening, good for a drive. We pulled through town slowly, the windows rolled down. In the square, a group of boys sat on the wall enclosing the courthouse lawn. Joshua's head swiveled as we passed.

The limestone buildings of downtown gave way to some older wood-frame houses, then a pharmacy, a gas station, a tire place, then a dirty white shop with blank windows. The sidewalks grew rough, cracked. We were only a mile or two from our comfortable apartment and its double deadbolts, but I felt the presence of those old enemies, decay and neglect. I slowed, leaning toward the passenger side to gaze up at the houses on that side of the street. Joshua's hair was still wet from his shower and he smelled sweet: bar soap, laundry detergent, warm skin.

"What are we doing?" he said finally, as though granting me a favor.

"Research for a job I'm doing here in town," I said, pulling the truck over to the side. A few impatient drivers rushed around us.

"Where's the handwriting?"

"It's not quite like that. It's more like . . . reconnaissance."

He glanced at me. A word of war, of video games. I hadn't meant to offer a branch, but he seemed interested. "Recon? Are you on a stakeout or something?" He was teasing me, and I took the time to enjoy it. He leaned toward the windshield and peered out.

"OK, maybe more like surveillance." I pointed to the specific house, a gray square-faced place with two front doors. One stood partly open, the screen hanging crooked. The porch sagged under the weight of a couch and a stack of boxes and milk crates.

"Did a murder happen here?"

"Do you think I'd be sitting here? Do you think I'd bring you along? A little boy is missing. This is his house."

"I bet he's not missing the house," Joshua said.

Part of me wanted to agree with him, but I knew better. How could I explain to him how complicated it was, to love and hate a place so much? To know your home's lack but still defend it—even yearn for it. To see glossy color photos of it and be angry it still existed without you. "He might be. This is his home, no matter what it looks like. If a stranger took him, I'm sure he's missing it very much."

"Did a stranger take him?"

I pictured the grocery list clawed into pink paper. "No," I said. "His mother took him. His father wants him back."

"Oh." He sunk back in his seat and picked at a spot on his window with a fingernail.

"There's a part of me that hopes the mother gets away," I said, willing him to react. I wanted him to agree with me, but why should he? I was asking too much of him. Most of the time I asked too little, except his entire stock of faith.

"Why?" he said.

"I can tell from her handwriting that she loves her son so much, and all I can tell from the dad's handwriting is that he's probably not the kind of man who should've been anyone's father," I said. "That's a problem, because I'm supposed to help the father get his son back."

"Did you help?"

"I'm helping. But it's hard to do what's right. Right doesn't always feel right." I watched the back of Joshua's neck. "And if the mother did take him, then—" I thought of the ridiculously attractive young babysitter. "Then she might have done a terrible thing in order to get her son away."

I looked up at the house and thought I saw a face—a woman, young, dark hair—peeking out from behind a curtain. The curtain dropped.

A dark vehicle screeched to a stop next to our truck. I turned my head and saw the glint of the streetlight flash on the hood of a black SUV just as it started to back up and parallel park behind us. I pulled forward to make room, then did a U-turn toward home.

Back through town, Joshua slumped against the passenger door, as far from me as he could get.

I took a deep breath. We were supposed to talk about math, but I didn't think math was the problem. "Would it be the worst thing, for the little boy to live with his mom and not his dad?"

He began to pick at the spot on the window again. "No."

"No?"

"But why?" he said.

"Why what?"

"Well, why couldn't he see him?" he said. "Sometimes?"

Shards of memory: the glint of sun on the new boat oar. Lake water at the back of my throat.

We drove on, stopping for a red light a few blocks from the apartment. The truck rumbled lightly under us as I calculated the silence ahead. He was only thirteen. At least five years until college, and then what? In the silence, he might become the very thing I feared. Or worse: I might lose him altogether.

The image that came to me now was my mother, leaning against a kitchen counter, then turning away. I'd had a broken arm and she'd said—what had she said? *This isn't how I raised you.* To talk back, she meant.

The light changed but I sat staring at the bright green circle, immobile until the car behind us honked. I pulled through the light and to the side of the street, threw the truck into park, and turned to him. What were the words we had agreed on, over time?

"Joshua, you know your dad had some—he was sick, and I didn't think he could get better," I said. "I worry that I was wrong, but I don't think so. I worry about a lot of things. If there's something you want to talk about . . ."

I was leaning toward him, pleading. He was unmoved and silent.

"I can tell you one thing," I said, turning back to the steering wheel. "You're not like him."

I was about to start the truck again when, finally, in a voice as even and unconcerned as though he were asking about math, he said, "How do you know?"

"Because I do," I said, gripping the wheel with both hands. "I know him and I know you. I'm in a pretty good place to judge. You're smarter, kinder. You're already a better man than your dad had a chance of being."

He let his head fall against the window. "Did you read it in my handwriting?"

"No. I didn't read it anywhere," I said. "Haven't you ever heard of intuition?" I wanted to place a hand on him, but didn't. "I don't need to see it in your handwriting. I can just feel it."

He looked at me, and I knew what he wasn't saying. I didn't rely on intuition. Sometimes I didn't seem to have any.

But then his eyes went wide. I turned my head to find a dark figure outside my window. I threw my elbow on the door's lock button as a set of knuckles landed on the glass.

I finally recognized the gold buttons of the uniform, and then the sheriff's hat. I cranked down the window, still shaking.

"Ms. Winger, is everything fine here?" He ducked low to see across the expanse of the front seat.

"We're just having a little talk, sort of unexpectedly. I—Sheriff, this is my son, Joshua," I said. "Joshua, this is Sheriff Keller."

The sheriff leaned across me and put out his hand. "Well, nice to meet you, sir. Your mother thought you were too good a guy for us to meet, but here we are."

Joshua pumped the offered hand a few times, giving up a smile kept tight and cautious.

"School going OK, then?" the sheriff asked, pulling back outside and leaning on the window with folded arms.

"Yeah, it's OK. Except math." Joshua shot me a look. "But I'm on it."

"Good, good." Keller nodded. "Ms. Winger, I was just over at the Ransey house to talk with Bo."

I glanced into the sideview mirror at the vehicle behind ours. A black SUV. Of course.

"Damnedest thing, I thought I saw you out at Sugar Creek Park yesterday after our chat, too. I'm running into you everywhere I go." I looked away from his self-satisfied grin. "I was just reassuring Bo Ransey how hard we're working to get Aidan back. I left you out of that. I don't think he needs to know my methods. But I told him I have all my best people on it."

The process was tainted, irrevocably. Meeting Bo—even twice, even having a conversation with him—might have been forgiven. But I had broken my own rules by going to the house, and what had I gained? Nothing useful. Seeing the Ransey house had confirmed something for me, given me a moment of relief. Now I saw that I had driven there for that very thing, a sense of superiority.

Joshua scooted in from his side of the seat. "How many people do you have?"

"Ah, son. It's a small town," Keller said, smiling. "My best people is just one guy. Me."

Joshua's laugh was full and loud.

"And my chief deputy. And your mom, of course. She's been the consummate professional," Keller said, giving me a heavy-lidded look. "She's so good at her job I'd like to have her come back by to help me out with another lead."

Extortion. None of this would have happened if I'd just minded my own business. "A new lead?"

"Maybe, maybe nothing, but I have to follow every single lead I get, even if it is a far shot in the dark," he said, turning his head to give a sharp look to a car passing too quickly. The car slowed, an arm poking out the window to wave. "Frank Hart," the sheriff said, shaking his head, and then turned back to us. "Trying to make my town a better place to live, all the time, so of course I'm going to track down every last bit of a lead. If I can't spend too much time on the hocus-pocus, it's because I have a boy to get home before the trail gets cold."

I rubbed my arms, feeling the evening chill now. There was

something in his tone that I remembered—a sudden memory of a knock on the tin-can trailer I'd rented on a patch of no-where in Tennessee. The state trooper with the apologetic eyes.

I hadn't thought of that man in a long time. That man. He was the one who'd found me and had to report me alive—but he'd also set me free. *You don't have to sit here, waiting*, he'd said. *Is there someplace you can go?* There hadn't been, but I had hoped some-day there would be.

I turned and studied the sheriff's face.

"—shoot anybody?" Joshua was asking.

"Joshua."

"Well, now, we don't like to do that if we don't have to," Keller said.

I said, "So. Your best man is on the case."

"He certainly is," Keller said. "I've been out to the Ransey place quite a lot in my tenure. I send my chief deputy even more. He's on Ransey duty most of the time. If Mr. Ransey needs atten-tion, we've got it to spare—but he doesn't get to decide what we pay that attention to. Understand? Now, I don't want to keep you. Good evening, Ms. Winger, Mr. Winger."

I sat for a moment after he was gone, finally coming out of the conversation as if from a deep sleep. At last I rolled up the window.

"Mom," Joshua said. "Did you hear that?"

I wasn't sure what I had heard and what my mind had filled in. "What? Did I hear what, honey?"

"He called me *Mister* Winger." He turned in his seat to watch the sheriff pull away. Keller flipped the siren to let it *whoop-whoop* at us. I laughed at Joshua's surprise, relieved by how good it felt to take air deep into my lungs. How long had I been holding my breath?

I leaned over and put a hand on the back of Joshua's neck, gently. "Well. Why not? I was telling you. That's who you are."

Joshua, of course, brushed my hand away.

Chapter Eight

The Dairy Bar parking lot was full, a crowd gathered around the picnic tables. I would have pulled back out again and gone home, except that Joshua seemed interested in dinner out, even a crappy malt. But I couldn't help thinking that most of the people had come to gawk or compare notes on the Ranseys in what amounted to their own front yard. I made our order at the window—to go, I confirmed twice.

When I turned back from paying, Joshua was walking off toward the tables. "Hey," I called, but the girl at the window was pulling me back for my change.

"I need quarters," she yelled over her shoulder.

"We all need something we don't have," said the woman coming up behind her in a matching Dairy Bar shirt. I recognized the old woman from somewhere and decided she must have been the one smoking out the back door earlier that day, a long shift. The woman's eyes were sunken and her voice scratchy. "Give the lady some dimes, peach. Dimes is spending money, aren't they?" The woman looked over at me with a smile that didn't reach beyond a grimace.

I waved the dimes away, but the girl was insistent it would mess up her drawer. I remembered that all-encompassing concern and took pity, waiting. By the time the change had been sorted out, I'd lost sight of Joshua.

"He's over here." Grace stood at the edge of the lot in the spotlight of a streetlamp overhead, waving me over. A few faces had turned to see who was yelling and who'd been yelled at, and they all seemed to be watching openly as I made my way over. "He and mine are tight, I guess," Grace said. She had a big cup of something icy in her hand and gestured with it toward a picnic table where Joshua sat with an assortment of kids, including one who might have been one of the boys from the school hallway. "Shane Junior or Shay, we call him," she said, pointing with the cup again. "I wanted to name him Brad Pitt after his daddy, but my husband wouldn't hear of it. Here he comes."

I turned into a chest of brown polyester and brass buttons. In the sheriff's path again. Then I saw that the collar of the uniform shirt was unbuttoned and pulled open to reveal a beefy red neck and the face of the same cop who had handed the sheriff his strawberry malt earlier. "She told you the kid's George Clooney's or whoever's, right?" he said around the mouthful of chili dog, his cheek distended. "Every time I meet someone new, they're embarrassed for me. Shane Mullen." He wiped one of his hands on the hip of his uniform pants and held it out. I shook it, reading his nametag.

"Chief Deputy Mullen."

"Just Shane is fine," he said. "Unless you run up against the law before I get this dog finished."

"No plans to," I said. "Anna Winger."

"Oh, I know," he said. He had chili at the side of his smile. Grace reached in and swiped at him with a napkin, rolling her eyes at me. "The whole courthouse is talking about you coming in," he said. "Exciting week."

"I would imagine, what with a murder and a kidnapping already this week, my visit wouldn't inspire much notice."

"We notice when the boss starts dealing in witchcraft—"

"Shane, shut up," Grace said. "Brad Pitt would not be such an asshole."

"—or magic or whatever you call it," Shane said. "The sheriff's a straight shooter, one of the old kind of cops, like you see in the westerns. White-hat dude, for sure."

Grace had missed a small patch of chili sauce on her husband's cheek. I stared at it. "I would have thought all the sheriff's office would be white-hat dudes," I said. "The good guys. And gals, I guess," I added, thinking of the sullen Deputy Lombardi.

"I've always gone in for a nice pearl gray, myself," he said. Grace went in with the napkin again, and he grabbed it from her. "Woman, watch the sunburn. Brad Pitt would never put up with this. Let's get a move on so the kid can get his homework done. He's supposed to be grounded this week, I thought. What are we even doing here?"

"Getting chili down the front of your uniform, for one thing," Grace said. Shane walked off toward the boys. "He was supposed to be gone this week golfing and fishing but then shit hit the fan here and he got called back. All he got was a scenic drive and a sunburn he can whine about. All I got for my trouble is a morning off before he's back wanting dinner." She looked at me. "I liked what you said today about my handwriting. About me. I don't believe it for a second—but it was nice."

"If I spent more time with the sample, maybe I'd find something else to add," I said.

"Something I wouldn't like as much, I bet," she said. "I'd have you look at Shane's handwriting, but I don't think I want to know him that well. You could set up a booth right here, though, doing what you do and the line would go around the block."

"A booth—oh, you mean—" Like a kissing booth? Like a sideshow? I was stunned by that image in my head. "I don't think so," I said. Her husband, instead of wrenching his son away, had settled in to talk with the boys. "Joshua doesn't want me to do that kind of thing. In public. It horrifies him."

"Mine is horrified that I'm even *seen* in public," Grace said. "We come here for a little air and ice cream, he's never met me before. That's fine," she said, sipping at her cup. "I get to catch up on the happenings. Have you heard the latest?"

"Probably not," I said. "I'm only a subject of the grapevine, not actually attached to it."

"They're saying that girl, the one who got killed . . . maybe she was Bo's live-in something else."

I made a contemplative noise. I had seen the handwriting of the man sending notes of *love* to Charity, and it wasn't Bo. Those could be old notes, set on fire because of a new man in her life. But I also remembered how careful the *Spectator* had been to say she lived with her parents. "Maybe."

"And maybe the reason the wife moved out?"

"So then your theory—one woman comes back for her kid and kills the girlfriend, not the babysitter."

"It fits," Grace said.

"It would also fit if someone wanted to get rid of both the girlfriend and the mother and the kid all at once," I said.

Grace turned to me, stricken. "What do you mean?"

"The mother is missing," I said. "Until they find her, alive, with no kid, she's not just a possible suspect. She's a possible victim."

"You mean Bo," she said, shaking her head. "You don't even know him."

"I don't know any of you," I said, waving it away.

Shane and Shay were heading off toward a showy black SUV in the back of the lot. Everyone seemed to have a black truck here. "Hey, Angelina Jolie," he yelled. "You walking?"

"I got the keys, smartass," she hollered back. "Bo's OK. He's— I've known him since we were all kids together." She watched Shay all the way to their truck. "He was Aidan's age two blinks ago, you know? Well, of course you know."

"They'll find him," I said.

"They'll find *her*," she said. "Look, I know that what you said about me at the café today was wrong. You know why? Because when I think about that young girl with her head cracked open, I don't feel charitable toward the one who did it at all. Not even a little bit."

To the Dairy Bar and back to the white-walled blank of the apartment, greasy bags in our fists, I replayed the image of Joshua's hand swiping mine away.

At home, he ate everything, including the malt and burger I had ordered for myself but didn't want. He sat at the kitchen table with his propped-open math book serving as a screen between us. He flipped to a blank page in his notebook and glared at me.

"Just do the homework," I said, getting up from the table. "Let's just start by seeing how much you can do. I won't look." He ducked his head behind the book, and I went to the couch.

From there I studied him. He was all odd shapes and angles, elbows thrown out onto the table and knees sharp underneath sloppy blue jeans. He'd always been thin, too thin at times. When he finally started collecting girth, I'd been relieved. One less thing to worry about. But that relief was misplaced, I saw now. His new shape wasn't the return of something he had lost, but a different flesh altogether, a new body that would serve some purpose. A new purpose. Wasn't that what biology was? Kids grew into the next phase, and you wanted them to become adult, to take the form of their adult selves. Joshua was just reaching, biologically speaking, toward—

Sex.

My throat seized up, and I coughed to catch my breath.

Joshua turned his head. "What?"

"Nothing," I croaked, fanning my hand in front of my watering eyes. I grabbed at a notepad I'd left on the table and waved it in front of my face. Joshua watched.

Through the floor: *tap, tap.*

Joshua whipped around in the chair. "I'm not doing *anything*."

"No, I know. It might be a cry for help." Although if Margaret's broom could reach the ceiling, how much trouble could she be in? "Or maybe she hit the wall by mistake?"

We sat and listened.

Tap. Tap-tap.

I put down the notepad and slid into my shoes. "I'll be quick."

I paused on the stairs, in no mood to be neighborly: all my efforts to keep men from my life to the contrary, there was one living in my house.

In the hallway outside Margaret's apartment, I could hear the broom handle punching at the ceiling. I knocked and waited, long enough that I began to think something was actually wrong.

"Margaret? Are you OK?"

The door swung open, the old woman leaning on her broom. "Why wouldn't I be OK?"

"Are you sweeping your ceiling? You might use the bristle end."

"What do you think of that deal with the kid?"

"Margaret," I said. "Is anything on fire? Can you not reach something? What did you need?"

"What's that ruckus up there?" the old woman said.

"You have fantastic hearing, Margaret, to detect Joshua sitting at the table, silently doing his homework."

"I have a hearing aid," she crowed. "Never mind that. What's all that stomping up and down the stairs lately?"

"I don't know what you mean. Do you want me to take out your trash or something?"

"You, lady. You're running all over the damn place. I can't get a lick of sleep."

Margaret slept all day, except for the two hours her game shows played. The volume was loud, broom-worthy. "That's awful. I'm so sorry you can't sleep."

"I heard you was a police."

The Parks grapevine really was impressive to reach a woman who never left her apartment. "Not exactly. Just helping out where I can."

"What do you think about it, then? That boy gone?"

"I'm not sure what to think," I said.

"That boy," Margaret said, shaking her head. "That poor boy."

"They'll find him. We have to keep hopeful."

Margaret glared. "I mean that boy, Bo. He's got enough to bear. And that wife 'a his."

I felt strangely protective of Aidan's mother, had developed a sort of secret crush on her, for running, for eluding them all even for a few days. I couldn't think how she had outgunned a woman a foot taller and probably thirty pounds heavier and so

I couldn't help but assign that crime elsewhere. I kept my tone noncommittal. "What?"

"She's a real handful," Margaret said.

That was old-biddy code. I'd heard it before, names applied to my mother and then later to me. We were women who got ideas, who got a notion, who thought they were better.

"Who said that?" I asked.

"People just say," she said. "It's in the air."

"That must be what I smelled," I said. "I thought it was the fumes from somebody's hog farm."

"What?" She reached to turn the volume on her hearing aid higher.

"What about the babysitter? Charity Jordan?" I said. "What's in the air about her?"

"Well," Margaret said, frowning. "She died."

We didn't speak ill of the dead. I thought about that burned blue letter. "Did she have a boyfriend?"

"How should I know?"

"You seemed to be on the pulse of Parks society, Margaret," I said. "Never mind. You didn't need anything? If not, could you keep the broom off the ceiling?"

Margaret sniffed and brushed at the carpet with the broom. "Ride to the doctor," she said.

"What—oh. You need a ride? When?" This was not the question I wanted to ask. Why? Why me? "What about the van that comes around?"

"That's for church," she said. "For the doctor, I usually take a taxi, but the doc won't let me check myself out tomorrow. Says I'll be woozy."

"Oh." I thought of excuses, rapid fire, but none of them stuck. The best was the truth: that I didn't care enough, that I didn't want to get involved. Of all the neighbors in the building, why me? Because the sound of a broom handle could travel to my apartment? Because I worked from home and, maybe from Margaret's perspective, didn't seem to work at all? "Tomorrow?"

On my way upstairs, the best excuse of all came to me. Tomorrow—who made plans that far in advance?

Chapter Nine

The next morning, with Joshua out the door, I turned to my computer. Projects were stacking up while I played cops and robbers, while I got dragged into the lives of my neighbors.

First, I had in my email a new project from Kent: a scribbled kidnapping threat against a CEO of a Fortune 500 company in Chicago. For a moment, I let myself think about the apartment we'd left there, the noisy invented games of the children next door, the smell of barbecue on a Sunday afternoon. We'd lasted several years there, and I'd never, not once, had to take a neighbor to the doctor.

And then the trip downtown one day, like tourists. Chicago pizza, a trip to stores we never went to, Joshua lining up for some famous caramel popcorn he had to try. Not as though I was the criminal. Not as though I hadn't done everything I could think of to get on with my life. But then some northern Wisconsin grandma looks at me like she's seen a ghost. She'd been wearing a Sweetheart Lake sweatshirt.

I had forgotten about chance, about coincidence. I'd allowed myself to forget that unlikely things did happen. Chalk it up to a god, call it fate or the planets aligning or a bad sun on Jupiter, whatever woo-woo you believed in. Unlikely things happened all the time.

I opened Kent's file, blowing the scrap up on my screen and focusing on a few words: *I'll skin the fucking bastard.*

I studied the height of the letters, how much of each figure seemed pulled upward away from the baseline. Some of the uppercase letters had a careful pride to them. An educated author. I peered at the sample closely, planning what to say. It always occurred to me how much longer I spent reading samples than the author had spent writing them.

Second point: some pinching of the letters, which led me toward a diagnosis of narrow-mindedness. Typical of the kind of people who left threatening letters, whether they followed through with violence or not. I plodded through a few more features of the man's handwriting and, when at last I couldn't ignore them, I studied the curve of descending tails of *g*'s and *y*'s. Gaps.

Gaps in the strokes of those appendages meant that the poor jerk probably suffered more sexual frustration than anything else.

I felt a recurring sensation at moments like this: Who was I? What right did I have to dig into someone's life this way? I hardly ever came down on the side of mercy, but I hated speculation when real crimes happened every day. When they involved people at the top of corporate boards, the FBI cared, they jumped. When they happened to girls too young or naïve to know they didn't deserve it, nobody blinked.

Me, my mother, maybe her mother, too. Maybe generations of women who weren't allowed, or didn't know how, or were trained not to think, react, fight. Was it biology? Did I have no shot at all?

Because this was the question, the only question: Would any of my efforts with Joshua make any difference?

Maybe all the violence had already been passed down to him by biology, the anger marker on the chromosome I had passed him from my father finding a happy match in Ray. Or if not biology, then environment. Had I raised him too attached to me, so that now he would fight to free himself? Had I brought him up too strictly, so that now he could do nothing but rage against rules?

This was the science I didn't know. It made no sense, and it was all guesswork, all what-if, until I woke to a late-night call from the police or saw his face in a grainy security camera film on the news. It was all speculation, until it all went one way or the other.

I went to the kitchen for a cup of tea and when I came back to the table, I ignored the email in progress and picked up the notepad from the night before, still open to the empty page. I brushed my hand over the smooth page and reached for a pen from a cup on the table. *Joshua*, I wrote, knowing that the curve of each letter gave away everything the word meant to me. I tried to free myself from thinking about my handwriting. *Joshua*, I wrote again, pouring myself into it.

I was enjoying the curve of the *J* of *Joshua* in my own hand when it came to me: I had to settle for reality. Joshua needed help, and I wasn't the one he needed.

A psychiatrist? It was too much invasion. But—a good influence? A good, strong, intelligent, safe influence—who could help me guide Joshua through this rough patch? Some figure that Joshua could turn to, who could be a sort of spy in the house of adolescence, who could make certain there wasn't any real trouble brewing? What if—

"Sure," I said aloud to myself. I flopped back in my chair and threw aside the notebook. Because Joshua was making it clear that he was finished in the world of women. He was done with my coddling, my protection. He needed a man.

It had been a long time since a man had been in my life. So long that I tended to forget. No, that wasn't right. It was more that the desire had become a low-grade buzz, a thin wire of white noise that was pulled taut along my spine. The noise was easily drowned out.

There had been offers. That neighbor and his jackass John Henry. And then in Ohio, the client who'd asked the right questions at the right time. For six weeks, twice a week at noon, like a therapist. He might as well have been a stranger—a string of one-night-stand strangers, actually, for how little we spoke of it before, during, or after. Quick, repeated, trying to seek the enjoyment I never fully felt. When his phone rang, his hand would reach for it without hesitation. His kids, calling from their mother's. Too young to settle so completely, too old for a relationship built on film noir, I quit the project.

But the idea of finding a man for *Joshua*, a man who would crack the Joshua code for me, gave a clumsy strum to that wire of need. I found myself thinking of the sheriff. Then Mr. Jeffries. I stared at the open window on my laptop, tapping idly at the keys before hitting the send button on the email to Kent. One item off my list, but I felt no satisfaction, no possibility, no sense of hope.

Tap.

I glanced at the clock, then shut down the computer, letting Margaret's messages grow more insistent. When I thought about it, when I really looked back on my life, I couldn't remember the last time I'd felt much hope at all.

"YOU DRIVE TOO fast," Margaret said.

"Here?"

"You nearly took out that mailbox—"

"Is this the place?"

"Slow down. Well, you passed it."

I took a deep, steadying breath and pulled into the next entrance. "Here? Urogynecology?"

"I don't want to talk about it," she said.

"Fine by me."

"They're falling out," she said.

"Excuse me?"

"My lady parts," Margaret said. "I think you parked over the line there."

"It's a handicapped spot. Hop out—"

"Young lady, you wouldn't hop if you were here for what I'm here for!"

"—and I'll meet you inside," I said.

I took my time parking. Inside, everyone turned to see whose lady parts were falling out next. The waiting room held husbands of a certain age, daughters, one little girl sitting on her mother's lap. The magazines were outdated and the television in the corner silent.

"Ma'am, I have a form for you." The woman behind the desk held out a clipboard.

"Me?"

"You're with Mrs. Percy?"

I tried to remember the name on Margaret's mailbox. "I'm with Margaret. She just came in?"

"Yes, Mrs. Percy. We've taken her back already. I just need you to sign that you're taking responsibility for her after her appointment."

"A liability thing?" I walked to the desk and let the woman put the form in front of me. "Is this legally binding?"

The receptionist took a good look at me. "Your signature, phone number, and relationship to the patient."

I read a few lines. Crazy legalese. I wasn't adopting the woman, was I? "What are the options?"

"I'm sorry?"

"I don't really have a relationship to the patient."

Someone in the room behind me laughed.

The woman had color in her cheeks now. "Are you family?"

"No."

"Then you are a friend," she said. "Sign or I'll have to go get Mrs. Percy from her exam room and reschedule her for when someone else can bring her."

This bumped up against my concerns. In a lowered voice, I said, "I'm not sure she has someone else."

"Apparently not." The woman stared at the form until I picked up the pen and signed. After another second, I gave in. *Friend.*

"She's going to be about an hour," the woman said, taking the clipboard back.

I looked over the waiting room again. One of the women was staring openly. "Is there anyplace nearby to get coffee?"

The main hallway could have been any corporate office, with its low-pile carpet and framed still-life prints, but signs led to a set of doors that opened automatically onto a hospital setting: clinical, medicinal, familiar. The doors started to close, then bounced back again as I convinced myself to go through them. A few people looked up from their magazines as I squeaked through, concentrating on the cafeteria sign and trying not to look too closely at anyone's injury or pained face.

I'd almost made it past the waiting area when someone gasped, a tiny whimper meant for no one to hear. I glanced toward the sound. In a chair that had been designed to invite comfort, a young woman sat forward, awkward and careful, her hair hanging into her face. A piece of paper lay near her bright pink sneakers.

"Did you drop—" I had reached for the paper but stopped when she recoiled. Her hair swung away to reveal a violent red, puffy mouth. "Let me get it for you," I said. I left it on the seat next to her and hurried on.

I found the cafeteria and paid for the coffee with shaking hands. The round-cheeked woman at the register smiled at me. "Maybe it will be OK, baby," she said.

"Thank you." I was not the patient, Joshua was safe at school. Maybe it would be OK. "Thank you so much," I said, meaning it.

When I saw an exit, I took it. Outside the sun was shining, warmth beating down on the top of my head. I closed my eyes and returned to my skin.

The sidewalk led out and around the corner of the building. I could see the door back to Margaret, but also a group of trees across the street, the tops waving gently. I sat on a nearby bench and sipped the coffee. Maybe it would be OK.

These were not thoughts I'd entertained before. Inside, many people were having the worst day of their lives. I had already been that person. I didn't have to keep being that person. I kept running up against that person. From experience I knew the woman in the waiting room didn't want to be talked to. She only wanted to fade into that chair until they called the name she'd given them.

When the breeze in the treetops wasn't enough entertainment, I turned to the comings and goings at the clinic. Old people, being helped along. A woman with two young children, one of them crying and fighting her. At one point I thought I saw Stephanie from the Boosters hurry inside.

A sheriff's cruiser pulled up and parked in the fire lane, expelling two officers I couldn't identify. They'd called the cops on that puffy lip. I tried to see it from the side of authority. It had to be reported or nothing would ever change.

But that's not the way I felt. My pulse battered against my skin as I waited for someone to emerge.

My phone rang in my pocket. I answered distractedly.

"Ms. Winger, Mrs. Percy is ready to be escorted home."

"Oh—" I held the phone back and checked the time. "Oh, right, yes. I'll be right in."

I hurried across the lot, discarding the coffee in a bin near the entrance. As I opened the door, I spotted Stephanie back at the other entrance, this time leaving. She moved cautiously but fast, her arm around a figure in a baggy coat and baseball cap. It might have been her son. It might have been anyone, except for the pink shoes, bright, neon, and running.

Chapter Ten

I woke with the imprint of *Aidan's crackers* on my mind. When my cell buzzed on the kitchen counter the second the clock showed 8:00 a.m., I was not surprised. Maybe I could tell the future after all.

Sherry said, "The sheriff wonders if you can come in this morning."

"What's going on?"

Sherry paused. I could imagine her craning her neck to make sure the sheriff was at his desk. She whispered, "He won't tell me anything. I'm dying to know."

An hour later I had assembled myself and arrived at the same hazy glass door on the third floor of the courthouse. When I opened it, Sherry's smile drew me in and quickly dimmed. "I think they're on her trail."

"Yeah." I leaned on the counter. Sherry wheeled herself closer. Some officers talked quietly to one another in the back, one of them Chief Deputy Mullen. I nodded when he waved. The other was the young woman who'd given me daggers every time I'd seen her. Deputy Something Lombardi, but I couldn't think what I'd done to insult her. Beyond them, the sheriff's door was shut tight. "I think we had better get used to the idea," I said. "It's likely she's a kidnapper. At the very least. She might be a murderer, too. She— well, she's going to get caught." The thought of it made my gut go tight with anxiety. Call-in-the-night anxiety. Moving-box anxiety.

Sherry nodded. "I don't wish she'd get away with it so much as I wish—I wish she hadn't needed to do it."

"Exactly." We considered each other, but I was thinking of Margaret, who spoke gibberish all the way back to our building the day before. I'd put her down for a nap on her couch, trying not to take in too much of the surroundings. I didn't want to see my own future—elderly, alone—that clearly. "Didn't Aidan's mother have anyone?"

"Just the—"

The sheriff's office door opened. He emerged with his head turned over his shoulder. I took a step in his direction, but he hadn't come out for me. Behind him, a stout, stooped, gray-haired woman trailed, he the sheep dog, she the sheep. I could sense the sheriff's gentle impatience with the woman as she inched forward in prim little pumps.

When she looked up, her eyes, though heavy-lidded slits in a leathery face, beamed utter reverence. She nearly shined at the sheriff, reminding me of the collected portraits on his office wall. All those people leaning, grasping, reaching—the walls closing in with the weight of all that need. All those people depending upon him.

I just had the one depending on me, and that was enough. Though now that I thought about it, I should have checked on Margaret this morning. I should have offered to check on her, at least, and let her brush me off.

"I just don't know what we'd do," the woman murmured.

"Let's not think that way, now," the sheriff said.

On the way past, the woman's eyes darted all over me, then returned to the sheriff.

"You're a true hero, Sheriff," the woman said.

Keller, pink, directed her inch by inch toward the front door. I tried not to watch. There was something magical in the mechanics of how Keller led the woman to the door and coaxed her out. She didn't seem hurried to leave the sheriff's company, but she was leaving as fast as he could make her.

I watched, fascinated, until I realized I was the one here at his beck and call, for the third time in almost as many days.

When the door finally clicked behind my back, separating the sheriff from his one-woman flock, Sherry looked up from her papers and waited for him to come around to the counter.

"Ms. Winger," he said.

"Sheriff," I said. The nod I gave might have clicked in its efficiency.

Sherry said, "Sheriff, before you go, two calls came in for you. A little dispute over land at the Karpowicz house with the Martins. And then this one from the prosecutor. It didn't seem urgent, so I didn't interrupt."

"What's the—did you say *land* dispute?" he said.

"Yeah." She smiled. "The Karpowiczes' dog has been—violating some boundaries."

"Oh, hell."

"Yeah."

Keller laid the paper back on Sherry's workspace. "Can you?"

"Yep."

"Thanks."

The man certainly had some hocus-pocus of his own. First

the citizen promenaded out of the office and now a secret language, half unspoken, with his assistant.

The room seemed close, stuffy. I'd been too friendly, too open with both Sherry and her boss. I'd have to pull back.

The sheriff sighed and took a look all around the office before turning to me. "Well, Ms. Winger. Let's go have a talk."

Was that a question? Or a command? I'd already lost this one, already run over when bidden. I should have made an appointment later in the day, called the shots.

I started walking toward his office, letting *him* follow *me*.

Inside his office, the sheriff started right in. "I hear that you had an accidental face-to-face with Bo Ransey," he said.

This pitch was a few feet wide of my expectations. We sat. "Yes, when I went to my son's school, I ran into him. Literally."

"Did you get anything from that meeting?"

Another throw, another few feet. "Get anything?" I said. "You mean, like *vibrations*?"

"That's *not* what I meant. You don't get vibrations, by the way, do you?" He was looking at me mock appraisingly. "That might be a useful talent to have in my arsenal."

His arsenal. He could believe whatever he wanted.

"No, I didn't get anything—well." The memory of the meeting in the school hallway came back in sudden dramatic clarity. I felt something bright hiding in that dull scene and stretched for it. "Well, I guess that's not true, now that I think about it. I learned that he has another boy in his house, a nephew my son's age. They seemed to get along fine, I suppose. Although that kid is probably a menace to neighborhood pets. If the Karpowicz dog goes missing, check the Martins' backyard for shallow graves and then head straight over to talk to that kid."

"Yes, I've met young Master Ransey before. I don't know about his way with animals, but he does have quite an artistic talent. With a can of spray paint." He tugged at the bill of his cap, like the punctuation of his own joke, paused, and then offered, "That was his grandmother who was just in here."

I couldn't make out what he was saying, and then all the pieces snapped into place. "That lady was—?" The woman clawing at the TV camera in anguish the night Aidan went missing. The woman who'd fed the Dairy Bar counter girl change the night before. And today, in her church dress, unrecognizable. Each woman seemed like a different one.

"Mother of our friend Bo, grandmother to both the spray-can artist and his cousin, Aidan," he said.

"Huh." I had crossed my legs, and now the dangling foot jiggled a bit as I thought this information through. With effort, I forced my foot still. "She seems to . . . like you."

"Mrs. Ransey and I go way back. Well, as far back as I've been here," he said. "I guess the former sheriffs have always had the opportunity to get to know the Ransey family. Bobby comes from a long line of hell raisers."

"Bobby?"

"Bo's real name," he said. "His mother, she calls him Bobby." The sheriff began to dig under some file folders.

Bo Ransey was a guy you didn't turn your back on, but Bobby? Sugar wouldn't melt in his mouth. Names had power, or a lack. Like Joshua's name, which was an itchy collar my kid wanted to yank off now. Someday he'd be happy to have it.

I hated that anything about Bo Ransey reminded me of Joshua.

Keller found what he'd been looking for and slid it across his desk. "The Ranseys are about all I can handle right now," Keller said. "One of them calls me twenty times an hour. His mother has stolen, with her concern and her grandmotherly theories, most of my morning. There's a thirteen-year-old who seems to want nothing more than to spend the rest of his youth in my little jail, as is his legacy. And now—" He tapped a finger on the page in front of him. "One of them is starting to get sloppy."

I leaned in. The page had a small receipt copied into its center, the edges scratchy from having been faxed. It was for a credit card used at a motel in Indiana. If the total included lodging, the place was a fleabag. At the very bottom, a cramped, small script read *Beatrice Ransey*. "Beatrice?" I said.

"Bea Ransey, who you saw leaving my office just now, was taken aback to hear that she spent the night upstate this week. Nor does she remember signing her name quite in that way, ever in her life. Your expertise says?"

I hardly had to look. "Some of the markers look . . . familiar."

"Thought so. Seemed like it was about time Leely popped up."

I gulped, hard. The room seemed to tilt, the wall of photos leaning toward me.

Too strange. Too much. Not possible.

"Who—what did you call her?"

I imagined my face was white. I felt white. I felt as though a door had slammed somewhere, and I was on the other side. Somewhere else entirely, where doors slammed, and precious things were thrown up against them. One barking voice, gruff and animal, and then another voice, a woman's, in the rise and fall of a keening, desperate song.

I couldn't still be in the sheriff's office, because these sounds didn't belong here, or now. They were from long ago, so far back in years that I wasn't sure I'd ever really heard them. I had tried not to listen, because that's what my mother had told me to do. But now I remembered the wailing sound, a song with one word, drawn out long and ugly so that no one else could understand it. I knew the word: my own name. My mother begging, and the only thing she could or would beg for was her daughter, for a girl who didn't exist anymore, not in this room and not anywhere. My mother begged only for Lee-Lee, Leeanna, who was now me, the woman who had almost forgotten that song.

"Leely is the name Mrs. Ransey uses for her daughter-in-law," he said, watching me. "Leely and Bobby. I guess I took it up when she was here . . . do you need a drink of water?"

I'd only seen that stark image of Leila Ransey but now she came to life in my mind: wrung out, dark-eyed, anxious under the constant demands of her two-year-old. Maybe the little boy's cries rang out along the hallway of that cheap motel. I knew how alone she must feel, how in need of a trustworthy friend to tell her what to do. I knew the right thing to do, the lawful thing that any good friend should tell her.

Turn yourself in. Get a lawyer. Cooperate.

But if I were the friend, I wasn't sure what I would tell her.

Would I tell Leila Ransey how hard the years ahead of her would be on her own? Would I tell her how it would feel not to have anyone—really, absolutely no one? How almost anyone Leila knew would turn her in? How almost any move she made from here on out could lead to her capture? That, someday, something would?

"Ms. Winger," the sheriff said. "Are you OK?"

Leely. Not possible. Not funny.

Or would I tell her to do the only thing that had occurred to me? To run?

Yes, run. Stop using the credit card and run. And hide. And try not to pop your head out again. Live an unexceptional little life somewhere crowded and noisy, so that your presence will be drowned out by the cyclone of activity around you, and no one will think to ask you questions, but if they do, run *again*.

Or move to another town, a small one, and keep your head turned from the street, and try not to gather too many pieces of a life or too many objects or too many friends or too many hours in one place. You need to keep light, and fast. Because you will need to run again.

"Anna?" the sheriff asked gently. "Does the name Leely mean something to you?"

I remembered signing the form for Margaret, not even once thinking about the name I once used. You could·slough off another life, but it took a little practice.

"No," I said, straightening my spine and focusing all my effort on meeting the sheriff's eye.

This is what I mean. Look them in the eye, until you can't. Then run. "I don't know a single person by that name," I said.

Chapter Eleven

It took me a while to recover from the surprise of Leila Ransey's nickname. The sheriff left the office and came back with a little plastic cup of cold water.

"Why am I here?" I said.

Keller had been giving me all of his attention, and yet he still seemed to look even more closely now. He took off his cap and threw it in the corner of his desk. I'd never seen him without it. "You don't want to be here?" he said.

"That's not what I said. I don't have any work to do here—do I? That receipt? That was all?" My voice rose. Sherry was probably listening, as well as Shane Mullen and the other one. I started over, lightly. "My time isn't too precious to try and help here, but I don't feel like I'm doing all that much."

The sheriff rubbed his scalp with the flat of his palm for a second, reached for his hat. He sighed. "I know."

"You—what do you mean, you *know*?" My voice grew again, and this time I didn't care who heard.

"I don't mean you're not pulling any weight. That's not what I meant," he said, holding up his hands in the universal signal for *whoa, girl*. "What I meant to say is—here's the problem. You and I are not very central to what's going on right now."

I thought it through. I'd seen the unmarked cars lined up outside. "The feds took over, you mean."

"The feds, sure, and they've got first dibs on every guy I have. But it's Leila's game right now. Her move, for the moment. Here I sit." He sat silently with his hands folded on his desk.

I wanted to stand up and give the guy a chance to pull himself together. I'd seen this hands-up weakness: my mother, standing at the sink with her back to me. Someday, I would be an eighty-year-old woman and all I'd remember of my mother would be her back, her hands slack at her side. An entire life, worn down to a single moment.

"Leila Ransey is playing a game of chess against lots of opponents, least of all me," the sheriff said. "We got things rolling here, got the Amber set up, got a lot of local guys out combing the outskirts, the roads, the cornfields. And then got Aidan listed in all the places he should be listed and talked to about a hundred people about what I should be doing. I mean—" He stopped and seemed to remember I was there. He nodded and leaned over the desk, as though just now deciding he was all in, penny or a pound. "Remember when I said all that stuff about—how kids go missing, but they're never very far?"

From our first meeting. He'd seemed confident, almost cocky. His message had come in loud and clear. He was the guy who ran the place day in and out. He was in charge. "I remember," I said.

"Well, here's the thing. If the kids who've gone missing aren't really missing, as I said, how did that prepare me?"

"For when the child is really gone," I said.

"We get about five or six reports a year. Most of them just teenagers taking a walk. On purpose or not, they never get very far. Only one was gone for more than a day, and that was because he'd stolen a car that happened to have a full tank of gas."

"No little kids? Babies?"

"Zero," he said.

I glanced above his head at the wall of people, all of them depending on him. If all his officers were currently in the service of finding Aidan, who was out there keeping the faith with them all? Who was patrolling Sugar Creek Park, as that neighbor had assured me they had? "So what did you do? How did you know what to do?"

"You can't laugh," he said.

"Fine."

"Really now. This is a secret between you and me. How did I know what to do when the time finally came?" His knees bounced against the underside of his desk. "I got out the manual. I read a damn book."

I tried not to laugh but had to hide a smile. "That's not . . . awful," I said.

"Oh, yeah? You want to know that the guy you elected to protect you from the hazards of the modern world has to *get out the instruction manual*?" But he was smiling back. "I should have sworn you to silence first, I reckon. Too late now."

"Sheriff, really. Who am I going to tell?"

I had meant to keep the joke going, but the sheriff seemed to know how deep the truth was to this admission. He could see right through me and the empty spots on either side of me where others had been and no longer stood. Now I was embarrassed again, this time for myself. But then I thought of Sherry gossiping over her desk, of Grace rolling her eyes at me in the parking lot of the Dairy Bar, of Margaret tucked into her couch with a tattered quilt. And now, as stern as I'd wanted to be, here I was laughing with the sheriff, again. Things were changing, and it was my own fault. My own weak will, letting them in.

"I have something you can help me with," he said.

"Oh. No. That's not necessary at all. I have a job, you know. I'm sort of behind, actually—"

"Because I keep calling you in here."

"Not just that. Joshua—" The sheriff already knew about my visit to the school. Probably knew the reason, too. The grapevine, after all. "Joshua is in an epic battle with algebra."

"OK, fine. You have more than this case going on in your very busy life," he said. "But you seem interested in this case. You want to help. I didn't read that wrong, did I?"

I wanted to help, but I wasn't sure which side of the field I played for. I remembered Bo Ransey flinging off the hand of Deputy Lombardi as she escorted him from the premises. And Leila Ransey, skinny and shifty-eyed, out there alone with a cranky toddler. Did they have a place to sleep? Could she get milk without using the mother-in-law's credit card? I made sure I had control of myself, and then tried it aloud. "I want to help."

"And I need your help."

"Sheriff—"

"Don't go straight to shooting me down," he said. "Just listen? It's a little busy around here, what with taking social calls from Ranseys all day and of course everyone else because one missing kid means their kids are next." He waved his hand toward the outer office as though they were lined up waiting for me to leave. "And, you know, all the *dogs* trying to annex new patches of backyard. Meanwhile, I've got a little—" He glanced at the door and lowered his voice further. "A little internal issue with some missing evidence. Drugs, to put it bluntly. Now. If there was a way you could pull some weight around here that no one else could? You would help me with that, wouldn't you?"

When he had finished, I felt caught up. Caught. What choice did I have? I gave the smallest nod, noticing a headache I hadn't felt come on. Leely, if you're going to get away with this, be smart. Be smarter than you've ever been. Be smarter than me.

I WOKE SLOWLY. I'd come home from the courthouse with my head thick and gone to bed in all my clothes.

In my dreams I had visited places I'd long forgotten.

The room, now, was wrong. Before I knew where I was, when I was, I watched the room stretch and morph out of memory and into real life.

Leely Ransey had opened my memory like a can of tuna.

I remembered: my mother, her back to me. We wouldn't look at one another after a rage. He'd leave for the bar, for three days, for the woods, we never knew. We wouldn't share our relief. We didn't share anything.

Now, I sat up and held my aching head. I felt as though I'd been sniffing paint fumes. I looked around at the bare white walls. But I had, in a way.

Yellow. As a child, the walls in every apartment we ever had were yellow, or at least the bedroom I slept in. Another move, another yellow bedroom. At first, I probably hadn't noticed. When I did, it had seemed like a lucky accident. My favorite color.

And then I'd caught on. Room after room. Rooms I had lost track of and could never put into order. Some had windows with white curtains. Sometimes the curtains were dirty, and my mother would take them down and wash them again and again. Some of the rooms had no window and barely enough room for my small bed. Closets—holding pens, really—rooms that were not useful for anything else and therefore belonged, as much as anything belonged, to me. Lee-Lee.

Drowsing, I found that the name supplied itself. Just as the yellow rooms had returned, so had the name. I'd grown tired of the yellow rooms, hadn't seen the point. When I was twelve, thirteen, I refused.

"What do you mean, you don't want it?" My mother stood over me at the kitchen table of the new house, the newest new house, which was not really new at all. It was our new, someone else's old. Most of my clothes were that way, too, and the furniture. The table I sat at in the kitchen was from someone else's alley. My mother crossed her arms over her loose shirt. She always dressed in baggy clothes, jeans and long sleeves. Dark colors, though I thought she must love bright colors. I knew she did, because of the yellow paint. Daisy Smile yellow.

A can of the stuff left over from the last house was just feet away on the back porch. "I'm tired of yellow," I said. I sat at the table with a textbook, eating a bowl of cereal without milk with my fingers, one piece at a time. It drove her crazy, which was one of the reasons I did it. My mother always twisted her mouth at the bowl and checked, every time, that there was milk in the refrigerator. *The one thing I can do*, my mother would say at these times, peering close at the date on the carton, *is keep milk in this house.*

My mother did not check for milk this time. She stood at the counter and looked into the sink. "I'm tired, too."

Her voice seemed different. I looked over my shoulder. My mother's shirt was the color of a one-day-old bruise.

I turned back to the textbook, but couldn't think about anything other than the expression on my mother's face. It wasn't sad. I could do better than that, or at least that's what my English teacher wrote on the margins of my essays when I wrote a sentence that said something obvious or tried to say something that I wasn't really sure I understood. I stretched sometimes, using words I hadn't looked up, or repeating things I'd read in our text or during library study. My teacher was never fooled, which was perplexing and pleasing, in a way. How did they always know when I tried to be someone else?

I could do better than sad. I glanced over. My mother looked— used.

That weekend we didn't paint the room or even pick up the can to judge how much Daisy Smile was left. The next time I thought about it, the can wasn't there.

I opened my eyes and looked around, willing and also not willing to leave where I'd been. The walls seemed more bare than ever before. They were white, always white, because they were someone else's walls. We never hung things or put in nails. We never painted. If we moved, it was just too much trouble to make it right. Too much trouble, and too much time to spend, if we moved.

I swung my feet over the side of the bed to the floor and sat, staring at the pattern in the carpet I hadn't chosen. Underneath my bed were the flattened boxes from our last move.

Who was I kidding? If we moved? If? The only question, really, was when.

Chapter Twelve

To shake off my coma, I washed my face in cold water, changed into yoga pants, and went to check the mail.

At Margaret's door, I paused. I'd meant to check on her before now, but how did you get into the habit of *checking in* on people?

I knocked. "Margaret? It's Anna, from upstairs," I said to the door.

Shuffling feet and the chain sliding. The door cracked and swung open. She waved me in and lay back down.

"How are you feeling?" The table next to the couch had the glass of water I'd left her, but it was empty. I fetched more. "Have you eaten?"

She didn't answer.

I turned up the volume. "Margaret, have you—"

"I'm fine," she said. "I had some soup."

There was no pan or bowl in the sink.

"Can I make you something? Or call anyone?"

"If I had anyone to call, I would have called them," she said. Her hand fluttered as it reached for the water. "I used to have a lot of people."

This sounded like the beginning of a story. I sat down. "Around here?"

"I grew up here, missy. People used to stay where they were planted. They didn't run around everywhere." She sounded tired, and her wrinkled face was thin and drawn.

"What happened to them? Your people?"

"The same thing that happens to us all," she said. "But a little faster, maybe, than we'd have liked."

Her eyelids drooped. The apartment around us grew still and I sat and listened to the old woman's shallow breathing. The dense quiet reminded me of when my mother and I whispered around the closed door of the bedroom while my dad slept off a bad night, both of us trying to stay as still and small as we could. At a certain age, I'd enjoyed these times, like a game. Later, not so much. And now—I would have given anything not to imagine the moment I might have sat by my elderly mother as she napped on the couch, a future no longer possible. What if I had talked her into coming with us? What if she had lived a long life, without me there? In my old town, people cast off were sent to a home on the river, the loony bin. That place, Riverdale, was a cruel taunt, a threat. At least I was glad I'd never have to see my mother placed there.

We sat for a long while until I thought Margaret had fallen asleep. When I went to get up, she reached out to grab my knee.

"I don't think I ever ate that soup," she said.

Margaret fed and tucked in again, I returned to the apartment to find the time had moved maddeningly onward without me. I had less than an hour to work before Joshua's footsteps brought the outside world into the apartment again.

I dumped the mail onto the table and sat down to the neglected in-box, but my gaze transferred to my computer screen. *What do you want to know?* Kent had asked. And he hadn't been talking about Charity Jordan's death or Aidan Ransey's disappearance. He had meant mine.

A few keystrokes and I was looking at the website for the Vilas County *News-Review*. The news, always the same. Fundraisers. Fishing tournaments. School-board minutes. Lake houses for sale. Family names I should remember. I still felt nervous to click through the pictures of arrests, awards, weddings, deaths—as though someone on the other side could see me peeking. I rarely saw the names I wanted to see—or didn't want to see—in the news. What was Ray doing? Theresa? Such quiet lives, if they still lived there. I checked the clock and searched for their names directly. Addresses in Sweetheart Lake for both. They still lived there. They still lived.

I had to force myself to close the window and get some work done. Even a little.

I sorted the day's mail and plucked out a stationery-sized envelope. A lonelyhearts request. My ladies in anguish and doubt. That seemed like an easy, welcome task.

The letter was from a woman in San Francisco who wanted to know if she should marry her boyfriend. She had included several samples of the man's handwriting, copies of scrawled lists and a signature ripped from what seemed a very formal document, as well as a short note on stationery that was signed with a simple *Charles*. I looked first at the woman's note asking for help, noting the large, looping scroll of her letters with interest. Nothing too crazy there; the request was an honest one. Her signature appeared again on the check, which I set aside.

Now: Charles. The formal signature was sloppy, a little impatient. As though he'd had to sign the document in several places. The list was a set of notes from a household project of some kind, a checklist of purchases to make at the hardware store. I started to get a feel for Charles, for the ebb and flow of his hand on paper.

Then I took up the personal note. An original. An original was always better. There was always some doubt with a copy. Copies could be tampered with, for one thing. Part of the paper could be missing, or the whole thing could be constructed from multiple samples. Sometimes people sent me patchwork pieces in order to test my abilities. I could always tell them more about the owner of the handwriting than they had expected, and then I could tell them quite a bit about themselves, if they wanted to know.

In Charles's note, the script had strong lines. He had a very nice hand, actually, all the markers open and charitable. Why had the woman even thought to solicit my services? That's the sort of thing I wished my clients would put into their requests. But they didn't, because it might lead me down some path—like telling the palm reader that you were most worried about money and having her give happy predictions on your financial troubles. They didn't want to give me any signposts so they could be sure my work was genuine, not the work of a shyster. They believed enough to send me money, but they didn't believe enough to send clues.

I reached for the laptop to type up a response, but paused over the personal note Charles had written. I hadn't really read it before as much as parse its construction, a set of dots and lines that added up to a message for someone else. It was the encoding that I was paid to tear down, not the text. But a word had caught my attention: *sweetheart*.

I had a real dread of the word, but tried not to get distracted from Charles. *Sweetheart* seemed like a word Charles meant.

Satisfied, I typed up the response. This man is a keeper. Congratulations on your engagement. I finished it off with a couple of specific notes about Charles's handwriting so that his new fiancée felt that she had received her money's worth. But I knew the sentence that the woman would come back to again and again in the future. *A keeper.* It occurred to me how less than qualified I was to say so.

I set Charles aside and tore through a few more easy tasks, questions that needed a fast answer and a renewal of a discreet magazine ad that attracted the lonelyhearts. I could stand to see more letters from people like Charles.

Then I turned to email and picked through what was there until I saw a new message from Kent, recent. The Chicago businessman had some concerns about the assessment I'd done on the threatening letter he'd received. Did I have anything else to add to the report?

Without going back to my notes or files, I remembered the thoroughness with which I'd studied that letter, the careful thought I'd given in honor of the debt I owed Kent. I remembered all the thought I'd put into those gaps in the descenders of his *f*'s and *g*'s, how I worried over my access to that information about the author. I emailed back a quick reply, hiding my frustration and offering to take another look if Kent wanted me to. It was professional courtesy to offer, even if there was nothing more I could say.

I HEARD JOSHUA arriving home from the bus stop long before he got to the door. Maybe Margaret had a point about the noise he generated.

The door swung wide, hitting the back of one of the dining chairs. "Shit," he said.

"Joshua."

He appeared around the open door. "Hi, Ma." His backpack thunked down in its customary spot: in the way.

"Oh, hi, yourself. You know what I said about the swearing—"

"But you do it all the time!"

"I do not swear 'all the time,'" I said. "And you know it. Only when it's really the best word for the situation. One of these days, you'll need a fat, juicy swear word for the occasion, and all yours will be used up. Save it for when life get really tough."

He flung himself down into the chair opposite me. I was bent over the laptop, but on alert immediately. He was sitting? Down? I checked the clock. Usually he reserved this golden hour for vendettas against video game ninjas.

"Life already sucks," he said, resting his head in his fists, face turned toward the tabletop. "How much worse do you need it to get?"

"I didn't get any calls today from the school," I tried, each word leaving my mouth with a calculated effort at lightness.

He raised his head and gave me a twitchy sneer that might have turned into a smile if he weren't so determined to remain sullen. "Funny, Mom. Really, really funny."

I reached for a batch of paperwork on the table and started to flick through it. Casual, casual. "Is something going on?"

He was silent, face down for so long that I wondered if I hadn't walked too directly into the topic. But then he sighed and emerged from behind his arms. "You wouldn't understand."

"You could try me." Now I turned the in-box upside down on the table and began to sort. The cell phone bill, unearthed just in time. My hands nearly shook from the effort of not looking at him. I was the one who had made his life difficult. Could I take a direct hit, if he said so? "I might understand," I said.

"Never mind."

"Oh." In my hands, an expired rebate form, a notice of a tenants' meeting I'd missed. I really needed to get it together. If I hadn't already known it, here was the physical evidence I was losing control over the order of my life. "Why?"

"Why what?" he mumbled, arms crossed, knees jangling. He watched me dig through the stacks.

"Why 'never mind'? Is it guy stuff? I wouldn't understand because it's guy stuff?"

He replied with a snort.

I tried again. "I wouldn't understand because . . ."

"Mom, *whatever*. You just wouldn't understand, that's all. It's not guy stuff. What's guy stuff? Just. That's it. Whatever. You wouldn't understand because you're my *mom*."

"Oh." I considered arguing my position, but then I didn't know what my position was. "I guess you're right, because I don't understand what you mean."

"See?"

"No, I really don't."

"Exactly."

The exchange brought back the efficient shorthand at the sheriff's office. Joshua and I were having our own kind of half conversation, far less successfully.

"I'm still willing to listen."

"Mom." It was less a word than exhale. "You won't think it's hard at all. It will be all easy for you."

"Oh, yeah, I see what you mean." And I did. *Leave him*, Theresa would say, had said already when no one else would. *You can stay at my place.* As though moving a mile away changed anything. "Some things, you have to make your own decision."

"Yeah." He leaned forward for a moment and then collapsed low into the chair, more despondent than ever. "I have to figure it out for myself."

"Well, no, that's not exactly right," I said. "You could take the advice other people have for you. Sometimes others can see things in a way you can't. But—but you may not believe them. Or deep down, you will, and you'll hate them for being right." I stopped. Who needed this advice more?

He was still listening.

"Eventually," I said, clearing my throat, "you'll make your own decision. But it doesn't hurt to try your problems out on other people, like, like a referendum on what you should do. Do you know—"

"Yes, I know what it *means*. Social studies class, you know?"

"Exactly. Just like social studies class."

Joshua sat chewing on his bottom lip. I picked up a large, flat envelope that had fallen to the floor, just to have something to hold onto.

He leapt to his feet. "What's for dinner?"

The referendum would not come to a vote today. I felt the immediate loss of his attention. "I don't know yet. Is there something you wanted?"

"Can we have something *good*? We never have anything *good*." He sat back down, pushed the chair from the table, and swiveled the chair from side to side.

"What are you talking about? We just had burgers last night. You ate about six pounds of them, so don't tell me they weren't good. Did you bring this in?"

"What?" He stopped the chair's tilt-a-whirl spin and looked at the envelope I held aloft.

"It doesn't have a stamp on it." Without postage, it couldn't be from Kent. And his human resources job, now that I thought about it, was probably the Chicago CEO's threat I'd already received. They were sorting through disgruntled employees to find the author of that note. That was human resources. So what was this?

I was by nature paranoid, but I'd also heard unlikely stories from Kent and others that came back to me at times like these. Mail without stamps—that seemed to dredge up some warning I'd heard. Like email from people you didn't know, with their unsolicited attachments. Computer viruses or—something. This envelope could have its own kind of attachment. I dropped the envelope, and before I could say anything, Joshua picked it up. "I'll throw it away," he said.

"No!"

He looked up, startled. I stood and grabbed the envelope from him.

"What? Why?"

I rubbed the open flap of the envelope with a finger and then peered at my fingertip.

"You are so weird," he said.

"I work with the FBI and the police, Joshua. You know that. I have to be careful."

"Like someone would be after *you*," he said. "Who would be after you, Ma?" He rose and stretched tall, taking a swat at the ceiling to see if he could reach it yet. "Air ball." With a squinting glance over his shoulder, he made for his bedroom.

I waited for the click of his door, and then sat back down with the envelope. The label was typed, but then every label I ever got was typed. No return address, no postage. Someone had left this for me at our mailbox or at the front door of the building.

Who would be after me?

The kid had no idea how much worse his life could be.

I shook the envelope over the table, watching for flecks of

powder. I sniffed at it, holding it out several inches. Finally I reached in for the single sheet of folded paper inside. Standard-sized copy paper. White, no watermark.

Before I shook the paper loose, I knew. A call in the night. A stranger on the street using an old name. The tourist magazine. Around and around we went.

Chapter Thirteen

I called Kent but got his voicemail. Did anyone use voicemail anymore? I hung up, paced the floor awhile, closed the blinds, and peered out between them. When I got his recorded message the second time, I took a chance. "Kent, it's me. I know it's after hours, but if you have a second, I could use your opinion on something."

But my voice must have given me away because the answer came in a text—Sending cavalry—and then with a buzz from the front door. I buzzed him in and waited for the knock.

"Kent, you didn't have to—" The sheriff filled up the doorway.

I was sick to see him. To see him so often. To see him so near, and here, *here* in the place that belonged only to me and Joshua. He was supposed to be on the other side of a desk, and now he stood next to me, looking down at the unfolded paper resting on the table where I did my work, where I ate my food, where my son did his homework. Eight at night, and I could smell his shaving cream. I went to the window and opened it to let a little air in. He watched.

The panicked call now seemed like a mistake. I wasn't taking my own advice. I was still standing here, still planted in this spot when I should have the moving boxes out.

The sheriff took his time with the letter. All I wanted to do was crumple the thing and fling it away.

"What does it mean to you, Anna?"

My disgust rose. Why did he take this very minute to call me by that name? Just now, when I was feeling closed in? I'd given the sheriff credit for being able to read people, but now I questioned that skill.

"I don't know."

He was watching me closely. Of course he was. He was always watching, always studying everyone else for detail, for weakness. He was just like the rest of them, always wanting to know, to know, to know. They were like children, with their unending questions, like cats, with their maneuvers to be under my feet, to trip me up.

"Let me tell you why I think that's bullshit."

I whipped to face him. "Excuse me?"

"I said, I think it's bull that this letter doesn't mean anything to you." Keller pulled out the chair Joshua had been spinning in not so long ago and sat on its edge with his elbows on his knees. He gestured for me to join him.

Invited to sit in my own home. I edged around the table and took my customary chair. The laptop had been put away; the rest of my in-box had been sifted, the trash emptied, studied, replaced. Between us now, at last, was the table. Let him try to take charge when he's sitting on the receiving end of *my* desk. I clasped my hands and leaned over the table.

He smiled. "Good. Here's why I think this means something to you that it doesn't to me. It's simple really." He held the paper up with both hands, pinching the edges of the top corners so it hung over his shoulder. "See that?"

I'd seen it. I'd seen enough.

"Look at it. What does it say? Just—what does it actually *say*?"

I glared at him, then at the note. Large black letters printed wide across the page, as large as the paper allowed. "It says," I said, my voice sounding choked to my own ears. "It says 'I *know* about you.'"

"No, did you hear yourself? What it says is: I know about you," he said. "No emphasis, no underlines. Just straight. Four words, that's it." His voice was low and calming. I thought of the people who were supposed to be able to make animals easy with the tone of their voices. I didn't want to be soothed. I'd never told him how much I could read into four little words. He had no idea. *Skin the fucking bastard.* Four words was all you needed. "It hardly means a thing," he said, "without having you here to read it to me."

He put the note on the table, printed side down and far from me. An offering. Maybe he could read people a little bit.

"Here's what I think," he said. "That's a sentence that could frighten just about anybody. Everybody has a little something they don't want out." I raised an eyebrow, and he shrugged. "Sure. Sure I do. Everyone has something they like to think is hidden. You could know someone really well, for years even, and still not know everything about them." He sat back, seemed to go somewhere else for a second. "And if everyone's got a secret, then what's the most general stab-in-the-dark threat I can make? To say 'I know you,' when you have no idea who I am at all? That's something none of us wants to get in the mail. Most people don't even know themselves. They don't like the idea that someone else does."

The thing hadn't come in the mail, though. It had sneaked

into the building and then into our apartment, in disguise. I hadn't mentioned the Sweetheart Lake magazine.

"Of course this sort of threat would be more keenly felt by someone who was . . ."

"Hiding something?" I said.

"I was going to say someone who was private," he said. "But yes, for someone who had a real secret, I'm sure a message like this would be a big deal, like the world was closing in. In fact, it might seem like the anvil she's been waiting to fall out of the sky and onto her head."

"Is that some sort of children's story reference? A cartoon? What?"

"I assure you I'm taking this matter seriously," he said.

"You seem to think I'm either overreacting or predicting doom *and* overreacting. Is this how you investigate every crime around here—"

"Where's the crime? There's no crime I can see," he said. "Have you considered that this is some sort of joke? You know better than I do what these things look like."

"I'm suddenly feeling very sorry for Bo Ransey when he had to call *you* for help."

That stopped him. We both rose from our seats.

"Ms. Winger, are you sure these are the words you want to spend your breath on?" The volume was up. We were back to formality. It was Ms. Winger again, the desk between us in every way.

"You know, when you're right, you are on the mark, Sheriff." I met his volume. "These are not the words I want to spend my breath on. The words I want to say are—"

Down the hall, Joshua's door flew open. "Mom?" He rushed down the hall, stopped. His eyes shifted from me to the sheriff and back. "What's going on?"

I felt a crushing weight of weariness fall onto my shoulders.

If someone knew? It was so unlikely, and yet, why not? I'd been so careful, but it was never careful enough. In the age of two-second internet searches, why couldn't someone track me down to the spot where I stood? A new name, thanks to Kent. No property, no utility bills, no credit cards. Don't get arrested, don't be a hero, don't get quoted on the news. It was easy to stay invisible: don't get a life.

But if someone was curious, all they'd need was a bit of know-how, a little bit of access, maybe a few hundred dollars for a private investigator. It wouldn't even take someone good. It wouldn't even take the investigative powers of the sheriff.

I suddenly had the feeling that someone did know. Maybe not the person who wrote the note and took the effort to place it in our mailbox. Maybe that person was just guessing well, like the sheriff said. But if anyone knew, it was Sheriff Keller. He had the world of investigation at his disposal, databases and background checks and all that. Hadn't he been referred by Kent to begin with? And he had a reason for checking on me—he had to keep the woo under control.

If he knew, how soon before someone else? Sherry? Sherry and then her friends, her neighbors. Stephanie and Grace and the Boosters, the guidance counselor Mr. Jeffries, the school, the students, the Ranseys, all of them. The grapevine.

Or maybe Sheriff Keller would keep it to himself—in his arsenal, wasn't it? What had he said about the Ranseys the day he'd parked behind us on the street and knocked on my window? That he was just trying to make his town a better place to live? His town? His town, his citizens, *his* problems when they got into fights and lit things on fire and drove too fast down his streets—and yet here was one of his people—one of those little pink stick figures in the game of Life, if that's how he wanted to play it. One of his own in trouble, and he didn't seem as interested in making the town a better place for *me*.

Our problems had come in the night and could be packed upon our backs and taken away again, if the sheriff decided that his town couldn't harbor them, if he decided that his town would be better for everyone else, would run just a little more smoothly, if we weren't in it.

I was being irrational, and I knew it. My head was thrumming with anger, but beneath that was a feeling in my gut I didn't like, something alive and crawling that made me want to duck under the table or into a corner. An old instinct.

I held my body tense, willing it to keep still, just now, just this once. The sheriff was not going to hurt me. That wasn't his game. But if he had his own motives, whatever they were, they had nothing to do with me. I wouldn't let him have anything to do with me.

"Nothing, Joshua," I said. "The sheriff was just leaving."

I HADN'T MADE anything good for dinner after all, but it didn't seem to matter. We both picked at our plates, and I reached again and again for my water glass in an attempt to wash the brackish taste from the back of my throat. The old taste to go with the old fears. No amount of water would drown it out. Joshua poked at his food. "What was he doing here, anyway?"

"I don't want to talk about it."

"Was it because of that letter?" he asked. "Or something else?"

"It's not really anything for you to worry about."

"But you were yelling."

"I said—"

"Why won't you tell me?" he said. "I live here, too."

"Fine, Joshua. Fine." I went to the kitchen and found a bottle of wine. I returned to the table and pushed my plate away so that the full goblet had its rightful place in the center of my vision. I had never been much of a drinker—alcohol hadn't done much for my life. But I suddenly understood how a drink could be the thing to reach for when other things were lacking: lover, friend, mother. Life. Safety.

"The letter," I said. "I just wanted the sheriff's opinion on it."

Joshua's fork dropped to his plate with a clatter. "What did he say?"

"He thinks I'm overreacting." I swirled the wine, watching its color cling to the inside of the glass. I could already feel my desire for the rest of the bottle recede. There would be no hangover tomorrow. There would only be sharp, acrid clarity and the damn sun in the window again. "He might be right."

Joshua scooted his plate to the side and crossed his arms in its place, nesting his chin there. "I have to ask you a question."

"Sure."

"You won't like it," he said.

"Now I can't wait."

"Mom, stop trying to make it funny. It's not funny." His chin slid deeper into the hollow of his arms. His voice became a mumble.

"What?"

"I said," he said, sitting up so I could hear his exasperation. "I said I have to ask you about Dad."

"Oh. You have to?" Sometimes I wished I'd killed Ray off. Ray could have died a glorious death in the military, in a fire, rescuing small children or puppies. But I never could have lived with those stories. Ray as hero.

I steadied myself. "OK," I said.

"It's for a project at school."

"What do you mean? Like—"

"It's a family tree. They're making us do it in history class, like, personal history, you know, what's it called?"

"Genealogy," I said, my voice stretched thin.

"Yeah. We have to try to research our family as far back as we can." He rolled his eyes. "My teacher would wet his pants if I could trace my family back to the Mayflower or Spain or something."

"We are not from Spain."

"But what about Dad?"

I hated that word. It was too familiar. Why couldn't he use something less—affectionate?

"Your father was not from Spain."

"That's what he isn't. I need to know what he *is*."

True. "So what do you need to know?"

He reached for his backpack. After a little digging, he came up with a notebook with frayed corners and a mechanical pencil. He gave the pencil a few clicks. "Well, I need to know his name."

Something inside me plummeted. I'd kept every shred to myself. Sweetheart Lake and all that had happened there—it belonged to me, didn't it?

But I could have spared him a *name*. Names had power, but even this I'd withheld. I could have spared him, even just a little, but I hadn't.

"Ray."

"Winger?"

"Oh. No." I didn't want to say it. Magical thinking again. "Give me your notebook."

With my own pen from the cup on the table, I wrote out Ray's name in thick, clear letters that reminded me of the typewriter hand Joshua had adopted. At the last moment, I misspelled his last name. As bad as I felt about keeping secrets, I didn't want to open up this particular vault.

He leaned closer to see what I had written. "What about his parents' names?"

I drew two branches and supplied the names of Ray's mother and father, using the same fake name. I'd never known them; they'd died before we met. Across the table, Joshua nodded his approval. "What about his sisters and brothers?"

I looked up from the notebook. I didn't know. Or I couldn't remember. "He didn't have any," I said. Best to keep it simple, in case I had to be responsible for these facts later.

"Do you know anybody before that?"

"No. No, that's all I know." I drew a line from *Ray* and added a name carefully: *Joshua*. I added another branch from Joshua's name and added my own.

Joshua pushed up from the table with his elbows to see what he'd collected. "That's not very much."

"We're a small family, I guess."

"Well, what about you?"

"Me, what?"

"What are your parents' names? Do you have any brothers or sisters?"

"Don't you think you might have met my brothers and sisters if I had any?"

He raised his eyes from the notebook, a line frowned into the freckled spot between his eyes. "I never met my dad."

"Well, that's different."

"How? It doesn't seem different."

"Well. It is. It just is. I don't have any brothers or sisters. We can put down my parents' names."

He watched my hand move across the page. "Are they—are they dead?"

His solemn face creased with concern, but for just this minute he gave me no comfort. Here he was, the justification of all those hormones flooding, bodies grinding, DNA strands replicating. But just for this minute, when my hand had just filled in the name of my mother—and my father, too, despite everything—I felt only loss. Nothing would change it. Nothing would cure it. If the presence of Joshua next to me didn't fix all that had gone wrong, then there was nothing that would. "They are."

"When did they—"

"My mother died in an accident. A car accident." The truth was inadequate.

"What about your dad?"

I don't know. I don't know. I don't want to know. "He died," I said. "Of old age."

The end. The period at the end of a sentence and the conversation, and I knew we both felt it. Joshua took the notebook from my hands and studied our tree. It wasn't a tree, really. A little bush, perhaps. A little patch of weeds, grown wild and stomped out.

And where the world might have once seemed vast, now it was tiny. It was really rather small.

Chapter Fourteen

On Saturday, I reported for Boosters duty at the school, dodging practicing kicks by a group of cheerleaders with skinny stilts for legs and smiles full of braces. The Boosters booth was a squat little green-painted cinder-block building next to the home team stands.

I arrived at the front, like a customer. Stephanie waved me around to the back and handed me a T-shirt. I'd worn a button-down green shirt, the only green item of clothing I had in support of the school colors. But she was right. Next to the rest of them, I looked like an accountant. I threw the T-shirt on over my other shirt.

Lines quickly formed on both ends of the service window. The Boosters' play clock started early, ended late.

Stephanie put me in charge of popcorn. I got the hang of it well enough: fill the pan at the top of the machine with kernels and oil, push some buttons, flip a lever, watch and listen for the popcorn to pop itself down to a certain threshold of pop-to-silence, and then flip the lever back and dump the popcorn into the bin.

I was given a saltshaker and some red-and-white striped cups to fill. Newbie job. Stay out of the way.

The pros grabbed at everything coming their way, yanking potato chip bags from where they hung by clothespins, filling soda cups, taking orders and yelling them back. Stephanie and Grace were adding up figures in their heads and giving change. One woman who had shown up in tight white jeans and high heels—"Kelly," Stephanie had cried, "you *made* it!"—had promptly been put in command of the nacho cheese and chili dog sauce bins. "Are there . . . aprons?" Kelly asked, holding her charm bracelet back to stir the cheese sludge as it warmed.

The double lines ran all the way to the fences for the first forty-five minutes, petering out only when a shaky national anthem started up on the field.

I loaded the popcorn machine again: kernels, button for oil, lever, *pop*.

"—anyone with a baseball bat could have killed—"

I looked up, trying to pick up the rest of the sentence out of the noise of the popcorn. Volunteers were resetting their stations and cleaning up spills, rushing by, bumping into one another, squeezing through narrow passages. So much movement that at first I had trouble locating the conversation.

"—meth heads are *strong*," Grace was saying to someone over the counter.

The woman on the other side sipped at a straw, nodding. She had a paper tray of nachos and a popcorn cup tucked to her chest with a pudgy arm. "She could have done it, that's what I'm saying. Didn't you think once that she was after Shane—"

Grace waved the idea away. "He's just doing his job. They're a mess or he wouldn't have to be over there night and day. Hold on—hey, Tara!"

Deputy Lombardi, in uniform, walked up to the counter. "You guys seen Russ?"

"Anyone left at the station to keep the lights on?" the other woman said.

"I saw him earlier," Grace said. "Shane's off duty but here to watch Shay play. Keller might be in the stands. What's up?"

"You didn't hear it from me, but the Jordans just found a suitcase packed with panties and lingerie stuffed into the corner of their garage," Tara said. "Looked like someone was ready for a romantic getaway."

"Charity's hope chest," Grace said. "Now, where do you suppose she thought she was going? And with which fella?"

"Bo," said the other woman. "I mean, all that time with his wife gone, what do you expect?"

Tara shot her a disgusted look, reaching for a handful of popcorn and then edging away. "Yeah, so if you see Russ . . ."

Grace and the other woman waited in silence until she was out of range, then made eyes at each other. *"Russ?"* Grace said. "Notice how she has to find him, tell him in person. Not like his radio's broken. It's ridiculous. She wouldn't leave Shane alone all last year, and I'd just about had it, though Shane always tells me I have *nothing* to worry about. These skanky girls."

"The sheriff's single, though," the woman said. "How in the world, I have no idea. You know I'd—"

"What's burning?"

Stephanie was at my side, pushing me out of the way and reaching for the lever to dump the popcorn, but it was too late. Smoke billowed out from the pan, a tongue of flame licking its rim. The woman on nacho cheese screamed.

"Kelly, please," Stephanie said, propping open the back door to let smoke out. Volunteers were shoving to get past her and outside. "Your shift is over, anyway. Can you all get out of the way so I can find the extinguisher?"

Suddenly Sheriff Keller stood in the open door. He tracked the smoke to its source, reached up to a shelf above the sink, and grabbed the extinguisher. In mere seconds, the fire was out.

Stephanie looked at me. "Grace, can you make a sign that says we're out of popcorn?"

"I'm so sorry," I said, not looking in the sheriff's direction. "Is there anything else I can—ruin for you?"

"Go stir the nacho cheese while Grace makes the sign," she said.

"I'll pay for the burned popcorn," I said. "And the machine."

"It's not the first time that thing has been on fire," she said, moving away from me. It was clear she didn't want to be near me. When I turned toward the back door, Keller was gone.

AFTER THE HALFTIME rush, I staggered out of the Boosters hut to the fence, my new Parks High School shirt stained with nacho cheese and my hair smelling of smoke. The game was a goner. I checked along the bench for Joshua.

"He's on the field," Mullen said. I hadn't noticed him there in his street clothes and Parks High green ball cap pulled low.

I peered into the fray of boys on the field until I found him. He was running along the edge of the field nearest us and, just as I spotted him, caught a long pass and fell wildly, ass over helmet into a group of players from the opposing side. I gripped the fence, my heart in my throat. "Oh, my God—"

Mullen was clapping. "Stop being a mom for a second," he said. "That was a fine catch."

Joshua hopped up, Frankenstein monster's padded shoulders on top of skinny white legs. He passed the football to a referee and ran back to the other boys, who pounded at his back and slapped at his helmet.

"Was Charity Jordan Bo's mistress?"

Mullen went still. "Where did you hear that?"

"Just . . . in the air," I said. "Is Leila a drug user?"

"After just one shift in the Boosters kitchen?" he said. "What else did you learn?"

That a very young woman officer had a crush on the sheriff, but I didn't say that. And after the episode with the fire extinguisher, I couldn't deny that he was the kind of guy women got crushes on. So was Shane, I noticed. No wonder Grace was on alert.

"They found a packed suitcase in Charity's garage," I said.

He stared at me, licked his lips. "That's news to me."

"I think it's news to everyone," I said. "I guess she had some big plans coming up."

"I guess so."

"So the drugs . . . are they homemade in Parks or do they come in from other places?"

Mullen leaned back on the fence and watched a play on the field. "If we knew the source, Russ would clamp down on it. But it's out there, no matter what we do."

"Any new leads on Leila Ransey?"

"Most people ask about Aidan," Mullen said. His eyes flicked behind me, along the stands, and then to his other side. "Leila Ransey was supposed to be off somewhere, getting clean, but we can't seem to find her to make sure her *hands* are as clean as some people want us to believe."

"Some people? Her family?"

"I think the Ranseys are all she's got," he said. "Bo and Mama Ransey. Bea, I mean. I'm talking about local do-gooders, sticking their necks in. Russ threatened a warrant, but it's no good. She's not here. Town's too small to hide a missing woman for this long."

A matter of opinion.

"And that receipt, anyway," he said. "She's on the run now."

"She used her mother-in-law's credit card," I said. "How'd she get it?"

"Stole it," he said.

The thing that really bothered me, though, was Charity's death. It didn't make any sense. If I hadn't seen that grocery list and those cramped, scared letters crowded into the only space they were allowed to take up, I might have been picturing a base-ball bat in Leila's hands, too. But she hadn't used it on Bo—why bother with killing Charity? And where could she be?

Something occurred to me. "I forgot something at the booth."

"Hey," Mullen called as I walked away. "Keller hasn't depu-tized you, has he?"

At the back door of the Boosters booth I stuck my head in and surveyed the damage. The rush was over and the volunteers left behind were busy cleaning up.

"Hot dogs, definitely short on hot dogs," Stephanie said, jot-ting some notes onto a notepad on the counter. When she saw me, she whipped the notes over.

"Can I talk to you?"

"Grace, can you watch the cash bag? I'll be right back." She followed me outside, pulling at the neck of her T-shirt to fan her-self. "What's up?"

"I want to help," I said.

"I think you may have done enough for your first day," she said.

"No, I mean—with Leely."

She stared at me.

"And Sommer House, right? That's what it's called?" I threw myself into the void. "Your card. It doesn't have an address and—well, I have what you might call relevant experience."

"If the sheriff sent you—"

"He didn't."

"I don't know where she is," she said, her eyes darting all around us. "I really don't."

"But you know where she used to be."

She sighed. "She hates that name. Leely."

I did, too. "What can I do?"

"If you have actual relevant experience, you'll know already," she said. "Practically nothing. The system is stacked against her."

"I don't think she killed that woman."

Stephanie looked at me as she had when I'd given Grace a generous reading of her handwriting. "The problem is, you and I and the real killer are the only ones who believe it."

Chapter Fifteen

On Monday morning, Sherry called again. Early, but I was wide awake, facing a large mug of tea and the day's work. After the call I would be disappointed I hadn't been in bed; with any luck I could have missed the call entirely. Sherry said, "Sheriff wants to know if you'll go check out something for him."

"He—what?" I had already written off the entire experiment with local law enforcement the night he'd been in the apartment. Yes, I'd been drawn into the Ranseys' case through a few odd parallels between past and present, and finally, I hated to admit it, through the magnetic charms of the sheriff. That man, I'd found myself thinking after he'd left. I was sitting at the table where he'd lectured me on things he knew nothing about, and now he had another bug up his ass? He was something else. He really was. "I thought I was done with all the samples he had," I said.

"This is something new, I think," Sherry said. "He wants you to go meet with someone at the high school."

"Does it have something to do with Aidan?"

"I wouldn't say so. I mean, Aidan is two. His mom and dad went there, you know, like years ago, but we all did." Sherry's voice was taking on a lilting, singsong quality the longer she talked, as though she didn't often get asked for theories.

"The high school," I said, remembering that Aidan did have a relative at that school. "Could it be the junior high school? It's the same building."

"Oh, maybe," she said. "I don't know what he teaches. He was a few years ahead but I remember him anyway. When I was in the sixth grade, Joe Jeffries was all-state football, and what an *ass* he had—"

"Joe Jeffries. You mean the guidance counselor."

"The sheriff called him a teacher, but, sure, if you know who he is, then you're probably right. *Hot*. I wish I got assignments like this."

"I'm supposed to go see Joe Jeffries."

"Soon, like today. And report back to me when you're done."

"Back to you?"

Sherry's voice lost its song. "Don't sound so surprised," she said. "The sheriff trusts me."

"No, that's not—look, that's fine with me," I said. "In fact, it's more than fine. Did he happen to mention what I'm supposed to be asking Mr. Jeffries?"

"He said Joe would know," she said, still wounded.

"Did you say you all went to high school together? You, Bo, your husband . . ."

"Jimmy," she said.

"Jimmy, of course. Grace and Shane Mullen—"

"They were a few years ahead."

"Leila?"

She didn't answer right away. "She was there."

"Was she a friend of yours?"

"It's going to sound bad," she said.

"Say it."

"She was . . . in a different crowd," she said.

"Which crowd were you in?"

"The fun one," she said. "You know. We just had laughs, drank on the weekends."

I thought back to high school. "So which way did she go? Jocks and cheerleaders? Nerds?"

"Stoners," she said finally. "Kind of. I mean, really? I don't think she had any friends at all. She was more like a ghost."

THAT AFTERNOON I went to the café early and waited for school to get out and Jeffries to disentangle himself from football practice. I hadn't wanted another meeting in his office—Joshua aware of my presence there, the other Boosters ladies talking it over later—but now it seemed like a better option than meeting in broad daylight in the center of town.

Too late to make a change of location. Anyway, I had a crisp copy of the *Spectator* and a fat raspberry scone slathered with butter in front of me. Rather a nice assignment from the sheriff. Out of the apartment, out in the sun. The leaves were turning, and it wouldn't be long before the wind became chilled and unwelcoming, and I'd find any excuse to stay inside. Across the street, the courthouse rose above the square in cold, limestone majesty. The world, soon enough, would seem as though it had been cut to match.

Jeffries arrived earlier than expected and greeted me warmly. He left his satchel by the side of the vacant chair and went inside for a cup of coffee. I watched him through the glass door. The old man behind the counter lit up at the sight of him. Jeffries gleamed like the statuette on a trophy. Today, all my senses piqued, I couldn't help but notice.

He came back out, sitting across from me and stretching his legs into the sidewalk.

"Thanks for meeting with me on short notice," I said.

"Please. It's a pleasure." He shrugged out of his suit coat and folded it carefully over the next chair. "May I?" he said, one hand over the knot of his tie. I smiled. He pulled at the knot until it hung loosely around his neck, and one button at the neck of his shirt had been sacrificed to his comfort. "I'm glad to get this chance to follow up with you. About Joshua."

I tensed. "This isn't about Joshua. The sheriff—"

"No, I know," he said. "I have good news for you, though, if you don't mind. Whatever you said to him—well, it worked." He sat back, elbows on the arms of the chair, his hands folded over his stomach. "I've heard some good reports already. Homework finished, at least."

"He was getting hung up on the aesthetics, I guess you could say," I said. "But I'm glad to hear good results so soon."

"I'm amazed to receive results so soon. He's really turning himself around, from what I hear. Our head librarian—we monitor first lunch together every day—she mentioned how industrious he was. Usually, library periods are treated like recess."

We smiled at each other until I finally looked away. I liked the affection in his voice when he talked about the students. He seemed to understand them, to accept the wildness in them that might make other adults—me—nervous. If Joshua still needed a mentor, here was the best candidate. It made sense. It made so much sense that I nearly cried from relief. He already took an interest. He seemed willing to share his insights. A local sports god.

I couldn't ask if he played video games. Instead I said, "The sheriff seemed to want us together?"

"Right," he said, a strange Mona Lisa twitch on his lips. "You're saving me from a pile of work in my office."

"What about football practice?"

His hand stopped on the way to his satchel. "It was in-service for the teachers today. No classes for the students, as you know, so no practice."

"Oh," I said. "Right." Except if I'd known about it, I'd forgotten—and where the hell had Joshua gone at seven this morning?

Jeffries extracted a manila envelope from his bag and slid it across the table. "This is what we're dealing with. Keller said you might be able to help. Not solve the case or anything, but maybe—I don't know—give us some ideas."

The envelope was heavy with a set of eight-by-ten glossy photos. I slid them out onto the table and held one, then the next, by the edges. There were six altogether, each one capturing a different section of bright graffiti on the side of a brick building. When I placed them side by side in two rows, the spray-painted words connected and congealed into a smattering of swear words, epithets, drawings that might have been sexual—they were terribly drawn, but I sensed the intent.

"Is this the school?"

"One of the outbuildings," he said. "The school keeps lawn equipment there. There's been a rash of these lately around the county. A bridge, I think. Nothing yet on the school itself. They did us that bit of courtesy, I suppose."

"Kids."

"I—well, I suppose that's the going consensus," he said. "Keller came out when they first went up, or when Griffin—the maintenance guy? Carl Griffin?—when he discovered them. We had the yearbook advisor take those pictures. Keller thought maybe you could wave your magic wand over them and tell us who left us the mess."

Magic wand. I wondered what the sheriff actually said, if he thought I could really help or if he weren't playing some sort of trick on us all.

"I can try to tell you something about them," I said. "It's not foolproof and won't stand as evidence in court. But getting some kid to confess might be easier if you've already figured out he did the deed."

"Anything you can offer."

I gazed down at the prints for a while. "It's more than one kid."

He leaned forward.

"I would say three separate people. To be fair, I can't say definitively that they are boys, but I think you're safe to say that. From the—" I waved my hand toward the corner where a sexual organ had been reconstructed by someone either sloppy with the paint can or inexperienced sexually, or both. "Probably young."

"We get sixth graders when they're eleven or twelve."

"Thirteen. Maybe fourteen, tops," I said. "Again, not definitively—these just seem so . . . juvenile."

"I understand," he said, looking off into the distance for a moment. "There's a line—a maturity line. Not always determined by age."

"There's one boy who's hesitant," I said. "He only has a couple of examples of his work in this entire, uh, project. Probably didn't want to be there. If you could find him, he'd break down and feed you the other two. The other two are more practiced. One of them is rather a pro with his lettering. No drips." I turned the photo around, pointed. "That's your ringleader, your idea man. He's very confident. His work is all over the wall—he's your Picasso. You need to get that boy into art class, Mr. Jeffries."

"Joe."

I glanced up but returned quickly to the prints. It was fascinating, the interplay of ego and ethics that played out on the side of this brick wall. One boy was all bravado, sweeping gestures and full, round lettering. Another boy was less so, but willing. I could almost picture the second keeping an eye on the first, to guide his own efforts. His lines were thicker, slower, clumsier— but they, like the strokes of the first boy, were well represented. He'd enjoyed himself. He had wanted to be there. "Here's your number two," I said. "He's a follower. Probably not heading up the junior high student council, but you guessed that already. He's a lefty, too, by the way."

"A lefty who is not on the student council. Got it."

I grinned at the prints. "Like I said, it's imprecise as an identification tool. What would work much better is to look for a dumping ground for about six nearly empty spray-paint cans, and then use the fingerprints on them as your evidence. Or have the sheriff go around to the places that sell the paint to see who's been buying a variety. Will they sell spray paint to young kids around here? Lots of urban areas don't."

"We're a little behind the crimes in Parks."

"Your third guy here," I said, drawing a finger over the blocky letters of a shaking-lettered obscenity. "He doesn't want to be there, and probably hasn't done it before. He's your weak link." I peered at each print, searching for the work of this particular boy. "Righty. Not very tall. Not as tall as the others, I mean. None of them are tall, or they would've painted higher on the building."

Joe took earnest notes, as though they could somehow tell him what to do next. For the third boy I described a sense of self-preservation, a wavering ethic of right and wrong. He was clumsy fisted—perhaps chubby, for all the grace lacking in his few attempts at lettering—and he probably stumbled through a great deal of his miserable days with his head turned toward his buddies. He was sloppy. He would still have some of the paint under his nails.

I had been jotting notes for my report back to Sherry, and when I finally pulled myself out of them, I'd nearly forgotten Joe was there. He was silent, watching the progress of my pen across the page. I turned my notes away. "Sorry. I—I get caught up, I guess."

"No wonder. It's really interesting. All very logical, but with just a little touch of something like—"

Don't say hocus-pocus. Don't say magic. Just this once.

"Psychology. I'm afraid to let my handwriting near you."

"Most people are," I said.

Joe turned a new page in his notebook and started sketching something.

"You don't have to do that."

He huddled over his page like a seventh grader preventing a classmate from cheating. "I want to. If you see something horrible, just—just break it to me gently."

He turned the paper over and held it in front of his chest.

It read *Will you have dinner with me next week?*

My eyes darted quickly over the lines, closures, and the dot of his question mark, putting on the show he had probably wanted me to give for students: furrowed brow, finger tapping on chin. The show was, first, the show, because I had the feeling he wanted to see my consideration. But the show was also a cover. My thoughts scurried. I gave the page real attention while he gave me the chance.

But it was rude to meditate for too long over the particular slant of that question mark, when the question was still in the air. And—suddenly I wanted very much not to study the handwriting too closely, to do what other people would do. To stop thinking about flight, to stop thinking about the worst possible thing that could happen, to say yes instead of no.

When he stood to leave, he touched, very delicately, the top of my hand with a finger. Just an acknowledgment of my hand by his before he walked away.

"Ah, I almost forgot," he said and came hurrying back to the table. "This is from Keller. Something you're working on for him, I guess?"

He handed over a sturdy package that had been sealed expertly. It was heavy.

"Oh, sure," I said. Actually, I'd imagined that this meeting with Jeffries was my penance with the sheriff for being nosy, but it looked as though I'd be doing as much work as he wanted me to.

I WALKED TO my truck admiring the way the sun threw anonymous shadows across my path, each its own small Rorschach test. The day had turned itself around so easily on the chance of a full sun, a cloudless sky. Nature's own hocus-pocus, because where I had felt closed in last night, I now felt more free and alive and hopeful than I had been in years. The pieces of my life were drawing themselves, finally, along a straight line, like characters on a page.

I opened the driver's side door and tossed the envelope onto the passenger seat and took a last look around the square. A couple stooped over a little boy dangled between them. A woman in pink jogging pants led a tiny dog across the street, talking to it with a high-pitched, smoosh-mouthed voice. On the low retaining wall around the courthouse green, a group of boys taunted and jeered and fought—

One of the boys was Joshua.

One boy tugged at Joshua's shirt, nearly pulling it off his skinny back. I almost cried out, but stopped myself and looked feverishly around for Jeffries. He could put a stop to it.

But then the two boys broke apart and shook their stretched shirts back into place. They grinned and laughed, and drew back in for more.

Now I knew what I was seeing. Just boyhood in the wild. Like his video games, but in person, in the sunshine. Joshua wasn't just on the receiving end of the attacks, either—he was in the fray. He leapt in the air, pretending to land on the feet of one of the other boys, slowly enough to let the kid pull back. The other retaliated with a slow-motion punch that landed in the air to the side of Joshua's face. From this far away, I could only hear a few yipping words. They were like dogs let loose in a park.

Four or five boys, plus Joshua, wheezing with laughter. They moved around fast enough that I kept counting them, trying to make sense of all these *friends*—

One of them, Steve Ransey.

"Oh, no." I slid behind the wheel.

These boys? Out of all the students in the local seventh grade, out of all the boys who played sports or played in a band or collected Japanese anime, he had to choose boys who hung around the square after school waiting to be old enough to talk someone into selling them beer? Joshua gave up precious video game time to hang out with members of the Future Criminals of America? With a baby thug? With—

An artistic talent, Sheriff Keller had said. An artistic talent. With a can of spray paint.

Across the street, Joshua and another boy tackled the smallest of the group with fake pummels. Steve sat on his haunches in the grass, hooting and slapping his leg. The leader, the follower, and the pudgy and reluctant mascot. Perhaps they were all in there, right now. And so, now, was Joshua.

Later, reporting back to Sherry on the phone, I gave in and said, "Do you sometimes wonder if you're a bad mother?"

Sherry had been a little cold at the beginning of the conversation, still stung from the earlier insult. But she'd warmed up again—Sherry either couldn't stay mad, or really liked taking reports from the field.

"When I gave Jamey his first bath in the tub, I dropped him," she said. "He was so slippery. I still do something nearly every day that makes me wonder if I should have got a dog instead. Or a fish. Something that didn't need me so much."

"Just wait," I said. "Just wait until they don't need you at all."

Chapter Sixteen

The next morning, Aidan's suspicious gaze appeared in the *Parks County Spectator* again. He was a feature of the paper, like the sun-cloud-umbrella icons for weather in the top corner, or the box scores of all the high school sports played in the state the night before. Aidan Watch. If it had been television news, there might be some logo to ensure that everyone knew they were tuned to the right minute-by-minute coverage of the story.

I scanned for the updates. The forged credit card receipts were reported: the hotel, food charged at a grocery store (no diapers, the story reported grudgingly), a full tank of gas at the state border. Leely was out there spending her mother-in-law's money, but it wouldn't be long. I worried for her.

How had it happened that this family of trouble had become my trouble? First Aidan, then Leila, and now Steve.

When Joshua arrived home the night before as though he'd just gotten off the bus, I hadn't said anything about Steve Ransey or the spray paint. I couldn't think of the right thing to say. I couldn't even think how to say that I'd seen him with the other boys. He'd never believe I'd been working on a project for the sheriff. He'd suspect me of *recon*.

I'd gone to bed early, but couldn't sleep, tossing and turning and flipping over my pillow. Thinking of all the things I should have demanded he explain. The teacher-in-service—where had he been all day? Why was it a state secret that he had a day off school?

This morning, I was ready. I went for the paper early, then sat at the table in wait for him to come to life. He was slow this morning. Once, I went to make sure he was getting dressed. "You had better not be playing video games in there," I said to the door.

I tapped my spoon against my mug and turned back to the paper. In lieu of real movement in the case, the news staff had adopted some gimmicks. A time line. Lapsed time: nine days and counting.

Nine days. I hadn't realized.

The time line was sleek in the face of no facts. I focused on the pulled-out boxes that offered real-time notations for when Charity left the house (8:45 a.m.) and the discovery of the body (10:08 a.m.). On day three: *Sheriff's office consults local handwriting expert to study ransom note. Note confirmed to be written by Leila Ransey.* Part of the public record again. How long before my name showed up?

Then: *Sheriff's office consults psychic to locate Aidan. Private sources say psychic provided information that could lead to Aidan's body.*

Aidan's *body*?

A *psychic*?

It had to be a joke, a mistake. The paper had got it wrong, and Keller was on the phone with the editor right now, demanding a correction. Had to be.

The door to Joshua's room opened, and he came down the hall with purpose, grabbing his backpack and reaching for the front door deadbolt almost before I registered his presence.

"Hey," I said.

He stopped, hand still on the lock. "What?"

"I need to talk to you about some things. Important things."

"I'm late for school already, Ma."

I glanced toward the clock. "Why are you so late?"

"I gotta go."

"Well, there are some things we need to talk about tonight, then, so you need to come home right after school. Or practice, I guess."

His eyes shifted away. "Can't we just talk over dinner, like normal?"

"Oh, when do you *normally* talk to me over the dinner table? I thought that you normally didn't talk to me at all."

He rolled his eyes. *"Ma—"*

I resisted the urge to ask him to call me something else. Anything else.

"If you're missing your bus, I can drive you," I said. "We need to talk about who you're hanging out with these days."

Joshua stared at me with eyes dark as holes. "Oh, yeah? Well, we also need to talk about who *you're* hanging out with these days." He flicked the deadbolt and reached for the doorknob.

"Wait," I said. "What did you just say?" I couldn't imagine who—the sheriff? Margaret? The Boosters? What hanging out had I even done?

He opened the door and stepped through it. The words he was using didn't make any sense. I stood and started for the door, but it was already closing. "What are you—Joshua—"

"Mr. Jeffries. We need to have a *referendum* on that." He pulled the door closed as my hand grazed the knob. His pounding foot-steps receded down the hall and away while I stared at the closed door.

Downstairs, the tap of Margaret's broom.

Cautiously, as though the door might explode inward, I stood back from it, returned back to the table, sat in my chair.

Who was that? That boy who had closed the door in my face didn't remind me in the least of the boy I'd raised, the boy I had such hopes for. He seemed like an image of someone I'd once known, like the photo of Aidan, nine days into his disappear-ance: a face I recognized, but a boy I didn't really know.

I looked around for distraction and saw the package Jeffries had delivered from Keller. I sliced it open and slid out the bundle of paper inside. Paging through, I found the same form, over and over. Each page was headed *Evidence* and divided into columns filled in by hand with times, dates, and signatures, begging for careful study.

I reached for my phone.

Sherry's voice said on the other end, "Parks County Sheriff."

"Hey, Sherry. It's Anna," I said, suddenly not sure what I was about to ask, or how. "Uh, Winger. Is the sheriff available?" I'd never called the sheriff before. He had always demanded *my* time. "I mean, I need to talk to the sheriff."

"OK, yeah, he's back there. Let me forward you. Hey!"

"What?"

"I thought maybe you might want to come over to our house on Sunday. We're having a cookout."

"Oh." I couldn't think of anything to say. "What's Sunday?"

"Just a Sunday. Friends, neighbors, some family. Bring Joshua, too."

I couldn't imagine it. "I'll try."

"You'll try? Come on, say you'll come. You have another offer?"

"Such flattery," I said. "I'll check Joshua's football schedule and let you know."

When Sherry forwarded the call, I heard a faint click and then a ring. Then another. I wondered if he would answer at all, if Sherry had announced me, and now his punishment for the other night was to let the phone go on and on.

Finally the sheriff answered with a sigh. "You're talking to me, then?"

"Is that how you always answer your phone?" Immediately, I knew this was the wrong way to go. I tried again. "I owe you an apology. You were trying to help and I was—I was just scared, I guess. And I took it out on you. For that, I am truly sorry."

Silence. I waited it out.

"'For that,' you're sorry," he said.

"I'm also sorry that I insinuated—no, let me say it right." I cleared my throat. "I'm sorry I said rather directly that you weren't doing your job. That is not the case. You're doing your job as well as anyone could. Aidan's case, for instance—"

"I'm not patting myself on the back for that one."

Aidan's body. My nerves leapt. "What do you mean? Why not?"

"Ms. Winger, the little boy is still missing, if you haven't noticed."

"Can I ask you a question?"

"You called for more than just plying me with half-assed apologies? Shoot." I heard him let out a small puff of air and pictured him relaxing back in his chair, throwing his boots up on the corner of his desk.

"Did you actually hire a psychic to help find Aidan?"

"Aw, hell. Where did you—is that in the *Spectator*?"

"This morning," I said. "Really? You did?"

"How did they ever . . ." Paper rustled in the background.

"It's on page two, with the time line."

"The *time line*? Oh, this is perfect. That's what we need. By-the-minute recapping, in case you missed it on television, on the radio, in earlier issues of the paper." He went silent. I let him read. "You're in here."

"Yes."

"Is that OK?"

"I don't know what I'd do about it if it weren't."

"Good attitude. Good," he murmured. Still reading.

"So how is it that you don't believe in what I do, but you believe in psychics?"

"Is that what's bothering you? That your science has been mocked, but I'm willing to listen to what Madame Zonda has to say?"

"That's not really her name, I hope."

"It is not," he said.

"But you hired her. You said you didn't believe in my sort of—woo, wasn't it? You didn't believe in me, but you went ahead and hired someone who depends on *vibrations*—" I heard the strident screech creeping into my voice. "You said my work wasn't real, but then you ask me to do more of it. I'm confused, I guess."

I wished both that I could see his face right now—that I had gone over to do both the apology and the accusation in person—*and* that I had never called at all. What was the point? Why did I care so much? If he didn't put any stock in what I did for a living, fine. He would stop calling. Except that he hadn't stopped calling. There was something there, a little bit of his own methods, his manipulations, that I wanted to understand.

"Two things," he said. I thought he was talking lower, or holding the phone closer to his mouth. I felt as though a hand had been placed on my arm; again, the calming, measured tones spared for me. I wondered what I must seem like to him. Recluse. Bitch. Wack job. He probably called me Madame Zonda behind my back. "I didn't hire that psychic," he said. "I never would. Never. I know some say they've had luck using them and all, but no."

"Oh," I said. "Who—"

"The Ranseys hired her. Mrs. Ransey."

The older woman, the penitent believer in Sheriff Keller, believed in the other side, did she? My sense of rightness came flooding back. Of course—and I'd insulted his methods again. "I'm sorry I thought that you—never mind."

"That's what the time line says, right?"

I laughed, a weight lifting. "The media," I said.

"Such as it is. Now the second thing?"

"Huh?" I'd forgotten his opening pronouncement. "Oh, yeah. What's the second thing?"

"I said I didn't put much stock into handwriting analysis," he said. "But I happen to think we're more than just the magic we believe in. I'm not saying I'm lining up to have my signature read or anything. That's what you do. There's more to me than what I do, though, so I expect the same of other people. And I never said that I didn't believe in you."

I sat, transfixed, trying not to breathe into the phone. I could pretend that I had already hung up, or that the line had broken while he spoke. More manipulation? Maybe this was just a prelude to asking his next favor?

He started laughing. "So you don't take compliments well. It's one more thing we both know about you. And you're mad I sent you more handwriting, even if I don't completely buy in?"

"Can we talk about that? What am I looking at here?"

"Those are copies of some chain of custody forms for our

missing evidence," he said. "Standard procedure, especially in a drug case, is to prove beyond a shadow of a doubt that the drugs collected from the suspect upon arrest are the drugs in evidence. If the chain is broken, that's reasonable doubt and my arrest walking out the door."

I paged through the sheets. "I don't see broken chains, but maybe I don't know what I'm looking for."

"I don't know, either," Keller said. "But the chains are definitely broken because the drugs are gone, replaced with useless powders. The good stuff goes up someone's nose or veins. So the chain of custody can't be right. You see?"

"And the person who signed in last isn't your best suspect?"

"Well, but look closer. Each one is filed last by a different person. Can my entire command be on the take? The whole place? I don't want to believe that," he said. "Oh, man, I really can't believe that. Now, I put a ringer in there for you, one sheet that's different from all the others. That's a sample you can go by or maybe it will help you see something I can't see. I don't know. Could you take a look and let me know if there's anything—I don't know—interesting or odd? Anything at all, doesn't matter how small."

After the call, long after, I was still thinking about what he'd said about belief. We are more than the magic we believe in. We are more.

It had never occurred to me to be *more*. My life had been chiseled down to the smallest portion. My own doing. I had only ever made plans to be less, to be nothing more than alive.

Chapter Seventeen

I worked all day on a stack of samples from candidates for an executive position at a giant international conglomerate. Another subcontract from Kent, ever the savior. The company sold enough dangerous products that its human resources department took special precautions when assigning away power. I didn't want to know about this company, what they sold or made or built. I didn't want to think about how many corporations there were like this one, or how few, and how much of the world they ran. I pictured myself taking the check for this job into the bank on the courthouse square, signing up for a college fund.

The time by which Joshua should have been home came and went.

Not that I hadn't expected him to pull a little rank, after this morning's performance. Today, at last, I'd resigned myself to the problem of Joshua. There was a little photo of him, fairly recent, sitting nearby. I'd only unpacked it three months ago, but it was already forgotten among the other knick and knack. He looked so young in the photo, even though it was a year old at best.

So? He was growing up.

In a secret part of my mind, I had hoped for something more, something concrete and fixable. A bully. Trouble with a teacher. Body issues. Depression? I could learn, get him help.

But no. Thirteen. He was just thirteen, rushing headlong against every barrier I'd set up around the two of us. He had to rebel against me. I was all there was.

It was just like when he was two years old, and wanted everything in sight, raving *Mine! Mine!* with his fists flailing. Or when he was six and seven and did the exact opposite of what I said, just to see what I would do. Once, when I was walking him to first grade, I'd reminded him about looking both ways at crossings just as we reached one. A lesson we'd gone over and over. Before I could finish the sentence, he'd taken a big step into the road. A car rounding the corner had to squeal to a stop. Scared, Joshua played as though he hadn't heard me. But I knew him—he was much easier to know then—and I'd seen the wayward expression in his eyes, the extra stretch he put into that last step.

He was a lot like me.

I should be comforted. It was normal. Isn't that what I'd wanted, for him to have a normal childhood? Why I'd sacrificed so much? All I'd given up—but this refrain seemed familiar, as though I'd absorbed the common lament of mothers everywhere through sitcom television. Maybe the way we lived wasn't that different from the way other families did. Maybe he was just thirteen. Maybe he should be craning his lanky limbs beyond me. He should be thrashing around, doing exactly what I told him not to—

Where the *hell* was he?

"A referendum on who I'm hanging out with," I said to the closed front door and the silent hall beyond.

All this because I'd sat at a café with Joe Jeffries? Working, by the way. Had he not considered that? The dinner invitation was a complication. My acceptance was a complication. I wish I had Grace's phone number, to call and ask. Was it wrong? To go out on a date with the kids' guidance counselor?

And while I had this imaginary friend on the phone, I might have some other questions. What did you wear for a dinner date in this town? People would see us. We would be much discussed, and I wondered if that weren't the sort of thing Joe liked, anyway. Another woman would have nodded. Exactly.

A former sports hero? I plucked at the keys on my keyboard. He wasn't even my type. A spokesperson for manhood, for good-natured, hearty masculinity. Together, his features portioned themselves out well, but that was a trick of the eye. If you looked closely, each feature was just a bit too large for his face, his face too full of wide, white teeth. If I could have said I had a type, I would have chosen something else entirely. Someone who could keep his long limbs in check, for one thing. Someone who sat on the other side of the table at dinner and kept any accidental brushings of their knees to a minimum. When we walked side by side, his arms should not *swing*. I should have said no. I really should have said no.

Finally the tramping of Joshua's feet came to the door, and his key rattled in the lock. He closed the door, locked the deadbolt, dropped his backpack hard upon the table. As though it were any day. As though the vapor of our conversation from that morning didn't still hang in the air. "Hey," he said, already halfway to the refrigerator.

"Hey, yourself." My mind raced through things I didn't want to say. Not yet.

He rummaged in the fridge and came to the table with a tough slice of old leftover pizza and a soda. It was a dare. So this was how it was going to be. Chewing, waiting, watching. A game of chicken, and I was a chicken.

In two more bites, the snack was gone. He went back to the kitchen and started opening cabinets. I listened as he systematically scanned every shelf.

"There are those crackers—"

"Found them." He came back to the table with his hand in the open box. He sat down again and, his full attention offered, dropped cracker after cracker into his mouth.

"How was school today?" I said. "*Was* there school today?"

"Uh-huh."

"I'm worried about the boys you're hanging out with," I said.

"Uh-huh."

"What kind of answer is that?"

"You didn't ask me a question."

"OK, fine," I said. "Why are you hanging out with Steve Ransey?"

Joshua's hand stopped midway to his mouth. "What's wrong with Steve Ransey?"

"He's—" Except I didn't know what he was. I'd heard things and accepted them. All I knew for myself was that he was trouble when he thought he could get away with it, and humbled and wary when he thought he wouldn't. What did I actually know? That his baby cousin was missing. That his home had been shattered, and that he still had to return to it each day. Where was his mother? The sheriff thought he was a spray-paint vandal, but I didn't know that, not for sure. At last, I said, "He's not from a good family."

Joshua started to laugh, choking a bit. He coughed wet crumbs onto the table.

"Oh, stop it," I said. "What's the matter with you?" I got up and reached over the counter for a rag near the sink, threw it onto the table near his hand. "Seriously, what is so funny?"

"'He's not from a good family,'" Joshua repeated, twisting his voice into a scratchy posh accent. He dragged the rag over the surface in front of him once, missing the mess. "What are we, like the family of the year or something?"

"There's nothing wrong with our family."

"Yeah, there is."

"What's wrong with our family?"

Joshua spun his chair around once, gesturing to the empty living room. "Where is it?"

"You are my family."

"Where's everyone else?"

"Who? We went through the family tree for your project—"

"That wasn't a tree. It was like a stalk of corn," he said, drawing a tall line in the air with his finger. "Where are the rest of us? Why is it just you and me?"

I stood up and brushed past his knees to get to the kitchen. I needed to start dinner, do the dishes, keep my hands busy. I couldn't let my mind follow the trail he was seeding. I'd lose it, I really would. "What's wrong with it being just you and me? I haven't minded."

"Mom, don't get mushy."

"Well. I'm just being honest," I said to the sink. "This is just the way it's worked out for you and me. We're alone, but together."

"But you grew up with other people, didn't you? You haven't always been alone but together. It's not the same for me. It's not the same."

I grew up with other people, but he wouldn't want to know them. "It's so much better, Joshua."

I did my own search of the cabinets, then opened the takeout-menu drawer.

"How do I know which is better?" he said. "I never had it the other way."

"Trust me on this one. The way you grew up—"

"You always say that. Trust me, trust me. Why should I?" He stood up and met me at the door to the kitchen. "You don't trust me."

"Of course I trust you. What are you talking about?"

"No," he barked. "You check up on me all the time, and you go through my backpack and you don't trust that I can pick my own friends and make my own decisions." Joshua's hair hung in his eyes, but he wouldn't swipe it away.

Standing so close to him, I noticed for the first time. He was taller than I was.

I didn't say anything. The backpack thing was true, anyway, or at least it had been.

"You keep us here like prisoners."

Tap, tap.

"Keep your voice down," I said. If Margaret came up here to point out how badly I parented or ask me to take her somewhere, I might shove a handful of Chinese takeout menus into the old woman's mouth.

"Why should I listen to you? You—are—a—liar!"

"Joshua. Stop yelling, and calm down."

"You're yelling. Why can't I yell?"

Tap, tap, tap.

I took a breath and concentrated on speaking in a controlled voice. "I am not yelling—"

"Well, why the fuck not?"

"Joshua!"

"I mean it. Why aren't you screaming mad? We have nobody, and that doesn't piss you off?" He paused to gulp for air. I hated the gasping, desperate look on his face. I hated the rise in his voice. "Why don't you ever talk about it? Why don't we ever talk about anything?"

He stood up and stomped back to the kitchen to fling the box of crackers onto the counter. He hadn't closed the box, of course—a few crackers skittered across the surface. He made a fist and gave the counter a pound. One of the crackers became a circle of buttered dust.

"Stop that. If you make a mess, you're going to clean it up."

"That's fine for you to say."

"What are you talking about? Why are you so upset?"

Another fist, another cracker pummeled. Downstairs, Margaret gave a tentative *tap, tap.* Her arms were probably giving out.

"Why don't you have any friends?"

"I—" But I stopped. How about that? He was right; my first instinct was to lie. "What does it matter to you if I don't have any friends? Which—" I remembered laughing with Grace at the Dairy Bar. But Grace wanted only jokes, not questions. And Stephanie didn't want my help. Then: Sherry's invitation for that weekend. "As a matter of fact, I do have a friend."

"Mr. Jeffries? That douchebag? I suppose he comes from a good family."

"You don't know a thing about him."

"I know what they say," he said.

"Oh, they. We're listening to *them* now."

"Who else is there?"

"What do they say, then?" I said.

"They say he likes little boys, for one thing."

I was stunned to silence but fought it. "That's just gossip. Why would you even believe that? How do you know he's a douchebag? I don't even know if he's a douchebag yet."

"He's one of the douchebag coaches," he said. "Steve says—"

"Oh, Steve says. Then sure." As I came to the kitchen door, he thumped another cracker into dust with twin fists, one, two. "You're making a mess."

I eased past him for the broom, laying a hand on his arm as I went, but he shrunk away from my touch.

He said, "You've made a huge mess of our *lives*."

My hand, stretching for the broom closet, swung around and struck Joshua's cheek.

"You don't know," I said, choked. I could hardly speak through my rage. "What I made of our lives. You have no idea."

"Look around, Mom. There's nothing wrong with Steve Ransey. Everybody likes him and the guys he hangs out with." He used his thumb to mash a shard of cracker into fine silt. "I'm the one who's always new. I'm the one who doesn't come from a good family."

I turned and put my shaking hands on the counter. I had done the one thing I'd never wanted to do. When I looked again, the red outline of my hand showed on Joshua's cheek. "You're having trouble—making friends—"

"*Had* trouble. I *had* trouble making friends." He picked up the box from the counter, folded it closed, and returned it to its home in the cabinet above his head. He started brushing the crumbs into a tidy pile. "You're too late. You weren't paying attention."

If he had wanted to hurt me, he had struck the exact spot. Like an expert archer. "When was this?"

He opened the door below the sink and swiped the cracker dust into the trash can, then let the door bang shut. I tried to remember. In Chicago—but I only came up with Joshua watching out the window as the children from next door played basketball on the sidewalk or chased each other down the block. Pennsylvania—I wouldn't let him have a bicycle because it was too dangerous, the hills obscuring riders until it was too late. Ohio. I remembered all the times I went to pick him up from school, finding him alone and anxious. I had enjoyed how much he wanted my company, but now I wondered why I hadn't noticed. I was all he had.

"I've been here," I said. "I've been focused solely on you for your entire life. See, here's the thing you don't understand—" I was warmed up now, ready to tell him what kind of life he might have had. He needed to hear the whole truth, because this grass-is-greener defense didn't work and he needed to realize it. All I'd given up. I was angrier than I had ever been, and I was tired of having to explain myself. He had no idea what I'd saved us from. "You have no idea—"

"Mom," he said, his voice strong and clear. He had a hand on the doorway to the hall, making his escape. "I've never had a single friend until now. All those schools. Not a single one."

"I—never knew that."

"That's the problem. How come you never figured it out?"

"That you didn't have any friends?" My heart was wrung out.

"No, I mean..." He searched the ceiling for the words.

"Figured out you and me," I said, hesitant. "That just you and me wasn't enough?"

He wouldn't look at me. He didn't say anything, but I knew that I had hit my target as well.

Why hadn't I ever figured that out? How had my son come to the conclusion so far ahead of me? And then I remembered. "You were always enough. For me."

But that, too, was a lie.

Maybe he could tell. Maybe he could see right through me.

Joshua swiped at his dangling hair, and turned on his heel toward his room. "Don't bother ordering anything," he called over his shoulder. "I'm not hungry anymore."

Chapter Eighteen

Lying in bed in the dark, I saw my hand reach out again and again and slap Joshua's face.

I finally got out of bed and went to the kitchen to pry open the cork from the wine bottle. Filled the glass, took a big gulp, topped it off. To hell with precaution, with moderation, with tiny steps and looking both ways.

Reach, slap. The image was maddening. Reach, slap. I had held that infant boy, newborn and wailing, with that same hand.

In desperation, I reached for the packet of signed forms the sheriff had sent and forced myself to read, line by line, to pay attention to dates and times, to codes I didn't understand. I got out a pen and pad and made some notes.

After almost an hour, I had calmed down enough to understand the forms. The first line was the intake, the evidence showing up on the docket as it arrived from the arrest. The second line was the next person to have their hands on the evidence, and so on. Seizure to storage to testing and all the transportation between these stations, each step signed off by one of the members of the county's office or by a lab tech. The forms were easy enough to follow once I had the idea, to watch each packet move from the possession of the accused through the system of testing. Presumably until the arresting officer and the evidence went to the courtroom—except that each of these forms stopped short of that step, incomplete. I could understand suddenly how important this chain was. Without assurances that the chain was unbroken, the case could never hold up, once the drugs weren't drugs, according to the tests. Charges dropped, time wasted, tax dollars down the drain—and of course there was the problem of the drugs back out on the street once they were switched out with the white powdery substitute.

Someone was taking a lot of risk. I wrote down in my notes: *How much money at stake?* Then: *Powder identified?* Then: *Who/ when/how drugs discovered missing?*

But that last question I thought I could answer myself. Each form stopped right around the time the evidence left storage for testing. I pawed through all the forms again and came up with one that stood out. The ringer Keller had mentioned. I set it aside. All the others held true to the theory: someone was breaking the chain prior to testing. The implication might be that the drugs were never really drugs. The arrest had been made on the evidence of a white powder that turned out to be baking soda or something.

It was genius, really, to swap out the drugs so early in the process. After testing, there was proof that the drugs were actually drugs. Before testing, it was just a bad arrest. A ding to the office's arrest record but a fattening of someone's wallet.

The form that didn't quite fit the mold had a long line of signatures, starting with Deputy Tara Lombardi's logging in a piece of evidence at 9:00 a.m. on one day and a series of signatures I didn't recognize and then to Sherry, signing the piece back in. I studied the form's details until I realized what I had: the evidence form for the supposed ransom note found in the Ransey house. I went back over the ins and outs. What had Sherry been doing with it? Oh, right. Taking it to the copy shop for the likes of me, when the original was obviously available.

Nice one, Sheriff.

I went back over the chain: Lombardi plucks it up at the house first thing, signs it over to evidence. So early. Had Aiden even been missing that early? Then, a day in, someone whose name I didn't recognize jumped in to claim it. Probably one of the feds, dusting it for prints. I went through it all, timing and dating it as though I was building an Aidan Watch time line. The chain was clean. The evidence hadn't been stolen or lost, but then the street value on a badly phrased ransom note was pretty low these days.

I drank deeply from my wine and checked the clock with bleary eyes. When I finally slipped between the sheets this time, I wanted to be so tired, so wrung out, or so drunk that I could slip off without seeing or hearing anything from tonight's mistakes. I kept my hand on the glass and turned to the signatures in the larger stack of the forms.

Some of them were purposefully complicated. Others were hurried. Some mechanical. There were a lot of tiny dust marks from the copier down the page near the signature column. Should have taken it to the copy shop, because the copier he'd used on these was throwing off too much toner.

I studied each signature in turn, my own hand stilled over my notes. There was something odd, but—I rubbed my eyes, looking toward the clock. Pushed the wine glass away and tried again.

Light had started showing at the edges of the living room blinds before I finally gave up, squared up the forms and put them away, poured out the dregs of wine, and took myself to bed. I hadn't forgotten what I'd done to Joshua, but my preoccupation had shifted enough that I might be able to sleep. I had a lot to put right in the morning in my own home. After that, I could worry about the sheriff's evidence locker.

I WOKE IN the dark from a choking dream. In my sleep, there had been a word, a long word running on and on, coursing its way across a field of blue: white script across an ashen sky. The script's loops opened up into wide nooses, flicking around my neck and yanking me up, out of bed, and into the dark. My ceiling became a gallows. Awake, I sat up gasping, my hand at my throat. There was a figure in the doorway.

"Mom," Joshua said. "Your phone keeps ringing."

I fumbled to the door and down the hall, still inside the dream. Still expecting the unending word trailing along behind me to loop around an ankle to drag me back. The predawn light at the living room window reminded me of some other emergency, long forgotten, in one of the old houses we'd lived in—Wisconsin. Some gray morning, bad news. The past, the dream—I couldn't imagine who would be on the other end. I picked up the phone from the counter. "Hello?" I croaked. I had to clear my throat and repeat myself.

"Ms. Winger?" A woman's voice. I was in no condition to place it. My head shrieked at me for being upright, for daring to open my eyes.

"Yes."

"This is Pamela Harris. From Riordan."

"Oh." Riordan was—a company. A client? I could not make these pieces fit together. Anachronisms at six in the morning.

"I know it's early. Very early, but we have a problem. I'm sure they'll call you eventually, but—I thought you should know."

"Yes?"

"The chief executive of the company," the woman said, helping me come awake, because I suddenly knew what the call meant.

"The man who got the threat," I said. "Is he—?"

"He's dead," the woman said, her voice clipped. "They found his body outside his car in the office garage last night. Shot."

"Oh, my God."

"Yes. You'll be happy to know that they didn't literally skin him."

"I'm so sorry."

"He had a wife. Three kids," she said. "And business partners and employees who actually didn't mind coming to work every day. I know you don't think about those people when you wave your wand, but I wanted to make sure that you heard it from someone—" Her voice broke. "We trusted your strange mumbo jumbo, and look what it got us. We might as well not have bothered. Someone high up in security will be calling you at a normal hour, I imagine. They'll be polite, but I'm not going to be. You need to quit selling your snake oil, Ms. Winger, before someone else gets hurt."

The phone went dead. I put it down, waited.

I checked on Joshua, but he was back to sleep, his head shoved under his pillow. I pulled his door closed and returned to the front room, wide awake and shaking.

He was dead?

Snake oil?

The gray light at the window drew me. I stared out at the sleeping street, at the row of hazy houses on the other side. I felt as though I were the only person awake in the world. The time was a gift. I had time to process. I had time to look the whole thing over, to be ready for the next call.

Still I sat and watched the walls turn gold as the sun rose. I had the feeling that the phone call had interrupted me in the middle of running a race, a marathon, and that I was obligated to get back to it, to start at the exact spot where I had stumbled out for the phone. The dream? But the dream had been nonsense, just another thrilling ride in the human psyche.

I lay on the couch with my back to the window, a throw pillow under my head. The gold wall—

The walls painted yellow for me were long in the past by the time I went to say good-bye to my parents. I don't know why I bothered. The terrible place they lived—the last place, as I thought of it, an old diner not quite turned into a house—was squalid and stale-aired, a mess. He wasn't right. His hands shook, his eyes rolled. Something in his coffee? Something in his head. I was less worried about his hands by then, because he had trouble raising them.

But I hadn't come for him.

"Come with me," I'd said. Though I didn't forgive her. In some ways, I hated her more than I'd ever hated him. For putting up with it, I supposed.

"You'll be back. What's out there?" my mother said.

"Something else," I said.

"Everywhere has troubles," my mother said. "Don't believe that the grass is always greener."

But how did she know? She'd never been anywhere else. None of us had.

"I'm going to have a baby," I blurted. I hated that anything of the baby would stay here, even the words spoken. Here, the mice in the walls and the crickets clawing the air after the lights went out. A last effort to get her to come with me. Out there, she'd be away from him, and with her grandchild. With me.

It should have been enough.

But this time she turned her back on both of us. Why had I always felt so guilty leaving her, when she was the one who left me, right there in that diner?

I heard Joshua's alarm sound, the strike of his hand to silence it. It jangled and cut out once more before I heard his feet hit the floor. He stomped to the shower and through his routine while I waited.

At seven, my phone rang. I was ready.

"Ms. Winger." The sheriff.

"How did you get mixed up in this?" I asked.

"What are you talking about?"

"I was waiting on a call, and I thought—"

"You were waiting this early? Business must be thriving."

"We'll see," I said, wondering if I would ever get work from Kent again. Things got around. You started to collect—for lack of a better word—an aura around you, if you made mistakes or if jobs you worked on didn't somehow end the right way. I'd seen it happen.

"I need your help with a little policing today, if you can make the time."

"Policing?"

"Well, it's right up your alley, I think. It's a busy day, but maybe I could meet you at the crime scene and get your thoughts?"

Crime scene. I felt sick. "Is it Aidan?"

"No, no. Aidan's still out there. Nobody's hurt. This scene's not even a little bit bloody. Here, let me give you the address."

I rooted around for some paper and a pen, and ended up sitting at my computer. I listened to the sheriff give road-by-road directions, staring at the address scrawled in my own careless hand. What would I say about this handwriting if I were given the assignment? That the woman who wrote it was hungover, that she was exhausted and weakened from a battle with her teenage son? That she was lost in the confusion of having been completely wrong about something she'd been certain of? The distraction of it all might have shown up in a comparison to another sample of handwriting—but the rest would be lost between the spaces of the words. I could tell so little from handwriting, after all. What value did any of it have, if the threatened men were going to die anyway? If the woman who asked about her fiancé knew all along that she would say yes when he proposed? If the company that wanted to hire an honest executive candidate turned around and made a dishonest man of him on the job?

I couldn't tell any of them what they wanted to know, in the end. I couldn't tell the future. That's what they wanted: a guarantee on what will happen, how things will turn out. Madame Zonda might have her vibrations, but I didn't know what would happen in three minutes' time. I had only one concern: what was on the paper. And what was on the paper didn't add up to much. Against the grim light of morning, against the reality of a man killed, it didn't seem like anything at all.

The sheriff was saying something. "I'll meet you there, then—"

"I'm not sure I'm as good at this as maybe you were led to believe," I said.

"Led to believe by whom? You?"

"By everyone. I'm—I'm not sure I should be shilling what I think right now."

"Well. How about I don't pay you and then you won't be shilling a thing?"

"I meant—Sheriff, I don't know if I'm any good at this, or if this, whatever this is, is good for anyone else."

"What happened to you?" he asked quietly.

"I made a mistake. I might have cost a man his life."

"Everyone makes mistakes on the job," he said. "Even doctors, and you know they're killing way more people than you are. Police make life-and-death decisions every day. You know, so I hear. The bullets in my gun get pulled out and cleaned every week, but those same six, they've gotten me through some lean years."

He was trying to make me laugh. I took it as a triumph of will that I could even recognize the effort.

"Seriously, Anna," he said. "People mess up. I don't know what happened, but I'm sorry it did. Listen, you have to learn how not to take your job so personally. It's just work. You have to punch in every morning, do what you can, and punch out at night."

"That's what you do?" I'd seen all those people on his office walls. They needed him. They looked to him to solve their problems. I saw it clearly in an instant: I was doing the same thing to him right now. "Never mind. You probably need to get on with your day."

"I do. But so do you. Hey, anything to say about those evidence forms yet?"

I wasn't sure I'd ever be able to say anything about those forms. "Let me spend a little more time," I said.

"That's fine. See you this afternoon. Oh, and wear long pants."

"What?"

"Long pants. There's tall grass where we're going. Gets itchy."

"Pants."

"Exactly."

The phone hung up. I retreated to the shower earlier than normal, so that I wouldn't have to face Joshua right away. Drying off in front of the mirror, I caught sight of my naked self, and stood still, taking a closer look. I bent over the sink and stud-

ied my face. The longer I stared into my own eyes—the longer I
built constellations from the freckles on my own skin—the more
I was willing to believe that the woman looking back at me was
someone else. I was willing to believe anything now. Anyone's
hocus-pocus, anyone at all. I'd believed in my abilities, in the
science of analysis, the way that other people raised their eyes
to the sky. The way some people played the lottery or the stock
market. The way certain people could say they were saving for a
rainy day, and believe that this day was not the rainiest. People
needed to believe in something; they needed a little hocus. But
my magic hadn't saved anyone. Not the executive in Chicago. It
had come too late for my mother. It had come too late for me, too.
And now, it didn't matter. I had believed that my job had saved
me, but I wasn't saved.

By the time I got out of the shower, Joshua had left for school.

At my computer with my wet hair still dripping into the neck
of my T-shirt, I set aside Keller's evidence project and called up
all my notes from the executive's threat, the original assignment, my response. I took another look at my copy of the sample,
finding again the same characteristics I'd noted the first time.
My phone should have rung. I traced my notes to the response,
checking each detail off as I'd reported them.

Everything added up; I started to feel the fury of the wronged,
until, suddenly, the bulleted list came to a stop, and one significant detail from my analysis remained. I checked again, then
searched my Sent folder for the original email. All of it came up
short.

The gaps. I'd never reported the likelihood of the writer's
sexual impotence.

I put my head in my arms on the table. I hadn't been wronged;
I'd been distracted. By Joshua, by the sheriff calling, Sherry, the

Boosters, Jeffries, Margaret. This was what happened when you let your guard down. You got caught up. You got caught.

Tied up in personal matters, I'd made the worst sort of mistake. Not just an error, but a lapse of my authority. I'd taken what the handwriting told me and dismissed it. Dismissed a man crippled in one way from being powerful in another.

That wasn't just bad analysis. That was bad human understanding. One or the other, and it didn't matter. The man was dead, his killer at large, and the phone still hadn't rung to tell me what I already feared: that my career was over, that the whole business was a bunch of bunk.

On the table, a short pile of assignments and queries sat, untouched. I brushed the top envelope with my hand to make sure it was really there. These people actually thought I had something to offer them. I'd made a mistake, but not the one Keller thought I'd made. No, the mistake had been long ago and it had nothing to do with handwriting. The mistake had been in believing that there was anywhere I could go that would change me from one kind of person to another.

I shoved the work away, shut off the computer. There was nowhere I was supposed to be, no one I could talk to. Joshua was right. I didn't have anyone.

And all he had was me, some prize.

And worse, I'd taught him there was even a part of himself that was unspeakable. I'd taught him to hate the very thing he was becoming. To hate himself. I'd saved him from a snake, only to poison him myself.

All that work to protect him. I'd done it for him. *For* him, that was the part I'd wanted him to understand. Why hadn't I been able to make him understand that last night? I was going to lose him and I deserved to. What else had I taught him, except that he didn't need anyone else?

Chapter Nineteen

I drove toward the meeting with Sheriff Keller, the radio off. The only sound was the wind in my ears from the open window, and the pinging of gravel against the bottom of the truck. Dust billowed out behind. On either side of the road, long threads of grass waved me along, or away—I didn't know. I didn't know anything. I drove, turning left or right when the directions told me to. "I give up," I said to the countryside, not sure whether I meant it for Joshua or myself. I had spent the morning looking over the evidence-form signatures, waiting for someone, Kent probably, to call about the dead man in Chicago. The call hadn't come, and all the signatures on the forms were blurring together.

At the same time, I knew that I couldn't actually give up. Give up parenting? Hardly possible. Give up working? Again—not an option. I would have to work the lonelyhearts and maybe the human resources clientele harder. After today, though, I was done with law enforcement. It was too much, too dangerous. The people drew too close. Their life-and-death matters began to matter to me.

I would try the only thing I knew to do. We'd go. Another town, another school for Joshua. Maybe further west, somewhere really new. Montana, Idaho, maybe as far as the West Coast. I wanted trees. I wanted land. I wanted wide space, and no one but the two of us allowed in.

I consulted the directions again. I'd taken the last turn, and now my handwriting gave out. Something—on the right. I scanned the right side of the road ahead and checked the rear-view for something I might have missed. Nothing but the waving husks of dry cornfields, all ending at a woods a half a mile or so back from the road. And then I saw it—a glint of steel low in the woods that took shape as the sheriff's black truck. The truck disappeared behind a crest. A set of indentions in the tall grass, not quite a driveway, appeared. I turned and followed the faint trail. When I rose over the small hill, the sheriff emerged and threw a hand up in greeting. I parked behind him and got out, surveying the lonesome stretch of nothing around us.

"I forgot to tell you to wear some good hiking shoes," he called.

"I'll do OK," I said. "Back there?" I gestured toward the stand of trees.

"Good guess," he said. "Unless you've got some ideas for Bob Banning about his soybeans next year. Ready?"

"Should I have brought a day pack or something? A tent?"

We started off toward the trees, the sheriff leading. He grinned over his shoulder. "You didn't strike me as the outdoorsy type."

"I'm not. I'm really"—my foot found a dip under the thick grass, my ankle twisting a little—"really not."

"Careful," he said. "The grass hides all sorts of things."

"One of those things wouldn't be snakes, would it?"

He stopped and turned, his hand on his gun. "Where?"

I held up my hands in surrender. "You are itching to use one of those bullets."

He set his jaw, grim, and relaxed his trigger grip.

"I'm kidding, Sheriff. Kidding."

"I didn't take you for a kidder, either." He turned on a boot heel and started off again. He swung a hand out to scatter the tops of the hip-high grass.

"I'm not." We walked the rest of the way into the woods without speaking, my head down to watch for whatever it was the grass might hide. We followed a grass path through the trees, stepped over a trickle of a rocky creek.

"What is this place?"

"This is the old Werner farm."

"You're kidding now, right?" I paused and looked into the trees on either side. On foot, the narrow lane seemed wider. It opened up onto another grassy hill. Ahead, I thought I saw a roofline through the trees.

"The house was back here with the barn. The Bannings farm the land now—you know Bob? No, I guess not. Anyway." He stopped to let me catch my breath. He didn't seem winded at all. "The old house got sold and moved into Smith County. But the barn's still here. You'll see."

We walked on, the trees closing in behind us. Maples and walnuts, no pines to speak of. I greeted the trees silently, old friends, as we continued up the low rise. At last the weathered gray barn was revealed. The high roof caved in on itself in one spot, and the big sliding door on the front was off its rails, propped askew against the entrance.

I had been going along with the drive, the hike, the history lesson, thinking that eventually I would know why I was there.

Now that I stood in the middle of an abandoned farm, sur-rounded by nothing, I still had no ideas. The fact that I had gone along with a man I hardly knew to an isolated location without telling anyone where I was—I hadn't been thinking clearly. I leaned my head back on my shoulders to see the widow's peak of the barn, where white paint peeled off in slow strips.

"Not up there," Sheriff Keller said. He went up to the loose door and eased it open a foot. "In here."

I hesitated.

"That does sound creepy doesn't it? Look," he said. He walked back to me, fiddling with his gun holster. "You can hold onto this. You can unload all six bullets on me if you need to." He took the gun out and offered it to me on his palm.

I wiped sweat off my forehead with the back of my wrist. "Pretty sure you're not supposed to give that up. Plus I don't know how to shoot," I said. "I'll have to lick you with my bare hands if you try anything funny."

Keller's gaze felt heavy. When I met it, he looked away.

"We'll fix your gun inexperience some other day, Deputy. How about if I stay out here, and you take a peek inside? You'll see it, don't worry." He walked off a few feet, reholstering his gun and leaving me to the black slash of the barn door.

I tiptoed up to the entrance as though the barn were asleep. I put one hand on the unhinged door, turning sideways to duck my head into the opening. Rays of sunshine cut through cracks be-tween the uneven slats of the high walls. A shaft of light beamed through the hole in the roof.

I saw the writing immediately, but didn't rush to it. The inside of the barn felt like a church. The air was cool, and the light hazy and silver. I took a slow breath and slid inside.

Ambitious shoots of green inched their way through the cracks in the wall and back out again toward the light. Through the opening up in the rafters, I saw the outstretched limb of a hearty cottonwood. A set of ladder steps led up to a loft that spanned the length of the barn. I smelled hay in the dark corners, wool, mildew, rot. Lingering smoke. Neglect and decay. I stood at the foot of the stairs and peered up into the dark upper floor.

On the long wall of the loft, vandals had been at work. The entire wall was covered with spray paint. I hardly needed to focus to recognize some of it as the work of the boys who were already troubling the school.

In the doorway, the sheriff said, "What do you think?"

I waved him inside. "I think you and Mr. Jeffries are looking for the same thing."

He snorted, lowering his head to fit the bill of his cap through the door.

"What?"

"Ah." He sighed. "Nothing."

"No, really. What?" I stood with crossed arms.

"Oh. Already, huh?"

"What are you trying to say?" I thought of Joshua's pronouncement that Joe liked little boys. It was pure crap, the kind of thing boys say to cut someone down. Surely the sheriff wouldn't be making juvenile jokes.

"It's nothing. Nothing." He wouldn't look at me. "Joe Jeffries likes to compete. He always has, and he probably always will." He shuffled the dirt floor with a boot heel and looked down at the line he'd scraped there. "I just mean that if there's something new and shiny to have, Joe Jeffries will want to have it first."

Now I saw the joke he was actually making. "New and shiny, huh?"

"Or elusive. You know. Hard to get."

I turned back to the job at hand. "Will this ladder hold?"

"It did for the kids, so I imagine it will for us. If we go up one at a time."

I put a foot on the lowest rung and put all my weight on it. When nothing creaked, I started the climb. At the top, I leaned over the side. "Do you smell smoke?"

"Yes, ma'am," he said, grasping the ladder and making his way up. "That's why we're here. A little graffiti, Bob Banning don't mind. A little fire? Well. He minds."

"Or a big one."

"Exactly. The place is a tinderbox looking for a match." He reached the platform, rising from a crouch straight into the sloped ceiling of the barn. The top of his head slammed into a low rafter. He hissed in pain and flinched away, both hands to his head.

"You're OK?"

"Not as OK as I was a minute ago. I think I ripped my hat."

"You've got about a hundred of those, though."

He took off the hat to show me the flap of fabric torn from in its crown. "Two," he said, as though I had accused him of something. He patted gently at the back of his head and looked at his fingers.

"Bleeding?"

"I'll live. So? What do you think?"

"Of the artistry?" I went to the wall and studied it. "What I said. You and Joe are looking for the same kids. Here's some of their work. Three boys, probably between twelve and fourteen. The school isn't that big, is it? Small town, small-town school?"

"It's got more than three boys between the ages of twelve and fourteen. And I can't force a confession," he said.

I turned back toward the long wall. Some of the paint seemed dull. I studied a particular foul phrase for a second. It was a different author. "Some of this is older than the other stuff. It's layered."

"It's an old hangout," he said, gesturing toward a dark corner. In it, the remnants of squatting: a plaid blanket thrown over old newspapers, fast-food bags, and empty bottles of beer and cola. "Like I said, Bob's not worried about the paint so much. So over the years . . ." He waved his hand over the tableau.

"But the fire—"

"Right. He thinks the last set of kids here might have had a campfire down below. There are signs of one just under the loft, pretty recent."

I was back at the wall, walking the length of the loft until I found a prolific section in the most recent layer. The vandals had put down a fresh layer of white paint with a roller, and then unleashed themselves upon their canvas. "Advanced planning. Nice. Here's your pro," I said, one hand upon the section I was sure was Steve Ransey's doing. His hand was as steady as any trained artist. In blue: his Mona Lisa, her monstrous breasts exposed.

"Your follower right next door." I drew a pointed finger along the bottom of a large red *SMITHIES SWALLOW*. "Smith County rivals, I'm assuming. Classy. And here's our clumsy fellow," I added, letting my hand pause over another rendition of his favorite four-letter expletive, this time in green.

Keller had followed me along the wall. "What about that one?" He had his hands stuffed into his front pockets, gesturing with a nod to the wall beyond my shoulder.

I turned. I could have taken my time. I could have spent a few minutes drawing it out for him. But I realized the instant I saw the words that, as with most of what happened in and around his town, he must already know. "That. That is Joshua's handwriting."

He waited as I kneeled on the loft floor next to it. I traced the outline of a big black *L* with my finger.

"It's dry," he said.

"I know. It's just been a long time. Since I saw . . . it's not important."

"It's him, then. You're sure?"

I sat back on my heels and took in the words. In black, unsteady letters:

LIAR GO TO HELL

"Absolutely sure."

The sheriff stood behind me. "Just the four of them, you think?"

I nodded and bowed my head. I thought of the package of photos placed in my path, the requests that had brought me along to this spot. The sheriff was the shepherd, and I was the sheep. "You knew it was Joshua, didn't you?"

"I thought . . . maybe."

"You didn't bring me out here to tell you for sure, though," I said to the loft floor. Behind me, his boots shuffled in place. I wanted to fly past him, off the loft and through the door, down the lane, into my truck. Reverse, retreat. "You didn't need me to tell you what you already knew."

"I didn't know. I had a feeling."

"A vibration?"

"Why are you mad at me now? I didn't put the can in your kid's hand. I only brought you out here—"

"To make sure I knew how badly I was falling down? Sheriff Keller, I hardly need anyone to tell me." I stood and faced him. He took a step backward. "I have the reminder living in my house, remember. When he's not brightening up the walls of old barns, he's finding new ways of making me feel like shit for giving birth to him."

"I didn't know that."

"Will you arrest him?"

"I brought you out here," the sheriff said quietly, "so that you could talk to him yourself. Bob's not interested in sending these kids to jail."

I remembered the reverent face of Bea Ransey leaving Keller's office. All those years, someone had kept her no-good son from being sent up. Keller did the same for Steve. All these boys from troubled homes—and now Joshua. Another boy from another desperate family. "You save them all, do you?"

"I haven't saved anyone lately." I could only see his outline against the little light flooding in from the ruined roof, could barely see how he hung his head. The register of his voice had turned toward darkness—a switch thrown in the dark. I could feel him in the air; I really could feel something like . . . vibrations. Coming from him. Somehow, in the dark, I could understand something that I hadn't before. He was laid bare. I could read his voice as easily as I could read the love written into Aidan's name on his mother's grocery list. "I've been working ten days, days and nights, on Aidan's case, but I'm no closer than I was the first day," he said, his voice gone thin and hoarse. "Nobody is getting saved on my watch."

I could nearly hear his heart beating through the words he chose. I had never met anyone who said exactly who they were. But he'd gone silent, waiting for what I'd say.

"Keep talking," I said.

A beat passed. The stilted loft air thickened; I couldn't breathe, because I could read this, too. In the next second, he reached across the void for me and I was enclosed, the bare skin of my arms electrified against his. He put a hand against the back of my neck and pressed his mouth against mine. I met him, freeing my arms to reach for his hair, his rough cheeks and jaw, to drag my palms down the front of his shirt to feel his chest. I didn't have enough hands for the skin I needed. I wanted to grab fistfuls. I leaned into the flat of his hands, pressing my body into his.

He put a hand on either side of my face and pulled away. He could see me, though his face was still shadowed. He dipped toward me again, and drew his tongue lightly over a corner of my mouth.

"What are you doing?" I said, starting to smile as his mouth grazed my ear.

"Licking you," he murmured. "With my bare hands."

I laughed. He smiled against my lips and slid his hands under my shirt and against my hungry skin.

Chapter Twenty

A woman's voice woke me from a doze. I lurched for my shirt. Where—?

I took a moment, not quite believing the dark, the dank smell.

"'s the radio."

The afternoon rebuilt itself in a rush of memory. Oh, no.

Keller lay on the old wool blanket next to me. "The radio. It's wherever my pants are." He rose up on an elbow and blinked into the corner of the loft and up at me.

"Back there."

"Right." We both peered down the length of the loft. "You're going to make me do that walk naked?"

"Your radio."

"You've got that shirt." The smile he gave me—if he could just keep doing that. If he could just keep me from thinking too much.

"Go on, I want to watch you fetch your boots," I said.

"Hey," he said, rising to a hunchbacked position under the eaves. "I've got my socks on, and so my dignity."

"If you say so."

He leaned low to kiss me. He had just begun to convince me when the radio squawked again. He groaned and pulled away. "Right back. Don't forget what you were thinking there."

I watched his ghost figure cross the dull light. The socks were ridiculous, but the rest of him required serious contemplation. He rifled through the clothing on the floor and came up with the radio from his belt. He stood with his naked ass to me and called into the dark with authority, "Yep."

"Sheriff Keller!" It was easier to hear Sherry's voice now that she had been liberated from the folds of his pants. "Oh, I'm so glad—look, Erickson's people called, and they've got something going down, I don't know what. He wants you to meet them here, *pronto*, he says."

I sat up.

"Any ideas? Does it sound like they found him?"

Sherry said, "I don't know. I just—maybe. It's big, whatever it is. He's bringing his own media, he said."

The muscles across his back tensed. He glanced over his shoulder to make sure I was listening, and then up at the opening in the roof. "His own media. I'll be there as soon as I can."

"Did you go take a look for Banning?"

"He call?"

"Yep."

"Let him know it'll be taken care of?"

"Sure, but, Sheriff? Pronto?"

"Pronto." He threw the radio to the floorboards and said, "As soon as I'm wearing pants."

"Aidan?" I said.

"Something to do with him. The attorney general is on his way." He stood looking at the pile of clothes at his feet.

"There's no way to know, is there? Good or bad?"

He sighed and pulled out his boxers. I watched him dress, keen for his movements, for the details of his body before they were buttoned away. "Only by getting back to the station and hearing it along with the reporters, I guess," he said, zipping his uniform pants. "Aren't you going to get dressed?" He reached down for some of my things at his feet and walked them over.

I crumpled the clothes against my chest.

"What's wrong?"

I shook my head, but I knew. As soon as I got dressed, and we climbed down from our bed in the sky, as soon as we slid out of the broken door and scrambled down the hill toward our trucks, it would be over. Whatever it was, this magic. In the half-light of the loft, I had shed more than clothes. Outside the barn, I would never be able to live with this. I stood and, finding each piece in turn, retreated within my wardrobe. "What time is it?"

"After five," he said.

"I'm late."

"I guess the attorney general is trying to make the six o'clock report, so there's not another day on Aidan Watch. Do you think—"

"What?"

"Nah. Nothing."

"Seriously?" I fumbled with the knot in the lace of my shoe, rushing now. Joshua would be home any minute. I hadn't left a note. Most of all, I didn't want another scene. I didn't want another fight. I would do anything to avoid it. I would even cancel the date with Joe, and not because I had the scent of another man's cologne on my neck. I didn't want any of this. All I wanted was to sit Joshua down and talk. Really talk. I was tired of talking around things, of withholding. Sparing him the truth wasn't working anymore. Maybe telling him the truth would change things.

"OK," he said. "Do you think—knowing what you know about Leila from her handwriting—do you think she could have done anything to hurt Aidan?"

"No." I stood up, dusting the back of my jeans.

"Not a chance? Not a single chance that she would do something—"

"No. Not even to keep him from his father." We faced each other at the top of the ladder, the sheriff's head ducked under the close ceiling. I thought for a moment. Could I say that? How much had I hurt Joshua to keep him from Ray? But the sheriff meant something else. "Not even to save him," I said.

He nodded. "What do you think I'm about to go see?"

Only one image came to mind: Leila Ransey, shadowed face, hunched shoulders, shackles at hand and foot. Arms empty. "I don't know. Madame Zonda could tell you."

"I was really counting on *that* woman to be full of shit." He waved me toward the ladder, holding the top rung. Body sore, I took my time. He followed, quick, skipping the last rung with a stretching step to the dirt.

"Look, before I go . . ." At the barn door opening, I reached my hand out into the sun. "Those forms—they're not originals."

"Oh, come on now. This again?"

"That's not what I meant." What I wanted to know, really, was if he needed them back. When we left in the night with all our things packed around us, did I need to drop them into the mail? "I'm not sure I understand it all yet but—I'll have something for you soon."

I crouched to slide out the door, but he grabbed my arm and pulled me back into the barn. "What?" I said.

"Don't—don't leave it here." He stepped closer, pressing the length of his body against mine, his lips against my temple. "You know what I mean."

I closed my eyes and accepted the full embrace of his breath and touch, enjoying the way my body felt stretched and skinned. Bruised, even.

I knew what he meant, but it was already gone. I broke away and slipped out of the barn, the sun in my eyes.

WE DROVE THE dirt roads like teenagers, kicking gravel and skidding at corners. Near downtown Parks, we parted ways. I decided to take an extra turn around the courthouse to see if Joshua was using my absence to hang out with his artisan friends, but the square was busy. One side of the street had been blocked off, a series of media trucks parked in a row and guarded by a variety of uniforms.

As I inched forward against the blocked traffic, I remembered the sight of my arm reaching out of the barn, sunlit. And then: the same hand darting out to connect with Joshua's face. Then: the sheriff's hands on me, his weight pinning me to the rough blanket.

We would have to go.

Finally I was able to take an alley to get around the square toward the apartment, but when I tried to pull back out onto a street, traffic there had backed up, too. People were gathering in front of the courthouse. Before I could talk myself out of it, I threw the truck's gear into park and pulled out the keys.

I crossed the street and waded into the crowd.

"I think they got her," someone said.

"But did they get the boy?"

I pressed between and around people to get closer. A podium

was centered at the top of the steps, bathed in TV lights, with a rope boundary keeping the crowd at bay. On the other side of the barrier, TV news crews were setting up. I found a space at the rope and craned my neck to see over a cameraman's shoulder.

Sherry stood just inside the propped-open door at the top of the stairs. I waved, hesitant, and then with gusto until she looked my way, checked around her, and came down. She made her way through the crews and leaned over the rope to whisper in my ear.

"You look like the same kind of hell that he does," she said. "I made him go clean the hay out of his hair."

My face was hot. I saw the sheriff at the door now, and he did look better. His hat was gone, his hair combed. He leaned out of the door and surveyed the scene.

"Do you know what's going on?" I said.

The cameraman backed into Sherry. "Watch it," he said.

"Watch yourself," Sherry said. "Or I'll get the media pool moved to the other side of the building."

"You don't have that authority," said a woman with a shell of banana-yellow hair. She held a microphone in her hand and had managed to create a two-foot space between herself and her crewman.

"Which side of the rope am I on?" Sherry said to the newscaster. She turned to me. "Nobody's told me anything, but if I had to guess—"

"We're live in Parks," the reporter said, her voice stretched broad. "Where Indiana attorney general Arnold Erickson has called a press conference. We've been told he will be joined by Parks County sheriff Russell Keller but we don't know yet what news the men will share with us today."

"If I had to guess," Sherry said, "I'd say we've got our woman."

The reporter glanced our way. "Speculation has it that we

might be hearing about the capture of the fugitive mother of a little boy who's been missing from Parks for ten days. Police have been looking for Lila Ransey—"

"Leila," I said.

"—since her son was reported missing from her estranged husband's home here in Parks."

Movement at the courthouse door. A man wearing a suit and tie and a foul expression came through, followed by a number of town and county men, but not the sheriff.

"Attorney general Erickson has taken the podium," the reporter said. "Let's listen."

The man at the podium adjusted the mic to his mouth and dove in. "Ladies and gentlemen, thank you for coming. We wish we had the best news for you, but unfortunately we cannot say what we'd like to say today. Aidan Ransey, two years old, is still missing."

I glanced at Sherry, who shook her head.

Erickson raised a hand to quiet a rising murmur. "Please let me say what I have to say. Aidan Ransey is still missing. But we do have new information that puts his situation in a different light." Erickson's mouth was grim, but he found the cameras in the crowd and looked deep into them with serious eyes. Projecting into the heartland for future election-year footage. "The good news is that we have safely located a person long of interest in this case. Sheriff Keller?"

They had her. They had Leila Ransey. I watched the sheriff—*Russell*—exit the door with someone in his wake. The crowd shuffled and strained to see.

The sheriff guided the woman out from behind him. She had lank bronze hair and wore a black, doughy coat that was much too large for her and too hot for the weather. She lurched into the middle of the men, swallowed behind the podium. Leila Ransey, no more than a girl. Skinny, even frail. Her face and neck were pale but blotchy, and her eyes darted around the crowd, past the cameras, out to the square.

The sheriff held the woman at her elbow as though she might fall over and leaned into the microphone. "We'd like to thank Mrs. Ransey for coming in today, as soon as she heard we were looking for her," he said. "Mrs. Ransey has been very cooperative. We'll be leading a renewed search effort in conjunction with state and federal agencies, revisiting all witnesses, all interviews. If you have information, any information at all that might have a bearing on this matter, we ask you to come forward now. We need all the assistance this town, this county, this state, even the nation, has to offer to Aidan and his parents."

Aidan and his parents. I had to dodge the cameraman to see Leila again. This was the woman they thought killed someone with brute strength? There was so little to her. The collective group seemed to be holding its breath, not sure what to believe.

"I'd like to apologize to the Ransey family for any semblance of lack of effort on my or my office's part. That is not the case. Not at all. But from here on out, we will not be making any assumptions. We will be bringing Aidan home." He stopped to clear his throat and turned a degree to include more of the crowd. For just a blink, his eyes landed on mine, then bounced away. When he began again, he seemed less certain. "We will do everything in our power to bring Aidan home. We'd like to thank Mrs. Ransey again for coming forward. Mrs. Ransey, would you like to say anything?"

The sheriff gestured the young woman to the podium and stepped back. She seemed drunk, or high, or—scared. When she raised her clasped hands to her mouth, the long sleeves of the coat covered her pinkies.

"Please bring Aidan back," she said, her voice low and raw.

The attorney general and the rest of them eyed the crowd.

Leila gripped the sides of the podium and stood on her tiptoes to speak into the mic. Her voice rang out, loud. "Why would you take him away from the rest of us? What have you done with my baby?"

The sheriff was watching Leila uneasily. His eyes flicked into the crowd, straight to me this time, and back.

"You bring him back, or I swear to God—" Leila Ransey lowered her head in anguish, one long wail rising out of the speakers, bouncing off the buildings across the street, and washing back over the gathered crowd.

The sheriff reached out to guide her away, but then came a screech of tires. The sound seemed to come from everywhere at once.

"Liar!" Someone raged across the courthouse lawn and through the throngs.

Sherry poked me in the side. Bo Ransey had left his truck in the street, the door wide, and was running toward the podium. "Liar!" The cameraman swiveled to capture the scene and struck me in the shoulder. I tottered and fell to my hands and knees, putting my fingers in the path of some heavy hiking boots.

"Hey, ow!"

The crowd surged. Sherry pulled me to my feet, guiding me under the rope to the other side.

"You liar!" The people parted for Bo even as the sheriff's men rushed in and the camera crews crushed closer. Bo Ransey, sweaty-faced and pale, dressed in paint-spattered pants. He made a move on the rope, and was met with force by a phalanx of officers. The pixie-faced deputy, Tara Lombardi, reached out and grabbed Bo's arm, almost tenderly. "You lying bitch—" Bo spat, shaking her off. Two more uniformed men grabbed him and marched him toward the courthouse, the young deputy running behind. Leila Ransey was scooped up and taken back inside, the official party gone within moments and the podium left empty under the lights.

Sherry ran up the steps behind the group, casting a wordless shrug over her shoulder at me. I watched after them until they were all inside. There was something in the scene that worried at me, but I couldn't place it.

The cameraman swung around to train the lens on the crowd and found me, solo and inside the barrier. Before I realized what was happening, I was staring into the camera lens and the reporter with the yellow hair was reaching in with a microphone to ask me for my thoughts. I only had one thought—my face showing up on the bar TV at the Clipper in Sweetheart Lake, Wisconsin—and reached for the lens. I pictured Bea Ransey sending the TV camera stuttering with a haymaker and reached now to do the same.

WITH NO ONE to stop me, I ran up the steps to the courthouse door and let myself in. I'd scraped my hands during my fall outside and had a small rivulet of blood on one palm. One of Keller's jailers stood to the side of the ladies' washroom. He took one look at the blood dripping from my hand and went back to his phone.

At the sink I rinsed the scratch thoroughly, waiting until the blood stopped. When I turned off the water to reach for a paper towel, I heard a noise behind me and realized one of the stall doors was closed. A woman was crying behind it.

"Are you OK?" I said.

She didn't answer. I heard a sniffle, then some toilet paper being pulled from the roll.

What did I care? I patted my hands dry and just as I was about to throw the towel away and leave, the stall door opened and Leila Ransey stood there in her overwarm coat.

"No, I'm not OK," she said.

Words failed me. I had nothing to say to this woman, nothing to ask her. Maybe I was projecting something upon her that had been put there by other people, or maybe I was projecting something more personal upon her, something quite like self-loathing. I was less sorry for her, up close.

She was unsteady on her feet as she washed her face and hands. Leila, face dripping, found me watching her in the mirror and decided she knew which side I was on. "He's not such a big family man as you want him to be," she spat. "Just enough to do whatever she—"

The door to the hallway swung open and struck the wall with a bang. Leila and I both startled backward. Deputy Lombardi stood there, her eyes narrowed at me. "Aren't you an interested citizen lately?" she said. When she turned to Leila, her expression sharpened even further. "*Mrs.* Ransey," she said. "You've already taken so much of everyone's time, so how about you hustle through your nervous breakdown and let's go?"

Leila hurried by me with a look backward that I couldn't read. When they were gone, I stood in the quiet bathroom and worried for Aidan, perhaps for the first time. I'd been pinning my hopes on his mother, and now—now I didn't know who the kid could come back to when or if he ever did make it home. His grandmother, but then she'd raised his father in the first place. And now this frail, bloodless woman who let life pull her along. Leila Ransey was no match for the kind of life I thought we had in common and, if she had killed the woman to steal the child and was somehow fooling everyone, I had to agree with Grace Mullen. I didn't feel as charitable as I once had.

Chapter Twenty-one

I hurried through the crowd and then the traffic as best I could, the clock in the dash ticking away the minutes as well as the moral high ground I usually enjoyed when telling Joshua he always had to let me know where he was. I tapped my fingers on the steering wheel. Something from what I'd seen pulled at me.

Leila didn't have Aidan, at least not with her. Bo didn't have Aidan. Bo thought Leila was a liar. Leila thought—

What have you done with Aidan? You bring him back.

What did Leila think? What did Leila believe? I knew who I believed. The mother's confusion had been real, her grief alive. She seemed just like a woman who had been blindsided by the news that her son was missing. But she also seemed to believe her son was out there, that he could be returned. Maybe she hadn't had time to process it; maybe she didn't know about the odds of a child missing for this long coming back unharmed. Maybe she just had a mother's hope that it would all work out. Or maybe she knew where he was.

You bring him back. That demand seemed oddly—directive.

It was like seeing Joshua's scrawl on the barn wall. *LIAR GO TO HELL*—it wasn't a statement. It was a direction: you, you go to hell. And of course he meant me.

And then I knew what had really caught my attention. Deputy Tara Lombardi's gentle reach for Bo Ransey's arm. I'd seen her do that before, seen him shake her off on the courthouse steps when she was escorting him off the premises. He'd shaken the smug look off her face, for once.

But what if that wasn't the whole story? What did I know about either of them? Only that Deputy Lombardi hadn't thought much of the suggestion that Bo and Charity were a couple. Only that Deputy Lombardi didn't think much of Leila Ransey, *Mrs*. Ransey, either.

I thought back over all the times Tara Lombardi had passed through my life, her eyes slashing and her doll-baby voice full of suggestion.

I'd seen her name somewhere, too, and struggled to remember. The newspaper? No. That evidence form Keller had given me placed Lombardi at Bo's house early the morning Aidan was taken. So early as to be ahead of the call to 911?

But then I remembered the neighbor walking his dog in Sugar Creek Park. The park was normally safe as houses, he'd said. A sheriff's car had been patrolling even that morning. The very morning before Charity's body was discovered.

I flung open the door to the building and ran up the stairs, fumbling for my keys just as Margaret swept open her door and started yelling about the noise. At the top of the stairs stood Joe Jeffries.

I glanced down at myself. I could smell the raw scent of my afternoon: hay, wool, sweat, sex.

"I thought—was it tonight? I thought—"

He turned. "Anna—"

"I'm running incredibly late," I said, opening the door wide and gesturing him inside. "And I haven't even told Joshua I'm going out."

"Anna—"

"Maybe we'd better reschedule—I might be needed at the sheriff's—did you hear? Or, look, the truth is—"

"Anna, *listen.*" He waited for me to pay attention. "I'm here because I heard something troubling. I don't know if it's . . . is Joshua here?"

"Of course. Or he might be . . . well, I guess not practice."

"He didn't come to school today."

I stopped. "What are you talking about? I heard him leave this morning. He was on time, for once."

The hallway was dark, and beyond that, Joshua's door was closed. He'd be in there until I rousted him out, the headphones on, the hair in his eyes.

Joe took a step toward me, and I backed away. I could still smell the sheriff's cologne on my skin.

"Is he here?" Joe said.

"Probably in his room. Who said he didn't show up to school?"

"*I'm* saying he didn't show up. He was reported absent in homeroom, but that's nothing to get alarmed about. But then—"

"I've been out all afternoon, but I was in this morning. He didn't stay home today." But then I remembered the in-service day. He hadn't stayed home that day, either. "Let me—wait, let's just check."

The hall, only ten paces, grew longer; by the third step, my mind had turned toward the time that had passed since I'd seen him. I was just being paranoid. Aidan was missing, so any boy could go missing.

When I reached Joshua's door, I could feel the quiet beyond. I knew the room would be empty. I swung the door open.

His bed was unmade, the floor littered with magazines and video game cords. The boxes that still held his clothes, open and overflowing.

"One of his friends was spreading a rumor today," Joe said.

"Which friend?"

He stared at me, his mouth slightly open. "It's the rumor you need to care about."

"What did he say? Where's Joshua?"

"His friend was saying—look, I don't want to upset you. But it was all over football practice today that Joshua was running away."

"That's—" Absurd. Completely wrong.

But I couldn't say it. I saw the look on Joshua's face as he called me a liar. I felt the black force of the words meant for me on the barn wall.

Jeffries cleared his throat. "Have you seen him since this morning?"

Besides the call to the phone in the early hours, I hadn't talked to him since last night, not since he'd blown up at me. Not since—not since I'd hit him. "No." I opened Joshua's closet door. The mess that met me there seemed right. "No. He couldn't have run away. It's ridiculous."

"He hasn't been having any troubles lately? At home?"

I glared at him. "You know he's had some issues lately. At *school*. Where could he be?" I pushed past Joe into the hallway. "Joshua? Are you here?" I pushed open my bedroom door hopefully: dark. The bathroom: dark. The front room was wide open, not a single hiding place.

Joe came up behind me. "I know he's had some problems with

his schoolwork. But to run away? Does that seem like Joshua to you?"

I turned in a slow circle, taking in the empty room. Something wasn't right. What was it? And then I saw. His backpack was missing from the table. "His backpack."

"What?"

"I don't know," I said. A shrill alarm began to ring in my ears, and I raised my voice to be heard over it. "I don't know."

"OK," Joe said. "Let's be calm. What about his backpack?"

"It's not on the table. It's always, *always* on the table." I thought of the pack's dense bulk, the thump it made when he set it down. "He hasn't been home." I ran back down the hall to his room and pulled back the sliding door of his closet again. On the floor sat a stack of books: *Our Land and Its People*, math.

Oh, God.

I fell to my knees. Joe came to the door, his cell phone already out and to his ear. I picked up the copy of *Huckleberry Finn*, its edges frayed from its crushing life inside the backpack. "He's been carrying this around forever."

"Are all his books there? Yes, hello," Joe said into the phone. "I need to have the police—Keller. I need the sheriff. Anna, are those the books for his current classes?"

My hands shook as I sorted through the stack.

"The sheriff, yes," Joe said into the phone. "We might have a runaway situation. We're not sure. Anna, your address."

I was going through the books again.

"Anna, what is your address?"

"He didn't run away." I was running a finger down the spines of the books and found the loophole I needed, the hope. "His history class stuff is missing." He must have gone to school. Who would run away with history books weighing them down?

"Hold on," Joe said into the phone. "He doesn't take history. Shepherd Ave. And—" He went to the window and looked out. "Crest and Shepherd—Shepherd Village. Second floor in the front. Yes. Yes. No. The *sheriff*."

"Why would he take his history book with him if he weren't going to school?" The missing book was a dangling prize. I wouldn't let go of it. He'd gone to school, of course he had. He was mad at me, and lying low in the courthouse square with Steve and Caleb and Shay and the rest of them. Or they were out at the barn smattering the day's outrage on the walls. I would forgive truancy. I would forgive vandalism. I would forgive anything, if he'd just walk through the door.

Joe came over and put a hand on my shoulder. "World history is a freshman class. He's in social studies. That's the book right there." We both gave our full attention to *Our Land and Its People*. "The sheriff should be on his way. Is there anything else missing? Clothes? Favorite objects? Can you tell?" He dragged a hand through one of the boxes.

"No, wait," I said, standing up. "He's doing a project for *history* class. Personal history. The genealogy project. He's been working on it so hard in the library—you said so."

Joe grimaced. "I said he'd been working on something. I don't know anything about a genealogy project. I doubt Michelle Grivner's got the seventh-grade social studies group doing genealogy. Last week they were doing reports on the Industrial Revolution. Milah—the librarian—said they'd ransacked that section of the stacks. She sent a group of them to see the principal."

I stared at him, waiting for the words to make sense. "Social studies is history, isn't it?"

"Hell," he said. "I don't remember what it means. Geography. Culture."

"The genealogy project?"

"If he was enjoying it, maybe he was doing it for fun . . ."

He didn't finish. Neither of us believed this.

There was a hard knock at the front door. Joe went to get it.

I sat on the edge of Joshua's bed, shaking and sick. The room was spinning. I slid off the bed onto the carpet, listening to a commotion at the front door, more people arriving. Joe got out his phone and yelled into it for a few minutes. It seemed hours before someone showed up at the doorway. I couldn't look up to see whose legs walked into the room. Someone knelt at my side and placed a hand on my shoulder. I pushed it off.

"Anna," the sheriff said.

He leaned low so that I couldn't help but see him. "Anna, what happened?"

"It didn't work," I said. My breath felt short, as though I had been running, running. In my dreams, in real life—always running. I'd hoped for a finish line, but I had only fooled myself. The race could never stop, and now that I'd hesitated, I couldn't win.

We had to go. We had to run. Run, Leely. That's what I would have said.

Running was a way of life. Running was a prayer, a church, a religion. Running was a god, the only one I'd ever truly believed in. You don't need hocus-pocus. You don't need magical thinking. You don't need anything or anyone. But the worst part was that I knew, and maybe had always known, that the running would never get us anywhere.

"It didn't work," I said. "I lost him."

Part II

Chapter Twenty-two

On the day I died, I dragged the new oars down to the lake. I pulled them by their shafts across the yard. They were heavy, but I was saving myself the second trip. The blades rode flat along the ground, flattening two tracks through the wet grass.

The air was cool, but down on the dock, the slats were already hot. I noted a lone fishing boat out on the water. Inside, two men hunched silently over their tackle, their faces turned out across the lake. Beyond them, mist rose off the water, nearly hiding the far shore.

I got to work. Ray had already dragged the rowboat from where it had been stored upside down under the porch since fall. Now I pulled it from the side of the hill, flipping it and pushing it to the water's edge. The bucket we kept tied to a piling had already been fastened into place. I filled it with green lake water, flushing spiderwebs out of the boat's bottom boards and from under the benches, then baled the water back out and pushed the boat into the water, guiding it along the dock and tying it in place.

At last I slid the new oars into the rowlocks, one at a time, stopping to admire the gleam on the blades. At the end of last summer, one of the old cracked ones had split wide, useless. We'd splurged for new instead of knocking around at rummage sales all season, waiting for something cheap to turn up.

The lifejackets. I ran back up to the house, spending twenty minutes digging through hideaways and corners as quietly as I could around our closed bedroom door. At the last minute I remembered the bungee cords to secure them. Down on the dock again, I patted at the jackets to beat out the dust.

I didn't notice the fishermen this time, not until one of them spoke. "Morning," he said.

His voice was quiet but large in the vast emptiness of our lake. *Our lake*, though many people lived on it. Many other people came to fish on it, like these men. These two men. They had drifted close to the shore, only a few feet off the end of the dock. There would be no fish there, nothing worth catching.

Their boat sat low and heavy in the water, barely clearing the sand. Two men. I glanced up the slope and stairs behind me.

"Didn't mean to scare you," the man said. His friend seemed content to remain silent, but his eyes roved over my bare legs. I'd gotten wet putting the boat in, and now I turned cold. I held the jackets in front of me.

"Morning," I said.

"Trying your luck?" He lifted his reel a bit. The gesture seemed strangely dirty, as though he'd unzipped his pants and shown me his dick. I didn't say anything. The men glanced at one another. I kept picturing one of them stepping out of the skip into the water. Up to his waist, maybe, nothing more. They were big men, but I imagined them moving fast. "Not much biting this morning," the man said. "You fish?"

"My boyfriend," I said. "My boyfriend likes to fish." He didn't.

Ray preferred red meat to fish, didn't think fresh fish on the grill was worth the guts, not worth the mess or the trouble. He liked burgers from the Clipper in town, with beer. He was up at the house now, sleeping off a late night. He didn't like the quiet of fishing, either, or quiet of any kind. He couldn't sit still for very long. Even out on the boat, we were always rowing, always moving, and always turning back before it got too late or too cold or too anything. He let me row more than was probably gentlemanly and took over when I was too slow for his taste. He wasn't interested in spotting eagles' nests with me. "We're heading out in a few minutes," I said.

"Should'a been out before now," the guy said. "Too warm and bright for anything now. Muskies don't much like a hot tub."

The other man looked back out at the lake, bored. The mist had started to burn off, and I could hear the faint sounds of the summer camp around the bend from us, children laughing and splashing. Their canoes would come out into view soon. We usually hated the camp kids and their noise. Now all my hopes leaned toward them.

"Isn't your guy Ray Levis?" the talkative one said suddenly.

He might know that Ray didn't fish, but then the first rafts in the battalion of camp canoes nosed out into the lake. I felt the darkness—imagined, it seemed—pass and took a deep breath. "You friends with Ray?"

"Wouldn't say that," the first man said.

The other guy looked at him, a hint of a smile at his mouth. He mumbled something his friend thought was funny that I didn't catch.

The first man looked up at the ridge to the house, but I didn't think he could see much past the stairs and the deck at the top. The house lay a hundred feet too far from the water, tucked into the dark woods. We wanted to cut down a few trees, but then it wasn't our place. We had no say in which trees lived and died. Ray sometimes walked among them and mimed an *X* on their trunks, choosing which ones needed to go.

"Would have guessed Ray'd be down for the count," the first man said. "After what he drank up at the Clipper last night."

My back went up again. I didn't want to be nervous but it seemed like I couldn't be anything else lately. I clutched the life-jackets to my gut.

Just weeks ago, that's when I'd realized. That night I'd been a little slow to meet him at the door when he came home, and then I hadn't wanted any dinner. Ray had big brown eyes, like bites of a rich dessert when he was happy, but like holes in his head when he was mad. That night, he had turned and watched me. "You've been sick for a while now."

It sounded like an accusation, so it probably was. He didn't know that I always felt sick, always, but had taught myself the trick of hiding it most of the time. To be discovered—to be noticed—was the surprise. "I have?" I said.

"Yep."

"I'm sorry." This was the best thing to say. I thought it over. "Are you sure?"

This was not the best thing to say, but I really couldn't decide.

"Couple of weeks." He looked me over, studying me hard while I wished he would forget it, think of something else to say or worry about. I didn't have the strength to keep up my side of an argument, and sometimes not arguing was as bad as starting one. "You're not pregnant, are you, Ell?"

It was best not to laugh until Ray had laughed, but I did. I was brittle, dead already. Such a thing had never occurred to me. "No way."

"Good." He turned his attention back to his plate. "You know what I'd do if you got pregnant."

I thought I knew.

I hadn't given getting pregnant any thought. But I was sick. I'd been sick a long time.

That night we'd spent the evening in front of the TV, but I didn't follow a single thing happening. Inside, I nudged and poked at the idea until a tiny crack formed and a hairline fracture of light showed itself. I thought I knew what Ray would do if I got pregnant, but suddenly I wondered wildly, forgetting who I was for a moment, forgetting the person I'd let myself become, what would I do? Me, not him. What would *I* do?

The little crack of light was hope. I'd been prying at it ever since.

So: the boat, the oars, the jackets. If I set up the boat and had a nice lunch ready when he woke up, had the right kind of beer in the fridge, cold, if I just made sure everything was right, I could tell him.

There was a cold heavy stone in my gut that had nothing to do with the baby growing there. But what had he even said? He hadn't really threatened anything, when you came down to it. He'd been in a funk that night, anyway. Now that it was getting warm and sunny, spring finally here, maybe it would all be OK. Maybe we'd be fine, all of us.

We'd be fine if these two men would just go. One of them, at least, had been at the Clipper to see Ray empty a few. "We were celebrating," I said, blushing a little. I'd nursed a drink or two, to make sure Ray and the ladies at the Clipper didn't notice I hadn't. Nothing went unnoticed around here. Unless they didn't want to notice.

"That's a thing Ray Levis sure likes to do," the second man

said. This was the first time I'd heard his voice and I didn't like it. Didn't like the sound, the leering swagger that lived there, and didn't like that I'd heard it, either.

"What were you clinking glasses over, then?" the first man said. I thought I recognized him now, and maybe the other one, too. We got strangers in town all the time, what with the weekly rentals all around the lakes, the fishermen trying out other waters, the summer camps, the flea markets. But this guy didn't just know Ray by reputation or through the long history of small places with very few shoulders to rub up against. He drank at the Clipper, and if Ray was the kind of man to have friends, that's what he'd be.

The lifejackets smelled like mildew but I hugged them tightly, afraid again. For a moment I couldn't figure out why. I'd been afraid of something my whole life. My dad's belt, looped. The back of my mother's head, turned from me. Then boys, their hands fumbling and grabbing. Then Theresa and the only currency I cared about, which was her attention and her presence. Scared that I'd lose it, and then I had.

In my childhood, being near Theresa, I had realized that some people didn't go around frightened the way I did. I admired them. Later, when I knew more, I hated them, envious. There was even a part of me that had grown to pity them. They were just babies, the way people cuddled and cared for them. Toddlers, unaware.

So I had been afraid, but this was different. I was not scared now of bruises, not of people seeing the bruises, not of what Theresa knew and couldn't stand to watch, or whatever it was that Ray might do.

I was afraid of the mist burning off the lake and the wide sky opening up over the far shore. My teeth chattered. I could barely keep the lifejackets in my hands.

I was afraid that I could have changed everything, and hadn't.

I was afraid that everything could yet change, or not, and I was the one who had to decide.

I was afraid of choices I had let go, of decisions I might never make. I was afraid I had turned down every opportunity to be someone other than who I was now. I was afraid I would never get back to someplace real, someplace on the map that would feel like a place to start.

I was afraid of the future. I didn't think I'd ever thought about the future before, beyond fantasies. Fantasies didn't require anything from me, but real life, the real future, did. I held the lifejackets against the slight swell of my belly. I had never had a future before.

What had we been celebrating? Just the fact that we had enough money in our pockets for one of us to get shit-faced. Another trip around the horn of a weekend. Another scraping by.

The men in the boat had long ago given up on hearing my answer. They had drifted a polite distance away, where they might ignore me completely. The talkative guy motioned for the other to pick up the oars, and there was no question that they meant to make the distance far more than polite. The first guy took out his phone but we didn't get much reception out this far. When he put it back in his pocket, he turned resolutely away from me so that no one would feel as though they had to say anything in parting.

Later, the guy with the phone could say I was alive and well and alone until such-and-such time. Alive and alone, at least. No one had spoken for my well-being in a while. But I hadn't been hurt at 12:39 p.m., and these men turned out to be above suspicion, churchgoers and family men, one of them a grandfather, the other a veteran. He walked in the Fourth of July parade over in Rhinelander every summer.

One of the men would say to the papers that they'd noticed two lines in the grass, like the feet of a body being dragged to the shore. It hadn't been my body, of course, and by the time people were curious about where my body was, the grass had dried and the twin tracks from the oars had disappeared. But it was the kind of thing that got people thinking.

The men paddled away, and I dropped the lifejackets and cords into our boat and took the stairs two at a time.

I didn't know what I was going to do, but I knew I was doing something. I was making the choice as I went, hoping I would know what I had decided when I reached the deck or the yard or the car or the road.

At the top of the stairs, Ray, his bare chest tan, sat back in a folding chair. His eyes were holes in his head.

"Who were your friends?" he said.

I had a lot of experience with knowing when I was in trouble. A part of me observed us from a high branch of a nearby tree. Maybe from the bald eagle's nest we'd spotted last week. I was an eagle, and all these human problems down here were none of my business.

"They seemed to be friends of yours," I said.

"No friends of mine." And that was true, because Ray didn't have friends. He had twenty or thirty guys he could buy a beer for down at the Clipper, but hardly anyone would buy a round for him. So he admitted, when he was in the mood to count his grievances.

"One of them was at the Clipper last night, I guess," I said. This was fact. The guy knew Ray was somewhere sleeping off a bender. Or maybe that had just been a good guess. I was musing about this when Ray reached for me.

Chapter Twenty-three

Men and men and men. They stormed the apartment and tried to find something to do that wasn't already being done. They poked around, moving items from place to place and back again, taking papers and the game system from Joshua's room.

I sat in the front room and watched their sensible black shoes and boots walk into and out of my field of vision. The sheriff kept close by, stepping away now and then to respond to his hissing radio. Each time he left my side, he directed another officer to be my guardian.

"Do you want anything?" someone said. The voice was unconvinced it could offer me anything, maybe hoping I wouldn't need anything. I looked up. Tara Lombardi, the young, smug deputy who was supposed to have a crush on the sheriff but might be dating a hooligan instead. The one who might have been on the scene of a murder a little too soon, who might have patrolled a crime scene just before a body was found.

"No," I said. The only thing I wanted was for the sheriff's radio to hiss and crackle and say *He's OK*, for the good news to come

in quickly—good news was always better when it was fast—and
for all these people to leave. I wondered if the rumor about my
whereabouts had already sneaked out the sheriff's office door. If
Sherry knew, soon everyone would.

I answered the same questions again. Had I noticed any
strange behavior? Had he been hanging out with any new
friends? Was there anywhere I hadn't thought of that he might
have gone? Could he be at a friend's house without telling me?
They stopped asking this after a while, so I knew the friends
and football teammates had been called, no extra boy discovered. Could I sign this form? And this one, for the release of the
things in his room? It was Mullen who was filling out the details
and who placed the clipboard gently on my knee. I signed, then
watched as he checked it over and signed his own name, tapping
his pen a few times before committing and then tilting the clipboard away from me.

Could he have gone to his father's house?

"No," I said.

As though his father's was a place in the realm of reality, a
place the kid could just *go*. I felt the officers looking at one another over the top of my head. "He doesn't have a father."

"Technically speaking . . ." Lombardi started.

He couldn't have gone there. He didn't know the town name.
He didn't know his own father's name. All the lies we'd lived. He
might have gone anywhere, thinking he was chasing down the
truth. But I couldn't forget the feel of my palm against his soft
cheek. "He and I had a big fight," I said. "He's never—talked to
me like that. And I . . . I hit him. I've never laid a hand on him
before."

I was ashamed, and started to cry. I had never meant to hit my
kid. It was the promise to myself I had kept all these years.

"Enough," Keller said. "Let's give Ms. Winger some air here."

Mullen hustled the crowd away. The sheriff sat on a couch arm and leaned down so that I had to see him. "I don't want to get into any details you don't want to share," he said, his voice low. "I'll only ask once. Are you sure?"

He smelled like hay. I concentrated on not gagging. "He doesn't have a father."

He waited, then pulled away. "OK."

The party of men grouped and regrouped in the rooms of the apartment and in the hallway, fidgeting like a first-grade choir. The radio hisses came further apart. The extra people began to peel off in pairs and out the door. The neighbors across the street, who had been on their lawn all evening, went inside. The night passed as I sat staring at my own knees, listening for a phone, the radios, for Joshua's shoes on the stairs, and for everything to be fine.

"Anna."

I blinked up. The sheriff. I hadn't forgotten he was here, but I'd almost managed to forget that I was. Tennessee, Kentucky, Ohio, all the way through Chicago, apartment after apartment and never a single yellow wall among them. Somewhere back there, in a strange cupboard over the window in Kentucky or out in the storage shed in Chicago—that's where I was. Lost. I was still there, and Joshua was still there, and when I woke up from this nightmare, we would be together. He waited just there for me now.

"It's time to get some rest."

"I'm not tired."

"People in distress always say that."

"Did you read that in the manual?"

He slid his hand up and down the kitchen doorway. "I've sent all my people on. I'll stay—"

"No."

"I think you need—"

"Please don't."

I saw that he wasn't here at all, either. He was back in the musty barn. His problem. Kentucky, Tennessee. I was back then, and if I chose to move on, I would take a different way. I'd never see that barn. I'd never see this town. I would take a different turn and never spot the familiar sign of the Dairy Bar. I would have Joshua by my side. I'd have everything I'd ever wanted, if only I'd never come here.

"OK," he said, and closed the door quietly on his way out.

Finally alone. The clock over the door said 4:00 a.m.

I walked to Joshua's room and stood in the threshold. They'd been too careful with his things. The tidiness was the worst insult. Everything was in its place but the boy.

But that was a lie. None of it was in its place. I had made sure of that, hadn't I? That nothing about us had a place to call home?

Joshua, alone, dark road, the driver doesn't see him—

I tried to turn off these thoughts, but the worst-case scenarios were patient. As soon as I discarded one, another rose to the surface.

Joshua, alone, fallow field short cut, he twists an ankle—

Joshua, alone, black alley, an arm darts out and grabs him—

I went to the window and yanked up the shades. The street below was silent and gray. Up and down the block, nothing moved.

If he walks up the block now, I won't be mad. If he walks up the block now, I will make everything right.

Something moved in the corner of my vision and my eyes leapt toward it.

A black truck, Indiana plates. And, inside, someone—

I recognized the sheriff, his black hat tipped back against the frame of his open window. He stared down the empty street.

He was back at the barn, but he was also here. Where was I?

I turned to Joshua's bed and lay down on the covers. I pressed my nose into his pillow to find his scent. His shampoo, because he wouldn't use mine. The gel he used on his hair to get it to hang straight into his eyes. Under all these perfumes was the scent I craved. Dirt under the fingernails, sweat on the back of the neck. I was here. I breathed in what was left of my son. I would never change the sheets. If it came to it, I would never change a thing ever again.

I DIDN'T SLEEP. Up at dawn, I made coffee I didn't want. The apartment was too quiet. After several hours at home by myself, I slipped out the back door and around to my truck and drove downtown. I made it through security at the courthouse without too many pitying looks. Deputy Lombardi wasn't on duty to dump out my purse this time. At the door to the sheriff's office, I lost my nerve.

The first time I'd come to this door, another boy had been missing. Was still missing. That first time I'd stood here, hesitating to go inside, I'd almost run.

What would have happened if I had?

Joshua might still be gone. But would I still be standing here now?

Because I wasn't here to work a case, pass along information, or even look at anyone's handwriting. I was here to see the sheriff—simply see him. To see—Russ. If I'd walked away the first time, I wouldn't be seeking the sheriff to help steady my anxiety.

Or maybe I would. Wasn't this where family members of the missing came to do their hoping?

This wasn't the headquarters of Joshua Watch, though. The courthouse square was empty; no posters or news vans.

I reached for the doorknob again. I couldn't stand being here. I couldn't stand not being here. I should have stayed home, in case Joshua came back.

I let my hand drop from the door and turned for the stairs. Two steps away, the door to the office opened behind me and the voices of two men bounced down the hall.

"Anna?"

Russ, of course, and one of the hard-eyed officers. I stared at their boots.

"Go ahead," Russ said. "Tell them I'll be right down."

I watched the other man's feet walking past. "Ma'am," he said.

"You should be resting," Russ said. "Has something happened?"

I nodded: yes, I should be resting. And then shook my head: no, nothing had happened. I found I was still nodding when I should be shaking my head, and then still shaking my head long after I should have stopped.

"Come with me."

I followed his boots down the hall, past the elevator. There was a window at the end of the hall that looked out over the courthouse green, nearly the same view I'd seen on my first visit to his office. The same jeweler, the same karate school, all the snug businesses living under the shadow of all the protection there was.

The sheriff took out a set of keys. A door opened up into a dark, windowless vestibule, crammed to the ceiling with storage containers and boxes. He squeezed through and, using the keys again, opened another door that swung out to reveal his office. He took my elbow and led me toward the chair in front of his desk.

"Secret passageway," he said. "In case Bea Ransey comes calling."

I began to nod, then stopped. Some people could understand how I felt, but most didn't and never would. Bea Ransey was not a joke.

My throat was tight, my eyes puffy from crying. I didn't want to cry. But then—Joshua's schoolbooks, pulled from the closet. The sight of his cereal bowl in the sink from the morning before, the morning I'd hidden from him in the shower. The alarm in his room going off at the customary time.

And now, this joke that was not funny. I buckled and fell into the chair.

"Hey, now. I'm sorry," Russ said. "I don't know what I'm thinking." He unloaded a pile of paper from another chair and brought it close to mine. He unearthed a smashed box of tissues from his desk and held it out. When I didn't reach for them, he pulled out two and put them in my hand. "Now, come on, Anna. We'll find him. Remember how we talked about kids not getting far? Remember? The odds are with us on Joshua."

"Aidan," I said, gulping around the lump in my throat. I pushed the tissues at my nose. "Aidan's been gone for—almost two weeks."

"Aidan is a different case. You can see that."

"But he shouldn't still be gone. What if Joshua is—is a different case?"

"Joshua is a runaway. He's on his own—now, hear me out. I'm not saying that to upset you." He was using his talking-to-horses voice now. I felt myself start to relax against my will. "What I'm trying to say is that Aidan was taken. He's got an adult in charge of things. Joshua's got no resources. No matter how smart he is, he's just a kid. He'll make a mistake, and when he does, we'll go get him."

"But—" But there was no way to make Russ understand what I knew, which was that Joshua was more than a different case. He was a *special* case. He was more accustomed than most people of any age to flight, to starting over, to lying low, to going unnoticed. I hadn't given him these skills on purpose, but I must have been teaching them by example.

All I could hope was that he learned quickly that being a special case was no fun.

"What about—what theories do you have?"

He stared at me just long enough. I must be playing the type. Bothersome loved ones must do this. They develop theories. They come visit. They take up time.

"What theories have *you* come up with?" he said.

"Two boys missing from the same town within two weeks?" My mind raced. I knew I sounded desperate. "Did Aidan have any contact with Joe Jeffries?"

His head snapped up. "What's this?"

"He's new in town."

"He's actually old to town."

"Joshua said he had a thing for—little boys."

Russ wiped his face with his hand. "I can't believe you're going to make me defend that dipshit, but I'm pretty sure *that* rumor falls under the category of idle. The stuff kids say about teachers they don't like. Anna, I think we have to be honest with each other. If you're willing to entertain crazy theories about guys who held your hand last night while we combed your apartment, then you should be willing to entertain the craziest idea of all."

I felt a little hope flutter inside me. He would know what to do. That's why I had come. He would know, and he would save us both.

"You need to consider the possibility," he said, slowly searching my face and laying a hand on my arm. "That Joshua went to find his dad."

"But—"

"I know. He doesn't have one. Let's call him whatever you want to call him, but—the craziest story might be the right one."

The craziest story was the one I had written. He would never understand.

I shook the sheriff's hand off. "You're wrong."

He pulled back, rubbing the palm of his hand on his pants as though he'd just pulled it from fire. "I have been known to be wrong. A time or two."

The door to the office swung open.

"Oh!"

Sherry, a stack of folders in her arms, jumped backward. She looked between us several times. "I thought you went to interview—I'm sorry. I'll come back."

"That's fine," Russ said. He stood and went to the far side of his desk. Once there, he didn't seem to know what to do. He swept his hand over the mess. "You can—whatever."

Sherry stood in the doorway. Finally, she dropped the files and came to my side. Without knowing how she got there, I was suddenly inside Sherry's arms, held fiercely.

"You poor thing," Sherry whispered, rocking us both. "I have to believe it's going to be OK. I have to believe it."

Every nerve in my body bucked the embrace, but I held on. I needed someone to believe for me.

Chapter Twenty-four

When I arrived home, there they were. Not just the man from Russ's pool of sunglass wearers they'd left outside the apartment, but two more. And instead of the brown-and-tans I'd come to know as the county uniform or the black-and-blues of the state troopers, these were wearing suits with unimaginative ties. Feds.

My mind leapt ahead to Joshua. He's found. Or—

I hesitated on the sidewalk, and they turned in my direction.

I couldn't move. All the logic I could muster told me that any news—good or bad—would have come from the local guys. From Russ.

"Anna?" the taller of the two said, taking off his sunglasses. And then the reason for their visit started to work its way up from the millions of years between this moment and the last time I'd given my job the least bit of thought. Somewhere, under all that had happened in the last thirty hours or so, was another problem altogether. I'd forgotten about the dead man and the note of warning I'd told him to ignore.

"Kent."

He met me where I stood and took my hand. With his sunglasses off, his eyes were too blue and piercing. I looked down at my hand in his. So many people touching me today.

"You've already heard," he said.

"Yes."

"So—onward. With the guy dead, it's a new game. Who called you?"

"His secretary."

Kent's eyes went distant, then refocused. "Really. How interesting." He threw a grimace over his shoulder at the other man, who hung back. "Hear that, Jim? Anna, you're already helping us." He pulled me gently toward the door. "Jim Kaleb, Anna Winger."

I met the other man's eyes in way of greeting and then turned back to Kent, who curled over me like a funeral director around the bereaved. He was taking too much care with me.

"You've already heard about Joshua, then."

"Keller called me." He pulled me into his ribs a bit and let me go. "I'd tell you not to worry, but I know you will anyway. And that's your job. I just need to talk to you about your other job. Can we bother you for a few minutes?"

Put that way, I could only say yes. All I wanted to do was go upstairs and make sure Joshua hadn't sneaked back on his own and then sit with my phone in my hand until someone called. Today. It had to be today. If Joshua was gone another night—

I couldn't bear to think about another night. How quiet the apartment had been, how every noise the refrigerator made became the sound of a key in the lock. Once around six, one of the neighbors had walked by the door and slowed down. Probably Margaret. The night before, when several pairs of heavy, regulation footwear marched up and down our hallway, I had heard the telltale broomstick striking.

Now, walking through the building and up the stairs with Kent and his partner, I imagined all the faces pressed to peepholes as we passed and all the phone calls among the Booster moms to discuss the ruckus. My life as a well-hidden woman was over. In an instant, I felt the old panic. When Joshua came home and everything quieted down, we would pack up our things and find another place to start over. But Joshua was gone. And if he didn't come back in a day or two days or a week or a month, this was where I had to be. I would remain here, under glass for the entire county to stare at and whisper about, for Ray to find me, until Joshua came home.

"I can make this easy for you," I said as the two men settled in on my couch. I'd pulled the dining room chair Joshua normally chose from the table and sat across the coffee table from them. "I messed up."

Kent and his partner exchanged a look. Jim slid a notebook out of his jacket. Kent leaned forward on his knees. "How do you mean?"

"I was distracted that day, I think. It's hard to think about it. Was I distracted enough that I missed something, and this man's family has to bury him?" I took in a deep, shaking breath and looked at each of them in turn. "I left something out of the analysis. I didn't mean to. It was a mistake. But I don't know how much of a mistake, and if hearing the entire analysis might help now."

"I've seen the write-up," Kent said, glancing at Jim as though he wished he'd come to talk to me alone. "It seemed like sturdy work."

"No, there was nothing wrong with what I said. It's what I didn't say." I watched the other man jotting down notes. "This is all from memory, Mr. Kaleb. I hope you'll put that in. I don't trust my—current state of mind."

"Of course," Kent murmured. "Do the best you can. Do you remember what it was that you left out?"

I tried to call back the moment when I'd meant to finish off the analysis but had been distracted by my personal life. I remembered exactly what I'd left out and why. It had seemed to me that the letter writer's secrets were being exposed when they didn't have any bearing. Those damn dangling y's and p's. But I knew better. Something that seemed unconnected might be the connection that mattered.

"Based on certain indicators in his handwriting, particularly in the descenders, I would say that the letter writer had some—" I paused, watched Jim's hand scratching across the page. "Sexual shortcomings."

Jim lifted his eyes to mine and tipped his notebook away.

"That's interesting," Kent said. He rubbed at his cheek. "I'll have to think about that. Was there a reason why you left it out?"

"Like I said, it was a mistake. I meant to include it in the end, but—well, I was distracted. Like I said."

"Joshua?"

I swallowed hard. I was pretending to be myself, sitting here and talking in a code I'd already started to forget. But I hadn't forgotten for a moment that he was gone. His empty room seemed to ring silence down the hall. My phone, in my pocket, was a brick. I was as distracted as I'd ever been. Talking about *murder*—and the only thing that mattered to me was the silence.

"Yes," I croaked.

Kent and his partner exchanged looks again. Jim flipped his notebook closed and stood. "I'll be at the car. Thank you for your time, Mrs. Winger." He fidgeted with the notebook. I noticed he left it in his right hand to avoid having to shake mine or to avoid having to decide if he should. That was fine. I was tired and didn't want to be touched anymore today. "I hope your boy gets home. Soon. And safe."

I remembered those words, used for another boy. "Thank you," I said.

Kent waited for the door to close. "I have a son about Joshua's age."

"You do?"

"How long have we known each other, and you had no idea our kids were the same age?"

"I wouldn't say—"

"What?" he said.

"I wouldn't say we know each other."

Kent nodded. "I guess I wouldn't, either. But I know thirteen-year-old boys." He took a wallet out of his jacket and flipped through a few photo holders. "This is my third, my runt."

I leaned in to take a look. I didn't want to. The snapshot was of all three boys, all tall and thin like their father, standing in a patch of grass with the sun in their eyes. The youngest had pronounced ears and a military haircut. His arms, dangling at his sides, were painfully thin. "Good-looking boys," I said, with effort. "Three. I can't imagine."

"No one can imagine your life very well."

I stared at him.

"I mean—no one can imagine another person's life very well."

If Kent weren't here, I would have checked my phone for reception already. Four times. "Did any of your boys run away from home?"

He cleared his throat and put his wallet away. "No. No, you're right. I don't know the first thing about what it's like from that side."

We sat in silence for a minute. Finally, he said, "Impotence, then? Is that what you meant?"

"Do you think it has any significance for your investigation?"

"It was significant to my investigation," he said with raised eyebrows. "But now that it's a homicide—"

"Right, of course. Different investigation."

"But it might mean something. I don't think you have to have testicles—pardon me for the bluntness—to know that a man's sexual health can affect the rest of his self-worth. We'll have to throw that piece into the mix and see what comes up. It could be nothing." He folded his hands over his crossed knee and stared at his own fingers for a moment. "It could mean nothing."

"But you don't think so."

"Everything means something to someone, right? Some kid gets rapped on the knuckles by the nuns in grade school and a quiver shows up in the handwriting two decades later?"

I granted him a small smile. "One of the Booster Club moms suggested I set up a sort of kissing booth for handwriting analysis. She wanted me to find the quiver in her handwriting."

His mouth twisted into a hesitant smile. "Did you find one in Joshua's?"

I was caught off guard, even so. I nodded, unable to speak.

Kent stood up and ambled to the window, his hands in his pockets. "I always wonder what my kids really think about it all."

"He hid from me, wouldn't write anything down."

"Doesn't mean he was doing anything illicit," he said. "Normal thing for a teenage boy to want privacy."

"He's gotten in with a bad crowd."

Kent considered this and the street outside the window. "But then what do the parents of those in the bad crowd tell themselves?"

A stone seemed to lodge itself in my throat. Kent knew better than anyone living where Joshua had come from. "What are you trying to say?"

He left the window. "Your son's not the bad crowd or the good crowd. He's not much of anything but thirteen. They have tempers outsized for their bodies. And desires you don't even want to know about. Pent up like firecrackers, and just as dangerous to themselves. He's just a boy."

"I just want him home."

"He'll be back soon. But that will only be the beginning. If they bring him home kicking and screaming—" Kent looked away, and I had to wonder if he had not lived through something, too. "If they bring him home before he's come to some conclusions on his own, he might be hard to handle. He might not be the boy you raised."

I imagined the scene. I'd rush to Russ's office or to the juvenile hall in Indianapolis or wherever they had him. I'd run to him, elated at the sight of him again, and he would shrug his shoulders. He would let the fringe of hair shadow his eyes. This was what I expected, even as I realized how little I'd come to expect.

"He's the boy I raised, all right. The very one."

"Well, then. Let's bring him home. If there's anything I can help you with, you know to call me? Yes? Good." He walked to the door and stood there with a hand on the knob. "I wonder—"

I stood, felt for my cell phone through my pocket. "What?"

"I just wonder—what's Joshua running from? In particular, I mean. Maybe you have some ideas. But could he have been running toward something? They're asking you these things, I hope."

"They've already asked. About—Chicago." He'd loved it there.

"And before that?"

I looked away. "They've been nothing if not thorough."

"Of course, of course."

"Just say whatever it is, Kent."

He came away from the door. "The police are being thorough, Anna, but they are just strangers following a checklist. You know him." He looked around the room. I saw him noticing the bare walls, the single framed photo of Joshua in the corner. "If he doesn't come back—" His eyes dug into mine to make sure I understood the possibility. "If he doesn't come back and you've done nothing but wait for someone else to rescue him?"

I took a shaking breath. I couldn't even be insulted that Kent still knew I needed his help. "What do I do?"

Kent smiled gently. How lucky his boys must be, his wife. "I would say do what you've always done," he said. "Whatever you have to."

KENT HAD ALREADY left when I realized I could have shown him the evidence forms from the sheriff. They were confounding me for some reason. I'd never figure it out now.

I was supposed to rest, but couldn't. I was supposed to stay near home, but no one came through the door. I was supposed to keep my cell phone close, but it didn't ring. My assignment was to do nothing. The world seemed quite content to go on without me, without Joshua.

My skin was itchy, jumpy. Something had to happen today. Joshua had to come home today. He had to.

I pulled my phone out of my pocket, put it back. These motions didn't give me even a second of satisfaction. I pulled out the phone again to dial Russ, but put it back down. I wouldn't do it.

Whatever you have to.

Down the hall, Joshua's room radiated emptiness. I walked

to it, opened the door. I looked again in the boxes he'd never unpacked, opened the closet door again. Got on my hands and knees and bowed to the dust bunnies under the bed. The police had been over the room; I'd been over the room—who had not been over the room?

I fell back on his beanbag chair and looked around. His desk was dusty. His game system was gone, though I didn't understand why.

From the closet, the spines of his textbooks mocked me. *Huckleberry Finn*—oh, God, he was a runaway, wasn't he?—math, *Our World and Its People*.

I reached for the social studies book and flipped through the pages, stopping once to stare longingly at a note Joshua had made in the margins.

The text was all agriculture and war, famine and migration patterns. I shook the book upside down. Nothing fell out. I ran the book's pages like a flip book forward and backward, checked the blank pages inside the back cover.

What had Joe said? *History was a freshman class.*

I flicked through the pages one at a time, willing the book to tell me what I could almost understand. And then I did.

Chapter Twenty-five

The school secretary didn't want to tell me where the library was. "You understand, of course," the woman said. She was younger than I was, pudgy cheeked, her hair cut short and matronly. "We can't have just anyone running around the school."

"I'm not just anyone. I'm a parent."

"You wouldn't want people running loose in the school, with your child—" The woman had the decency to stop talking. She blushed.

"So you know that my child is not in the building, and at the moment I couldn't care a lick who's *running loose*. I need to talk to your librarian. Urgently. I urgently need to talk—"

"It's not a good time right now." The woman pushed her chair back a few inches, as though readying for me to launch myself at her. "It's lunchtime, and Mrs. Chandler is busy."

"I don't want to talk to the principal. I want to talk to—is Joe Jeffries here?"

The woman picked up her phone. At last. I stepped back from the desk. Now that I was getting my way, I could give a few inches.

While the secretary spoke quietly into the phone—I could tell it wasn't Joe she'd reached and wondered whether there was such a thing as small-town school security—I glanced around. In the back was the principal's office, the door closed. Around the corner was probably the nurse's office and sickroom, the vice principal's office. I might be able to find Joe's office on my own. There was a student sitting with his back to me, waiting for one of the doors to open and a figure of authority to wave him in. Health trouble or trouble trouble? And then realized the boy was Steve Ransey.

I walked over and stood in front of him. "Steve," I said.

He was hunched over, his elbows on his knees. He didn't look up, so I knew he'd recognized me before I had him. "They already talked to me," he said.

"I'm not the police. I have different questions."

He kicked at the carpet. He wore work boots, as though seventh grade was a break from his job on a road crew. Or a chain gang. He was bigger than Joshua, heavier and thicker.

"What?" he asked, voice cracking.

Still thirteen years old, though, no matter how tough the uniform.

"You don't know where he might have gone?"

"That's the same question."

"OK," I said, sitting in the chair next to him. "When did he start spray painting on barn walls?"

Steve's eyes shifted all around without alighting.

The secretary walked up to us. "I don't think we can allow this."

"Allow what?" I said. "This is my son's friend. We're just consoling each other, isn't that right, Steve?"

Steve nodded at his boots.

The secretary made a small sound and hurried off.

"She's going to go get the principal or the vice," Steve said.

"Let her. I'm not doing anything. And neither are you at the moment. Why are you sitting here?"

"Waiting on the nurse," he mumbled.

"Are you OK?"

He managed to look at me for a beat, then away. "Yeah."

I'd used the mom tone on him, I realized too late. "Did the police ask you about the spray paint? And the barn?"

"Yeah."

"Then I guess I can't ask you about that. Did they ask you about . . . social studies?"

His face shifted subtly, curious. "No?"

"Are you in social studies with Joshua?"

"Different periods."

"But the same teacher?"

"Mrs. Grivner. She's kind of a bitch."

"I like her already. Did she ever assign you a project where you had to map out your family? Make a family tree?"

He laughed, a snaky little hiss of a noise. "Wow, that's lame. We did that in, like, second grade."

"Oh, yeah?" I said, my mind trying to race ahead, to make sense of it.

"And it wasn't fair. Some people had, like, really *simple* families."

The secretary marched back into the room and past us looking triumphant. Someone equally tiresome would be here soon to there-there me out of the building.

The poor kid. Living not with his own parents but his uncle. And what a jerk I'd been, to judge his family. "Joshua's family tree was too simple," I said finally, knowing I was admitting to the very thing I had denied when Joshua suggested it. "Where's the library?"

He shrugged toward the door the secretary had come through. "Down there, on the right. But it's closed. It's lunch."

Lunch. Hadn't Joe said something about lunch monitoring? With the librarian?

"Where's the cafeteria?"

"Follow the *smell*. And the noise."

"The whole place smells like cabbage to me. Why aren't you eating?"

He shrugged and turned his head away.

"Did you spend all your money on spray paint? Is that the kind of sick you are?" I remembered the sad gray house where the Ranseys lived and, from my own family history, the shame of reduced-price lunch, or of not having even that much. Like a sign hanging from my neck: *special case*. The last year of school I'd hidden out behind a bank of lockers during lunch, munching from a box of generic-brand saltines with Theresa, who started bringing things from home to share.

I opened my wallet, found a five, and held it out to Steve.

He made the snaky sound again, but it wasn't a laugh. "I'm not going to take your money."

"Why not? If I'm giving it to you."

He shrugged. I missed Joshua so much, my chest hurt. "What does Joshua eat for lunch?"

He sat silently for so long that I thought he might have decided against another word. His boots shuffled on the floor. The secretary coughed to remind us she was nearby.

"French fries. He has them, like, every day."

I nodded. "You'd tell me if you knew. Where he was?"

"Yeah."

"Have you seen your aunt yet?"

He shook his head slowly.

"Can I buy you some French fries?"

"OK."

He let the money be placed into his hand and hastened away. I stood, gave the secretary a look, and followed the smell and the noise before someone came along and told me I couldn't.

I FOLLOWED THE low buzz of voices until the sound grew into an unrestrained roar, meeting only a few students on the way. No one gave me more than an eyes-quickly-away glance. Down a long hallway, past rooms with small windows cut into them so that I could see they were dark, past framed photos of sports teams, the athletes with knobby knees, and portraits of proud and baby-faced class valedictorians, past a trophy case that was hopeful in its near emptiness.

A great blaring bell rang overhead, and students flooded around the corner and past me, around me, until I was an island in a fierce current of elbows and backpacks. I stepped back into the lee of the trophy case and waited, looking back when the students noticed me and stared. I didn't recognize any of the kids, but at last came Joe Jeffries's perfectly styled hair.

"Ms. Winger, what—? Is there news?"

I appreciated that we had returned to formality. "No, I need to talk to the librarian. You said she talked to you. About Joshua."

"The sheriff's already been all over—"

"I know, I know. I'm just trying to work out this one loose thread about the history project."

He looked at me with a grim mouth. I could see how I must look to him. I was a sad and desperate sack of a woman who was about to waste a lot of time when I should be at home. Resting and waiting.

"Look, I know. But I have to do something."

He sighed and watched the last of the students disappearing down the hallway. "Did you check in with the front desk?"

"Yes."

He raised an eyebrow.

"I've gone a bit renegade. Don't make me go talk to that secretary again."

"This way." He took off, leaving me to follow. We passed the portraits again, the wide, unsuspecting eyes of so much youth. Past the classrooms, their doors now propped open and the bustle of the students starting to fade as they settled at their desks. Before we reached the front office and watchdog secretary, Joe turned and led us down a narrower hallway. Another turn and I was rewarded with a long stretch of windows that revealed shelves of books.

"I don't know what you're going to find out," he said over his shoulder in a library-appropriate voice.

The library was high ceilinged and cold. I followed Joe across a wide expanse of tables and study carrels, some of them manned by kids in headphones or thumbing at their phones. They all had phones. Now I saw how odd it was that Joshua didn't.

The librarian stood behind the desk, smiling expectantly. She was wan, her cheekbones sharp in her long face. Her hair, curling and long, had been twisted up and into a sloppy bun.

"Milah," Joe said.

Before he could continue, I put out my hand. "I'm Joshua Winger's mother."

The woman reached into the handshake but ended up holding my hand. "Oh," she said, covering her mouth with her other hand. "Has anything happened?"

Waiting for the worst. Both of them. Joe with his concern and now this skinny librarian and her surprise—everyone was just waiting to hear Madame Zonda–inspired news.

Joe moved us over to an empty table away from the students. "No news. Ms. Winger just has some questions for you."

"For me?"

I sat across from her. She seemed sincere, not at all like she'd been asked to placate a disturbed woman. "Joshua was working on a project during library time?"

"He certainly was. He seemed very engaged."

"But it wasn't for class."

"Well. I don't know," she said. "The students do all sorts of research. Unless they're making a mess or getting too loud, we don't ask too many questions."

"No, I'm telling you," I said. "It wasn't for class. I've gone over it with—" I glanced at Joe. Better not to mention Steve as a source. "I've gone over it a couple of different ways, but whatever he was doing was personal."

The buzzer sounded again. All the students would be back in place now. All the students except mine.

"Some of them research their favorite baseball teams during library," Joe said. "Or their favorite supermodels or . . . we have a lot of websites blocked."

"So library time is all about the internet?" I asked.

"Most of them have access at home, so many will research in the books or use the time to write their papers or do their homework," the librarian said. "Or ask questions of us. It's really just study hall."

Joshua didn't have access at home. At home, the internet was for work. My work. "Was Joshua using the web for his project?"

"Some. I helped him a bit."

"Can you show me? Please?"

She and Joe exchanged looks, and then stood and led me to one of the study carrels. A girl sat there, tapping into the keyboard. The site in front of her looked like it belonged to a pop group. She hastily clicked the screen empty as we approached and gave up her spot without argument.

"Do you remember what he was looking for?" I asked.

Milah frowned. "A genealogy project, wasn't it?"

We gathered around the empty carrel, Milah leaning into the keyboard. "He was researching some distant relatives. Cousins."

"He doesn't have any cousins," I said.

"Well," Milah said slowly. "Everyone has *some* cousins. Down the line."

"We don't." Of course it wasn't true. "How would he have started? Wouldn't he have started with a name or something concrete? How do you do this?"

"Well, he could have started with himself." Milah tapped a few keys, Joshua's name appearing in the search box. When the results came up, she ran her finger down the few entries, tried a few more keystrokes. "But he doesn't have a web presence that I can see. Good for you. He's too young. Or he could have started with you. Your name is—"

I hesitated, glancing at Joe. Then gave the name I went by. No reason to call up the old newspaper stories now.

Milah typed my name, tapped around.

"You're not here, either." She shot me a look of renewed interest. In this day and age, it must be unusual not to come rising to the surface when someone tried to fish you out.

Joe shifted impatiently. "I'm just not sure how this is relevant."

I didn't want it to be relevant, either, but it was. I was willing to admit it now.

"Try this name," I said, saying it aloud for the first time in thirteen years. And spelling it the way I had for Joshua, the wrong way, the just-in-case way.

Chapter Twenty-six

Eliot Ray Levis. One *l*, one *t*. Sometimes he got mail addressed to Elliott, two *l*'s, two *t*'s, and it pissed him off. Or Lebis. Or Leeves, Leaves, Levi. *What does that say?* he'd crow, holding the offending catalog or envelope to my face. *How can they get away with being so wrong all the time?*

Milah clicked around on a few things then looked back at me. "Not much on that guy, either. I don't think Joshua would have the skills or the credit card to take this search as deep as you'd need to go. Some real estate stuff . . . nothing new, at least."

I let out the breath I was holding but didn't feel any better. I had to catch her attention before her search dug up thirteen-year-old headlines or chat rooms. "How could Joshua have spent all his library time on this if we're coming up tilt within ten minutes?"

"Oh, I didn't say he spent all of his time on this," she said, finally closing that search window and looking away from the screen. "He mostly used the reference section, which is why I noticed him specifically." She glanced at Joe. "They don't usually bother with the dusty side of the room."

"Reference section . . . like encyclopedias?"

Milah stood up and started toward the table we'd left earlier. Behind it, a wide array of books: thick, tall, old. "I think he was more interested in—"

She stopped.

"—maps."

I ARRIVED HOME without paying attention to how I got there. Underneath my skin, my veins thumped. I couldn't think. I couldn't stop thinking.

Maps.

But where was he going? No one had thought to ask, to look over his shoulder to see what trip he was planning.

Jeffries had gone and fetched the boys: Steve, Shay Mullen, another boy from the pack I'd seen on the courthouse lawn. Stephanie's kid, Caleb.

"He was always talking about Chicago," Shay said. His mouth didn't open very wide when he talked. I leaned in to hear better. "But then it was all about some woodsy place? Remember?" he put this to Steve. "He wanted to go camping?"

"I don't know," Steve said. He seemed embarrassed to talk to me now. The French fries, probably. I'd hurt his pride, even if I'd cured his stomach illness.

"Where?" I said, my heart in my throat.

"I can look it up when I get home," Shay said.

"How will you look it up?"

"Online," he said. "On the chat on low keys revenge."

"Two?" Steve said.

"Yeah," Shay said, flipping his hair out of his eyes and pulling up the waistband of his too-tight jeans.

"What? What's low keys revenge?"

"*Lo-ki,*" Shay enunciated. Someone across the room shushed him. "The god of mischief. *Loki's Revenge.*"

"Two," Steve said. "The next generation of the game."

"Oh, it's a game," I said. "And it's online? But Joshua doesn't have online access."

"Yeah, he does," Steve said, that hiss escaping him again.

"He plays all the time," Shay said.

"And there's a chat," Caleb said. "You know, where you can talk on the screen with the guys you're playing with. All over. Not just in Parks. Not just your friends, I mean."

His game system?

"But he didn't have online access at our place—"

"The neighbor," Caleb said. "Really easy. One of your neighbors doesn't keep their network locked down."

And here I thought I'd been the one running a secret online enterprise from our apartment.

"When he talked about going somewhere, going camping," I said, "did he mention anyplace in particular?" I glanced at Joe, then Milah. "Did he mention Wisconsin? Sweetheart Lake?"

Shay looked at me sharply. "Yeah, that's it."

Funny how the name of the place stuck in your head once you heard it. The boys confirmed they'd all heard that name, that maybe Joshua had been looking it up online during one of those library hours, too.

Now, driving home, I raged at myself. How had I wasted a minute trying to pretend I didn't know where Joshua had gone? He'd gone to find Ray. Of course he had. The police had asked. Russ had leveled with me. I wouldn't let them consider the possibility, because I'd hoped it wasn't true. Because my only hope was that it wasn't true. Because it didn't seem possible. Joshua couldn't go to his dad's because he didn't have one. A dad? That was the stuff of greeting cards and sitcom TV. Joshua didn't have a *dad*. Neither of us did, not anymore, and we were both better off for it.

When I pulled up in front of our building, Russ was standing outside. He didn't have his hat.

"Been looking for you," he said.

My hands began to shake so badly I had to grip them together. Just like everyone else, expecting the worst. "Joshua?"

"No, no, sorry—no news there, not exactly." He looked me over. "Have you had some news?"

I should tell him about Ray. Ray, for God's sake. Of course Ray. I had been using more magical thinking. And now: one name. One name, and I'd call down the power of the nation's security forces to retrieve my son quickly and quietly. But that seemed . . . oily. As Kent had said, if I went out and yanked him back, I'd get back the boy I deserved. I couldn't begin to explain that, or what it cost me to say Ray's name again. What it would cost me to explain what he'd done and how much I'd let him get away with.

"Can we go inside?" he said.

I looked up, then away.

"Oh." He turned his head down the street, watched a car coming at us too fast. The driver slowed down when he spotted Russ. He stared after the car until it turned a corner. "I guess I can tell you here, then. Nothing bad, now, nothing bad, but it's not that helpful, either. Just. Just a mystery solved."

"Aidan?"

"No—"

"Nothing? Even with Leila home again?"

He grimaced. "I can't really talk about it."

"Oh."

We stood uncompanionably for a moment.

"We got a match on that . . . that *threat*."

I couldn't understand him, but then I remembered the en-velope, the flyer, the mean, bold letters: *I know about you*. The memory of that day rose to meet me; pieces fit together.

"Joshua," I said.

"Found a photo file of it on the hard drive of his game thingy. Does that surprise you?"

I could no longer be astonished by anything Joshua knew, said, or did. He'd signed me up for the Sweetheart Lake travel mag, too. No one else could have done it. No one else could have been as cruel.

"It would take a lot to surprise me at this point," I said.

We stared at one another for a long moment, until I felt we were deciding something I hadn't realized we were going to decide just now.

"OK," he said. After a few seconds of silence, he started down the sidewalk to his truck. That day in the barn was over and now tainted.

"Wait," I said, and hated the sound of my voice and the chis-eled impatience I saw in his face when he turned back. "The handwriting—"

"I can't talk about that case, I said."

"No, not Aidan's note. Those evidence forms."

He wouldn't meet my eyes. "What about them?"

"I couldn't figure it out for a long time," I said. "They were all blending together. I couldn't get a handle on it. But I think all the signatures are signed by the same person."

Now I had his attention. "That can't be right. The techs—"

"Well, no, before the samples go to the lab," I said. "By the time the evidence goes off for testing, it's too late. That's where they're finding the problem, right? They come back from the lab as—something else, not drugs." I paused to make sure we were talking the same language.

"Listening."

"The arresting officer in each, and then the person who logs it into your storage, and then the person who claims the sample back to send to the lab. Sometimes they might be the same person, right, but on your forms, they're many names, all different—but all signed by the same hand. He tried to make them look different, pretty successfully, actually. Does that make sense to you? Is that—"

"Well, it would explain some things," Russ said. "Is there no way to tell who's doing it?"

"I could—don't take this the wrong way, but we've had this talk already. I need the originals," I said. He rolled his eyes. "Sheriff, the copier you used has dust or nicks on the glass, for one thing. It shows up as little black dots all along the page, right where the signatures begin. It's distracting. Get me the originals and I'll see what I can do."

He nodded once, curt. "Yes, *ma'am*. Anything else?"

I was telling him how to do his job again but was too tired to argue. What were the other questions I'd had for him? I didn't think I'd ever see this man or this place again, and saw no point to having this conversation. But maybe really pissing him off would keep him and his security service away from the apartment for the night. I only needed one night. I grasped at any of the threads from my notes that had been left untied. "When the drugs come back from the lab and it isn't what it's supposed to be . . . what is it?"

"Why does that matter?"

"It doesn't," I said. "Not to me. Just wondered. Missing cocaine, missing crystal meth." I paused, looking for the worst thing to say. "I would have thought it would matter to *you*. Enough to *ask*, anyway."

"We're working on it, Ms. Winger." His tone was as clipped as the click of a typewriter key. "And—I think I'll be using more traditional methods to solve my evidence leak from here on out, so don't worry about any further calls from me. I thank you for your service to your community."

For a moment I recalled the slanted doorway of the barn and my arm sticking out of the shadows into the daylight as we parted. *Don't leave it here*, he'd said, when it had never happened, when the place we'd gone had never existed.

"Of course," I said.

I turned to go but when he called after me, I stopped and looked back.

"You know, for a while I wondered what team you were on," he said. "It seemed to me that you had a dog in this race when you couldn't possibly."

"Meaning?"

"I thought you wanted Leila Ransey to be innocent. Tell me I'm crazy."

"No," I said. "I wanted Leila Ransey to get away. It's not the same thing."

I turned and walked toward the door, fighting the urge to look back again. I knew what I would see if I did, and I meant what I said. I had wanted Leila to get away. I wanted us all to get away.

Chapter Twenty-seven

I packed as though I would never return.

Clothes. Shoes. A jacket. I packed a few towels, a blanket. I threw pillows on top of it all. I might have to sleep in the car. My computer. I dragged the collapsed boxes from under the bed but didn't begin to fill them all. Light. We had to travel light this time.

I packed a bag for Joshua: underwear, socks, T-shirts, his winter coat, his snow boots. I began to see what was missing, what he'd taken with him. I developed a theory as I sorted through his things. The first time you run, you don't know what to take. You leave behind what you need and cart along what you don't. The first time I'd run, I had nothing but the clothes I'd stolen from the woman in the next hospital bed, but that hadn't been my choice.

His game system was still in county evidence, but I packed his new headphones, carefully wrapping the cords and tucking them into a corner of the cargo area behind the backseats.

I packed until I was exhausted, almost midnight. Everything

felt as though I were doing it for the last time. Maybe I was washing my hands in this sink for the last time. Maybe I was closing this door for the last time and descending these steps for the last time. But there would be other sinks, other doors, other steps. That was not how it felt. So little of my old life offered itself up to be taken along, I felt as though I were packing for my own execution. I packed for the trip, but not for what came after. I couldn't imagine what might come after.

At the bottom of the stairs, Margaret's door opened. I saw the glint of her glasses in the dark crack, gave a nod, and tried to slip past.

"Where do you think you're going?"

"Nowhere, Margaret, don't worry."

"That's bull, lady. I know bull when I see it."

I glanced toward the back door, propped open for my last trip through. "Seems like you already know it all."

"What'm I supposed to tell that police when he comes to check on you?"

"He won't."

"What did you tell him?" she said.

"Margaret, I need to get on the road."

"Nothing? Slip out of town like you came in. You don't know a thing."

Agreement rose to my lips, but I swallowed it.

"Tell me, then," she said. "Just in case."

I had thought of this—so many just-in-cases. But I hadn't taken care of any of them. I'd never left a forwarding address, never told anyone where I came from, where I was going. Why start now? Joshua. What if the police found him on his way to Sweetheart Lake and brought him back? What if he changed his mind halfway there and came back on his own?

But if I believed that, I'd be waiting here forever.

"Home," I said. The word caught in my throat. Whenever I thought of home, I thought of dusk and mosquito bites, the lake like a photo on a wall calendar I took for granted. The trees hulking over the houses, gods waiting to pass judgment. Red dirt in my socks and the smell of burgers from the Dairy Bar drifting out into the night. I thought of rental house after rental house, all dumps, and the sad bucket of yellow paint always stacked in the basement. "Home. Joshua's gone home, and I have to go get him."

Margaret opened the door wider, her worn slippers appearing over the threshold. She turned her bad ear toward me. "And where is that?"

"I'll call the sheriff's office from the road."

Margaret reached out to stop me, but I slipped past and out the back. The SUV didn't seem loaded for a new life. The far back was full and covered, but otherwise I might be taking a Sunday drive or running an errand. I got inside, buckled in. The sounds of the night came through the open window. After a moment, I started the engine and rolled out into the street.

A mistake, leaving so much behind, leaving the spot that Joshua knew to return to. By the time I had driven through town and past the courthouse, seen the disk of light from the lamp against the closed blinds of the sheriff's office, passed the neon of the Dairy Bar, and took the exit north, I had begun to believe that every move I made from here on out would be the wrong one.

The road was dark even lit by the half-moon, uncluttered by other drivers. I drove just a little fast. To keep my mind where it needed to be, I began to note every county marker I passed, every sign to towns I wouldn't be visiting. I was in the lull between one city and the next, just fast-food billboards and the oc-

casional cluster of lights. But this was the way: north, only north
and toward every mistake I had ever made.

"Where you headed?"

I looked up from the cup of tea, still full and long gone cold,
and found the source of the question through bleary eyes. The
waitress, swinging a coffeepot from her wide hip as though it
were an appendage. She wore a stained uniform and broken-
down sneakers. How many hours did this woman spend awake
when everyone else was asleep?

I was in a truck stop in the middle of the night on the bypass
around Chicago, and no one was here because it was where
he wanted to be. I didn't want to be here, either. After several
hours of the gray ribbon of the interstate, my sleepless night had
caught up with me. I was hoping a little pick-me-up would get me
through the city and through the night.

"Home," I said.

"Ah, yeah? Where you from, sugar?" She slid into the other
side of my booth and set the coffeepot down on a napkin. "You
don't mind, do you? I don't have enough to keep me busy, but
every time I look like I got nothing to do, those dudes"—she
jerked her head over her shoulder at a couple of truckers, the only
other customers—"decide they need to hear the pies again."

Earlier the truckers had been arguing amiably about who'd
seen the worst pile-up in their careers. As far as I was concerned,
they'd tied. I had been trying to shut them out. I had a lot of miles
left to cover. Dark miles on bare, two-lane state roads.

They were doughy men of that age just shy of old. "They're
lonely."

"Everybody who comes in comes lonely. They were each one
lonelier an hour ago."

"They didn't come in together?"

"They found true old-fart love right here at the Quick-Stop, honey. Love to hear themselves talk, I mean," she said. Her name-tag said *Mary Jo*. "What're you going to do when you get home?"

"Pick up my son," I said. "He's—visiting his father."

"I hate those visits. You drop them off as well raised as they're liable to get, and then you pick them up and they're an inch taller and full of shit. It takes six weeks to scrub the taint off them. You just got the one?"

I nodded.

"My boys, when they go down to visit their dad and his mom and dad and his brother and that guy's little band of assholes, they come back sounding like they've been to jerk camp. Be lucky you only got the one. He can't gang up on you."

The truckers exploded into laughter. I looked over at them but Mary Jo wasn't bothered.

"When they sit separate, they all want to talk to me." She fluttered her hand in the direction of the other booth. "They sit together, and they're just little boys. They're all the same."

I lifted the tea to my mouth to keep from having to answer. I'd met plenty of men to prove Mary Jo's theory, but I couldn't believe it applied to all men. What about Joshua? As much as the last few days had staggered me, I wouldn't believe it. I hadn't kept him from every danger, but I had to think that he was still—possible. Joshua was still a possibility.

"Mary *Jo*," said one of the truckers. "Can we hear the pie list again?"

The waitress let her head dip. "They don't want any pie. I'll bring you some more hot water, hon. And a new tea bag. That looks awful."

I needed to get back on the road. My phone said it was almost three in the morning. The phone got service here, so I could tell I had no messages, no texts, no news. But I stayed, watching Mary Jo refill the truckers' coffee cups and recite from memory what the men wanted to hear. I stayed and waited for the hot water and new tea bag I didn't really want, not knowing why I stayed but knowing that it was universal. Everybody who comes in comes lonely.

Blueberry, rhubarb, Dutch apple, cherry, and when Mary Jo brought me a slice without asking which flavor, I picked up my fork and took huge, gulping bites as though it had been months, had been forever, since I'd tasted anything so sweet.

I WOKE ANGRY, my head at an odd angle and my shoulder wedged against the steering wheel. A car horn blared. I jerked upright and the horn cut out, the silence left behind strange. I was parked in a rest area I barely remembered stopping for, and the horn had been my own.

I crawled out of the truck and stretched. After the truck stop, I had lasted only another couple of hours before my lack of sleep had caught up with me. I had a lot of miles left to cover, twisting roads better attacked in daylight. Now my neck was stiff and my head cried out for caffeine and aspirin. Two other cars were parked at the other end of the lot, a few tractor-trailers at ease in their area. I rubbed at my face and arms, walking quickly to the restrooms past the raised-fist map of my home state.

A few minutes later, I was hurrying back to the truck, guzzling a Coke and shoving a candy bar in my pocket when I realized I'd attracted someone's attention. A police officer peered into the passenger window of the SUV.

"Good morning," I said. I'd found aspirin in the vending machine and had all the hope in the world that relief would kick in any second. I could still be in Sweetheart Lake by noon. "There a problem?"

He straightened and held me in his gaze. "Report of a vagrant."

"Is he in my car?"

"Can I ask where you're traveling, ma'am?"

I supposed *no* was the wrong answer. "Just on vacation."

"No particular destination, then?"

Something about his tone struck me as off-tune. I glanced toward the other cars in the lot, hoping someone else was awake. I couldn't end up a televised true crime mystery, not after all this effort. "Visiting relatives. I haven't seen any vagrant, but I haven't been here that long."

"Not too long? Not several hours, and honking your horn for the last two minutes?"

I turned my head to look at the other two cars more closely. One was an open-bed truck marked but unreadable—Department of Transportation, probably. The other was dark, unmarked. "Am I the vagrant?"

The trooper walked around the back of my car, made a show of checking the license plates against a notepad he pulled out of his pocket. I imagined his handwriting: short, squat blocks of letters marching across the page. "Not if you get in your car and get moving."

"That was the plan," I said. He didn't move. I took another sip of my cola.

"Are you Anna Winger?"

A dribble of cola went down my windpipe. I choked, nodding my head. My hand reached toward him. Joshua, oh, God. Joshua. "Is it—my son?"

The trooper stared off toward the ramp back to the highway as though the answer he had to give troubled him. I began to shiver. I'd been riding the right lane all the way, looking for anyone hitchhiking. At overpasses, I slowed and searched the dark reaches, and once I'd seen a pair of shoes up high in the underbelly of a viaduct. It was dark, the road blank, but I stopped and rolled down the window. When no one answered, I turned on the blinkers, got out. But just a few feet closer to the shoes, I could tell that no one was wearing them. The shoes were lined up, left behind, the sort of thing I had to discard before I started assigning meaning.

The trooper sighed and finally looked me in the eye. "Not sure. Got a message, says you're to call in. Parks County, Indiana?"

"You mean the sheriff? Sheriff Russell Keller. How—?"

"Reported you missing."

I waited for a punchline, but none seemed likely. "Missing? But my neighbor—I said—"

"ATL on your plates. Attempt to Locate. You're free to go, but I got to call it in."

I was caught between anger and astonishment. Some sort of *alert* on my vehicle? Was that even legal? Was that even—ethical? What the—was this the game now? When I left his jurisdiction, I had to check out? As if Ray weren't enough, now I had to flee someone who could have me trailed by proxy across state lines, while he was serving the community, handing out handshakes and medallions?

"He would go to a lot of trouble to keep tabs on me."

"Ma'am?"

"What am I supposed to do?" I said.

"You're to call this number." He ripped a half sheet from his notepad and walked it to me.

Up close the trooper seemed a lot younger than I'd taken him for. He was freshly shaven and the collar of his shirt didn't quite fit. I glanced down at the paper in his hand and could read the digits there, just as squat and thick as I'd predicted. I should tell the kiddie cop a few things about himself, shake his faith a bit. But that would take time I didn't have. I dug the keys out of my pocket.

"Ma'am? Please take this."

"What does it matter? I'm not missing. I may never be missing again." They were wasting my time. "Besides, I know that number if I need it."

I DROVE FOR hours before the road finally split and veered into pines. I rolled down the windows, breathing deeply, taking them in. In all the places I'd been since, I hadn't found anywhere that smelled just this way. Maybe I'd chosen all those prairie towns to make sure we'd never settle in, that we'd never find it hard to leave again.

I was getting close, and nervous. An hour or so still before I reached Sweetheart, I drove into a little town that seemed familiar. This old house with the big rock outside and all the flowerpots. That little church.

A new gas station stood where something else used to be. I pulled in, filled the tank. Inside the station, I bought a bottle of aspirin and another cola and tried not to look too closely at the guy at the register. I was close enough to Sweetheart now that I might start to recognize faces. Or they might start to recognize me.

Outside, I held the door for a woman coming in. She paused. "Riverview High?"

I looked up. I'd gone to Riverview, but not with this woman, surely. She was older by at least twenty-five years, her eyes sinking deep into round cheeks.

"Mrs. Brightman." Just saying the name made me want to throw up, but I wasn't sure why. Not yet. These were deeply buried associations rising to the surface. I reached out and held the rim of the nearby trash bin and brought the cool soda can to my forehead.

"That's right! And you are—now let me look at you a second. I have a good memory for Riverview kids." The woman studied me, murmuring under her breath, until at last I saw the past rush up and grip her, and the woman's eyes widened. "Oh. I should have—you're the Winger girl, aren't you? I—hadn't—" She tried to start over. "How *are* you, dear?"

We were on the same terms at last. Mrs. Brightman, the Riverview High school nurse, remembered me now. I let myself remember Mrs. Brightman, her medicinal green smock, the little white closet of a nursing station, and the rough sheets on the cot. Mrs. Brightman's cool hands taking my temperature, her cool voice as she asked if there was any reason I was there, a test I wasn't ready for perhaps. A voice that never strayed, never pried. Not even when it should have.

How *am* I? Would everyone always use that tone of voice on me?

"We see quite a few from Riverview," Mrs. Brightman was prattling. "My husband, Richard? He taught at the elementary in Rhinelander for years and years, but now we've both retired. Don't get into Sweetheart that much. Are you in town to visit—family?"

"You could say that." And she would, I knew. "I need to go, as a matter of fact."

"Won't keep you." Mrs. Brightman looked me up and down, and said, "Well, you turned out just fine, didn't you?"

I launched myself off the sidewalk, across the parking lot, and into my truck. But then I couldn't start it. I pressed my shaking hands to my thighs. I found the control for the windows and rolled them all down.

I was still sitting there when Mrs. Brightman emerged from the station with a half gallon of milk. She walked past my window to her car and noticed me watching her. "It was so *good* to see you," she said. "Leeanna Winger, I've just remembered. An old lady's mind. Be thankful for your youth."

"Mrs. Brightman, my youth was a horror show."

The nurse dropped her keys. Her eyes weren't hiding in her cheeks now.

"If I turned out fine, it is my own doing," I said. "If I turned out fine, it is despite Riverview High, despite my teachers, and despite you."

"Leeanna—"

"I don't go by that name anymore," I said. "That girl is dead, just like you predicted. A lost cause."

"I never thought that." The nurse raised her chin, as though her pride were at stake. It was. It most certainly was, and I meant to drive away with it.

"Why didn't you help me?" I said.

The milk jug dipped heavily in her arms.

"Why didn't anyone help me?" I said.

The woman's eyes would no longer meet mine. "I didn't know," she whispered. "It was a different time . . . a different—things are different now."

I searched for something smug and cutting to say. The only thing I could think of was one of Margaret's. "That is bull and I know bull when I see it." If I ever saw Margaret again, I'd have to tell her. But if I got the chance to tell the story, I'd have to embellish a bit, because it didn't feel good at all to say it. Not when it was true, and not when saying it couldn't change a thing.

Chapter Twenty-eight

The town rolled into view, and it was like any other town I had passed on the trip.

Life went on. In Sweetheart Lake, the town I'd fled thirteen years ago, groceries were being bought and sold, kids were sitting in classrooms, and their parents were over in Rhinelander or St. Germain showing real estate or selling hardware. It was the off-season, so when the road veered from the highway, and I passed the first signs of town—the Stag, open only for dinner now, the road toward Theresa's grandfather's cabin on Midnight Lake, and at last the little market that sold eight kinds of jerky and wooden bears that the artists carved with chainsaws and axes right there in the parking lot—the place seemed just as I'd left it. Quiet, and willing to let me leave. I could turn around now, and nobody would ever know. No one would ever care.

At first what I noticed was how much I remembered. The forest station. My heart gave a little leap at the visage of Smokey the Bear and his fire safety sign. The risk of forest fires was *HIGH*. That little frame house next door had been turned into a café.

I drove so slowly, a truck behind me pulled around on a double yellow, just to be rid of me, and I nodded, yes, yes, this was all what I had expected. The same gas station on the left. The same curve, and the main street stretched to the horizon.

Among the T-shirt shops and knickknack stores, the same stores I'd browsed in my youth, I parked and got out, legs stiff. The same store where Theresa and I went to get *I Heart Sweetheart Lake* T-shirts to wear to Senior Day at school, a joke that not everyone understood. *That's not funny*, the other kids said uncertainly. Was it that T-shirt shop, or had it been so long that the places I remembered had as many cat's lives as I had, closing and reopening, closing and reopening so that I couldn't tell the difference now? Could anyone tell the difference?

Still there: the famous fudge store, where the tourists pressed their greasy hands to the glass to watch local kids making the candy every summer. The bookstore with its half-timber façade.

So much the same, but I could see what had changed, too. The town had a sort of grit to it that I didn't remember. Another real estate office with a for-lease sign in its own window. A family restaurant closed for the season or maybe forever. The old bank had been turned into a gift shop that specialized in dog figurines, dog mugs, kitchen towels with dogs on them.

A white-haired couple, late-season tourists wearing high socks and bright new tennis shoes, stepped away from the dog store window and into my path. The woman and I, face-to-face, did the awkward lurch people do when they are just trying to get by, the woman laughing after the second dodge failed. "May I have this dance?" the man said. I didn't laugh. I wasn't there. I was already around the corner, aghast at how much had changed, how much for the worse the town had fared in the decade-plus I'd been gone.

"Excuse us," said a woman's low voice. I stood back and let the woman pass. On her shoulder, a little boy lay his head. He stared back at me, his thumb in his mouth.

My breath caught in my throat. The boy reminded me of Joshua. But he looked nothing like Joshua, now or when he was that age. Trick of the light, trick of the mind—for just a moment I'd known him. Would every mother's son remind me of my own, until he was back with me?

I watched the woman and the boy until they turned a corner, and then I went back to my tour. The town had expanded. Streets had been rerouted and buildings torn down to make room for a couple of fast-food places and a shiny yellow convenience store. In the distance, the pink neon of the Dairy Bar. At least that was still intact.

The town I remembered was here, and not here. I could see both at the same time, the ghost and the actual.

I thought I might cry or throw up, but I couldn't tell which. I'd expected the town to be the same, but not this much the same, and I'd expected it to be changed, but not this changed. I had no right to say that Sweetheart Lake had been better before, that the old bank was more useful than a dog souvenir shop. I didn't get a vote. But I felt the changes in a deep place in my gut that I hadn't known would be there. My grief made no sense, except that I knew it wasn't just the buildings torn down, the changing of the T-shirt shop guard.

It wasn't the stuff. It was the time. The time spent and gone and, at the moment, nothing to show for it. That little boy on his mother's shoulder would grow up in town and not know the difference. The town would be fine to him, until he left and came back and saw how the one place where he should be necessary would go on without him.

I turned to look back down Pine Street and stood there for a good long while with no fear that anyone would recognize me. Ray himself could walk by. I was invisible.

I HAD TWO addresses culled from the internet and a choice to make. Be a coward and go find Theresa first as my backup, or be brave and find Ray—and Joshua—alone. The thought of seeing Joshua, of wrapping my arms around him for as many seconds as he would allow, made my chest tight. But Ray. How angry would he be by now? What would he risk in front of Joshua? If I went to Theresa first, I'd have a witness—maybe. Maybe Theresa would talk to me. Or maybe I'd have to spend real time trying to make Theresa understand, real time I should spend finding Joshua.

Joshua. The right choice was Joshua. I wasn't sure I was brave enough for the right choice, but I drove that way, hoping I would gain courage as I went.

The town was still too small. In no time at all, I had passed the address I'd memorized by now and had to circle the block again. On the second try, I parked. The houses looked as though they'd been purchased from a catalog. Ray's house was white and boxy, the lawn a little patch of deep green. I stared at the curtains, hoping for movement. Or if I waited long enough, for Joshua to emerge on his own.

The entire street was still, except a lone car crossing at the next block. No one walked by or came to the window. There was nothing to do but go to the door and see what would happen. I imagined what Russ Keller would say about a plan like that.

I slid out of the truck and approached the house, wishing I had something, anything, in my hands. With every step, I expected the door to swing open and for someone to shout me down. But the door stayed closed, the curtains stayed drawn. I reached the stoop and the doorbell without incident, and had nothing to do but push the button.

A dog yipped. Claws scrabbled against the floor inside and up to the door. No steps. No voices.

I gave the door a chance to open, glancing uneasily up and down the street. A neighbor would be watching. If they knew me, they'd stick their heads out of their doors and tell me when to try again. But I was a stranger. They'd watch to see what I did, dialing the local posse if they saw me heading toward trouble. My out-of-state plates had already been noted.

I had decided to go when I saw the corner of an envelope poking from the half-open mailbox. I tugged on the envelope until I could see it was addressed to—David Cotter, Jr. I opened the mailbox and dug the rest of the contents out. Let the neighbors call the police. I had a few things to report, too. Cotter, Cotter, David, Christine Cotter. One of the magazines was a woodworking magazine. I dropped the mail back into the box and walked, unhurried, to my truck. Relieved. This was not the place.

Chapter Twenty-nine

I parked in town, bumping up against the curb and then shoving the meter full of quarters. An upstanding citizen.

I walked Pine Street, taking a better look in the storefronts and seeing no one I should have known or who should have known me. I moved from one window to the next, not engaging. The summer tourists were back home and the winter tourists not yet on the horizon, the kids in school, the college students back on campus, the working people at their stations. I was a single woman walking unhurriedly down a bare street, worthy of note. But maybe that wasn't such a bad idea, being noticed. I had to figure out where Ray was, but I wasn't sure what would happen when I did.

I reached the north end of town where the streets had gotten their makeover and looked around. What I needed was a headquarters. A phone book. A phone, since mine hadn't been able to find service in the last fifty miles.

And then I saw the answer: the Clipper. It was right where I left it, the siding still weathered like a shack on a dock, the sign still pale and unwelcoming. Inside, it was dark. In the second it took for my eyes to adjust, I wondered at my own idiocy. This was one of Ray's hangouts, and I'd walked right in.

"Ahoy," said a voice from the direction of the bar.

My eyes finally found the source of the greeting. A middle-aged man with a round belly over the top of his pants sat on a stool at the back of the bar. He didn't look familiar. I hoped I didn't, either. Someone wanting to make conversation would *ahoy* him back. "I'll have a root beer," I said, sitting as far away as I could. I glanced around at the framed ads for fish sticks and beer, the tables with fishhooks and lures caught forever underneath thick shellac, yellow with age.

He put the root beer in front of me and slid a menu across the bar.

"Do you have a phone book?"

"Stolen," he said.

That jibed nicely with what I remembered about the place. I ordered the first sandwich off the menu so that he would have something to do while I made a plan.

I still had a visit to Theresa in my back pocket, but that prospect seemed further from reality every time I thought about it. We'd been friends thirteen years ago. If I'd stayed in Sweetheart, would we have found a way to bridge the next year, let alone a dozen or more?

All along, I had been thinking of Theresa as the young woman I'd left. She would look the same, she'd be in the same job. She'd lean out of the door of her same house, her face opening up into her wide grin. She might even cry. I had imagined the reunion enough times over the years, but that part never changed. Theresa might cry with relief to see me again—alive, well, strong. But we'd been estranged by the time I'd left. She couldn't stand to watch what was happening to me. I'd also seen the town now. I'd *seen* thirteen years. Things could be so different than I'd hoped. What if Theresa hadn't thought of me at all? Or, if she had, if she remembered all the times the girl I'd been had needed her, had leaned on her without taking her advice. If she thought of me at all, maybe all she remembered was how one-sided our friendship had been. No big loss. A relief, really.

I'd felt the same way when I'd seen my mother's obituary in the online edition of the hometown paper. My father's name, not listed. Good. I'd clicked away immediately, but it was too late. I raced to the bathroom to throw up and then back to the computer to find the notice again. To know—I couldn't not know. To see it through, though I knew I hadn't. I had already missed the funeral by months. Anguish that felt strangely like release. Nothing tied me to Sweetheart Lake anymore.

The barman came back with my sandwich. He tucked himself back onto his stool to watch the TV in the corner. I took a big bite. When I glanced up, the barman had turned his attention my way. "Hungry, huh?"

My mouth was too full to do anything but nod.

"From around here?"

Now I was thankful for the food in my mouth.

"Got a place up here?" he said.

A *place*. That's what we used to say. If you're not from around here, you still might have a place. You might be a neighbor, a summer neighbor, and bring the kids or grandkids to fish and boat and splash in one of the lakes. You might turn your place into a rental, shilling it out by the week to Chicagoans willing to pay fifteen hundred dollars or more to sit around the fire pit and slap at mosquitoes. You might visit two weeks a year or you might come up every weekend of the summer, but a *place* gave you a little heads up over a tourist, which was the worst thing to be.

"Just visiting," I said around a mouthful. "Just *touring* around."

The sea captain grunted. "Off-season. Got it to yourself."

"That's the way I like it." I shoved another giant bite into my mouth and looked away.

Bells jangled at the back of the building, and a couple came in from the alley.

"Ahoy," the woman cried. She was skinny and held together by tight, bad jeans and a tighter sweater. She grinned, showing off a missing tooth deep in her mouth. The guy with her was solid, thick from head to boots, his skin so red that he could have been spit-roasted.

"Betty Spaghetti," the barman said, sounding pleased. "Jim. You're in a little early."

Betty chose a stool and hopped onto it. "'s Friday somewhere."

I stopped chewing. As far as I knew, it was Friday *here*. Joshua had been gone three days. The food in my mouth had turned to concrete. I put a napkin to my lips and spit it out. Three days, and here I was, a lady who lunches. I pictured Joshua standing by the side of the road, hungry. Arriving at last at his father's house, only to find the unwelcome mat rolled out.

I shoved the plate away. Betty, Jim, and the sea captain, whose name turned out to be the landlocked Chuck, sorted out the need for brews and burgers and the predicted score of a game that was not yet being played. Betty looked away first, noticing me. "Hey, girl. How's that working for you?"

"What?"

She gestured toward the half-eaten sandwich.

"Oh, it's good. Highly recommend."

Betty blinked. "Are you a reviewer or something?"

The men both turned to look at me.

"No. Just a . . . tourist."

"Off-season, baby," Betty said.

"No good fishing in the damn lake," Jim said.

Chuck refilled Jim's beer. "Duke and his kid got some walleye this morning, they said."

"Duke is a liar," Jim said. "And so's his kid."

Betty leaned down the bar. "They don't like Duke because their wives like Duke too much," she stage-whispered. "What's to see this late in the year? The *colors*?" The missing tooth winked at me. I was Betty's big catch of the day.

"Seeing some—" Old friends? Relatives? "Sights."

Jim snorted. "Trees, trees, and more trees."

"Lakes," Betty said, defensively. "Are you staying on a lake? You got a place up here?"

"No," I said. "Might be heading home again, soon. Indiana," I added, before they asked. They would have asked. They all nodded.

"Got a cousin lives down near Tell City," Jim said.

Tell City meant nothing to me. But then I thought of a way out of my deadlock. "I used to have a cousin up here," I said, as if I'd just remembered. "Ray Levis?"

"You're Ray Levis's cousin?" Betty had an uncertain smile on her face.

"No shit?" Chuck said. "Been sitting here all this time."

I'd made a mistake. The Clipper could still be Ray's hangout. He might be due any minute—it was Friday somewhere.

"Distant," I said. "Like, three times removed or something."

"You been to see him yet?" Betty said.

So he was still here, despite the address from the web being a bust. "I went to the house on Elm."

"He ain't been there for a while," Jim offered. "He gave up city living a while back."

City living. Only someone who had lived in Sweetheart Lake his whole life could say it with sincerity. But if Ray had given up the city, and the city was Sweetheart Lake, that meant—

"His place is out on Dam Lake," Chuck said. He checked with Jim. "Is that St. Germain or is that Eagle River?"

"That's Sugar Camp," Betty said. She laughed. "I remember, because *Sugar Camp*, come on."

"Unincorporated," Jim chimed in. No town, then. Ray Levis lived on some quiet county road with as many inches of lakefront as he could afford, and if there was someone who could live without people, without even a town to call his own, it was Ray.

Chuck began to draw a squiggle-line map for me on a napkin. "You'll have to go out there. He doesn't come in much anymore. Not sure he even has a phone."

"Ray Levis," Betty said, shaking her head. "Whatever happened to that deal? You know . . . with that girl?"

Jim frowned at her. "What deal?"

"Don't you remember that fuss with the cops and that woman who kept saying that Ray had killed her sister?"

I let my root beer mug thud to the bar.

"Weren't her sister. Her friend," Chuck said. "You want a refill?"

I shook my head and dug into my purse for cash. I had to listen carefully to hear around the rush of blood in my ears.

Chuck got Betty a refill. She wrapped her hands around the mug. "Yeah. What was the girl's name?"

"That was a bunch of bullshit," Jim said. "That was twenty years ago. Never heard from that girl again."

"Which is why it makes sense." A slur was creeping into Betty's voice, but she had adopted a serious expression, as though the matter, twenty years old or not, would be decided right here at the Clipper, today. "Right? You *remember*. The blood they found. I mean, if anybody'd heard from her, then it could be bull."

"Someone heard from her," Chuck said. "Didn't they?"

"Ray Levis didn't even hunt." Jim slapped his hand on the bar.

Betty snorted. "Lots of men in this county don't hunt. Except for new ways to make their women miserable."

Jim crossed his arms and watched the TV with resolve, so Betty leaned over the bar at Chuck. "You knew him. And, wait, cousin-girl, you knew him." She swiveled on her stool to look at me.

"Not really," I said.

"Wouldn't hurt a fly," Jim muttered.

Chuck stood to take my money, offered the change. When I shook my head, he folded the bills away and stood staring at me, kindly, intellectually, the way I might study a signature I'd seen by accident—someone's signature in line at the bank, say, or a hand-lettered sign in a shop window.

"I don't want to speak ill of your *family*," Chuck said. He slid the hand-drawn map across the bar. "But the way I remember Ray Levis is, if there ever was a guy who would hurt a fly just to hurt a fly, it was him."

Chapter Thirty

The Northwoods were for getting lost, getting forgotten.

A certain breed was drawn to dense woods, to the sparse population. People with grudges and grudges against them. People with bad families, bad credit, bad exes.

That was always the problem with my escape plan. I watched the trees fall away to each side of the road through the truck's windshield. I was always trying to find a hiding place from the best hiding place in the world.

The road curved through the forest and around the lakes. The colors, Betty had said, but it was the green that made my heart ache. The pine trees on one side of the road were skinny and exposed, trimmed away from the telephone wires, but beyond their knock-kneed youth were the elders, all rough trunks and black needles. The river crossed under the highway and fell into place on my left, the water tumbling around rocks and smoothing to green glass as it deepened.

When the paper napkin map said to turn, I did, and then again, until all I could see past the scrub near the road were pines and the dark knees of white aspen. Trees, trees, and more trees, as the guy in the bar had said. He might feel differently about the woods if he'd been living in Parks County, Indiana. Town of Parks, tree population: three. Here the sun cut lines of gold through the thick canopy like spotlights.

The map guided me through a series of turns, the roads twisting around an unseen lake.

My family had never had a *place*, of course, since we'd barely been able to keep a roof over us at all. But Theresa's family had, and I'd spent weeks of several summers in a row as the assumed guest. The family compound was a tradition, all the cousins finding a way to converge. At Theresa's, I would find myself surrounded by a matched set of adults, the women shy in their suits and the men pale-bellied. Adults who threw their heads back and laughed, who didn't seem in a hurry, or anxious, or angry. At Theresa's, we spent the sunshine hours running around the land in our suits, jumping off the end of the dock whenever we got hot. When our stomachs growled, we went up to grab hot dogs and bags of chips and ate with our water-pruned fingers back on the dock, as if we feared the lake wouldn't be there if we stayed away too long.

It was one of those summer days on the lake with Theresa when I had met Ray, though neither of us brought it up later, when things went bad. When Theresa couldn't stand to be around me because I had gone back again. Back then Theresa worked at her parents' T-shirt shop but on her day off we went to one of the coves to sun ourselves. The inside of my mouth was sore from too many sugary candies, and I was stupid from the heat.

"Yuck," Theresa said, kicking at the water.

"What?" I was leaning back on a boulder. I was hotter than a human should be allowed to get.

"Why do they have to die here? I want to swim."

"What's dying?"

"The mayflies," she said.

"They don't die at the water's edge, dumbass," said a male voice high above us.

We both turned and looked up. Theresa pulled her towel from the rocks and tucked it around her. She's grown into her suit that summer, maybe a little too much. Some of the men in town had started watching us as we passed by, but it wasn't me who caught their eyes. The guy above us, though, wasn't looking at her. I smiled and he smiled back.

"They die everywhere," he said. He was older than we were by a few years, tan and muscular in a way that the guys in our grade had yet to figure out. He wore wet jean shorts, and that was all. His hair dripped onto his chest. "They die everywhere and then the water brings them to the edges. It's not some big plan to ruin your swim today."

Theresa didn't like being called a dumbass. And she didn't like having someone crouched over us, talking down. And maybe she didn't like that the guy—the man—doing the talking hadn't given her a moment's notice. If he'd flirted with her at all, I might never have learned the man's name. "What are you even doing up there?" Theresa said, pouting like a baby.

"Jumping off the high dive," he said. He looked at me. "You want to come up?"

"Don't you dare," Theresa said under her breath. Theresa was safety in human form to me, but she was also too careful for a girl who'd never faced a single barrier in life. She could wear makeup. She could go on dates. She could drive and hold a job. She could wear short sleeves without anyone asking about her bruises. In a year, she'd be gone, in college probably. I would be here. If she hadn't told me what to do, though, I wouldn't have taken the dare.

I was already rising and looking for a good handhold in the rock.

I climbed, certain until the very end. He reached down and pulled me up the rest of the way.

"Look at you," he said quietly, and did. I couldn't breathe. "What's your name?"

"Leeanna," I said.

"Well, Ell, what are you going to do? There's only one way down."

He still held my hand. I shook it off, gazed out at the lake for a moment, and then ran toward the edge. Behind me I heard someone screaming and someone laughing. I stretched toward the water, knowing I would climb up again. Dripping, shaking, the lake water in the back of my throat. I would do it, just to fly again.

I shook off the memories and followed the road deeper into the woods, past turnoffs for a summer camp and a series of rentals with cute names. *Pining for Home. Honeymoon Hideaway.* Past the white arrow signs for a hundred families, and then I saw the one I'd been looking for and dreading: *Levis.*

The feathered arrow signs were supposed to look hand painted, but they weren't. At least not by the owner. That kind of sign would have given me some advanced notice. Who was this Ray Levis? This lake-living, place-owning Ray Levis who wouldn't hurt a fly? My gut twisted into a fist, but I drove through it.

At the last turn into his gravel drive, I paused. It was not too late to turn around. Up ahead I could see a clearing, a deck, and a steep drop to a lake. Trees blocked the house. Again I hoped to see Joshua strolling across the open lawn with a paper plate of sandwiches, going down to the dock. I drove up the lane into view of the house, a single-story ranch. I figured I had the element of surprise, and so parked and walked quickly to the door and knocked, all business.

When nothing happened, I turned and took a better look at the property. There was a shed to one side of the house, a neat stack of cut logs, a hammock, a picnic table. The deck that overlooked the lake stood empty but for a grill. I heard a splash down at the lakeside and followed the sound.

Steps led from the deck down to another level, with a table and chairs and more steps down to the water.

At the end of the L-shaped dock stood Joshua.

He threw a stick into the water. A black dog leapt in and paddled out to fetch it.

A sob caught in my throat. Joshua turned—

It wasn't Joshua. Just the one person I should have been prepared to see.

Ray, wearing a ball cap and the same profile as my son, turned all the way around and stared. We regarded each other as the dog swam up from the lake to a shallow spot and launched back onto the deck. The dog dropped the stick, shook water off its coat, and, catching sight of me, bolted up the steep stairs, howling.

I turned and fled, bile rising in my throat.

"Magic!" Ray yelled. "Magic, no! Knock it off!"

I heard his footsteps up the stairs and didn't know whether I was running from Ray or the dog.

"She won't bite!"

I found the door of the truck before the dog could bite or not bite, and hopped inside. I was shaking: my hands, my whole body. My heart battered against the inside of my chest. The dog ran up to my window and sat below, crooning. I locked both doors of the truck just as Ray reached the top deck but couldn't begin to roll up the window. I held onto the steering wheel to keep from shaking. He came to the driver's side and scolded the dog. The dog's tail thumped against his leg.

He took his time meeting my eyes. I waited, wave after wave of nausea washing over me.

"I can't believe it," he said. "Do you know—?" But he wouldn't ask whatever it was.

"You had to expect I'd show up," I said. "At some point." I glanced toward the house to see if Joshua had come out yet. Surely the dog was doorbell enough.

"Fifteen *years* ago."

"Thirteen."

He turned to face me through the window. He was too close. I wished I'd rolled up the window while the dog was still yowling.

"Thirteen, then," he said. "What the—what does it matter? Thirteen years ago, your friend tried to convince the cops I'd killed you and dug you a grave in the woods."

"No, you would have weighted me down in the middle of Sweetheart Lake."

His hand froze on the dog's square head. I glanced toward the house again and back at Ray. Now that I'd brought it up, it felt like anything could happen. Probably best not to turn my back. I was here.

"Really, Ray, tell me that wasn't a plan you had in the back of your mind all along."

"I never—"

"You'd better think hard about what you *never* did before you say so," I said. "There are very few things you *never* did."

He contemplated the open lake. "I guess you wouldn't take an apology."

"Is that the apology? No, I don't really need an apology."

"I looked for you. I hired a private eye."

I remembered the call. Three moves from state to state hadn't been far enough. The call in the night, no one saying anything when I said hello. I had calmly stripped our lives out of that apartment, packed Joshua and what little I could grab, and driven through the night, looking for a place to land. I remembered every trigger, every flight. "I know," I said.

"That was you, wasn't it? That time." His face stretched into an awkward, triumphant smile. "You hung up."

"I hung up and moved to a different state."

"But," he said. The smile disappeared. "They thought I killed you."

I wanted to say that he had, but he wouldn't understand. "You almost did."

The dog shifted and whined at Ray's feet. He knelt on the pink dirt and scratched at the dog's ears. "We're going in circles here. If you're not here for your apology—why are you here?"

I took a last look at the house, but there was no movement at the windows, no one coming out to see who was in the drive. "But—"

And then I knew. Joshua had never made it to Ray's.

Ray stood, saw the look on my face. "What?" He stepped up to the truck. I slid away from the window. "Oh. Look," he said. "I'm not that guy anymore."

I took a deep breath and let it shudder out. "Why would I believe that?"

"I guess you wouldn't." He backed away, his hands raised. "But it's true."

I thought of my dad, angry as long as I'd known him and probably before I'd been born. I didn't believe him. I couldn't.

The dog barked and darted out from under Ray's hand to meet a small white car pulling into the drive. Ray went to meet the driver. A woman got out, scratched the dog's ears, and straightened to accept a cheek kiss from Ray.

"It's been a weird couple of minutes," he said to her. The woman watched Ray with concern as they walked up to the truck. I unlocked the door and slid out, the dog racing over to sniff at my legs.

Ray swept his hand in my direction. "Mamie, this is Leeanna Winger."

We looked each other up and down, me looking for signs that Mamie was the same kind of girlfriend I had once been. No bruises visible. She was sturdy, almost plump. Her hair was a fading blond, cut short and left to do whatever it wanted.

Mamie's mouth fell open. "You mean—"

Ray nodded and Mamie jumped into his arms. When she twisted her head on Ray's chest to see me, there were tears in her eyes. "It's been such a long road," she said.

"You can't be serious," I said.

The couple parted slowly, their dog wedging in between their feet. "It's just," Mamie said. "Well, you wouldn't believe the looks he gets in town. The way our neighbors would pull their daughters away from him on the street. It was just—we had to move."

A hot rage was beginning to boil in my belly. "You had to move? Out to the lake? You poor, poor people." I had moved six times, eight, whenever a cloud looked a little too gray, whenever someone gave me that don't-I-know-you look.

"You don't understand—"

"No, I don't think you understand," I said.

"My wife knows everything about me," Ray said. "She knows what I did."

"Oh, really? There's nothing I could tell her that would surprise her? That you beat me? That you broke my arm?" I turned to the woman, who was nodding. She had the decency to look ashamed, as though she'd let him do these things. "That you kept me so tightly under your thumb that I was afraid to breathe? That you threatened my life? That you did, in fact, try to murder me?"

Mamie said nothing, but she was clearly not alarmed.

"I told her everything," Ray said. "And I told her that I didn't kill you. She's the only one to believe me."

"Well, Mamie," I said, giving her a wicked smile. "I guess it's lucky you were right."

The woman stiffened. "I loved him. And I believed in love."

"I used to love him, too. Believe me, it was no good place to be."

"He's done counseling and anger management, and he's just really worked on—"

"Oh, God," I cried and pressed my hands over my ears. "I care so little. I'm glad you can parade up and down Pine Street with your head held high now, really I am. I'm so very happy that you're fulfilled and counseled and managed. But I didn't come here for this."

"So, why did you come?" Mamie said.

I dropped my hands, helpless. If Joshua wasn't here, then where in the world was he?

I hesitated, looking between the two of them. Mamie had taken Ray's hand, and Ray was as lost as I'd ever seen him. A little saggy at the corners of his eyes, a little thicker through the waist. And—diminished, I supposed, in his baggy shorts and tennis shoes. He didn't look so big or so strong. He seemed a little square, actually, the exact kind of guy he would have made fun of back when we were together, and if the guy had any balls and defended himself against Ray's taunts, the kind of guy Ray would have beaten to a meaty pulp.

The man standing before me now was a mystery. He seemed

genuinely happy to see me alive, curious to see why I'd come. I
wondered: Is it possible? Can he be this different? I might have
doubted my memory, except that Ray and Mamie had confirmed
the facts with their grim silence. Can he be different enough?
Can he deserve what I was about to give him?

I said, "I have news that should surprise you both."

Magic sat at my feet and swept the dirt with her tail until I
reached out and laid a hand on her black head.

Chapter Thirty-one

Ray raged, silent, at the kitchen table.

Mamie reached for him, but he drew his arm out of her grasp. The house was small, tightly furnished. I was the thing out of place and kept banging my knees on things until we sat down to have tea. Like civilized people. I gazed in wonder at the framed cross-stitch of a basket of fruit on the wall, the ruffle-edged throw pillows on the couch.

Ray had begun to resemble the man I remembered. And then he went pale.

"What?" I pushed away from the table, hard enough to make the ice in my tea clink against the glass.

Ray put his palms on the tabletop and regarded them. "*How old is he?*"

"Thirteen, honey," Mamie said. "She's been gone—"

"But he's practically—" His mouth opened and closed like a fish pulled out of the lake. "How tall is he?"

Mamie laughed. I managed to turn the corners of my mouth up. I was sure it was charming for his wife to see him so flummoxed—an understandable reaction from a man finding out he'd fathered a son he didn't know about. But it was not the reaction I had expected, or even hoped for. Already I felt closed in by Ray's interest, by this place. I'd only come here to find Joshua, and now that he wasn't here, I wanted to be out the door and down the road. I had phone calls to make and a nine-hour drive to compress as tightly as I could. I hadn't come all this way to make Ray a father.

"Do you have a picture?"

"In the truck." When I stood to go get it, Ray's face slackened around hard eyes. He looked just like Joshua, calling me a liar.

"I'll bring it back." Not that the escape plan hadn't occurred to me.

I dug through two or three of the bags in the back of the truck before I found the framed photo from the apartment. At the door, I hesitated. I really could jump in the truck and be half-way to Oshkosh before anyone noticed. They didn't know where I lived—and I didn't even live there anymore. Let them find my ransacked apartment, my old phone bills and full trash bins. Let them talk to Margaret and the sheriff. What would it gain them? I was already free from that place, and the next time I alighted, maybe I'd ask Kent about changing my last name, too.

I looked at the photo in my hand. Except. As long as Joshua was gone, I was stuck being who I was, where I was.

Inside, Ray took the frame with shaking hands. "He has my—"

"Everything," I said. "He looks just like you."

Mamie studied Joshua over his shoulder. "I can see a little of you in him, too, Leeanna."

This was going to be a long night, if I had to start with *Leeanna*. "Can I use your phone? I'm afraid it's going to be long distance."

MAMIE SENT ME to their bedroom for privacy.

Ray had a startlingly normal bedroom. Sky-blue walls, quilt on the bed. It was crammed with a giant four-poster and accompanying suite. Another room furnished with pieces from another, bigger house.

The dispatcher wouldn't put me through. "Is this an emergency?" the woman asked. I had never met any of the dispatchers and couldn't picture her. "I can call a unit in to assist you. But the sheriff's off radio at the moment. He's entitled to some downtime."

"He put an *alert* on my license plate," I said. "If he's so interested in where I am, then I think he'll take my phone call."

On hold, I took the opportunity to look around. On the dresser sat a framed snapshot of Ray and Mamie standing with their arms around each other. It was recent, candid. They didn't seem aware of the camera. Some friend had taken it at a social gathering, maybe. Ray had a friend. He went to social gatherings. I waited for the dispatcher or Russ, trying not to tally my life against Ray's.

When Russ finally answered, he didn't sound interested at all. "I'm a busy man, Ms. Winger."

"Spray-painting blazes on all the cars of Parks County? Just in case they, you know, leave the area?"

"I don't have time for this." His voice was distant, as though he'd put me on speakerphone. I hated that.

"Do you have time for a check-up on my case? Or does my missing son cut into your *downtime?*"

"I'm not sure a woman who left the town her son was missing from is so concerned about getting her kid back."

"Don't be an ass—" A huge noise cut me off. It was the siren rising and falling with the flick of a switch. He was driving. Using his privileges to bypass red lights, probably. I was sick to think of the day in the barn now. I hated everything about him and that little kingdom of his.

"That is not the way to get a public servant on your side," he said when the siren cut out.

"I thought he was here."

He waited.

"He's not," I said.

"Where are you?"

"I'd rather not say. I might—"

"What?"

"Nothing." I might need Sweetheart yet. Now that I knew I didn't have much to fear here, what was to stop me from bringing Joshua back? We could get our own place. I imagined it for a moment, surrounded again by the pines.

"You should get your son back before you start burrowing in," he said.

"Has he called?"

"No." He sounded tired.

"Do I have to ask—or can you help me out here?"

"Nothing has changed about your case. We don't know anything more."

"Are you trying to know more?"

"This is at least the third time you've called my professional abilities into question," he said. "If you'll remember, I haven't found that characteristic charming in the past."

"It's just—I thought he was here."

He sighed. "I understand."

"I banked everything on him being here."

"Come back to Parks."

"There's nowhere else I can think of—"

"Come back," he said. "We're doing everything we can, but you should be here when he gets here. And he will."

"I don't understand it. This is where he should be."

The sheriff hit the siren again, and for a moment all I could hear was the giant white noise overpowering the phone line. When the siren cut out, the silence was keen.

"Hello?" I said, oddly panicked that I'd lost him.

He said, "He should be with you. Wherever you are."

I was so exhausted. The phone felt heavy in my hand. "I'll start home tomorrow."

"Your cell phone doesn't work up there, huh?"

"Trying to keep better tabs on me?"

"Keep you better updated," he said. "When you're back, I'll send Mullen over to go through everything again. Maybe there's something we're missing."

"Mullen?" The distance in his voice was no longer just physical.

"I'm out of the area a day, two at the most, and then I'll stop by myself. If that's—if you want me to." He cleared his throat. "I'm chasing down a goose on the Ransey case."

Aidan's image came to me. By now the thought of him out there on his own hurt me almost as much as missing Joshua. I imagined Aidan's small body in his mother's arms on the town square, his head against her shoulder, his thumb in his mouth. I didn't know why that's how I saw him, but the image made me worry for him even more.

"How are you so sure it's just a goose?"

"I'm not, which is why I'm going," he said. "Got to meet up with a local constable. He won't know anything. Long drive to confirm nothing is nothing."

"Where?"

"Well, I'd rather not say. I might want to build a secret fortress there."

"Did you ever figure out the evidence forms thing?"

"Anna. You're off duty."

Off duty sounded suspiciously like *out of line.* "Only trying to help."

"Just trying to keep my head clear, and when you're helping—well. Let's just say you're distracting."

He was distracting, too, but I didn't want to say it. I couldn't say it, and there was no point. Only Joshua mattered. I was the one who couldn't be distracted.

"I'll try to stay out of it," I said. "Good night."

I HADN'T WANTED to stay the night, but Mamie bested me. I needed an early start and didn't relish finding a room in one of the log motels where the snowmobile kamikazes camped out every winter. I was so tired the prospect of finding another place to sleep seemed as complex as a NASA reentry from space. So when Mamie started fixing up the couch, I gave up arguing.

"What's he like? What was he like as a baby?" Mamie was stuffing a giant pillow into its case. In the next room, Ray still sat at the kitchen table studying the photo. He hadn't said a word since I'd gotten off the phone.

I perched on the edge of a chair and rubbed my face. "He was a good baby. Quiet. Not a crier."

"Like one of those that always gazes around at the world through huge eyes," Mamie said. "They're seeing everything, and nothing meets with their full approval. Like old men."

They saw everything, all right. "That's my boy." I glanced over at Ray, but he didn't seem to be listening. "You two don't have any children?"

Mamie smoothed out another layer of thin blanket on the couch, her back a little too straight. The dog lay at her feet, her eyes rolling to watch everything Mamie did.

I sighed. "That was really nosey. I'm a little rusty on social graces."

"It's OK. We just—we found each other late, and then just never had any luck." Mamie finished her nesting with a last plump of the pillow and sat in a chair across the room. I could see the two of them there, each night returning to their spots. Mamie in her chair with the craft basket at her feet, and he in—in this recliner I couldn't quite settle into.

Mamie stared out the sliding glass doors into the dark trees. "No luck at all there, but we've had a lot of grace. I'm not ungrateful."

"Luck," I said. "In my case, bad luck. At least that's how I felt at the time."

"Were you scared?"

"To death." For a second, I let myself think of the blood that must have pooled on the dock. If he'd known I was pregnant, he might have held my head under the water long enough to follow through.

Mamie turned to look at Ray, brooding over the photo. "It's hard to imagine now. I'm—I'm just so sorry."

"You have nothing to apologize for." I hadn't lost track of Ray's apology, which hadn't yet come. I wasn't sure I wanted to hear it.

"But you know how it is. Men and their feelings, never the twain shall meet. We stand in for them in times like this." Mamie looked at me for confirmation. "You know what I mean? Like when Ray's dad was sick in the hospital. It was chaos, just utter—he was crazed from the drugs they had him on, poor soul. And I held Big Ray's hand and calmed him down, just like he was my own, because I knew Ray couldn't. They're not born that way, but they're not raised that way, either. It's just one of the things we do."

I didn't think that was true. I'd heard Joe Jeffries's voice, trying to tell me the truth about Joshua, heard Russ calming the startled animal right out of me with a few words. But I didn't want to get into it. "I've never been anyone's wife."

"Oh. I didn't mean—I just mean we *women*. Maybe that's not lady lib enough, but I think we do what we can, and some things are easier for me than for Ray." She turned her eyes on him again. "Like for instance. Right now he's stunned and he can't say what's in his heart. I don't think he knows all what's in there right now."

I barely stifled a yawn. "You do, though?"

"I usually do. There's a lot competing for his attention right now. Love he can't explain. And worry that he won't be able to explain it to me, that I'll take offense. Disappointment that Joshua doesn't have any half siblings. And regret. Thirteen years is a lot of time to miss." She avoided meeting my eyes. "Lots of regret."

Watching Ray rub his thumb methodically across the image of my son made me crazy. Given the chance, I'd leave right now and keep Joshua to myself forever. Regrets for leaving. Regrets for coming back. Regrets of such size that they seemed to be welling up and choking me from the inside. Or maybe that was the anger. I could still feel some of that, too. Thirteen years is a lot of time to miss. No one knew that better than I did.

Mamie hoisted herself to her feet. In the low light from the kitchen, she looked tired and older, and I imagined that's how I looked to her, too. "We all have some regret, Leeanna. Sometimes I think that's what we're made for. Humans. No matter what we do, we regret what we didn't."

I didn't answer. Mamie sounded to me like a woman who hadn't suffered, not quite as much as she thought she had.

Chapter Thirty-two

I slept badly. I woke once in the night from a dream—words scribbling across the same blue field of earlier nightmares. Everything hinged on reading the message and knowing who wrote it, but the words circled and looped around me so that I was tied up in them, noosed. Half awake, I tried to remember: Was it Joshua? Was it Ray? Was I chasing or being chased?

I lay in bed until the sun finally rose over the lake, straight into my eyes.

The clock in the kitchen said six thirty. I found a nearly full pot of coffee and a mug waiting for me. In the window over the sink, I caught sight of myself—puffy eyes, hair haphazard—and beyond my reflection, the lake.

The sliding door was quiet. Outside the world was already alive with chittering bugs and birds. This was my favorite time of day in the woods. Before mosquitoes, before the high, burning summer sun. Before the boats pulling water-skiers roared across the water. I'd always slept through the mornings as a kid staying with Theresa's family on the lake. But when Ray and I had lived on the lake—

My pulse jumped. I didn't want to think about it.

The sky over the lake was a tender blue.

I took my coffee outside to the deck. There was something unfair and unsatisfying about being the only one who seemed to remember just how awful those days were. Ray should remember, but he hadn't been very talkative. Or apologetic. And Mamie had all the facts, but she hadn't gotten her head bashed in. She didn't get her arm twisted behind her back. She hadn't heard her own body creak and snap. Something unfair about how well one person can know these things. Other people could never understand, no matter how much they thought they did. I caught myself feeling smug and started down to the lake.

Ray was sitting on the dock bench. Before I could turn around and go back inside, Magic jumped up from the dock and came to escort me down the steep stairs, her tail wagging a hero's welcome.

"Hey," he said.

"Good morning."

He turned back. The water was black where the sun had not yet reached.

"Or," I said, "maybe not a good morning?"

"A—confusing twenty-four hours."

"I think I'm only responsible for your last twelve or so."

"Always had to be right."

I sipped my coffee, thinking how easy it would be, just this one time, to bash *his* head in. Here was the mug in my hand. He might even get a little scald. "Is that it? The reason for it all?"

He slid over on the bench to make room for me. "Sorry."

"For the comment, Ray? Or for more than that?" If I ran for the stairs, he'd be too fast for me. I sat on the edge of the bench. If he'd really changed, here was his chance to prove it.

He nodded into the lake. "For everything."

For everything. Two words didn't quite cover it, but I guessed it was all he was capable of. It was probably all *locked in his heart*. Locked in his monstrous heart, if he'd actually been born with one.

Magic had had enough inattention. She put her chin on my knee and sighed. I switched the mug to my other hand and gave the dog a scratch on her neck.

"I want to see him," Ray said. "Joshua."

"Me, too."

"No, I mean. I want to get to know him."

I'd been waiting for this. Had worked the words over and over in my head in the night until I'd made sense of it. He'd want to grab his half now. Now that I'd done all the hard work of surviving his abuse and raising his offspring. He could do all the anger-management training in the world, and it wouldn't change my mind about this: he could go to hell.

"I think it's probably not the right time to be making plans like that. Obviously he and I have some things to work out. I think you might just—complicate things."

Ray was glaring at me with Joshua-brown eyes. "You're going to run off again."

"Don't even—you're not allowed to talk about it like that. Like I was some crazy kid taking a joy ride."

"He's my son, too."

I hated him, I really did. "I won't entertain clichés from talk shows, OK? I just won't. I could have gone my entire life not coming back here. You'd never have known."

"But now that I do—"

"Screw you."

"I can get a lawyer."

"*And* your lawyer."

Ray slapped his hand on his knees, the sound jolting me. "What am I supposed to do? Just ignore that you did come back?" He narrowed his eyes at me. "You *had* to come back. You thought he'd come here. He didn't, but that doesn't change the fact that you thought he wanted to. My kid has an interest—"

"He has a lot of interests. Football. Oh," I said, "and he's taking up street art."

"He wants to meet me, and that just drives you insane."

"Can you just go back in the time machine for a second? I left here thinking that you would kill me. *Kill* me, Ray. You said"—I lowered my voice to imitate him—"'you know what I'd do, right?' And I took you at your word—no, I didn't have to, did I?"

Ray's face went flat. "I've left all that behind me."

"Well, how lucky for you. How very lucky for you, indeed. I— have not." I looked around the empty lake as though the words I meant to say would be there. If those dream-supplied ribbons of words were ever going to surface, now was the time. "I've been on hold all these years, Ray. You have a lake house and a lake and a wife and a dog and *grace*, and I have put my life on complete hold for thirteen years with fear of you. All the time you were getting counseled and fixed, hooray for Ray, I was wondering when you were going to come *kill* me."

His hands lay in fists on his thighs. I took a shuddering breath, watching them, and kept going. "If it seems like I can't let go of what you've already left behind, it is because I haven't left it behind. I came here for one thing. And now I'd like to go home and maybe get on with my life. Maybe get a house and a—dog." I had almost said husband. "I have been on hold. I have been on ice. No matter how well your anger has been managed, I remember. And I don't forgive you. You stole—" I pictured Joshua, small, on my shoulder, his thumb in his mouth. What if I'd stayed? What if I didn't have him? "You stole everything, and you would have stolen more if I'd let you."

Ray's attention had returned to the lake. A boat with an outboard motor putted along the shoreline toward us, two men in camouflage caps casting into the darkest shallows. Ray let them pass, everyone but me nodding acknowledgment. The boat tugged along until I couldn't sit still anymore. I stood and strode down the dock, Magic at my heels.

The dog beat me to the stairs, but Ray was just behind.

"Wait."

"I will scream." I saw the rowboat at the dock and inside, two shiny red oars. I turned and fled up the stairs, the dog racing beside.

"Wait. Damn it, Leeanna." His fingers grazed the back of my elbow as I ascended the last stair.

I whipped around and faced him. "That is not my name," I said. "Not anymore. That girl is dead."

He looked away. "What, then?"

"You don't need it. Just for you? I'll answer to some of our old favorites—" He winced. "You want to catch my attention in the next five minutes before I leave here forever? I'll answer to bitch-face. Or whore. I'll answer to—"

The screen door slammed, and Mamie came out on the deck in a long robe, a mug in her hand. "Morning," she called. "You-all are up early."

I glared at Ray. "I'll get my things and be out of your way."

"Don't you want your kid to have a father? As crappy as I would have been then, Ell, I'm not such a slouch now."

Ell—he was the only person who'd ever called me that, giving me a new identity that was all his. I'd loved it, then. "I think he's doing just fine without a father, slouch or not."

"Fine? Missing for a week? He's just dandy."

"Shut up. We have some things to—"

"But why would you give me a chance? That father relationship was never anything you had much time for."

I shook my head. "You know what my father was for me. He primed me for one thing: a relationship like the one you and I had."

I turned on my heel and walked toward the house. I had a calm face for Mamie.

"Is everything OK?" Mamie said, reaching out to touch my arm as I swung by for the deck door.

"Leeeee-Anna!" Ray taunted at my back. "Just a damn minute before you pack your shit and leave forever."

I pulled at the door and left Mamie, open-mouthed, in my wake. Inside, I saw that nothing at all belonged to me. Except the photo of Joshua. I'd thought to leave it, a token, but just now I wanted it back. The photo was mine. Joshua was mine.

Ray walked in. His eyes dropped to the frame in my hands. "I know your dad was pretty messed up—"

"Don't talk to me about my father," I said. "Your memory is pretty bad concerning the years you were slamming me into walls, so I can't imagine you remember the stories I used to tell you about him. But why would you? It's all revisionist history in this little idyllic cottage by the lake, isn't it?"

"I think it's more like a course in denial."

I tucked the photo under my arm, making sure he saw me do it. "Thanks for the visit and the new outlook on life."

"Yeah," Ray said. "Oh, yeah. Look at Lee-Lee Winger now, running out when things get tough. That's what she's good at."

I had reached the kitchen door. I burst through it and hurried for the truck.

He ran up behind me and grabbed my arm, spinning me around. The frame slipped out. We both reached for it, but too late. The glass shattered on the driveway. I raised my hand, but I couldn't let it fly. As much as I wanted to hear a resounding belly flop of a slap on that man's face, all I could see was the shape of my hand on Joshua's cheek.

"Go ahead. You learned from the best," Ray said.

"I don't need to," I said. The glass was smashed and the frame broken. I reached down and slid the photo out of the debris.

"But you wanted to," he said. "I wonder why Joshua hit the road."

I stood. "I'm a good mother. I could have done better, but I could have done worse. Much worse, since I learned from the best there, too."

"Such loyalty," he said, shaking his head. "I used to wonder how you left her behind, but I'm starting to see. Are you even going to pay your respects while you're in town? Before you leave, you know, *forever*?"

I didn't even know where my mother had been buried.

The clock was ticking. No, the alarm was going wild, and I needed to get going. The longer I was here, the more I turned into a person I didn't want to be. I wanted to be—home. Wherever Joshua was. All I wanted was to make sure he was safe. I'd thought, once, that when I was a parent I would finally understand my own. But I actually understood them less.

"You wouldn't be a father if I hadn't left," I said. "You know what you'd have done."

Ray, ashen, glanced toward the house.

I felt only grim confirmation. "Didn't tell her that part, did you? Sorry I won't be here to see her believe in love on this one."

"Ray, what's going on?" Mamie called. He nodded, and she disappeared into the house.

"You should at least pay your respects."

"Respect was the one thing my mother didn't earn." I pushed the photo of Joshua into his hands. "She never did a thing to stop it. None of it."

"Didn't mean her," he said.

"I need to—I've been gone too long." What if Joshua had come back? And I wasn't there?

"That's what I'm saying. You've been gone too long. You should go see him while you can."

I shielded my eyes. Ray was backlit, his expression lost in shadow. "Who?"

"Who?" Ray turned his head toward the deck, where Mamie stood with a box under her arm. "I mean your dad."

"My—? But he's—" He was dead. But when I tried to remember how I knew this, I came up short. "His name wasn't in her obituary," I said. And I'd put him behind me long before I'd left town. Only my mother's death had concerned me. Only my mother's death had released me.

"They were divorced by then," Ray said. "She left him. She just didn't get far."

Mamie had arrived in her slippers. She held out the box. "I'm sorry it's not nicer—"

Ray took the box and thrust it into my hands.

I swallowed the rock in my throat. "What—"

Mamie waited for Ray to say something. At last she said, "Your mother, honey. Her ashes."

My mother had been a single passenger in a single-car accident. One car, one passenger. One tree. The tree, an old oak that had survived the American Revolution and a thousand scrapes, had to be cut down. I'd read the online news story six months after the death, sitting in a cold apartment in Ohio, and imagined my father asking after the firewood from the tree.

"Why do *you*—?" I heard the twist in my voice. Ray, stoic, shook his head.

Mamie said, "Your dad—"

"For God's—don't tell me my dad went through anger management, too." I glanced a last time at the photo in Ray's hands, and turned for the truck.

Mamie hurried after me. "He's old. This might be your last chance—"

I slid inside, started the motor to block anything else Ray or Mamie wanted me to know. I'd already given last chances enough for a lifetime.

Chapter Thirty-three

On my way out, I bypassed the town. I had confronted Ray and had my mother's ashes in a tidy box. I never had to see Sweetheart Lake again.

Within an hour, my head pounded and my stomach roared for attention. I needed gas soon, too. When one of the towns presented a gas station—slash—fast-food option, I steered for its harbor.

I dug the aspirin out of the back of the truck and, inside, bought a Coke and two fistfuls of breakfast sandwiches, each loaded with cheese and eggs and awful bacon. Hangover food. I had a hangover from being in that house, from bumping against that furniture. From trying to understand and explain. What a waste of time.

The restaurant portion of the station was busy. I found a stool by a window and tore into my breakfast. I realized I'd left the truck parked at a gas pump and didn't feel as bad about it as I should have.

I was unwrapping the second sandwich when an old sedan

pulled up behind my truck and idled there, waiting. The woman behind the wheel rested her head on her shoulder, her arm dangling out the window, patient.

A little head peered out the backseat's window. The kid was small, jumping up and down. No seat belt or he couldn't have been monkeying the way he was. After a few minutes the mother lost her cool and turned on the kid, slapping at him until he sat down.

The mother's fault. Mothers took the brunt of everything that went wrong, but in this case, if she had just put the kid in his restraints, he couldn't have been as much trouble. He was just a baby. Another day I might have said something, but I was tired of judgments and still inside the restaurant, chewing, my mouth filled with egg, when the boy in the backseat fled the woman's hands and pressed his worried face against the window—

Aidan.

I stared, started to rise. But wait, *how*? The child slid out of sight and I still wasn't sure. I stumbled off the stool.

Too late. The woman was backing up the car and pulling around the gas pump and my truck. By the time I navigated the restaurant's tables and the other patrons to the parking lot, the car was gone.

"You're not serious, are you?" The dispatcher I'd bothered the night before was still on duty and tired. Tired of me, in any case. She put me through to the sheriff's administrative office, but it was not Sherry who answered. The woman who picked up instead wouldn't patch me through to the sheriff, either.

"He's not on downtime," I said. I had barricaded myself in the last known pay-phone booth in the Western world, and all the people leaving the restaurant seemed to smirk at me, cell phones casually to their ears. "Really. He's working, and this is—he's going to want to talk to me."

"Think pretty high of ourselves, don't we now?"

I had a sudden picture in my head. Deputy Lombardi. The young officer who was always watching me with junior-high eyes.

"It's about Aidan. Aidan Ransey."

"This conversation may be recorded to better serve you."

"Are there any grown-ups there I could talk to?" I said.

"My break is in a half hour," Lombardi said. "If you want to talk to your *boyfriend*, you might have better luck with the next shift. Although, I wouldn't bet on it."

I'd had enough. "Let's talk about how you say you discovered the ransom note in the Ransey house before Charity's body was even discovered," I said. "Because you were there all night, with Bo."

"Oh, look who thinks she's a detective."

"And who maybe had time to get over to patrol the crime scene just in time to leave that body there."

"What are you talking about?" Lombardi said.

"Just put me through and you'll find out—" I held the receiver away from my ear. The phone had gone dead. I really did hope the conversation had been recorded, but I didn't think so. I stared at the receiver. Call back? But what was the use? The criminals were running the jail. I hoped all the signatures on Keller's evidence forms led to Tara Lombardi, I really did. At last I had nothing to do but slam the phone onto the hook and get out of the booth.

The car with Aidan inside had had enough time to drive around town twice while I'd wasted precious minutes with Parks County's finest, but I pulled out of the station parking lot with intention, going the way I thought the car had turned. It was the same strip of town I'd passed through already, but now I paid at-

tention. I bore down on each gas station and then slowed down
to sort through the cars at the pumps. I started to doubt myself.
Had I passed it? Was it blue? Black? There was rust on the front
passenger door—or was it the back door? Did it matter? Wouldn't
I know the thing when I saw it?

Wouldn't I know—

Something about this situation had been nagging at me, and
now it came to me in a rush. Aidan. I'd never met him back in
Parks, but I'd seen him before, once. He'd been sucking his
thumb on the shoulder of a woman brushing past me in Sweetheart Lake the day I'd returned to town. Outside the store that
used to be a bank, Aidan had looked right at me.

I'd missed my chance to help Aidan, missed perhaps the only
chance anyone would have to bring Aidan home.

I drove on, head swiveling. The road kept offering places the
sedan might be—up ahead, like a shimmering mirage—and so
I pushed on. The trees began to edge closer to the road. I knew
where I was going. Back the way I came, back to Sweetheart Lake.

I HADN'T FOUND the car by the time I drove once again into the tidy
downtown of my youth. I'd been calculating the entire ride back
what evidence I had. Sitting in my truck in front of the fudge
shop as the town began to wake and the shopkeepers flipped
over their door signs, I wasn't sure I had anything but doubt. Had
the kid really been Aidan Ransey? What were the odds? And if
the boy was Aidan, then who was the woman? How likely that
a stranger had abducted Aidan and was brazenly carting him
around northern Wisconsin as though he was her own?

I'd got it wrong. Simple enough. Lots of little boys had blond
hair and mournful eyes.

I tried to bring back the image of the boy's face as he dodged the woman's slaps. It was the sadness that got to me. The kid had been jumping up and down in the backseat without joy, his face blank. Maybe it meant nothing, but if it meant anything, it was worth looking into, just to draw attention to a child who needed help.

I got out and opened the back of the truck, digging for my work stuff. Tucked into a pocket of my computer bag were some of the *Spectator* clippings I'd saved. When I saw the photo of Aidan's round face, the hairs on my arms stood on end.

I grabbed all the files and my computer and filled the parking meter with quarters. In the pharmacy I made fifty grainy color copies of the clipping, watching Aidan's face shuffle again and again to the top of the pile. The cashier accepted my money and glanced at the stack of pages.

"Have you seen him?" I asked.

The cashier was a young woman with fading purple hair, and a metal toothpick through her nose like a bull's ring. I wondered how hard it was for her to live in such a small town, or if she'd found her crowd anyway. "Cute," the girl said in an unconvincing monotone.

"He's missing."

The cashier looked more closely. "From Sweetheart Lake?"

"From Indiana. I think he might be—maybe someone brought him up here."

"Oh." The cashier fed me a receipt. "Why?"

It was the perfect question. I couldn't think why. "So you haven't seen him?"

"They all look the same to me, really. Small."

"Will you keep one behind the counter? If you see him—" What? What plan did I have? "Call the police, I guess."

The girl looked at me, blank.

"I'm working with the police. The Indiana police, I mean."

The cashier seemed to believe me less. "I'll keep it back here?"

Up and down the street, I handed the posters to skeptical shopkeepers. No one could say that they'd seen him. And maybe they hadn't. Or maybe they had and hadn't noticed him. There were no news alerts here, no Aidan Watch time lines in the daily paper. To them, he'd be just another little boy on vacation with his family. Just another tourist.

The woman running the real estate office said he looked just like her grandson when he was a baby. "I hope you find him," she said, displaying the copy I gave her prominently on her desk. "His poor mama."

In one of the last shops, a tourist T-shirt emporium, a teenage girl welcomed me through a mouthful of braces. Her skinny arms stuck out of a candy-colored Sweetheart Lake T-shirt too large for her.

"Is the manager or owner here?"

The girl went to get someone, her ponytail swinging.

I glanced around at the shirts, instinct drawing my eye to one that seemed closely related to the shirt I'd had in high school, the pair of matching shirts Theresa and I bought to wear together that the other students hadn't liked. It was pink with, inexplicably, a palm tree scene and the words *Sweetheart Lake Welcomes YOU!* blazoned across the chest. I pulled it off the rack.

"That one is sort of funny," said a woman's tentative voice.

I glanced up and did a double take. Things were funny, when you were least ready to laugh.

Chapter Thirty-four

Theresa. This time I was sure of what I saw. The only living person I might have wanted to reclaim from Sweetheart Lake stood before me, a little older, a little more chin, a little more hip. I looked at the shirt in my hand.

"Those shirts *were* funny," I said, finally.

Theresa's eyes flickered to my face and away. "I can't believe it."

"I'm sorry."

"I feel like—like I just got punched." She held her hand to her stomach. She couldn't seem to look at me directly. "How—I mean—I don't know where to start."

"I'm so sorry," I said.

"Stop it. There's nothing to apologize for. You made it out. It's what we—it's what I always wanted. I thought you were . . ."

I hung the shirt's hanger back on the rack with a clatter. "Murdered."

"Yeah."

"I didn't think it through. I should have written you. I should have called." None of it seemed like enough.

"Should-haves are like apologizing except no one's listening, is what my gammie used to tell us," Theresa said. "You remember her. Crazy lady."

"Sweet lady. Your whole family—"

"She's gone now. And my mom."

"It's not apologizing to say I'm sorry for that."

"Over ten years, but—well, I took it hard. So soon after—" She looked to the door, though no one had come in. "I thought he killed you. They told me he didn't, that you were living in a trailer in Tennessee—"

"For a while."

"—but I tried to find you and I couldn't. I didn't believe them." She covered her mouth with her hand. Over it, her eyes went soft and then snapped back. "I didn't know you had it in you."

"I didn't, either," I said.

"I didn't know you at all."

I dug in my bag, my wallet, and finally found a tiny photo of Joshua from Chicago. The photo wasn't that old, but he still looked so young. I paused with it in my hand. If I didn't find him, would every photo of him catch me like this? I held it out to Theresa. "This is how."

"What," Theresa said, smiling for the first time. "No *kidding*. That is—wow, is that his kid." She glanced up.

"I've seen him."

"Born again," Theresa said.

"He seems to think so."

"His wife is nice," Theresa said, studying Joshua's picture. "She might be an idiot, though, I can't tell. All that 'I believe in love' stuff."

"She's said that more than once?" I said. "Wow."

"I believe in what people do," Theresa said. "You know? Not

what they say. I know what he did. Except—what happened to you? All that *blood*."

I blinked away, trying not to remember just now what he'd done. Ray seemed a million miles in the past. And so did Theresa, even as she stood with Joshua's photo in her hand.

"Did you bring him with you?"

"Joshua? No. It's—complicated."

She handed back the picture. "If *you* say it's complicated, I'm going to believe it."

"He disappeared," I said.

"He takes after you, then, too."

It hurt. Apologies weren't allowed, but I could see how they were necessary, would always be necessary, and would never be accepted. We'd lived without one another for thirteen years, and now I saw how small the reunion would be. I'd be an anecdote to tell.

"He's here?" she said.

"I thought he'd figured out where his dad was."

"But you haven't found him." Theresa gestured toward the flyers nodding from the top of my bag. "Who's that, then?"

"Further complications. I thought I saw this kid here. He's missing from—from where I've been living." I handed her one of the copies, trying to drag the woman and child from my memory again. Was I *sure*? "I mean—I think I saw him. It's possible I'm losing my mind. They need to put me in the nuthouse. Is Riverdale still open for business?" Riverdale Center was a childhood taunt, the place where the crazies got sent. As an adult I understood it was a home for the elderly and fragile, not a psych ward at all.

Theresa looked like she wanted to say something but turned to the flyer instead. She studied it for a long time.

The girl who'd welcomed me stood outside the propped-open front doors, clicking through racks of clearance T-shirts. At this distance and angle, I saw that the girl must be Theresa's daughter. I supposed I didn't deserve to hear about her.

"I can't be sure," Theresa said.

An electric thrill shot up my spine. "You've seen him?"

"Well, I don't know. There was a woman with a little boy in here—yesterday, I guess. She was looking for a job, but we don't have anything. I wish I'd had her do an application."

"She's younger than us, brown hair, ponytail? If this was yesterday, she was wearing a . . . like a sleeveless black T-shirt and jeans. Not a job interview outfit."

"That's the one," Theresa said. "I thought she might be looking for a place to rob. That was the vibe."

"They passed me on the street. I was so caught up in my own thing."

Theresa gave me an appraising look. "No wonder," she said.

But it hadn't been about Joshua at the moment the woman and Aidan had swept past me. I'd been locked into a dead-eyed gaze with the past and had forgotten the present altogether. I hadn't been thinking about Joshua at all, and Aidan had looked right at me.

When had I become so self-involved?

The mistake with the murdered executive came back to me. I'd been caught up in my own drama then, too. If something happened to Aidan now, I'd never forgive myself. And Joshua— what was I missing? What had I seen and not paid attention to? I'd spent thirteen years with my head to the ground listening for approaching hoofbeats. Listening so hard for what wouldn't come that I'd missed everything else. How could I still be down there on my knees, my ear pressed to the dirt, while missing boys walked right past me?

"You didn't recognize the woman?" I said. "There's no reason for that woman to come back to the shop?"

"I was pretty straightforward. No job here. No jobs in town, really, since it's off-season. Doesn't mean she's not still in the area, though." Theresa thought for a moment. "She seemed like she might be from here, but I can't tell you why I thought so. Maybe she's got a place nearby."

Those winding roads, peeling off again and again to encircle the lakes. A hundred lakes, a thousand. The task was too big. A few color copies weren't going to bring Aidan in. If anything, I might scare the woman away.

I dropped my bag to the ground and ripped it open. At last I found the original news clipping again. Under the large color image of Aidan was the small, grainy photo of his mother. I stood and held it out to Theresa. "What about her?"

"That wasn't her."

"But do you recognize this one? That's his mother."

She took the paper. "Nope. But you know how many people come here every summer. It was slow, economy and all, but still—maybe she was here this summer with all the rest of the crowds."

But I knew where this woman had been for several days now, and where she'd been before that. That Indiana hotel receipt she'd signed seemed like it had been in front of me a year ago, not just last week.

Theresa unfolded the newspaper to read the front page. "Indiana, huh?"

I felt my face go red, as though I'd been caught in a lie. I hadn't told the sheriff about Wisconsin and now I wouldn't tell Theresa about Indiana. Holding my old life apart from the new, just as I always had. "We lived a couple of places. Before there."

"How many times did you move?"

"Lost count."

Theresa wouldn't look away.

"Eight, ten times, city to city. Six states. Joshua is tired of it."

I reached for the paper, but she had opened it to an inside page. "What's this place like? Will you go back?"

"Not sure. No plans until I find—"

"Hey." Theresa parachuted the newspaper open and folded the pages back. "I think I know this one."

She turned the paper around, and there he was: Bo Ransey. The story from the front page continued inside, with the photo of Bo in front of his tumbling front porch.

"You're not kidding, are you?"

"Why would I kid about that redneck? I'm sure I saw him over at The Shaw in Rhinelander once. Remember The Shaw? I don't drink anymore." Theresa dipped her head at the paper, so that I had a sense of how much drinking had gone by. Maybe I had been the cause. Another thing to apologize for. "But we still go for burgers sometimes. I wouldn't remember him," she said, "except he seemed like such an ass."

I rushed from thought to thought, but nothing lined up behind what I knew. Nothing made sense. Bo Ransey hadn't kidnapped his own child. He hadn't left town. Had he? Had he paid someone to do it? But then how was he still in Parks bothering the sheriff every day?

"Do you remember when you saw him?" I said.

"Sometime this summer."

"Not in the last two weeks?"

Theresa leaned on a T-shirt rack. "No, it was early this summer. May, maybe April."

If only I knew what it meant. I'd been given a handful of puzzle pieces, but not enough of them to build the picture.

"So," she said, handing the newspaper back. "I hate to bring this up, but you know your dad is still kicking, right?"

Ray and Mamie, now Theresa. They were determined to tell me the things I didn't want to know.

"I've been made aware of it," I said.

"He's at Riverdale, Lee," Theresa said. "A couple of years now."

Riverdale. So this was the news that Ray had wanted me to have. My dad was alive, and he was stowed in the bogeyman place of my childhood, the cuckoo's nest, a haunted house made real.

"That's probably fine for him," I said.

"I know how you feel about him, but—"

"I won't be going out there," I said. "How does everyone seem to know about his being alive except me? Never mind."

"Everyone?"

I sighed, picked up my bag, and faced Theresa over crossed arms. "I stayed with Ray and his wife last night. Please don't ask how that happened, because I'm still not sure myself."

"So he told you?" She sounded so surprised, I could tell there was more to hear.

"What? Just—out with it."

"He didn't tell you."

"I think you'll have to tell me to find out."

Theresa looked sharply at me. "You're changed. As changed as Ray thinks he is."

I felt the insult but let it go. I had changed. I wasn't here to morph back into the tiny Leeanna shape that allowed everyone to stay comfortable and uninvolved.

To get it over with, I asked, "How much has he changed?"

"Ray Levis," Theresa said with a deep sigh and a fast glance around the store. "Ray Levis is the guy who pays the bills at Riverdale."

I felt something in my body shift threateningly. If I didn't sit down, I might fall. I reached for a T-shirt rack. I hoped I was misunderstanding.

"Ray is the one who keeps your dad. There's assistance, sure. But it doesn't cover everything." She looked uncomfortable. "Also, they visit him."

"But—*why*?"

"He didn't tell you." Theresa shook her head. "I'll be damned."

"He thinks he's making it up to me. He has some nerve."

"I won't argue that. But I think he started out believing that if he did something for your dad, people wouldn't think he'd done something to you. That's not how it went. Karma must be really hard to buy."

I remembered Ray seated at his own kitchen table, rubbing the photo of Joshua. *We had to move. You wouldn't believe the looks he gets in town.*

What would I have thought if I'd been one of the bystanders?

"They wanted to think he'd killed me," I said, seeing it all clearly. "And then he gave them a reason to believe it."

Chapter Thirty-five

At the Vilas County sheriff's office, the chief was out. A bored officer with a walrus-whisker moustache sat at the front desk alone, his gut bumping the counter. He wouldn't say when his sheriff was due back, wouldn't get anyone from behind the security door to talk to me. He took my information down.

"Do you get missing kids from Indiana up here all the time?" I said, my blood starting to rise.

He finally rose to the challenge of noticing me, his demeanor telling me what they got most was crazy out-of-towners. "You wouldn't believe it if I told you," he said.

I slammed the door on my way out.

I found another sticky pay phone in the lobby and tried Sheriff Keller's office again. The Parks County dispatchers had traded shifts, but the new one was no more help. She wouldn't put me through to anyone else. "He's out on a call," the woman said. She sounded older, not smoking while she worked, but she was all business. "I can put you through to the nonemergency number and you can leave a message."

"But this is actually an emergency."

"Deputy Lombardi said you'd say that."

So now I had a reputation among the ranks. I did as I was told, leaving a message. But it felt as futile as it probably was. Who was going to get that message? And when?

I dialed the only other number I had memorized. The phone rang and rang in Kent's office in Indianapolis until voicemail engaged. "Kent, it's Anna. This is going to sound crazy, but what's new, right? Listen, I'm up in Sweetheart Lake. It's where—" I pictured Kent's precise way of talking, the delicate way he asked what I wanted to know. "My hometown, but you probably remembered that. Look, that kid missing from Parks, Aidan Ransey . . . I swear he's here. I don't know how or why yet, but he's here. I can't get through to Keller, but if you could get someone up here with one of your shiny badges, I could use the support. I need to get back to Parks and my phone doesn't work here . . ."

I looked over my shoulder at the lonely lobby. "Kent," I said. "I'm trying to do what you told me. I'm trying to do everything I can—"

The system beeped at me so that I wasn't sure if it had stopped recording or hadn't caught a word. I hung up.

The street outside the station was quiet. Maple Street. Of course. And a block away was Birch. In the other direction, Spruce. And don't forget Pine, the heart of Sweetheart Lake.

I retrieved my truck and took Maple to Railroad Street, crossed the river. In town the river was little more than a creek. The water was low now, the grass up both banks a fragile yellow. A breeze blew in through my window, pleasant but cool. When I hit a red light, I stuck my arm out the window and caught the wind with my cupped hand. Not just cool, but maybe a little cold. I stared out my windshield at the trees as if I'd just woken up

from a long sleep. I hadn't paid attention, but the maples had
begun to turn gold. It was October and, if I blinked, it would be
November. And Joshua, out there in just a thin jacket. He hadn't
packed for the Northwoods.

The car behind me honked to urge me through the green
light. I couldn't remember what to do for a second, but I did it
anyway, unconsciously, driving up Railroad as it widened and
led me past landmarks I knew, like the golf course, where Ray
had done maintenance for a few months one summer until he'd
pissed off too many people. I drove out of Sweetheart Lake, recognizing an old house turned into an antiques store, a motel that
still seemed in working order. I swung into a dirt turnaround
and back toward town.

When the Dairy Bar appeared, I turned in. I wasn't hungry so
much as empty. I took my time getting out and walking up to the
window, where a girl in a pink Dairy Bar shirt checked her hair
for split ends.

"A—malt, I guess."

"What flavor?"

"Chocolate."

The girl ducked out of the window.

I leaned against the counter and looked around. I was the only
customer. They'd shutter the place for the winter and reopen in
April when the summer tourists started trickling back. Theresa's store probably closed for a few weeks, but stayed open for
the winter visitors: the snowmobile adventurers, the ice fishermen. For the long-lost friends she thought were dead. Long-
lost friends she'd come to rely on being dead. People got used to
things, even things that were hard to get used to. They wrote the
stories in their heads and rewrote them until they made sense.
That's what I'd done. And now the story was unraveling.

I closed my eyes and imagined Joshua, wherever he was, safe and warm and being fed. If I believed it, maybe it would be true.

But I couldn't wish him home or pray him home. I could only rely on action. If only I knew what the best action was. I opened my eyes. The malt, whipped cream and cherry, too, sat on the counter. I slid a handful of dollars to the girl. "I never knew these were a chain."

The girl took the money. "They're not."

"How many are there?" Maybe I could find another Dairy Bar town, just to see the look on Joshua's face.

"They're not a chain." The girl slapped my change onto the counter. "Do you live in Indiana?"

I glanced at my truck. The license plate was visible, but the girl had extraordinary eyesight. "For now."

"There's one in Indiana and one here. If that's a chain."

"That's weird."

The girl looked up from her split ends with a look that I could read. I was the weird one here.

"I used to work at this one, this very store," I said. "One time I dropped a bag of malt and the powder went everywhere, coated everything white. One of the other kids tried to snort—"

"Did you want an application or something?"

Got it. "No, thanks," I said, and took my shake back to the truck.

An application. I couldn't laugh it off entirely. How long would our savings last? We'd have to stop jumping around so much, stop paying first month and last month, stop leaving mattresses behind. Stop wasting money. Stop wasting time.

I sat behind the wheel, the malt melting, unwanted. I had to stop wasting time, no matter what happened.

I swept past a trash can on the way out of the Dairy Bar's parking lot and threw in the malt.

Stop acting as though I knew what to do. Stop acting as if I had any confirmation at all that I had ever known what I was doing.

Stop—everything. God, couldn't the world just stop for a minute? I had to catch up. I had to find Joshua. I had to find Aidan. I had to find a way to start over. Forgive and be forgiven and start over.

Do-over, as the kids in my neighborhood used to yell when a game hadn't gone their way. I was nearing that place now, the school, the houses lined up behind downtown on tree-named streets. I turned in and rode up and down the shady, parallel lanes. A friend in elementary school had lived here. I'd been allowed to go to a birthday party in fourth grade there. The library. The school. The jungle gym where I'd played with friends until the sky turned dark one night and I grew afraid to go home. I climbed to the top of the tallest slide and tried to hide as the other kids peeled off toward home when their parents called for them. Mine didn't. They didn't come for me at all. A woman who lived nearby finally shooed me home. I knew I would never talk to those kids again. We didn't live in the same world.

Stations of the cross. I was beginning to feel loose, like my bones had slipped out from under my skin. I knew that I could not avoid the places we had once lived. That I would choose to see these places, like a punishment.

The first was easy: in town, a run-down one-story. Inside was a room that was probably not still yellow. Two streets away, a ranch-style trying to return to the earth.

I couldn't remember where all of the houses were, but found four in town before striking the main street and taking it south. I passed Greenhouse Lodge Road, where Theresa's family had had their place. Probably *still* had their place. I hadn't asked. So many things I hadn't asked. What would it mean to settle down in a single parcel of land and watch your life flower out around you?

And then the worst of them all: the old motel restaurant where my parents were eking out their existence when I'd left town. The motel's strip of rooms had been torn down long before we had to live there. Now the building had graffiti-covered boards on the windows. The cement stops from the motel's parking spaces were still lined up facing the woods beyond, but no one had visited in a long time. This was it—the last place. As far as I knew, this was going to be the place where my father breathed his last. He owned it, some kind of auction deal. All the apartments, all those years, but he owned this dump.

I got out of the car and looked the place over. Inside, I knew, was a smoky kitchen, torn booths, a long, stained Formica counter. A storage room with a single mattress on the floor, home sweet home.

Joshua had no idea what a terrible life was. Standing here, I was so angry at him. He was gone, and the empty space he left was like a deep sore, every move I made scraping at it, keeping it raw. He thought moving from town to town was difficult. Try staying in one place. One awful place with no one looking out for you. I had never run. Not, at least, until I had to.

I circled the motel parcel now. I couldn't stand this story I was compelled to tell myself. Because I had put up with abuse and ugliness, I was somehow better than my son? He'd taken matters into his own hands far earlier than I had. He was the smart one. I couldn't even be angry with him anymore when I thought of myself at the same age, the mousy girl afraid to make a sound. If it hadn't been Ray, wouldn't it have been someone else? Whose fault was it that I expected and accepted so little?

But I wouldn't take this one on myself. This was not my fault.

I kicked at the loose gravel at my feet. The house had been left to the rats and the vandals. My dad, the architect of my ruined life, was in an institution, kept by a stranger; my mother's brittle bones were reduced to ash in my truck. And here I was: home. I laughed out loud. The laugh gathered strength, rolling downhill toward hysteria until my ribs hurt and anyone who saw me might have believed me to be just who I was. The heir to this mess, this empire. Finally. I choked for breath. Finally we have a place and I am its queen.

I crouched in the dust and coughed myself into tears, then sobbed until I was dry, and the sparks caught flame. I was angry enough, at last, to go see the devil himself.

Chapter Thirty-six

It would not be a reconciliation. More like a visit to the zoo—to see the beasts.

I rose from the ground, dusted off. An RV heading out of town slowed down to get a good look.

"Damn tourists." Which made me laugh a little more, but I didn't want to kill the red coal that burned in my belly. I had to go see him now, before I discovered a secret store of pity and talked myself out of it.

The road to Sweetheart Lake was lovely in the afternoon light. I'd driven it four times since my return and could finally see the trees as trees instead of omens, the hints of lake behind the trees as water and not memories. I drove through town again, and this time nothing about it surprised me.

Riverdale was where it had always been, even if the town had remodeled the building completely and rerouted the roads all the way around it. I navigated my way through the new configuration, off the main road and onto a narrow access road, and into the complicated parking area. I threw the SUV into park and sat there regarding the building, which was not a haunted house at all, but a sprawling, squat box of medicinal glass.

The double doors swung out and a wheelchair emerged in front of a white-uniformed orderly. The chair held a person. Probably a woman, collapsed upon herself with age. She was aged to the point of agelessness—she could have been seventy or she could have been one hundred seventy.

The orderly pushed the chair down the sidewalk and around the corner of the building. He tapped the chair's brake with his foot and pulled out a cigarette. The chair faced the river, but there was no recognition by the patient of the fine sun or the orderly's smoke drifting across her face. No recognition that she was still alive.

I got out of the truck and took a few steps toward the door. When the orderly glanced my way, the brief acknowledgment was all it took. I retreated.

I hadn't regained safety in the truck yet when I saw a long, sleek car pass by on the main road.

The dark sedan with the rusted doors. Aidan.

The car moved fast, like a black fish rising to the surface and diving. Before I could get my truck moving, the car was gone. I made a bad turn trying to escape the access road and had to turn around, cursing all roads. At last I found the exit to the street and the turn I needed to follow the sedan west.

As I went, I scanned both sides of the road: storefronts, offices, gas stations. Restaurant parking lots and RV dealerships. A curve ahead. If I could just get around the curve and see a distance . . . but each curve provided a view of the next. I sped up, scoping out each turn, each potential hiding spot, as well as I could. I kept moving. I wouldn't lose Aidan this time.

The doubt returned.

But then around the next curve, *there*—just a flash of light off the trunk as the car turned into the pines. I glanced all around for a landmark. We were miles and miles from Sweetheart Lake. Why would the woman with Aidan even look for a job in town? I had to remind myself about desperation—the woman had a lot to lose, but perhaps she had lost a lot already.

I rushed to make the same turn as the sedan and was rewarded by a clear view of the car and the road we shared.

I stayed back, gave the car room, my thoughts leaping ahead. As far from town as we were, I knew this road. Ray had liked to drink at a place called Digger's, a backwoods pub that had been built onto an old house. And there it was, still open or at least it would be in a few hours, as forlorn and dusty as ever. After Digger's, though, the road was like any other in the area. There would be nothing but turn-offs, narrow gravel roads that splintered into private drives, a boat launch for the lake. Rentals would be standing empty this late in the season, and very few cars would meet us coming the other way. Wherever the woman was staying, I would have to follow and I'd be hard to miss.

And who would emerge from the car when it finally stopped? The woman? Or Bo?

The car took an abrupt turn onto a gravel road, kicking up dust. I slowed further, letting the car get some distance. When I reached the road, there were the white feathered signs pointing into the woods: *Reynolds*, *Carter's Cozy*, *Fuerole's*, *Hodag's Hide-a-Way*. I couldn't read them all before my fear of losing the car forced me around the corner—only to find the sedan stopped a few hundred feet ahead, brake lights bright. I hurried into a three-point turnaround, catching a brief glimpse of the woman reaching out her window for the mailbox at the end of a drive. She didn't seem to notice me at all.

I drove back to Digger's and sat in the lot for a while, my heart racing. I dug out my phone again. No service. Digger's was dark, the parking lot empty.

No phone. No houses anywhere in view. The Sweetheart Lake cops had already brushed me off as a nut. I wished for Russ—the Russ who would help me, not the one looking for the easiest way to brush me off, too.

I couldn't think of what to do but drive back to the road and take that private drive. Pull up the path behind the sedan, cut the engine, and hope that a plan would meet me halfway.

I retraced my route, nothing coming to mind. No houses, no cars. I found myself easing into the drive behind the woman's car and taking a look at the house. It was as pink as a birthday cupcake with white gingerbread trim like a chalet or someone's idea of one. The house was old, and was starting to look uncared for. It sat on a wide lot but the woods still came up to the house on two sides. Only the view to the lake had been cleared, but the view surely made up for anything the house lacked. The house turned its open face to the wide, smooth water.

As I got out, the screen door creaked open and the woman I'd seen leaned out.

"Hi," I said, managing to keep my voice from quaking.

The woman frowned. She clung to the door, half hidden. Where was her other hand? I stopped. Gun, knife, baseball bat.

"There's a no-trespassing sign back there," she said.

"I didn't see one." It was the truth.

"Oh. Well, there used to be. What do you want?"

"One of the old Northwoods families, huh?"

The woman eyed me. "What do you want, I said."

"I'm sorry to disturb you." I tried to keep from looking wildly toward the house's windows. If Bo was here, it was over. "I—I heard you were, uh. Looking for a job."

The woman stepped out, letting the door smack behind her. She looked suspicious, but the frown was gone and if she'd had anything in her hand behind the door, she'd dropped it. "How'd you hear that?"

"The owner of the T-shirt shop on Pine. Well, one of them. Never paid any attention to the store name, you see it so often."

The woman's scowl returned. She reminded me of a beautiful child who was used to getting her way. "That bitch. She was so—she thinks she's better than me because she owns a *T-shirt* store?" She looked me up and down. "What job?"

Something thunked against the door behind her. Inside, a child began to cry.

"Just a sec," she said. Her sleek brown ponytail swung around as she went to the door and opened it. A chubby little blond boy spilled out of the door onto the step, wailing. Aidan. It was really Aidan. He had a red spot on his forehead. The woman scooped him up and gave him a comforting bounce. "You're OK now, you're fine."

"Child care," I said. "A babysitter."

The woman patted Aidan's back. "I do plenty of that."

"You have a real skill," I said. "Yours?"

"How old is your kid?"

"The same age, about. Two?"

The woman bounced Aidan to her hip. "Mikey's two."

I watched the woman smooth the boy's hair away from his forehead and kiss his temple. Michael. The kid really did look like Aidan. And wasn't Aidan's middle name Michael? I remembered my hand writing it into my notes, the physical memory of the word leaving my pen. My nerves began to jangle and buzz. "Mine's a handful. I bet yours is, too." The woman said nothing. I stepped forward and tutted over Aidan's forehead. "Poor guy. I'm—Leeanna."

"Bonnie. How much do you pay?"

The job was a good ruse, but the details were killing me. "I'd want to, you know—make it worth your time."

Bonnie liked this. "My time is pretty valuable."

"You spend all your time chasing after your son, I'm sure."

"Yeah," she said, but there was a wistful quality to her voice. She set the boy down and watched him run a few feet. I took a step to follow, but Bonnie just watched. He found a stick and settled himself into a patch of red dirt to dig. "This one's my nephew."

Another loose piece of the puzzle. Nephew? Or cover story? "Oh, yeah? You seem like such a natural."

Bonnie peered at me as though she thought she was being made fun of. "Well. I have one of my own, too. I just don't—"

Don't know where he is.

But then the downcast image of Steve Ransey came to me. Of course. If Aidan was really her nephew—

"Custody is a bitch sometimes," I said.

Bonnie folded her arms across her chest. Her hands fists. "Such a crock. I was a mess but I can raise a *kid*. And who gets custody? Does this make sense to you? My mother. She raised me so damn well I had my kid taken away and who do they give him to?"

I shook my head, which was beginning to spin off my shoulders. This was really Steve's mom. But why steal Aidan? And to get away with it this long? Wouldn't the Ransey family tree have been shaken pretty hard as part of the investigation? I hated to doubt the sheriff again, but here it was: Aidan Ransey sat with dusty legs two feet from his own aunt. But maybe Bonnie wasn't the mastermind. I glanced uneasily at the house.

"I mean, I'm great with kids now," Bonnie said. "Don't worry. I was messed up when I was *young*. The place I come from—well, it's not all pine trees and fudge shops there, let me tell you."

She was talking about Parks, I realized. But maybe Bonnie had a point. No place was only pine trees and fudge shops. Even this place.

Bonnie sniffed. "So when?"

I'd been looking over the house and had lost the thread of our conversation. "What? Oh." The job. "Next week or so?"

"What's your kid's name?"

"Uh," I said, and Bonnie narrowed her eyes. "Josh." It was the only name that came to mind the way the truth would. "If you have some paper, maybe we could work out the details." I nodded toward the house. "How much I could pay you, how many hours."

I waited for the deal to fall through, for the woman to balk at letting a stranger inside the house.

Bonnie gazed out at the lake, twisting her mouth. "Yeah. Cool." She went to Aidan, propped him up, dusted off the seat of his pants. He began to howl and wave his stick at her face. She held him away from herself, forcing the stick out of his hand even as he began to scream. "Time to go inside, mister. None of that." Her tone was singsongy, ready-made for the audition. She led me up the steps, letting Aidan dangle over her shoulder. Aidan stopped crying and regarded me.

Bonnie held the door for me with her foot. "Welcome to the crazy house."

I stopped in the doorway. Inside, the house seemed normal if a little run-down and messy. "What's so crazy about it?"

Aidan, kicking for freedom, was let down. He stomped away, tramping toys as he went. Bonnie watched him disappear down a dark hallway and then turned back to me, her eyes flicking toward the open door at my back. "Long story."

Chapter Thirty-seven

I glanced over my shoulder. No one was there, but the trees had begun a seductive wave in the rising wind.

"I love a long story if it's got crazy in it."

Bonnie was sweeping a pile of papers and empty plates off the table.

I said, "You can leave that. I know about messes, believe me."

The woman moved the detritus in her hands to the kitchen counter behind her. The rooms were all wide and open. The disaster continued into the kitchen, where the sink was heaped with dirty dishes, and into the living area, where a lumpy couch held two cushions' worth of laundry to fold.

I sat at the end of the table cleared for me, casting about, while Bonnie's back was turned, for anything interesting on the table. "So how long have you been coming up here?"

The woman sighed.

"You called me nosey," I said, forcing myself into joviality. I hated the woman I was pretending to be. The Booster Club mom. "You didn't realize how right you were."

Bonnie's fake smile was weak. "Family's had the place for a long time. Like, forever. I don't come up much now."

"Weather's turning. If you're getting a job, though—you're not going home soon?"

The smile faltered. "Do you want some coffee or something?"

"Glass of water?"

As soon as Bonnie turned toward the kitchen, my eyes raked the table. Newspapers, shopping bags, flyers from the local grocery chain, a fast-food job application. I heard a clink in the kitchen and looked up. Bonnie was choosing a glass from the overloaded sink. She flicked on the tap and ran the glass under water. I took a quick look around the room. Nothing seemed out of place, really, for a lake house in which a child was staying the summer. Except there were no swimsuits or beach towels hanging off the backs of the chairs, no sandy footprints on the linoleum. The house felt empty, even with the three of us there.

Bonnie crossed the room with the glass dripping in her hand. "I'm going to go check on Mikey. Just a sec."

As soon as she'd gone, I turned back to the table. The newspapers were local, the headlines mundane. The bags held hot dog buns and insect repellent. There was nothing of interest until I lifted the edge of the job application and saw a scrap of handwriting on pink paper. My pulse quickened.

I slipped the paper out and into my palm just as a door down the hallway opened and Bonnie reappeared. I moved my hand to my lap and left the scrap of paper there on my crossed leg under the table. "He's OK?"

"He's the youngest kid I've ever met who puts himself to bed."

This seemed remarkably sad, but the mask had to be put back on. "Oh? You've really trained that one. Your son must be so well-behaved."

Bonnie snorted. She sat across the table, the hump of the stuff in front of her hiding all but her shoulders and head. "I don't hear much, that's part of the deal. But I doubt it."

The deal? "Why not?"

"Rotten role models. Who's he going to take after? Me? His damn father? His no-good uncle? My kid didn't have a chance. But if we're all bad for him, why not me?"

I took a drink of water and tasted dish soap.

Bonnie dug under the papers in front of her, shuffling so roughly that the newspaper on top slid off the other side of the table. I reached for it. "Leave it," Bonnie said.

The newspaper on the floor was a copy of the Parks County *Spectator*.

My stomach dropped. The boy really was Aidan. This woman really was a kidnapper. She reached over the mess and offered a pen and notepad. "See if this works," she said.

I coughed to cover the sound of crumpling paper under the table and shoved the stolen sample into my pocket as I reached for the pad.

I didn't want to see my own handwriting. I knew where the tight enclosures on *o*'s and *a*'s showed my need for control; I knew how many characters I could get through before my inner analyst lit up and started paying more attention to the lines of my own hand than what I wrote, how my script would come to a self-conscious halt in the middle of a word. Plus, my hands were shaking.

"I forgot my glasses," I said. "At home. Could you?" I handed the pad back. "How much do you think you'd need an hour?"

Bonnie brightened, brought the pen cap to her lips. A cry started down the hall, and she slumped again, sighing. "This is why I'm getting my own place."

Her own place? Who lived here, other than her? For the first time since being in Bonnie's presence, I wondered how much danger the little boy was in. How had he come to be here, and who was due back home anytime? "I'll go check on him," I said. "If that's not too weird."

Bonnie didn't seem to see anything wrong with the offer. She held her hands up in surrender. "Fine by me."

I stood and picked my way through the toy minefield. Bonnie was leaving the family compound. That might explain why she was searching as far away as Sweetheart Lake for a job, but what did it mean? What would happen to Aidan? What was "the deal" she'd made?

The hall was dark, all the doorways closed but one. I made for the strip of light there, my skin tingling. I could just walk in there and grab him? It was going to be this easy? Surely, the room would have a window—and then around the house to my truck. I pictured the back of the house and the woods. If I could find a path through the scrub without crackling leaves. If Aidan would play along. If all the pieces fell into place, I could get Aidan almost all the way to my truck before I'd be visible from where Bonnie sat.

I eased the door open and stuck my head in. The dark room held a set of bunk beds, everything in shadow from the heavy drapes over the window. Aidan sat in the lower bunk, his thumb in his mouth.

"Hi, buddy," I whispered. I closed the door behind me and made for the window, slinging back the drapes. It was low enough to the ground. I turned the lock. Halfway open, the window stuck and would go no further. It would be a tight fit.

I turned to Aidan. He watched me warily.

"You're getting so big." I took a step toward the bed.

Aidan popped his thumb out of his mouth. I stopped. "Do you want to take a ride in a big truck?"

His belly rose under his T-shirt with every breath. "Truck," he said.

"That's right. Want to go with me in the truck?" I moved quickly, reaching into the bunk and pulling him out. He lurched for his bed, but I held him tight against my hip. "Let's go to see the truck, OK, Aidan?"

He stuck his thumb back into his mouth. I grabbed a stuffed bear from the bed and handed it to him. He heaved it over my head. "OK, OK. No bear."

I carried him to the window and tried widening the opening again. The problem revealed itself—I'd have to put Aidan through the window first and then crawl out behind him. There would be a moment of terror for him, outside, alone, a stranger struggling out of the window after him, and this was when the scream would come. "We don't have much choice, buddy. You and me, we'll be friends. Can you be really quiet for your friend?"

Aidan whimpered around his thumb as I slipped his feet through the window. He kicked my hands away. "Easy, easy," I murmured, and then the door behind me opened.

"Is he giving you trouble?" Bonnie said. "Hey."

I pulled Aidan away from the window and jostled him against my hip. "Oh, we were just—looking at the squirrels. Josh likes to look at the squirrels."

Bonnie looked at the window. "Mikey's afraid of squirrels."

"Well, you didn't tell me that, Mikey," I said, wedging the false gaiety back into my voice. My heart was pounding in my ears. I couldn't believe my panic wasn't written on my face.

Bonnie reached out both arms, the notepad in one hand. A trade. I bounced Aidan playfully, but he dove toward his aunt.

I pretended to give my full attention to Bonnie's calculations, written in a lumpy script.

Bonnie walked past me and wrestled the window closed, Aidan clinging to her chest. "I'm going to need at least fifteen dollars an hour."

"Fifteen." I nodded quickly, my mind already racing ahead for a second opportunity. Or maybe now was the time to leave and bring back help. "Of course."

"Although," Bonnie said, rocking Aidan back and forth, "you probably don't need me that much."

Why couldn't I just wrench Aidan from Bonnie's arms and run? "Fifteen an hour is *fine*."

"Your kid couldn't be that much work." Bonnie placed her hand on Aidan's fluffy hair and turned him away. "Being a teen-ager."

I heard only the barest rush of air as something heavy swung toward the back of my head, and then all was black.

Chapter Thirty-eight

The moaning came from a long way off, then it was inside the room, inside my mouth, my own voice clawing at my throat. It was my own.

I could stop it.

Under the silence and my own ragged breath, I heard hisses. Whispers. The whispers stayed where they were.

I am the moan and they are the whispers.

They. Bonnie, holding Aidan in her tight arms and turning his face away just as the hammer came down.

And accomplice. With two-by-four? With baseball bat?

I reached to feel the wound, but my arm wouldn't move. Paralyzed.

My arms were tied. The room, dark. I imagined boots stepping over me to cover the window and began to shake.

Joshua.

A moan escaped, loud, unbidden, long. The whispers dropped away.

Joshua. All I had wanted. And now.

Baseball bat? Hammer? The entire back of my head was caved in, crushed.

The whispers rose and fell. I woke again without knowing I'd gone under.

Boat oar.

Joshua sat at my side in the dark room. Small Joshua, a baby again. He ran a small fire truck up my arm. "Go," I groaned. The whispers down the hall stopped. "Go. Before they—"

The door opened and footsteps landed all around me. A woman's voice. "Stay the hell out of here." Hands reached into my view and took him away.

My head. I passed out for a while and then the footsteps came back. Something nudged me.

Boat oar. It was new. I'd put it in the oarlock myself.

The moan came from somewhere deep.

Something nudged me again, and I reached for it. I hung onto it as it shook and stabbed at me. A woman's voice. "Get off, damn it."

I opened my eyes. The room was black but I could see a figure there. An oar. It really was an oar. The weapon of choice for lake people. My bound hands clutched at it—and, at the end of the long handle, not Ray. Not Ray at all, and not Bonnie or Bo. I hung onto the oar with all my strength, climbing up the handle like someone gasping for the shore.

"Drop it, or I'll kill you right now." The gravel voice.

I saw the shadow in the dark, let go of the oar, and fell back to the carpet. I knew. I knew, except all was black.

MAMA BEA RANSEY came back with the oar and poked me in the side. "Get up."

Some time had passed, but I didn't know: hours, days. The whispering had gone on for a long time. In and out of memory,

I heard the voices, felt the skin on my face grow hot with fever. I threw up, only able to wipe my mouth feebly. I thought of Joshua and I did not cry. I watched a thin line of sunlight move across the room and fade, but lost track. Slept. Woke. Slept. Heard Aidan crying far down in a well, and scratched at the floor, trying to reach for him. Woke and heard the whispers moving toward me: "Make them tighter. I have to do everything—"

"Let's just—"

"Pretty big talk, 'Let's just.' You do it, if it's so easy."

Slept. Woke.

My thoughts had risen all at once, but now they started to line up. Into sense. Into fact. I saw the curtains behind me and calculated how I might get through that window. I could not get there. I would never be able to move fast enough through the woods, even if I could reach the window and heave myself outside. Even if my truck still sat in the drive. I felt with my elbow at my left pocket. Fact: the keys were gone.

I had to try, though. I stretched and squirmed toward the window, managing only an inch or so.

Bea. Concerned grandmother. On TV. In Russ's office. I could not make order from this. Kidnapping your own grandchild and killing a young woman to do it. But—there was no sense to it. Not yet.

Exhausted from stretching, I lay panting on my side, curled around my deadened hands. The binds so tight. They would have to amputate my hands when I got out of here. I imagined trying to get analysis work, not being able to write. Saw myself, like a Winged Victory, armless. Saw myself armless, ditched in a shallow grave.

I braced myself for another effort toward the window. The door opened.

Bea Ransey entered the room, the oar at her side. "Get up," she said.

Chapter Thirty-nine

I got to my hands and knees, retched. The pain.

"If I were you," Bea said, "I'd keep what you had."

Another voice behind her, a whisper. "Oh, hell."

"Shut up," Bea said to her daughter. "This is your fault."

My head was heavy, my neck too weak. I let it drop.

"I said get up. Come on."

"How is this *my* fault? I didn't beat her brains in."

"We wouldn't'a had to, if you'd had half a brain yourself," Bea growled. "Jesus. Another ten minutes and you'd had her peeling potatoes and staying to dinner."

I grabbed at the oar. Bea shook me off.

Bonnie said, "I think she needs help."

"You'd pick her over your own kid? What do you think Bobby'd do?"

"I mean—I think she needs help up."

The oar dropped into view. I grasped at the handle and let it lead me upright. My head swam, the corners of my vision going to television static.

"No, no," Bea said. "That's right. Just going for a little walk."

My knees buckled but I was on my feet. The sharp blade of the oar slipped out of my hand. My hand. I was untied. My hands were swollen and the wrists scraped raw, but they were free.

The old woman jabbed the oar at me. I took a step, another. I used the wall to catch myself, pressing my palm flat and hard. Fingerprint. In the hallway, I scooted along the wall, letting my hand find purchase on the light switch plate. Fingerprint. We inched through the kitchen. All the blinds and curtains had been pulled. I used the back of a kitchen chair to catch myself. Fingerprint. I reached for the back of my head and brought back red-tipped fingers. Bea prodded me toward the door, but not before I found the doorjamb, the doorknob.

"Bonnie, damn it. Get the blood, will you?"

"What about the baby?"

"You can look after him and wipe up the gore, too. The things you and your brother—I swear."

The screen door slapped behind us. We stood under a night sky, the black trees waving. To my right, the lake and sky had become one. Bea heaved me by my elbow and guided me into the yard.

My tongue was too large for my mouth. "Where—" I choked.

"Oh, now, don't worry. We just need you to be somewhere else."

Bea took me to my own truck. The oar helped me step up, and then stuffed me in, like a loaf of dough into the oven. The television static came again. When I came to, I was curled on the floor, my head on the seat. We were moving.

Finally I understood that I would die.

Bea Ransey's face was lit by the dashboard. Her hair blew out of a knot in long strands. I had the feeling this was the first time I had ever really seen Bea Ransey. She was no church lady now.

She was no concerned grandmother rending her shirt on TV. Her eyes were black slits in deep wrinkles; she had the squint of an old ranch hand, even in the dark. The slits turned on me.

"Just so we're clear," the woman said. "I have more than one way to open up the back of your head. The other way, you won't be getting up at all."

"You wouldn't."

"You think you know me?" Bea Ransey said. "Best reason to shoot you yet."

I had no argument for this. I had started to think about other things I had never really seen before. Things that made no sense until they began to make perfect sense. "You wouldn't," I said. My mouth was stuffed with my bitten tongue. I talked around the taste of old blood. "You wouldn't leave my kid without a mother."

The slits turned on me again and then the linen skin at the sides of Bea's mouth pulled tight and youthful. She threw back her head and laughed. We could have been on a Sunday night drive. The truck turned. I felt the surface beneath the tires change. "I'm not the goddamned orphan prevention society, you idiot. I'd rather make your kid an orphan than see my grandkids with their own damn parents. Aidan with that slut? Steve's no-good dad had the decency to leave the state."

"My son—"

"I don't give a dang about your kid," she said. "It's my kids I'm saving."

"Why are your kids worth protecting"—we hit a bump in the road, and I lost my nerve for a second at the searing pain in my head—"and not mine?"

"Because mine are *mine*. They are worth fifty of you."

"Even though you tell your daughter how stupid she is. Even though your son beats his wife."

"You'll be wanting the rest of your brains spilled, then?"

"You have a pretty rotten sense of worth," I said.

"Nah. I'm worth a million, believe it or not. My kids'll do anything for me," she said. "Even if it's just to get their share someday."

I remembered the look Bonnie had given out the door over my shoulder, the apartment and job she wanted on her own. "They don't love you."

"My kids love being taken care of. Love not working too hard. Love having Mama to bail them out and give 'em ice cream money."

The words *ice cream money* nearly slipped past, but then I heard them.

Not money for ice cream; money from ice cream. Dairy Bar proceeds, funding Bo's hard living and Bonnie's imprisonment in the family's summer home. If I had just left the Dairy Bar parking lot instead of pulling into Parks. If I had only ignored blind nostalgia. How many times had I had that thought? *If I had just.*

"Your malts are really crappy."

Bea cackled until she had to wheeze for breath. "They sell real good, though. And those two little shacks keep me, my kids, my grandkids." She paused. "Half the town," she muttered. "You've no idea."

I did, though, because she'd already been clear. Worth a million. I didn't think she was rounding up. "They only fear you."

Bea gave the wheel a wide turn. Gravel pinged the bottom of the truck. "You wouldn't know anything about that, having a son that fears you."

Joshua. She was saying something about Joshua. "My son doesn't fear me."

"Sure, sure. Nothing to worry about with you in charge." She shook her head and squinted out the windshield with purpose. "Kids raised on shaky ground always bounce back."

We made a sharp turn, and the gravel fell away. The tires grew quiet. Tree branches scratched at both sides of the truck. The sounds of the deep woods went silent around us. We drove for a long time, the smell of wet and decaying leaves coating my throat. I tasted lake air.

Bea slowed the truck to a crawl, dragging through bramble and scrub, then stopped.

My focus darted between Bea's hands and the oar. The right moment—

But Bea was faster. "I'll get this," she said, sliding the oar away. "Get out, and try to remember who's got the gun here."

I had not seen a gun, but I believed in it. I slid out, using the truck's door to stand upright and stare into the clean black of my surroundings. A slim moon hid behind roiling clouds.

"Where—"

Bea's voice hissed in my ear. "Shut it." The oar handle nudged me forward. I stumbled, wondering if Bea could see anything. Maybe now was my chance to dash away, use the dark to my benefit. I hesitated.

"Do something funny," she said. "I won't even have to look at the mess."

She shoved me forward into the dark. The green smell of the lake gave me courage. "No wonder."

She sighed and prodded into my back with more force.

"No wonder your kids are no good," I said.

"You think you're better? Your father should have taken you out and drowned you like a kitten."

"I'm surprised he didn't think of that," I said.

"I'm pretty sure he did."

I staggered forward. "You knew him."

"Oh, hell, yes. I knew that piece of crap."

"We agree on this." I stopped, let the oar dig into me. "You knew him. From coming to your lake house?"

"Lake house," she grunted. "You sound like one of them fudge shoppers. Ain't no summer home, sweetie. That is my grand inheritance, or it would be, if I could outlive a few more cousins."

I stumbled over something, and Bea wrestled me back up. In the dark, I could identify the barest outline of a low roof against the sky.

Through my rising panic, I tried to think of something to say. "My dad—"

"Never thought much of him," Bea said. "Or your mother. Or you. Didn't put two and two together soon enough when you showed up in Parks." A flashlight beam appeared, pointing out the rusty locks on a metal door. Bea fidgeted with a ring of keys, then used a series of them to turn groaning locks. "Wished I'd realized it was you first time I saw you. I would have yelled across the street, 'If it isn't little Leeanna Winger from Sweetheart Lake!' You'd'a turned tail and we wouldn't be going through this dance."

The door opened. Bea's sharp fingernails squeezed and directed me. The flashlight lit a narrow path in the floor. The place, whatever it was, smelled like mouse droppings and grass, dank decay, and water damage. Like a garage. It was stuffy, hot, the air bad.

Bea reached for my hands. I fought, slapping her away.

The light swung into my face. Bea's voice sliced at me: "But you're the one that gave me the idea. Single woman on her own. Just her *kid.*"

I heard the threat and let my hands be guided together behind my back. It was thick tape this time.

"'Where is the father?' I ask myself," Bea said. "Everybody notices, but nobody cares enough to find out. Leely would have done that. She'd've stole Aidan and run and I'd never see my grandbaby again." Bea's breath came hot and snorting as she wound the tape tight. "You were the warning I needed and then— well, things fell together."

I didn't like the sound of that. Charity Jordan being murdered was not a flick of a domino. "You killed a girl and then stole Aidan so that his mother couldn't. Your sense of justice is screwed."

Bea grunted. She was using her teeth to tear the tape. "Justice is what I say it is. Bonnie'll tell you the same thing, soon as she gets her boy back. We all got our own right and wrong. Don't tell me you don't."

So that was Bonnie's deal. Watching over the kidnapped baby while everyone else in the family did boo-hoos for the cameras and played straight-faced games with the police. And her reward? A boy for a boy. And Bo's reward: his boy, all to himself.

"You'd have done the same for yours," Bea said. She pushed me up against a wall and let me crumple to the floor. My foot hit the flashlight, sent it rolling. The rough wooden wall caught at my clothes. "Hell, I'm pretty sure you did the same for yours already. We're not that different."

"I would never kill anyone."

"I'm not going to kill you." Bea began to tape my ankles together, the adhesive pulling at my skin.

I heard hope fluttering its wings in my chest, but couldn't listen. I knew what this looked like. "I would never leave anyone to die."

"Is that so?"

There was nothing to say. If Bea knew my father, then she probably knew where he was. Probably had even known how he got there and who paid for it. Mrs. Bea Ransey kept up on her Sweetheart Lake news; she probably got the *Vilas County News-Review* delivered to her Parks, Indiana, front door each week. Clicked her tongue over property values and obituaries. Stored away bits of news like a squirrel packing its cheeks.

Bea gave my head an awkward pat, leaving her warm hand on my forehead.

She wouldn't do it. She can't.

But the old woman was only holding my head so that she could find my mouth and force an oily cloth inside. I bucked and bit until Bea pinched my nose and shoved the cloth between my teeth.

As I gagged, Bea heaved a sigh and stood. She retrieved the flashlight, the beam brushing past a few dark shapes in the corners and then pointing unkindly into my eyes.

"I owe you, I guess," the woman said. "Least I can do is Josh'll never go needing, as long as I'm there. Of course, if his father comes along wanting him . . ."

I kicked at the woman's feet. I tried to cough out the rag and scream—scream at the retreating flashlight, at the door opening and closing, at the sound of the rusty locks squeezing back into place. At the black that descended and the silence that followed. Bea gone, and the wide woods of Wisconsin wrapping around me.

Chapter Forty

I worked on spitting out the cloth, making progress in incre-
ments I wouldn't have known how to calculate. Bea was gone
minutes, hours. Coughing, choking, spitting. And then I sneezed
twice in a row and the awful thing was away from me.

"OK." I heaved and grabbed for air. "OK."

When I had regained my breath, I raised myself up on an
elbow and screamed.

The sound bounced against the walls and back, filling the
shed.

I tried again, listening carefully. Cement block or brick.
Something sturdy. Not a shed, but an outbuilding, a garage.
Surely some of the sound escaped. I took a deep breath and
screamed long and loud.

I pictured the shadowed woods all around, the gray lake.
Houses—there would be a few, at least, and some more across
the water. But it was off-season, and the lake could be broad. I
thought of the ride in, the sound of limbs and scrub dragging
across the truck. The pines around the garage and a mile back

would be thick and cushioning. And the last paved road a half hour or better on the other side of that. I could spend all my energy screaming and no one would ever hear.

I fought the tape at my wrists for a while without progress, then I let myself rest against the wall. How long before someone realized I was gone? But I was already gone, and with Joshua missing, who would even think of me? Margaret would wonder. Russ would not be surprised. Ray, Mamie, Theresa. No one would blink if they never heard from me again.

I slid further down the wall and to my side and cried into the dirty floor. It was my fault, for teaching people to expect me to disappear. My fault, for spending all my energy saving Joshua and making sure there was no one left to save me. Not this time.

That escape from Ray, I had let everyone else save me. I had needed them all.

It was the little girl who saved me the first time.

That day at the dock, when Ray threw me down the stairs and picked up the oar, I had woken in the water, my chin just above the surface. My head was heavy. I lay back and let the surface of the lake hold me.

After a few minutes, I found the sandy bottom and walked my hands over the length of the dock until I could kneel in the shallows. Under the water, dark smoke rose from my skin. Blood. The ends of my hair dripped red streaks down my T-shirt. I reached for the back of my head, then stopped myself.

The dock was dark with blood.

The new oar lay on the embankment, cracked through the middle all the way from the blade to the collar.

Up ahead: the house we didn't own, the lives we wouldn't get to live.

I had decided.

I reached into the boat and grabbed one of the lifejackets. I stumbled out into the lake and walked until the jacket floated, lifting me along with it.

I had drifted around the bend and toward the camp's dock, when the girl's tuneless singing wormed into my fever dreams and woke me again. It was later in the day, the sun down a few notches. I hadn't gone far enough. The orange kayaks were tied up, twenty or more of them, and the girl sat at the edge with her back to me, swinging her legs. The seat of her swimsuit was dirty, her ponytail long and crooked, hooking out from behind an ear. She'd tightened it herself at some point with her own grubby little hands.

I didn't know about kids. She seemed young to be down at the water by herself, but then I'd always been the girl down by the water by herself. Shhhh, little girl. Or maybe I had never made a noise. Maybe she thought she imagined me, and then woke in the night with dark dreams.

The man in the truck saved me next. I had dragged myself over a long stretch of shallow water onto a low shelf of grass to get out of the lake, out of the way of the after-work water-skiers and tubers, the pontoons full of people with cocktails. I lay on the shelf of grass for a long while, letting the woods behind me fade into dusk. Our little rental house seemed a million miles away, and the time had stretched so that I wasn't sure if I had floated through the afternoon or a full week.

I crawled up the embankment and dragged myself upright to skirt the clearing and any buildings that might be there. I was reminded I was barefoot by a sharp rock.

"Who's there?"

I stood, quiet, waiting for him to go back inside. My ears were ringing and I was cold, quaking. I knew suddenly that he could see me, that he couldn't believe his eyes, that he didn't know what to do.

"Holy . . ." Barely a breath's worth. "Baby girl, how are you still standing?"

In his truck, I fell asleep again but he reached over and gently shook me awake. "Don't die, sweetheart," he said, his voice reverent, only a prayer. Maybe he only thought these things and I could hear them inside his head because I had already died and before I could be an eagle on the wind, I would be a ghost. His hand on my shoulder was warm and insistent. "Hold on, now."

And then the nurse. She wore scrubs with stick-figure drawings on them, as though a gang of children had decorated her that day. She leaned into my view. "Well now," she said. "That looks like it hurts, doesn't it?"

I hadn't seen it, didn't want to. Didn't want to talk about it. The man was gone. He'd let me out close to the hospital and pointed me in the right direction. "You understand," he said, his mouth barely forming the words. "Tell them what happened to you, baby girl. They'll fix you up."

By some luck the man had taken me to the hospital in the next county, not the closer emergency clinic where my file was thick. And maybe this place had a file, too. A list. When it came to emergencies, I was what they called a known entity. A frequent flier: bones, bruises, casts, ice packs, bloody noses.

The nurse had a sense of humor. "Now, what brings you in today, sugar?" she said. She turned my chin this way and that and took a long look at my neck. "Bludgeoned head, bruises in the shape of someone's fingers, or did you have some other complaint I needed to know about?" By now my whole body was stiff, my left arm cradled to protect the shoulder that had caught my fall off the deck.

"I'm pregnant," I said.

"Well," she said. "That's good news."

I knew she was being sarcastic, but I thought the news might be good. The news could be good.

"Did the daddy do this to you?"

I watched her realize that I wasn't going to say so. It was best to give away less than people wanted. "I got hit by a truck," I said.

"How many times?" she murmured and put down a few words on the chart. "They'll want to ask you about that, so get the color of the truck straight. In the meantime, we need to get you up to a room, Mama." Neither of us moved. I didn't know if I could.

I'd been in pain then, too. Fatigued. What had moved me off the bed and into action? Into the clothes I found on my roommate's side of the room as she slept, and later, with a twenty the nurse slipped into my hand at the bus station as she dropped me off, onto the bus and away? Away as far as I could afford, and then a shelter that didn't ask too many questions until I got a job and then the little tin-can mobile home, all to myself. And then the Tennessee state trooper at my door, when I'd only just settled in. "I got to tell them I seen you, miss," he'd said. "They think you're at the bottom of a lake, and now they can stop looking." And then the librarian with a little handwriting knowledge. Then Kent. Who hadn't I allowed to save me?

I lay in the foul dust of the forgotten garage, forcing myself back into the memory, sorting the moments of my life and the saviors. Not Kent, not the community center librarian before him. Not the trooper, the nurse, not the truck driver, not the little girl. Each had saved me and yet none of them had, not really. This is why people believed in gods, in magic, in wishes on stars. This is why people believed—in rabbit's feet and fate and crossed fingers. In yellow rooms—

Joshua. But it hadn't only been Joshua who had saved me. Not only the child I carried and thought I might keep and raise. I'd had no faith in that plan or my own ability to see it through.

What saved me was the child I had been, the child who had not been given a moment of freedom or choice or faith in anything or anyone. Didn't that kid deserve a chance, this many years later?

I remembered my mother's eyes shift away from me to the dirty sink of the old motel restaurant. *What's out there?* Something else, but it hadn't been enough. You can't trust blue skies, she had told me once. My mother had not believed in luck and so neither had I, because the only luck was the kind you made. From doing something, from standing on your own feet, from kicking down closed doors, from leaping into the wide open unknown from a lakeside boulder—

From rising out of green water, retching, to find that the girl you'd been had drowned. That girl was still there, under Sweetheart Lake, waiting for me to give in and crawl back into the water.

I hadn't come all this way—the apartments, the towns, and the curving roads through pines. Not all this way, just to die here nameless and unknown, alone. I believed one thing: it had to have been worth more than this. What was out there? Everything. Only everything. And no one was coming to save me, not this time.

I pushed myself up and swung my legs like a clapper in a bell across the floor, striking out for any tool—anything—lying about. Nothing.

"OK." Think. Think.

There was a hulking shape in the corner, just a bit darker than the dark itself. I remembered the sweep of the flashlight, the blink of something there. Firewood covered by a tarp? Or something more useful?

I inched toward the corner, but my mind raced ahead. Joshua. I needed to get out of here. The police. No, the woods. If that bitch so much as looks at Joshua . . . I'd have to find a road first, or another isolated house, and who knew if someone would even be there. I'd have to break in. Then what? A phone. Police. Would the Ranseys still be there?

My foot found something. I tapped at it with my shoe, the object answering with a metallic chink. Not firewood, at least.

I scooted around so that I could yank the tarp with my hands. It caught. "OK." I backed up into it, reaching my fingers through cobwebs until—

A lawn mower.

I used my feet to topple it, flipping it upright against my legs. Accumulated dust shaken from the tarp swirled over me. I turned my back on the thing and fumbled with bound hands until I found the bottom.

It had blades. Dull, but still there, still in place. *Blades.*

With a stretch, I found the right angle to saw at the tape. I fumed and rubbed my wrists raw. Bea's kids would do anything for her. I nearly laughed. "The difference between you and me," I said. The difference was that I would do anything for my kid. Big difference.

At last my hands broke apart.

I ripped the tape away and then tore at the binds on my ankles with fumbling, swollen fingers.

"OK." My voice was more assured now. I stood, shaking, and found the door.

Locked. I knew that.

I could still die here. All that maneuvering and I might still die here.

I couldn't. I had to get out. For Joshua. For Aidan. For Leila

Ransey. For myself and for the chance to take an oar to that silver knot of hair on the back of Bea Ransey's head.

I had to get out. And then through the brambles to the dirt path, the path to the gravel and through miles of forest on a road that no one else probably used. All to find the paved road that led, if nowhere else, back to the Ransey compound.

My skull was exposed, the fever raging. I couldn't think. My legs trembled under my own weight. I slid to the floor and rested my temple against the cool wall. Think, think. But I couldn't. I couldn't. I was getting tired and my head hurt beyond comprehension.

Joshua.

I came roaring to my feet, clawing along the wall away from the door and through a cobwebbed corner. I ran my hands high and low, high and low along the wall. Another corner, more dusty wall, and then my fingernails grazed a wide crack and a different texture. I ran my hand back and then down the crack to the floor, then up until it cornered and turned.

Another door.

There was something covering most of the door, heavy. A wall of thick pressed board. Building supplies? I shoved and pulled and pried, smelling the rot at the bottom of the wood when I gained on it. Water-damaged pressed plywood sheets, heavy as hell.

I strained at it until I lost track of time and my head began to swim. I listened to my own breath. If I died here—

I gave one last groaning push. The weight of the wood panels shifted.

I leapt backward, feeling the rush of air as the boards collapsed and slammed to the ground. My lungs filled with dust, but I fought through the coughing fit and rushed to the door.

It wouldn't budge. Wouldn't slide left or right, wouldn't be pushed or pried open. My fingertips grew raw and splintered. Nothing gave, even a little bit.

"God*damn it!*" And I heard the sound of my scream going out into the woods, free. This was the way. This was the only way. I had to do this. For Joshua. For the girl I used to be and everything she was due. For the beautiful life I had, for the chance to see the blue sky or black, just one more time.

Think. *Think*. And then I realized what I hadn't done.

I bent low and, with the last of my will, pulled the bottom of the door up and inward, toward me. A hinge somewhere above my head creaked and crackled.

Clear air rushed in, along with the sound of a hard breeze rustling the pines. I stood for a moment in the stage of the open garage door, torn hands, raw skin, the wound on the back of my skull furious from the exertion.

The trees waited to see what I would do.

I noted the spot of moonlight on the surface of the lake, and limped in the opposite direction. Hoping for road.

Chapter Forty-one

The trees began to say my name.

I stumbled through the woods, briar and brush, everything throwing itself in my way. Stumbled for miles without ever finding the dirt path the truck had taken. I did not find a gravel road. Just trees.

Trees, trees, and more trees, someone had said.

A million years ago.

I wanted to put my head down. My head, so heavy. But I fought on, banging into a tree stump, tripping over a fallen log in the dark.

"Trees, trees, and more trees," I said. I liked the way it sounded, my voice alive in the dead silence. Trees, trees, and more trees. The guy who'd said it first had been lost in the woods in his lifetime. He wasn't just making noise. "Trees, trees."

I felt the trees nod toward me for a closer look.

"I'm not crazy," I said.

The wind picked up. Dry leaves from under my feet rose into the wind and rustled all around me. The aspens would be lifting the bellies of their leaves to the wind, the loose yellow pieces dropping to the forest floor like coins thrown into a fountain. I wished I would live to see it. A storm was a beautiful thing.

The pines nodded deeply.

I warmed to their solicitude. "Trees, trees," I sang.

At the first gray of predawn, my foot hit gravel. I stood in the middle of a thin stretch of pale, crushed rock. From where I stood, the road seemed to lead out of forest and back into forest. But I knew it wasn't true. It was a road, and it would take me.

"Thank you."

The trees bowed extravagantly, showing me which way. I didn't know which way. I took their recommendation.

I started down the road, right down the middle. No one could miss me. I could not be passed by.

But after a while I had to watch my feet. The gravel kept rolling away and taking my shoes with it. The road was trying to buck me. I'd have to walk to the side of the road.

The scrub next to the road was thick and punishing. I was too tired, too slow.

What if the woman, the bad woman—I couldn't quite come up with her name—what if she came back to check on me?

The forest presented itself as the best idea of all. I returned to it.

And then the trees began to call my name.

They didn't have one voice, but many. *Anna*. The high wind made their song hard to hear. *Leeanna*.

I stumbled through the trees, patting as many as I could, thankful they could stand when I couldn't.

Anna, they sang. And just before I might have found the courage to answer, I tripped over a limb. I fell to my knees, pine needles carpeting the blow to my palms.

I let myself meet the ground, soft. I could rest here. All the rest of it would take care of itself. This was my job, my only responsibility.

Lie down among the trees, home.

IN MY OWN grave.

I blinked. Above, a canopy of trees and a daytime sky.

I was soaked. The rains had come and gone while I slept. It had not felt like sleeping and now waking did not feel like waking.

"Dead," I said, to test the theory.

The only dry spot was the ground under my body. I began to shiver. The trees stood straight and disappointed. They had gathered around to watch.

I reached for one of them and pulled myself up.

The wind had died back down. Nothing chirped or sang. The woods behind me were waiting. They'd heard something.

Then I heard, too.

A car coming, on the road.

I had lost the road. I stumbled from one tree to the next, blessing each one.

Through the trunks I saw a black truck. Just as I might have dreamed it. Just as I would have conjured it.

I propelled myself forward, body stiff, lungs burning. I was too late. The truck passed, kicking up clouds of dust.

Black truck, Indiana plates on the back.

It was the sheriff. I had no idea how or why. I threw myself into the dust, into the road, and tried to make any noise I could think of. I knelt in the road and grabbed handfuls of gravel to throw.

A half mile down the road, the truck's brake lights glowed red. It stopped, paused, and began to reverse toward me. It skidded to a stop, another cloud of silver dust billowing over me, into my eyes. The figure of a broad-shouldered man hurried toward me.

"Sheriff," I said, my voice a croak. I thought I had never been more happy. My eyes stung. I turned my head away, coughing. "Russ."

He pulled me gently from the ground and I let him.

"What the hellfire happened to you?"

Not the sheriff. I tried to stand on my feet. But still—someone. I would take any help now, any help at all.

"—looking all over for you," the man was saying. "—how the hell you managed it—"

I knew the voice.

"—what you're even doing here—"

Bo Ransey.

"No," I screamed, and swung my arms.

"Hey, hellcat." He backed away, raising his hands in surrender.

"Not after that."

"Can you get yourself in the truck?" he said.

"Not after all that."

"Didn't think so. Here—"

"Get away from me, I swear to God."

"We're at a real standoff, then."

I took a step backward into the brush. Wobbling.

"You're a mess," he said. He watched me take another step. "You're not going to get far."

"Sorry you weren't around to help?"

"How are you way out here and your truck is being pulled out of the Midnight right now? This lake isn't even on the same chain as the Midnight."

"I'm not buying that innocent look."

He raised his eyebrows.

"Or that one." I took another step backward, my shoe sliding in the loose gravel at the edge of the road.

"Where you going? There's not going to be anything left of you, you keep walking that way. Nothing but trees."

"The trees are—" My friends. My army. I didn't want him to know how outnumbered he was but then I lost my balance and slid down the embankment on my knee. I couldn't stand. "I want—a glass of water."

"Got a Coke in the truck."

I let myself slide the rest of the way to the ground. "I wouldn't take spit from you—"

"Forgive me for saying so, but you don't get to choose from a menu right now."

He came for me, hauled me upright and dragged me a few feet. "Jesus, you're a mess." He knelt and let me fall over his shoulder, sandbag-style. I struck feebly at his back. But he was right. I had no other choice. I'd have to go back to the Ranseys and give Bea a chance to get it right.

I welcomed the darkness when it came for me again. I only wished, in the blink of thought I was allowed, that since I was going to die, I wished he'd just left me in the woods.

Chapter Forty-two

——not out of the woods."

In my own grave. I opened my eyes onto a white ceiling. I tried to sit up, to run. I was tied again.

"Forget it. You're not going anywhere."

The voice. I did not trust it. I had a memory of talking to trees. I blinked into brightness.

"Is that bothering you?"

A hazy figure walked into my view, pulled the shades. The white room now gray, I could see the outline of the man who held me captive.

I didn't trust it.

"You're not," I said, my voice rasping and slicing at the words. "Wearing your hat."

"No," Russ said. "I'm a gentleman."

"Paying respects. To the dead."

"I don't think we're quite ready to get out the shovels."

I concentrated on the ceiling, willing this to be real. "Dead," I whispered, remembering how the tops of the pines nodded at me.

"Nope." He brought a chair to the side of the bed and sat with his hands in his lap. He fidgeted, boot heels tapping against the leg of the chair.

"Can't. Sit still," I said.

He looked at me sadly. "Go ahead and rest. I'll try to stop jangling."

I reached out my hand. Tethered.

He shifted to the front of his chair and smoothed my hand back down. "You're on some tubes. They want you to stay as still as you can. We'll try together, OK?" He held my hand in his. His warm hand.

He was here. He had come all this way. He had come all this way to—bring news.

I tried to swallow the bile rising in my throat. "Joshua?"

He didn't say anything. I squeezed his hand as best I could. He tried on a bemused smile. "Bo Ransey said you were pretty tough."

Ransey.

"Bea," I whispered. My throat burned from the effort. "Aidan. The lake."

He hushed me until I had to rip my hand away.

"Bonnie. Aunt. *Steve.*" I tried to rise from the bed. The back of my skull had some screaming to do.

Somewhere behind me, a machine beeped.

Russ squinted at the contraptions to the side of my bed and leaned in closer. "If they see you all worked up," he said in his horse-trainer voice, "they are going to make me leave."

I lay back. We regarded each other.

"You don't want me to leave?"

I remembered the moment when I had mistaken Bo Ransey for him. The wave of relief that was more than what it should have been.

"I don't want to leave, either." He took my hand again. "But I'm going to have to. It's been nothing but paperwork since you rousted that kidnapper I've been looking for."

I could barely mouth the word. "Aidan."

"He's doing fine, Anna. He's just fine. I'm just going to trust that you didn't go looking for him because you thought I wasn't doing my job well enough. Again."

I shook my head, regretted it.

"Stay still, now."

"Joshua."

"I wish you hadn't gone off on your own like that. When I saw your truck being pulled out of the water—"

I couldn't follow him. He'd been in town before Bo had found me, my truck already dragged out. He had been here for something else, and now Aidan was safe and so was I. And Bo was—

"Bo?"

"Shh. I'll tell you, if you just be still, is that a deal? I came up here on a lead. Bo Ransey followed me up here, vigilante that he is, and found you with your skull bashed in. Far from home but strangely not so far from an old stretch of property his family fishes and hunts from. Illegally, of course. They don't own that garage she put you in. They don't really own the house, either, which is how it never got tossed for Aidan. It's still in Granddaddy's trust, buried in legalese and decades of tax evasion."

I tried to rise up from the bed, but Russ gave me a look. *"Bo,"* I said, trying to convey more meaning than I was capable of. He was part of it, and he'd convinced everyone. I tried to remember everything Bea had said. There was something nagging at me, something not right among the things she'd told me.

"Bo found you, stopped by the old place to grab something to stop your bleeding all over his truck, finds his kid, his sister, and his mother, and she's mad as hell," Russ said. "And you know what Big Mama said?"

I remembered Bo's bright rage at the news conference. He'd really believed that his wife had taken Aidan. He'd believed with everything he had that Leila would produce their child if he yelled, if he pushed, if he pleaded. No matter what his hand-writing said, he would have done anything for Aidan. Maybe, I realized, his resentment lines had come from his rotten mother. And Leila, caught in a failing marriage made worse by her controlling mother-in-law. What if she had been scared not of Bo but of what it meant to leave the Ransey family, to defy Mama Ransey?

"She did it," I squeaked. "For him."

Russ stared at me. "You mothers are a hard lot. She said, 'Get the gun from my coat.' Bo got the gun, his kid, and you out of there. We found Bea and Bonnie heading south. I think you covered more ground with your head caved in than they did in that stretch car of theirs." He didn't smile. "I just can't believe—what were you thinking going into that house?"

"Police," I said. "Nobody." This was a good place to be a criminal, for all the attention you could raise. A good place to amass a million dollars in net worth out of ice cream.

He nodded. "That Vilas County cop thought you were a crank. I was out with the county chief when you came by. They just don't get that many missing Indiana kids in one week."

"Joshua." I was suddenly done with anything having to do with Ranseys. All I wanted was my son. Before I could stop the rush of misery, I was crying.

"We'll find him." He was nearly off his chair, on his knees. "I swear, Anna. I can't believe your kid. He's like a Green Beret. Did you teach him that?"

I cut a look his way.

"Oh, yeah. I know all about it now. You're quite the marathoner yourself, aren't you? None of that anymore, right? None of that jumping around, your ass on fire."

I let my eyes close. So tired. I listened to his breath, felt the weight of his hand on mine.

He hadn't known to look for Aidan here. He'd been here already. Another case, and there was really only one other case it could be.

He'd come all this way. For Joshua.

After a few minutes, Russ slid his hand away from mine. I wasn't asleep, but couldn't open my eyes or say a word. I felt him leaning over me, a light touch at my temple.

"I'm sorry," he whispered. "I thought he'd be here."

He came all this way. For me.

Chapter Forty-three

Drowsing, I became aware of an argument in the hall.

"I'm not going to disturb her," a man was saying. Not Russ. Not Ray, thank goodness. "Just need to drop off a few belongings."

Footsteps. I struggled to wake, my eyelids fluttering open to see Shane Mullen letting a large plastic bag slide off a clipboard onto the windowsill. The bag held a pound or more of gray sand. No, not sand. Ash.

"Yeeeyuk," he murmured. He pulled a pen off the clipboard and tapped his pen a few times on the paper there. *Tap-tap.* I was reminded of Margaret, poor Margaret. But who was the invalid now? "I'll just . . ." Mullen said, tapping a few more times on the board before writing something on the form and putting the pen back. He turned and saw that my eyes were open. "Oh, sorry. I didn't mean to wake you. I just—I brought you, uh, your mom, I think?" He shuffled nervously from foot to foot. "You're in no shape—I mean, you look great, but . . . I took care of the form for you. Do you need anything?"

I closed my eyes in answer. After I was sure he was gone, I

opened them again. The bag of ashes sat in thin stripes of light from the window shades. Ashes in a bag, bag in a box, box in a truck, truck in a lake. My computer, my photos, Joshua's things, all lost.

The stitches in the back of my head itched. My wrists were sore, and they had begun to itch, too.

The spare white room made me think of all the white walls I had never painted, the white blank page of a life I faced if Joshua didn't turn up.

I'd had the nurse turn off the television, close the blinds. The magazines the volunteers brought slid to the floor.

Later, I heard one of the nurses in the hallway use the word *depressed*. A nice round word, with the clip *tsk* of diagnosis to it.

"Hell, yes, she's blue," Russ boomed. "She's got sixteen stitches in her noggin and her son is missing. Give her a break. Give us both a break."

He left the nurse in the hallway and brought a chair around to face me. He held an officer's hat and a manila folder between his knees.

"How are your gabbing muscles today?"

I shrugged.

"Don't let's make that nurse right about you being depressed, OK? Do you want to be loaded up with zonk-out pills?"

"Fine," I said.

"Good." He opened the folder. "I came to commend you on your policing." He held out the folder like a platter, offering a wrinkled piece of pink paper.

"What is it?"

"You tell me. You had it on you when you were found."

Tramping through the woods, palming trees. Lying on the floor of Aidan's room, the back of my head open. I could have sworn that Joshua had been with me there. My memory couldn't be trusted. "I don't know."

"Well, let me tell you, then. Seems you found the other part of Leila Ransey's so-called ransom note." He held it up, showed me the dark pink hearts along the edges. It was ripped along one edge. "You never liked that note, did you? It never added up."

I remembered the pile of papers, clothes, dirty dishes on the Ransey's table, Bonnie sitting across from me, calculating the value of her time. "I took it."

"Damn right you did. That note wasn't for ransom. It was for help." He held out the paper. Unhooked from most of my wires, I could sit up on an elbow.

Mama Ransey, I don't know how to thank you. We do need a fresh start, like you said. Both of us. Actually, all of us. But you know

Same hand as the first note and the grocery list. I couldn't remember the exact wording of the original piece. Something about keeping Aidan with her and money.

"Bea offered to help Leila take a break," I said. "Only Leila didn't want a break from Aidan. Bea gave her a credit card and then turned Leila in for stealing it. This is why," I said, running a finger across the ragged edge of the paper. "This is why we don't like to work with copies. Copies flatten the texture, the tears on the page. It's easy to forget you don't have the full story."

"You have a curious obsession with originals given your faked Social Security card, but point taken. On that note, I brought you a little gift," he said, holding out a short stack of papers. The evidence forms, again, but this time the originals. I turned my head. "Oh, you don't care about my missing drugs anymore?"

I didn't care about anything but Joshua. Why couldn't he understand that?

"Well, I'm going to leave these here," he said. "We'll just see."

"I don't want to work with law enforcement anymore," I said. "Or with people, really. Except the lonelyhearts. They're all I have since I can't work with corporations anymore, either." I lay back, letting Leila's note drop to the covers.

"Lonelyhearts," he murmured, taking back the note. "And why not corporations?"

"Just some—mistake. I got sloppy."

"My experience is that you're paying closer attention than anyone has a right to. When you asked me about the powder? The drugs that weren't drugs? I was—*fuming* would not be too harsh a word. But you know what it was?"

He put the folder aside and went to the window. Pulled the blinds up.

"Hey," I said, wincing from the light.

"It's good for you. You need to get yourself together or they'll never let you leave."

"I'm healing like a good little human."

"Psychologically speaking, I mean. Your doc wants to put you in that place in town. River-something."

I made a noise in my throat.

"What?"

"Nothing."

"You didn't guess," he said.

I looked at him.

"The substances back in the evidence room that should have been cocaine and heroine. Results came back this morning. I think you can guess. Mostly starch, sugars, a little milk protein."

I thought about it. If I could guess, and he was certain I could—

"Dehydrated barley," I said. "Malt powder."

"And ice milk crystals." He beamed and counted off on his fingers. "Kidnapping, murder, attempted murder, and, forgive me for this one given the topic, but the cherry on top: drug trafficking between Parks, Indiana, and Sweetheart Lake, Wisconsin, out of the back of shitty little ice cream stands."

Russ came back to the chair and, sighing deeply, put himself into it. "And probably with drugs stolen from my evidence locker, but I don't have the link yet."

"Tara Lombardi," I said. "She was dating Bo."

"She told me," he said. "There's no accounting for taste. But Bo's clean."

I made a face. Bo had been added to the list of people I owed my life to, and I didn't care for the taste of that.

"I know what you think, but I'm telling you—he's not in on it. This is Bea's ship. The trouble is, I'm still not sure she's strong enough to have killed Charity."

"I assure you she is."

"You saw her? You saw her swing at you?"

I had to admit that I hadn't.

"But more importantly," he said. "Why? Why kill the nanny at all?"

It had always bothered me. I was right that Leila had no reason to, but who had? "She had Aidan," I said, prospecting.

"But Bea's the grandmother. She could have gotten Aidan any number of ways, pretended he'd wandered off . . ."

We both sat with it for a minute.

"You're trying to trick me into doing more business for you," I said. "I told you—no more law enforcement, only drippy love notes and hopeful prison pen pals."

"What's wrong with working with the likes of me? I'm all

right." He took in the bag of ashes on the sill and looked away. "What mistake did you make? Are you talking about that guy who got himself killed in Chicago?"

"Not sure if we'd be talking about the same guy."

He lifted his chin, nodded at the ceiling. "We are. Kent called. The only way I knew to get the whole of Vilas County looking for you was he had some crazy voicemail you left him."

Kent. I owed him again. The whole county searching—

I remembered the sound of the trees' song to me in the dark, imagined Ray and Mamie and Betty Spaghetti tramping through the woods, calling out my names. Well, at least I hadn't been going insane. Even if I felt a little sad to have the trees' song explained. The trees had guided me, kept me on my feet. If I didn't want the strangeness explained away logically, how was that a fault? A little magic when I didn't have any.

"Kent says to tell you that guy's wife had him killed."

"Because he—" Because he was impotent? Wait, no. It wasn't the CEO who was sexually frustrated, but the author of the note. "Because she—"

"Because he was cheating on her with his assistant. Kent says you sent them the secretary. When she broke down under questioning, they went back to the wife, and then *she* broke. A real detective you're turning into." He looked me over. "Maybe just one more case before you're retired?"

Tired being the part I felt most keenly. The tubes were gone, but I hadn't regained an appetite or the will to get out of bed. There was talk of putting my IV back in if I didn't start eating.

"One more investigation together," he said. "I'll spring you from this place for an hour or two."

I blinked at him. "You can get me out?"

"I told them I had you under arrest."

"Oh." I glanced into the hallway. "I'll never be able to almost die in this place again."

"Your reputation is completely soiled. You might as well go."

"My head," I said.

"You're doing fine."

"Can't walk."

"You haven't tried."

Out the window, it was sunny, probably warm enough. I didn't care where I was. "Steal a wheelchair," I said.

He went to arrange for my release while I still agreed to it and I lay back, trying to avoid looking in the direction of the bag of ashes. I would have to do something with them, something more like kindness than I had felt toward my mother in a long time. My eyes fell on the evidence forms and traveled over the signatures again. The same markers, over and over—the same hand. I looked more closely, then picked up the top page and wiped it with my hand. The dust marks from the copier—they were still there. They hadn't been dust. Here they were, on the originals, tiny taps of ink at the beginning of each signature as the author chose the identity he would use instead of his own.

I put the form back, gently, trying to let everything flooding my dizzy head take its turn.

Tap-tap. The hesitant hand of someone about to deceive.

All the notes and checks and receipts that had passed before me during the last few weeks—where had I seen that?

At last I located the blots of ink—dabs of indecision as someone either professed or denied a love, written in reluctance but later torn and burned and tossed into a dead girl's trash.

I reached for the call button and pressed it frantically. Mullen's second home, Russ had called it. Checking in on the Ranseys. Bea's million-dollar ice cream stand. Mullen, signing *my* name to the form releasing my mother's ashes.

"Get him back," I said to the nurse who hurried into my room. "The sheriff. Get that man back now."

Chapter Forty-four

Russ was quiet in the truck, his face gray.

"I'm sorry," I said.

"Nothing for you to be sorry about," he said.

Only that he'd had to arrest his best guy, his second-in-command. Only that he probably felt like a fool. There would be an investigation, of course, into the missing evidence, the chief deputy's finances and relationship with the dead woman. We both expected Bea Ransey to throw Mullen in for Charity's murder, and we were both fairly sure she wouldn't be lying. Bea Ransey, after all, had been establishing an alibi. She never left Parks during the time Aidan went missing. She was on the TV, in the sheriff's office, in the ice cream stand.

It was Mullen who had a little R&R scheduled that week, a trip cut short—and yet the sunburned hands of a man who might have driven all the way to northern Wisconsin and back that day. He was always at the Ransey house, Russ had said. Always at the Ransey house to keep an eye on the Ranseys, to find himself in the path of a cute young babysitter. By the time they met in the secluded Sugar

Creek Park that morning, a neighbor spotting the cruiser "patrol-ling" the area, Charity had already decided on breaking things off. She left her bag at home and burned his letter. She brought along Aidan—as a guarantee, maybe, to keep things civilized. Maybe she had threatened to tell his wife, to spill everything she'd learned about the ice cream business from being in the Ransey home. But she didn't know how much Mullen himself had to lose, how much stake he had in that ice cream shack. I remembered Bea saying how "things" had fallen together. Charity's murder was the first domino, after all, and nabbing Aidan away from a custody battle had been secondary. A crime of convenience, a cherry on top.

Russ was keeping his own thinking to himself, so I kept quiet, too, going along with whatever happened now, waiting for some-one to push me toward a next move. But when his truck turned off Railroad Street onto the access road and found without any problem the parking lot of Riverdale Convalescence Center, I reached for the door handle.

"You going to jump?"

"I can't go in there," I said. How had he figured out where my dad was? How had he figured out I had a dad and what did it matter to him, anyway?

"I'm not getting you a bed," he said.

"No, I—I just can't."

"With all the victories you've claimed today? I think you've got it in you for one more."

Two wheelchairs and their hunched occupants sat out front, a woman in scrubs standing nearby.

"I don't want to."

Russ got out and came around to my side. He brought the folded wheelchair out from the back of his truck, popped it open, and opened my door.

"It's not a mystery," I said. "I already know."

"You can solve cases before they're even presented to you?"

"There is someone I very much don't want to see in there."

"What if you're wrong?" he said.

"Take me back."

"Can't do it." He held up his empty hands. "I checked you out just now. You are no longer a guest at Eagle River Memorial Hospital."

I had the strangest sensation that I had left something there. Or—somewhere. But there was nothing. The clothes on my back, not even mine but bad castoffs from the hospital's lost and found. Everything else left behind or dunked into Midnight Lake. Everything—

"I brought along the ashes," he said.

"Take me—take me to Parks."

He came to the door and held out his arm. "I would gladly do that, if that's where I thought you needed to be. Please."

I hadn't known I could still have my mind changed for me. More of his hocus-pocus. Or did that even make any sense, now that I knew that the day I'd seen him moving Bea Ransey like a chess piece, Bea Ransey was the one who'd been leading the game? Maybe I gave people too much credit for always being on the make. Or not enough credit for wanting to do what was right.

"Fine," I said.

I let him tuck me into the wheelchair and roll me past the elderly women in theirs. "Morning, ladies," he said, taking off his uniform hat. His hair was red-gold in the sun.

"Running for office?" I said.

"Spreading my charm around," he said. "Otherwise, it's too much."

Inside, the woman at the front desk nodded at him and stared at me. He rolled me up to the desk and took a pen from the counter. He looked at the pen and then at me.

"Sign away. I can't see anything from down here."

He searched my face. "Which name are we going by these days?"

"Anna. For now."

He whisked me down a long, sterile hallway into a bright atrium. I'd never been to Riverdale, but it seemed like the hospital I'd just left. Clean. Bland, except for a palm tree growing in the middle of the atrium, its canopy crowding a large skylight.

"Even the old folks' homes in Wisconsin have more trees than Parks," I said.

"You don't remember seeing any trees? Near a barn?"

I held on as we sped through the atrium and down another hallway. The chair stopped in front of a door. A door like all the other doors, except that my blood pumped so hard I wondered if I could pop the stitches in my scalp. "I really don't think I can do this."

"I'll be right here."

"I'm not sure how much I believe in forgiveness."

He reached over me for the door handle. "I'm really sorry to hear that."

The door swung open. Across the room, Joshua rose to his feet.

"Hi, Mom."

I didn't trust any of it. "Joshua?"

"I'm sorry," he said.

"Joshua?"

Russ rolled my chair to meet him. Joshua leaned awkwardly into me for a hug but I grabbed him and pulled him into my lap. My whole body shook.

"Mom, don't hurt yourself."

"I don't hurt. Anymore."

Russ backed away and closed the door.

I gasped for breath, taking in the smell of his neck, his hair. "I was so worried."

"I know."

"You don't know how worried I was."

"I'm *sorry.*"

I pushed him up, holding him by the shoulders so I could feast on the sight of him. "I don't want you to be sorry. I want you to know how much I love you."

He shrugged.

He was still thirteen. I couldn't expect him to be anything else.

But it wasn't just that. He wouldn't look me in the eye.

All this. All this, and I'm still going to lose him. Which boy would I bring home?

I said, "I'm sorry, too."

He glanced at me, away.

"I messed up. I thought I was doing the right thing, but I wasn't."

He picked at the ugly shirt I wore. "So," he said finally, "what now?"

"What do you mean?"

"Do we—what do we do now?"

"I'm not sure." And I wasn't. The old fears had left me, but the weightlessness didn't feel safe, either. "I've been a mess since you've been gone."

He studied my face, the bandage around my head. "You look really *bad.*"

"That—I'll have to explain."

"Sheriff Keller told us about it."

"Us?" For the first time, I tore my eyes from him and saw that there were beds in the room. One was empty, the sheets rumpled and slept in. Joshua was looking toward the other bed, which was not empty. I didn't want to see the thin figure there, the way the sheet revealed the bony knee underneath.

"Oh, no."

"Grandpa," Joshua said.

"Is he—"

"He doesn't talk," Joshua said. "Or eat. Or look at you."

"This is why? You ran away to see—"

He shrugged.

"You ran away from me, but you had nowhere to go."

"Grandparents always like to see their grandkids." He frowned at the figure in the bed. "That's what I heard."

I squeezed his shoulders. "Oh, Josh. All this? Just for—"

He loosened himself from me and stood up straight. "I didn't know anything about him. Everything was such a big, dumb secret."

"Couldn't you have asked me?"

"You said he was dead."

I glanced toward the bed. Wasn't he? "I thought he was. I thought you came to find your—father."

His shrug was small this time. "I tried."

"But?"

"I think I saw him once," he said. "He didn't look—real."

"What did you do?"

He lifted a hand to his mouth and gnawed at a hangnail. He'd chewed his fingernails to nubs. "Nothing. He didn't see me."

No, he wouldn't have. He was much too selfish to notice anyone else.

I gestured for Joshua to roll me closer to the bed. My father lay on his side, eyes staring past me. He was skin and bone, an empty shell.

"I think he can hear us," Joshua said.

"I don't think he can." The old man didn't so much as blink at the sound of my voice.

I felt self-consciousness creep over the scene. I wasn't sure what I would say, even if he could hear me. I felt as though I'd said the things that needed to be said, in action, in my departure, in my absence. He'd spoken with gestures, and so had I.

I would never forgive him. He'd never given me a reason. But I wondered about those ashes in Keller's truck, if I wouldn't feel differently about them if I'd had a little more time to forgive my mother. I understood a little better now. She was scared. No one had ever taught her that she didn't have to be. But she had somehow taught me, and that was a lot.

I pushed back a few inches. "Your . . . grandfather and I have already said everything to each other we need to. Can you understand that?"

Joshua turned to the prone figure on the bed. He nodded.

"Joshua, I'm so *sorry*. I've made a lot of mistakes. You haven't even heard all the mistakes I've made yet. And—I can't change them."

The door opened a crack and Russ peeked in. "OK in there?" he asked.

"Yes, sir," Joshua said, standing taller.

I reached for his hand to keep him close. He seemed so grown-up just now. I remembered Ray pawing at the photo I'd left him, his misery at the years already lost. I couldn't change most of the mistakes I'd made. But there was one I could. Was Ray real? It wasn't my call anymore. We would have to figure things out together, this kid and I. This young man.

Russ glanced apologetically toward the figure in the bed. "Got some papers for you to sign to release this—fugitive."

He held out a handful of forms.

"Can't we do this later?"

"Why's everything have to be on your schedule, Ms. Winger?" Russ said. "I need you to sign—right below me." He dropped them into my lap.

At the bottom of the top page, a signature. His signature. It was an unsteady hand, half print, half script. A nervous hand, this one, but I didn't mind. He didn't look away when I signed and gave the papers back. I said nothing. It wasn't good business to give it away.

"I'm a fugitive?" Joshua shuffled his feet. "Will you arrest me?"

"Not this time," Russ said. "Although I do have some ideas on how you can repay some of the trouble you've put my team to, chasing you up to the hinterlands."

I pulled Joshua's hand to me before he could chew his nails. "How did you get up here?"

"Hitchhiked," Russ said. "He worked it all out in that chat room in his game. An eight-hour head start and the ride-share was a college kid going up to Canada, took him most of the way. We finally got a bead on him when a semi driver picked him up at a rest stop. We let him roll right into town."

"You knew I was here?" Joshua said.

"Had a guy in the lot the whole time," Russ said. I knew he meant Mullen, that he'd put his best man on the job and been let down a thousand times over. He'd had all that faith in other people and now he might have to see things the way I always had, with none. "I'm thinking about fifty hours of community service to run concurrently with any punishment you have coming from other quarters."

Joshua's eyes cut in my direction. "Am I grounded?"

"So grounded," I said. "As soon as we get home."

The word *home* had such a nice tone that I didn't want to say anything else. It had power no mere word should have. Did I mean Parks? I didn't mean Sweetheart Lake, but there were so many places we hadn't been.

Russ watched me with feigned casual attention. That heavy look.

I'd said *home* as though I knew where that was. What I meant was that I could make one. I could find a way to be part of something. An image came to me: bright pink running shoes rushing out of the hospital. If I went back to Parks, maybe I could find a way to put all this relevant experience to use. I hoped I could.

Joshua must have felt a little of the same hope. He settled on the armrest of my wheelchair without my pulling him in and eased an arm around my shoulders. He touched his temple to mine, careful with my bandages, careful with me.

I closed my eyes and enjoyed the solid weight of him against me. I was going to tell him, anything he wanted to know. Minus a few details, maybe.

I might start by saying, "On the day I died. . ." And he would probably stop me, call me dramatic, call me out for the wording. He would have an opinion on things from now on. I would have to hear them all.

No, I would say. Listen: on the day I died, I dragged the new oars down to the lake. But I didn't know it was the last day, and I didn't know I would get another chance. I didn't know you yet, but on the day I died, you saved me. You save me still.

On the first day of my new life, I bought sandals and pants at Theresa's store, along with a bright Sweetheart Lake sweatshirt. Theresa *tsk*ed over the state of the back of my head and threw in an equally bright bucket hat. We hugged for a long time, making the kind of promises I had never made. But if I brought Joshua up for a trial visit with Ray next summer, some promises, at last, might be kept.

One last errand. Not a lake, I said, directing him out of town. The river. Downriver from Sweetheart, on its way to somewhere else.

At the water's edge, I rolled up the pants and slipped out of the sandals. The water was freezing.

Someone should say something.

I glanced up. Russ stood at the top of the riverbank, waiting. Behind him, the sky was clear and bright. It had not been in my mother's power to trust blue skies, but I could. And greener grass, and yellow rooms. I felt only the water and a warming trill of nerves and possibility—I could dwell here. Here, where I was both certain and uncertain, but most of all grateful.

I pulled the zipper bag open and bent, the current rushing around my knees as I dipped the bag into the clear water and let the river draw the ashes. A cloud caught under the surface, brief, and then was gone.

For a moment, real grief gripped me. I tried to think of each fleck of ash rushing away from Sweetheart Lake at last.

I stood and picked my way out of the water, across the rocks. Up on the road, Joshua waited in Russ's truck, fully outfitted from the sporting goods store on Pine Street. Russ had put away his uniform and hat. For the ride home, he was wearing jeans and a gray Sweetheart Lake fleece with soft pockets. We would arrive back in Parks, festooned as tourists, lauded as heroes, a ragged family of hitchhikers and liars and whatever Russ turned out to be.

"Anna," he called. He pointed further downriver, where a large bird pinwheeled high in the air. An eagle, maybe. I slid my wet feet into the sandals, hurrying. I was ready to find out: the eagle, the man, whatever came along. Ready, just this last time, to get on the road.

Acknowledgments

This book started as a short story about ten years ago and has lived many lives since, giving me many people to remember here.

Grateful thanks to my agent, Sharon Bowers of Miller Bowers & Griffin Literary Management, and my editor, Margaux Weisman, for making this book possible. Thanks also to the good people at William Morrow, including Jena Kamali, Serena Wang, and Owen Corrigan.

Special thanks to Terence Faherty for giving me the heads up I needed to see this project the right way, and Midwest Writers Workshop for, among many other things, introducing me to Terry.

Also special thanks to Christopher Coake, who read this book years ago when it was terrible and said nice things, anyway.

Thanks to my first readers Yvonne Strumecki, James W. Ziskin, Lynne Raimondo, Kimberly Rader, Tricia David, Darian Ochs, Laurie Martin, James Burford, and Tiffany Rader and to Lauren Stacks Yamaoka, Kim Robbins Oclon, and Adam Morgan for enthusiasm about seeing the project to completion. Thanks to Lisa Stolley, Scott Blackwood, Mary Anne Mohanraj, and Don Pollack, for early encouragement on this story and to Roosevelt University's MFA program in creative writing for introducing most of these people into my life.

Thank you to Amy Clouse for her expertise in small-town sheriff's offices. Mistakes made despite her good counsel are, of course, mine. Thanks to Tom Jones for the corn knowledge. Belated thanks to Rob Ramey for his high school principal help.

Special nod to the librarian at Chicago's Edgebrook Public Library who put the book on handwriting analysis facing out on the shelf in 2007. I owe you one. Thanks to Michelle Dreshold for writing *Sex, Lies, and Handwriting*. To librarians in general and booksellers, too, much is owed.

My true gratitude goes to Dan Mayer and Jon Kurtz for giving me a beginning.

Special thanks, as always, to all my family and friends for how much they've put up with and for how much they participate in this alongside me. But the real hero here is my husband, Greg Day, whose support of this project has weathered its entire ten years.

I have struggled with how to acknowledge here the women who have faced domestic violence in real life, many of whom have not survived their abuse. They were much on my mind as I wrote this book. If you need help getting free of a bad situation, please call 1-800-799-SAFE (7233).

About the author

About the book

Insights,
Interviews
& More . . .

Meet Lori Rader-Day

Iden Ford

Lori Rader-Day tried writing fiction for the first time at age seven, when she turned her love for Beverly Cleary's Ramona Quimby into a rudimentary attempt at fan fiction. She discovered a love for dark stories by reading Lois Duncan. When she was twelve and had read everything in the children's section of her town's library, she was sent to the second floor to read among the adults. Scared of passing the circulation desk, Lori took a right-hand turn into the first open doorway—into the mystery room, where she discovered Mary Higgins Clark and Agatha Christie.

Lori dabbled with writing through high school and college, studying journalism at Ball State University in Muncie, Indiana—twice, without ever, not once, becoming a journalist. In 2006, she decided to get serious about fiction and started a degree program in creative writing at Roosevelt University in Chicago. She started writing and publishing short stories and just after graduation in 2009, finished the first draft of a novel that went promptly into "the drawer," mostly unseen by human eyes. Lori wrote and published two novels over the next several years, winning the 2015 Anthony Award for Best First Novel for *The Black Hour* and the 2016 Mary Higgins Clark Award for *Little Pretty Things*.

And then she opened the drawer. *The Day I Died*, rewritten, renamed, is the result, ten years after originally undertaking the story.

Lori's next novel is in progress, slated for publication by HarperCollins William Morrow in 2018.

Lori's all-time favorite writers: Agatha Christie, Shirley Jackson, Carson McCullers

Lori's favorite contemporary mystery writers: Tana French, Catriona McPherson, Gillian Flynn, Lisa Lutz, Ann Cleeves—visit your local independent bookstores and read them, too! ▶

Meet Lori Rader-Day *(continued)*

The book Lori rereads every year: *84, Charing Cross Road* by Helene Hanff

Other most often reread books: Jane Austen's *Pride and Prejudice*, Annie Proulx's *The Shipping News*

Favorite mystery TV: *Vera, Sherlock, Elementary, Miss Fisher's Murder Mysteries* ∽

The Day I Died Playlist

This list isn't a marketing scheme—I actually write to music most of the time and always construct playlists for my novels. To start, I'll gather a few songs I already own that seem thematically appropriate to my story (though I don't usually know much about the story when I start writing it). Sometimes it's the tune or tone of the track that gets it placed on the list. Sometimes it's much more literal: lyrics speak to me and to the themes of the novel. The list always grows over time as I discover new songs to add, and I'm constantly searching for new music to inspire a few more pages.

"WHITE BLANK PAGE" BY MUMFORD & SONS

I was an immediate convert to the music of Mumford & Sons. This song had resonance for Anna's career and for the dreams she has in the night, when the words trail and tighten around her. I originally heard these lyrics as "Wine Dark Page," so if someone would like to write that song, I want to hear it.

"WHERE TO BEGIN" BY MY MORNING JACKET

Well, truthfully, this book began years before it was finished, but I chose this song not because of my beginning but Anna's. Where does the strength come from to begin again, after you've lost everything? And then again? ▶

The Day I Died Playlist *(continued)*

"UNDER THE MICROSCOPE" BY MATTHEW SANTOS

This is just a tremendous song. Some songs demand to be written to. If Anna were asked to connect this song to her story, she'd point to that first meeting with the sheriff. He's paying attention, much too closely.

"RIPTIDE" BY VANCE JOY

"I love you when you're singing that song . . . I got a lump in my throat because you're gonna sing the words wrong." I was charmed by these lyrics, and imagined all the little moments between mother and child that Anna misses as her son starts to grow up and away from her. All the little moments in a life between people who love one another.

"COME PICK ME UP" BY RYAN ADAMS

A song about a couple having a not-happy ending in progress. When Anna remembers wanting to call Ray and let him know where they are, she knows it's not a good idea, but can't help wanting what would be easy. The devil she knows. (Not safe for work, this one.)

"OLD FRIEND" BY SEA WOLF

"Old friend come back home . . . Even though you always were alone . . . You had to push against the fates . . . Just to make it . . . Make it through the gate." I picked up this song from hearing it on TV at some point. I've gotten very good at recognizing good writing songs, and spend far too much money on iTunes.

"A NEW LIFE" BY JIM JAMES

Anna has plenty of new lives, but they haven't been as full as she needs them to be. Maybe this is the one she'll get to keep?

"MESS IS MINE" BY VANCE JOY

Even independent women wouldn't mind someone saying they'd take on all your baggage. If only you'd let them.

"LONG RIDE HOME" BY PATTY GRIFFIN

"Headlights staring at the driveway . . . The house is dark as it can be . . . I go inside and all is silent . . . It seems as empty as the inside of me." For when the ride home isn't just a road trip.

"GO INSANE" (LIVE) BY LINDSEY BUCKINGHAM

This is not an unproblematic choice, given what we've heard about certain guitar players and certain ex-girlfriend singers, but it reminds me that all the characters in *The Day I Died* get to have a voice. Also, I have a not unproblematic crush on Lindsey Buckingham.

"THE YAWNING GRAVE" BY LORD HURON

This entire album, *Strange Trails*, is one long writing soundtrack for me. This track is particularly haunting, evocative of dark walks through the woods and of what awaits if Anna cannot save herself. ▶

The Day I Died Playlist *(continued)*

"BLOOD IN THE CUT" BY K.FLAY

(NSFW) I heard this song on the radio (bleeped) long after *The Day I Died* was written, but I so wish I'd had this in the playlist during drafting. Something about the tough lyrics and delivery—and perhaps because of the lyrics "Take my car and paint it black, take my arm break it in half . . . Take my head and kick it in, break some bread for all my sins"—the song reminded me of Anna and everything she had survived to be able to tell this story. Not everyone is so lucky.

"LUCKY NOW" BY RYAN ADAMS

"And the night will break your heart, but only if you're lucky now." Hmm. I just realized this song needs to be on the playlist for my next novel, too. "Am I really who I was?" Ryan sings, and that's Anna's question to answer in the end. ❧

Reading Group Guide

1. When we first meet Anna, she can't admit that she cares about the little boy who's missing. What changes in this situation? How does Anna find compassion she didn't think she had?

2. Anna's only friend isn't really a friend. She knows that "one of us had been a drowning person, and the other, a life raft." How has being helped so much by Kent and others defined Anna's ability to connect with other people?

3. How does the Ransey family's history in the town of Parks color Sheriff Keller's approach to the case of Aidan going missing? How can media representation or other commentary hurt the chances of justice being served?

4. The Dairy Bar is a place that Anna gravitates toward, a place she can reclaim from a childhood she's had to leave behind. What are the touchstone locations of your childhood? Where is the place in your current life that reminds you most of a cherished place or person?

5. Anna returns to her old town and sees simultaneously what is the same and what is different, layers over time over top one another. (The word for this phenomenon is ▶

palimpsest.) Have you ever returned to a place you hadn't been in years? What changes or enduring artifacts stood out to you?

6. What complex feelings do you see between Anna and Theresa during their unexpected reunion?

7. Left for dead, Anna finds strength not just in her son but in the child she once was. What emotions are at work here?

8. What do you think will be different for Anna after the end of this story? How has she changed? ∾

Discover great authors, exclusive offers, and more at hc.com.